Cougar Boss

Kerry Belchambers

This is a work of fiction. All characters, locales and events are either products of the author's imagination or are used fictitiously.

COUGAR BOSS

Independently Published

ISBN: 978-1-6892-1362-2

First edition: August, 2019

Published in the United States of America.

For Rose

ACKNOWLEDGMENTS

I started working on this book a few years ago and in the beginning, it was a therapeutic way of getting my mind off of things that were troubling me at the time. As the pages continued, the story took on a life of its own and basically wrote itself.

These characters came to mean so much to me, they became real and I've learned so much from them. In time, the online support I was getting from my readers was so encouraging, I forgot everything I was going through and just wrote.

I'm blessed in a lot of ways, but I'm entirely thankful to my God, who gives me the strength to keep on going and to keep on writing.

I thank my Wattpad family for their love and support, as well as my real life family for being so patient with me. I hope to make you all proud.

Prologue

BOOK ONE: OLIVIA

I was late for my interview. One I'd worked so hard to get. A former employer had recommended me for a personal assistant position at a CEO's wife's mansion, where she preferred to work from, which I found a bit odd, but she was paying well and I had student loans and bills to pay.

I hurried along, hoping she'd give me a chance. I was ten minutes late. If I failed to land this job, I'd be kicked out of my studio apartment.

The moment I arrived, I was instantly intimidated by the extravagant house staring back at me. It felt as if I had no business there.

The mansion must've housed about thirty rooms and a dozen bathrooms or so. Workers were everywhere, and the compound was larger than three football fields.

The mansion was in a private estate which took approximately twenty minutes to get to from the main road, where the rest of the world, or rather poor people like myself, barely managed to exist.

This was a different universe and I was an intruder, wearing four-inch heels I'd gotten weeks earlier, which were squeezing the life out of my toes and a grey pantsuit I'd gotten using the remaining money I'd had left.

If I didn't get this job, in a week or so, I'd be living on the streets. I'd already asked too much of my best friend, Rex, and I couldn't bring myself to ask him to help me more, even though I knew he'd be more than willing to come to my rescue despite the fact that he was a struggling artist with as little to nothing as myself.

At the entrance, I was met by a serious looking middle-aged British butler. British. Talk about exaggerated wealth. Or perhaps I should've been grateful because it might've meant this ostentatiously wealthy people would pay me well. But then again that was if I passed the damned interview I was late for.

"I'm here to see Mrs. Gallagher about an interview on the personal assistant job," I said as the butler looked me up and down. He looked like a bouncer from a high-end strip club.

"You must be Ms. Olivia Williams." His tongue was heavy with that English accent.

"I am," I said.

He let me in. I was awestruck by the expanse space, elegance and luxury that immediately assaulted my eyes. I'd seen these kinds of homes in movies and extravagant home shows, but I'd never quite pictured it in reality.

The human-sized crystal chandelier hanging from the ceiling was the first thing that captured my eyes, then the artsy and luxurious looking, embellished unending staircase which seemed, as if, ascended to heaven.

My studio apartment was a quarter of a quarter of the space which directly met me at the entrance of the mansion.

"Second floor, third room on the east wing," the butler said.

Third room on the east wing, even the White House paled in comparison to this mutant of a house.

After the shock, I rushed up the stairs.

"No running," the butler said after me, forcing me to slow in my step.

I straightened up my outfit and windblown brown hair at the door, and took a breath before knocking. I didn't know who or what to expect on the other side as I'd not had enough time to prepare or research the position I was supposedly interviewing for.

I'd planned on doing so, but last-minute studying for assignments and constant countless side jobs to make money for bills that seemed never-ending had taken up all my time. I hoped the recommendation, coupled up with my skills would land me the job.

I didn't have full details on how much I'd be earning or when payment would be due; I hadn't had time to research on that either. I'd been too busy and desperate for the next job.

After knocking twice on the giant, shiny inlaid wooden door which was as intimidating as the rest of the house, a voice spoke from the other side, telling me to go in.

Mentally preparing myself and fully unaware of what to expect, I pushed the doors open, only for it to bump me back when I tried to walk in. On my second attempt, I realized it was a pull-not-push door.

Trying to hide my embarrassment, I walked in hoping my future boss hadn't noticed the mishap. When I approached the large mahogany desk, I was glad to note her attention had been elsewhere. "I'm Olivia Williams, I'm here for the interview," I said when she didn't barge.

My heart was thudding loudly in my chest.

"You're late, Olivia," she said.

I was so used to being called Livvy, when she called me Olivia, I felt like a child being scolded by a parent for something wrong I'd done.

Other than that, her voice was firm, calm and composed, which scared me because I knew there was a countless number of people who could've been present for the interview but I was lucky enough to be the only person available on such short notice.

"I'm sorry, I…"

The truth was, I'd been late getting out of my last job. It'd been my last day, and I'd changed my outfit in the car on my way to the interview.

I couldn't tell her so.

I'd planned on telling her I'd gotten lost due to inaccurate Google Maps locations or I'd been stuck in traffic and considering the distance I lived on the opposite side of the paradise I'd just stepped into, the excuse didn't sound too farfetched for me so I doubted it'd sound absurd.

What sold me out was my poor state of being unprepared. If I'd known what to expect, I'd have been a bit better off.

She looked up and turned her attention to me.

My breath caught in my throat and I swear I could feel myself shrinking. She looked like she was in her early to mid-thirties, her eyes were a clear bright blue and her flawless face was astoundingly stunning.

She was the most beautiful creature I'd ever laid eyes on in my entire life.

It caught me off-guard.

She looked at me, having momentarily abandoned whatever she was doing on her laptop, and gracefully directed me to a seat across her expertly-carpentered mahogany desk with her perfectly manicured fingers.

Reluctantly, I approached the chair while I hungrily feasted on the most thrilling sight to ever cross my eyes as I sat down.

Her hair was a dark honey color, like a late evening sunset across the sea. I envied her husband's freedom upon his fingers running through its soft silky texture.

For a person with grown children, she didn't seem to have the body of one who'd bore two, for every curve and crevice was in place, and every inch of her body and being was as perfect as the kingdom she ruled.

"I'm throwing a charity ball at the Eden plaza in a week. You'll find all the necessary details in these files. I need you to go through them. There's a list of three hundred people here. I need you to reduce the number to fifty so that by morning I can send out the invites. I'm giving you a week; this is your project. It requires a lot of work and attention to detail. If you manage to make this charity ball a success, we can discuss a longer term of employment."

I froze in place. I'd carried a file full of documents revolving around my skills, educational background and what-not. I'd expected questions and the whole shebang that went on during job interviews, but this, this was new.

For some reason, I was pleased by the turn of events, but I realized I was equally as scared because, what if I failed?

Mrs. Amelia Gallagher was trusting me with a project without checking out my background experience to see if I was qualified to know what I was doing.

I wasn't an event planner. I didn't know the high rollers of this community she dominated, yet she was giving me this huge responsibility. Was this how obscenely wealthy people conducted their interviews?

But then again, a previous employer had personally recommended me to her and I didn't know exactly what she'd said.

"Do you have any questions?" Mrs. Gallagher asked.

My mind snapped back to the present. I looked at her, once again awestruck by how beautiful she was. I'd never heard of her, yet at that very moment she held the key to my future.

I'd be lucky if I lasted that one week.

"Where would you like me to work from?" I asked.

She took the phone and almost immediately spoke into it, asking someone to come up to the office.

She had so many employees I wondered why she even bothered lifting a finger when someone she'd hired could lift it for her.

"How old are you?" she asked when she placed the phone back in its cradle.

"Twenty-eight."

I was on my fourth-year of my Masters in Business Administration, and had done a lot of other studies before deciding to settle for the corporate world. I expected her to ask me more questions, but she turned her attention back to her laptop.

A couple of breaths later, a knock came at the door, and the butler walked in.

"Francis, I'd like you to show Ms. Olivia Williams to her office," she said.

My office? I got an office?

"Yes, of course, Mrs. Gallagher. Ms. Williams, this way, please."

I got to my feet, took the iPad on the desk with the information regarding the charity ball event and followed after Francis.

"Olivia," I paused at the door when she called after me.

"Yes, Mrs. Gallagher," I said nervously, realizing I'd already started working for her. "If you have any questions, I want you to feel free to ask me. I don't want you making any mistakes," she said.

I nodded, pleased by the thought that she was willing to help me if or when I got stuck. At least I had a lifeline, though I doubted she'd take too kindly to me asking her questions after every five minutes. Hmm, maybe it was a test.

I nodded and left her office.

I expected Francis to walk me farther down the hall, but my office was directly facing Amelia Gallagher's office.

"This is where you'll be operating from."

I walked into an office that was probably three times the size of my studio apartment and slightly resented myself at the realization of how poor I was.

Amelia Gallagher's office was larger than mine and as expected, each corner of it was coated in luxury. It was heaven compared to my office, but nonetheless, what I walked into was more than anything I could've imagined.

I didn't know what I needed all the space for, maybe I'd find out.

The office was neat and elegantly furnished.

There was a large window with the view of a tennis court. Wait, these people had a tennis court in their backyard?

"I expect everything is to your satisfaction," Francis said.

I couldn't help wondering how long he'd worked for the Gallaghers and if he'd ever gotten used to being around such extremities. "It is, thank you," I said.

"I'll leave you to it then, good luck," he said on his way out.

I wanted to ask him a few questions but seeing as this was my first day, I doubted he'd be willing to answer. His loyalty was to these people and I was an outcast to him as much as I was to them.

I placed the iPad on the desk and went to sit behind the comfortable leather seat. I sunk into the softness and exhaled in pleasure, taking in everything on the desk. When the initial shock wore off from the luxury I'd come across since the moment I'd stepped into the Gallagher residence, I turned my attention to the work I'd been assigned by Mrs. Amelia Gallagher.

She had a lovely name, Amelia. It suited her. Noticing I was getting distracted, I focused on the work at hand.

Apart from a few names of very rich and influential people on the list of three hundred, I barely recognized anyone else. I switched on the Apple iMac and went online to figure out who the rest were.

I was gifted with a photographic memory and my IQ was well above average so going through the list and doing background research on those names was my forte; a strong suit that'd gotten me far in my school years as well as my professional background.

I applied my focus and attention to my work and got so completely busy and carried away, I didn't realize how fast time was moving until I was interrupted by one of the household employees, a kind old woman who brought me lunch.

I wasn't hungry until I took the first bite of the mouthwatering grilled chicken and spinach salad.

It was amazing to me how these people lived this way on a daily basis while the rest of us barely managed to survive.

I retreated back to work, knowing I was being slow due to the extensive research. I needed to minimize the number of people on the list but I didn't need to examine every detail of their life, but then again, I was better safe than sorry. I had a feeling Mrs. Gallagher would need reasons as to why I'd chosen the specific fifty.

By five in the evening, I was supposed to be winding up for the day. I'd gone through the entire list five times and had only chosen thirty. I needed to finish the assignment before the following morning if I wanted this job.

It was probably going to be the best or the worst job I ever had, but I was certain the pay wouldn't be so bad. All I needed to do was prove myself to Mrs. Gallagher even though I knew very well that I didn't fit or belong in that world.

I wasn't sure if I'd be allowed to go home with the work and I didn't know if they'd ask me to leave since my working hours were over, but I stayed until that moment would occur.

Sometime around eight in the evening, there was a light knock on the door. Francis walked in and for a moment, I thought he'd come to ask me to leave but, he surprised me when he placed a plate of food and a bottle of water on my desk.

By that time, the entire family must've already gotten home or so I assumed, perhaps had dinner and were probably somewhere doing what rich people did after a meal.

"Thank you, Francis," I said, expressing my gratitude.

He nodded.

On his way out, I asked, "Do you think I'm in anyone's way if I stay longer and finish up?" I needed to know if I'd be asked to leave and didn't want to go home with regrets.

"The doors lock at midnight so until then, you can resume with your duties," he said.

I exhaled and got back to work.

Half an hour to midnight, I was double checking the names and details. The second I was finished, I sent the data to Mrs. Gallagher and notified Francis of my departure.

When I got into my crappy little car, I drove past the fine imported vehicles on the parking lot that hadn't been there earlier when I'd arrived, and drove out of the Gallagher residence, wondering if I'd last a week.

Chapter One

I stood nervously in front of Amelia Gallagher, Queen of the Gallagher Palace, and waited for her verdict on the list of names I had compiled. I'd arrived half an hour early and the house had been quiet and empty with no sign of life present.

Francis had met me at the door, formally greeted me as though we were business associates then let me in. An hour later, Amelia Gallagher had called me to her office. Elegantly dressed like the royal highness herself, I'd been stunned a second time by the regal appearance of the woman.

She wore an exquisite pearl necklace with quaint expensive matching earrings, a white blouse that exposed her chest but covered her cleavage, tucked under a nicely fitting silver-colored skirt. She was like fine delicate china.

"This is the final list?" she asked.

I'd gone through it over a hundred times and I was certain those were the best guests to invite to the charity ball event. "Yes, it is, Mrs. Gallagher."

"Mrs. Anderson, Mr. Calloway, Patterson, Zeigner, Peiser…" she trailed off.

"You didn't say what I should base the list on so I checked their background, their line of business and philanthropic work they've been involved in for the past year and made the list from the most generous to the least in terms of donations."

I was so nervous while I explained, my hands were slightly shaking but I forced myself to be steady. If Mrs. Gallagher noticed the lack of confidence in my work, it'd be enough reason for her to fire me.

"Lauren Watkins is my event planner. Call her. Get me a couple of samples for the invites and visit the venue to see the progress she's made planning this event. You're in charge of this project. Make sure everything is done right."

I felt like I was in a reality TV show competing for a position or a prize, except there were no other contestants. I was in charge of planning a charity event that had a guest list of fifty of the most influential people in the world and I had no experience in this. The thought left me so unmotivated, I wanted to run out of there and go back to the other side of the world, where I belonged.

Mrs. Gallagher must've noticed my reluctance because she fixed her eyes on me, meeting my gaze for the very first time. I must've been one of those inconsequential faces that she could pass by the street and never remember we'd at one point breathed the same air.

My gaze wavered under her unyielding one because I couldn't pull off looking her directly in the eyes. God, she had beautiful eyes. Well, no wonder she wouldn't recognize me or pick me apart from a group of people, I needed to be strong and match her steady stance. I needed to stop being so afraid.

If I ended up losing the job, I wouldn't let the cause be it was because I wasn't confident enough with my skills or committed enough to my job. It'd have to be something else. I had to make Mrs. Gallagher remember me. And I needed to remember that if I didn't get this job, I wouldn't only be broke and homeless, I'd also have unimaginable student loans I'd be unable to pay.

"The person who recommended you said you're extremely hardworking, driven and committed. That is why I'm letting you do this. Take it as a challenge that determines whether you get to keep the job." Her voice was satin soft and I wanted to drink it in forever.

Focus, a little voice whispered in my head. Whatever attraction I had to this magnificent creature had to vanish and fast. She sounded confident in me. That was all I needed.

I went back to my office and called Lauren. Since I was going to be working with her, I needed to better acquaint myself with the project. We made an appointment to meet later on in the day and I got to work about those invitations.

There was a long contact list on the computer with the names of people the Gallagher family hired for projects, so it didn't take me long to get a contact the family used to design invitation cards. Even in a digital era, a tangible invitation was extremely important.

At the mention of the Gallagher name, it was confirmed I would have the cards before the end of the day.

On my way to meet Lauren, I realized my work might end up being easier than I thought. Someone had neatly arranged almost everything I needed to do my job in the computer. It must've been the previous assistant. If she'd been so well organized and hardworking, it made me wonder why she hadn't stayed on longer.

From the moment I met Lauren Watkins, I knew she didn't like me. She looked down on me, like I was help in the plaza and I was there to serve her instead of working with her. I'd never taken a liking to women who looked down on their own gender.

I could bet the remaining fifty bucks I had in my bank account, she'd probably come from the same poor background that I had, but in her attempt to fit in, she'd gotten completely sucked in and ended up resenting everything she'd come from. I admired and resented her in the same breath.

I followed her around the plaza trying to figure out how far she'd gone with the project but she kept treating me like a lapdog, just giving me little to satisfy me but not enough to figure out what my next step would be. It pissed me off.

I went for a bathroom break half an hour later when I got tired of chasing her around and tried to motivate myself by talking to my reflection in the mirror. I didn't look like I worked for an elegant woman like Mrs. Gallagher. I could see the fear in my eyes. Fear of rebuke, fear of failure, fear of standing up for myself. That was probably what Lauren saw too.

I needed to be bold and assertive. This was probably how every other person I'd interact with who worked for the Gallaghers would treat me. I needed to show them that I wasn't going to be a rug for anyone to wipe their feet on.

I needed to remake myself and I needed to start here. I'd not spent the entire day and most of the night working on a project someone else was going to steal from me. I was heading to the lobby to talk to Lauren when I overheard her talking to her assistant.

"Did you see how she was dressed?" the assistant said in a mocking tone.

"Where did Amelia find her? Good God, the woman looks like she fell from the wrong side of the tracks," Lauren said.

I usually didn't care about what other people thought of me.

Usually, I had too many problems to think about anything else outside my responsibilities but their conversation made me more aware of how lowly I felt being thrusted into a world I'd never set foot in.

"Don't worry, she won't last a week. I'm even shocked she lasted twenty-four hours," the assistant said.

"Amelia is too kind, taking in a stray and hiring her for such an important job. They're both lucky I'm here," Lauren said.

It was hurtful to hear them talk that way about me. It felt like I was back in school having to deal with a bully. Well, I wasn't a child anymore. I worked for Amelia Gallagher and I needed to remind these two women who they worked for.

"Lauren," I said, walking into the room as though I'd not overheard anything.

They both turned to me and looked me up, down then up again. It was offensive of them to seize me up as though we were in high school and they were the popular girls.

"I'd like you to run everything by me again," I said firmly.

The assistant snickered and Lauren gave her a look. It seemed they could talk about me behind my back but couldn't do so in my face.

"Erm, I'm sorry, remind me your name again," Lauren said.

I was trying hard to keep my cool but they were making it increasingly hard. "My name is not important, my employer's name is. Her name is Amelia Gallagher. I'm her personal assistant. She put me in charge of this project. Now, you can make this easy and tell me what I need to know or, I can get someone else to do your job."

"You can't do that," the assistant said.

I reached for my phone and looked at the two women.

"I've worked for Amelia Gallagher for years," Lauren said, crossing her arms over her chest in amusement.

I knew I was out of my element, and this woman had a point, but I wasn't going to let her disrespect me. "Then she knows you don't like to cooperate with her assistants."

They both stared at me, daring me. When none of them made a move, I pretended to dial the number and placed the phone over my ear. "Mrs. Gallagher, this is Olivia Williams," I said my name particularly firmly so they could remember it. "I've been at the Eden plaza for almost an hour and Lauren Watkins…" Their frantic waving at the mention of Lauren's name had me staring back at them.

The fact that they were threatened by the fake phone call put me exactly where I needed to be.

"Please hang up," Lauren silently mouthed.

I waited a bit, just to enjoy the suspense then made something up and pretended to hang up the phone.

"What do you need to know?" Lauren asked, being pleasantly accommodating.

How pretentious.

"Kate, go get us some drinks. What would you like, Olivia? Coffee, wine, water?"

I raised my eyebrow at how well the threat had worked. "It's Ms. Williams to you, and if I hear either one of you disrespecting me again, I'll get you fired."

They both nodded and I had an overwhelming moment where I experienced a surge of satisfaction at how good power felt. "Now, let's get this over with. I'd like to know every single detail."

We sat down and Lauren became very forthcoming with information. She told me everything that I needed to know and in a couple of hours, I was leaving Eden plaza with a smile across my face. I went to pick up sample invitation cards afterwards and headed back to the Gallagher residence, with a certain sense of pride I hadn't had before.

I went to Amelia's office with the samples so she could tell me which ones to send out and found her on the phone. I had to wait until she finished. I listened to the sound of her voice as she spoke, it was so calm. Her left hand was slowly moving over her laptop while she stared into space.

Since she wasn't paying any attention to me, I took the chance to study her. I didn't think I'd ever get used to just how lovely she was. Looking at her made me feel like my eyes were feasting on a deliciously rare delicacy they'd never encountered before.

Her thick hair was in curls that day, cascading down her shoulders in gorgeous waves, gently kissing her flawless, perfectly carved, marble-like face. Her acutely blue eyes were beautifully disarming and so alert, I felt like she could feel me watching her.

Her adroit character and the air she carried around her or within herself left me feeling like I wanted to know her better but I could not read her at all. It was like there was an invisible wall between us and much as I could see her, I couldn't see through to her.

Such a captivating mystery. She made me wonder if she noticed me at all. At the thought, her eyes met mine and I froze. I held her gaze for a couple of seconds and realized she was looking through me as she continued with her phone conversation.

How silly of me. Maybe I needed to make myself a bit more noticeable.

"Olivia."

My thoughts vanished at her controlled but commanding voice.

"I wanted to show you the samples for the invites."

She summoned me forward and automatically, my body moved as though under her spell. I got a whiff of her perfume and my nostrils bathed in the fragrance. That must have been how heaven smelled like.

I would've loved to see her smile. I bet she had the most beautiful smile in the world. *Focus*, that little voice again.

"Use this," she said, handing me one of the samples. "How did it go at the plaza?"

I remembered Lauren's foul attitude towards me and ignored that part as I filled her in on the details. She probably wouldn't care to know her employees were not getting along. I'd probably be the one to get fired, seeing as Lauren had worked for her for years in comparison to me.

"That will do, thank you," she said.

When I got back to my office, I gave the go-ahead to the company to print the invitation cards after sending all the relevant names of the invited guests. Now, for the hard part, liaising with Lauren and working together to make the event a success. I groaned and made the dreaded call.

The rest of the week moved on quite fast after that. I attended countless meetings and met a lot of people who worked for the Gallaghers to make the event a success. Since everything had to run by me so I could take it to Mrs. Gallagher for approval, I was extremely busy and at some point, I was afraid I'd screw things up.

Mrs. Gallagher seemed very confident in my skills and that comforted me. It didn't make my work any easier though. By Friday afternoon, I was so busy making sure everything was perfect for the following night, I thought I'd go crazy.

When Francis walked into my office, I grew a bit nervous. Mrs. Gallagher had sent me out for countless errands and much as I'd accomplished each and every one, I was still afraid I might've screwed up somewhere.

Francis never came to my office. He'd only done so once, the first evening of my working for Mrs. Gallagher, but never again. There was little interaction between us, seeing as I was cooped up in the office or constantly leaving the house for errands. But from what I'd seen, he was a kind man.

"Sorry to interrupt your work, Ms. Williams," he said.

A moment later, a man and a woman walked in after him dragging along with them a rack full of clothes.

"What's this?" I asked in confusion.

"It's just a fitting for your dress and accessories for tomorrow night's event," he said.

The woman walked over to me and started taking my measurements while I tried to absorb what Francis had just said.

"Please stand up," the woman said.

I got to my feet as she probed me. I'd known I'd be attending the event but I hadn't known clothing and accessory would be provided for me.

The man walked over to me and studied my face and body, making me feel a little uncomfortable. I'd never been self-conscious of my looks. I'd always been too busy to make an effort to bring out my features but Rex, my best friend, had described me as a quiet beauty. When I'd asked him what he meant, he'd said I didn't need make up or fancy clothes to enhance my appearance.

I personally thought my emerald-green eyes were a bit too big for my face because of my high cheekbones and small straight nose but Rex had said they sparkled and had the limitless capacity to be fiery.

My unruly brown hair could at times be a bit hard to handle or style so to make it easy, I just held it up in a tight bun that ended up giving me headaches.

I had full pink lips, which were probably the only feature I thought was appealing and as far as my body was concerned, years of hard work had gotten me in shape, with a slender, lean body on a tall physical frame.

Rex said I was a catch but from my lack of personal time and love life, I didn't really have a moment to think along those lines. In fact, I'd never been in a serious relationship. I'd had short-lived flings with women I met in school, but none of them had meant enough for me to take seriously.

"I want you to try on a few gowns, they'll give me an idea of what goes well with your body," the woman said.

I didn't have time for this. These people were getting in the way of my work. I wanted to say something when I met Francis' expression and realized this was mandatory. He was there to make sure I did as told.

I groaned and spent the next hour trying on clothes. The man, whose name I'd come to learn was Andre was a makeup artist, while the woman, Anna, was a personal shopper. Since Andre couldn't do his work fully in my office, seeing as he hadn't carried enough 'equipment' *his word,* he told me to go by his boutique for a full makeover the following day. Yeah, like I had the time.

"If you want to work for Mrs. Gallagher, you're going to have to follow her rules," Francis said when I complained after Andre and Anna left.

"I'm going a little crazy doing so much in so little time. I honestly don't have time for a makeover," I said.

"You need to present Mrs. Gallagher's image in the way you project yourself to others. You'll be with her almost every second of the evening."

If I was going to be by her side all evening, then I needed to look the part. I couldn't attend the event looking like my usual self. Besides, it was just one night and I needed a network of rich and powerful people in case I didn't end up working for Mrs. Gallagher.

I needed them to remember me and if I had to dress up to make that happen, then so be it.

Rex came by to see me that evening. I found him waiting outside my door when I got home. Seeing a familiar face was calming because the past week had been a whirlwind ride.

We'd met in school years earlier and had become instant friends. We'd struggled through life together and he'd come to my rescue more times than I could count. He knew about my new job, but he wasn't in on the details so when we got into my apartment, I told him everything that had happened.

"Wait, so tomorrow morning you are going for a fancy makeover then later on you're heading to a charity ball that will have some of the richest people in attendance?" he asked.

"Yeah, can you believe it?"

"And this charity ball thing is going to determine whether or not you get the job?"

"Pretty much," I said.

"Damn, that's a lot of work and a whole lot of pressure."

I'd been a bit anxious with all the planning and the work I'd put into the project, but now, I was more worried about how close the event was.

"I'm sure you'll do great. You're the hardest working person I know. This job will make a difference for you and I'm sure you don't take the responsibility lightly."

"Don't you think it's weird though, that instead of a normal interview, I had to do all of these things?"

"It is a bit weird, but I think it's the best way to see how well a person conducts themselves while employed, under pressure and in a new environment."

"Yeah, I thought the same thing too. Amelia Gallagher knows what she's doing."

"What is she like? Is she mean, bossy? Is she a control-freak?"

Quite the contrary, I thought. She was something special. "She's the most beautiful woman I've ever seen."

"What?"

"I mean, work-wise, she's a good boss. But every time I see her, my heart picks up pace and then I realize I'm holding my breath until she can speak. Her voice is…" I didn't know how to explain it.

"You have a crush on your boss?" Rex asked.

"A crush? No. I just think she's hot."

"Wait a minute, how old is she?"

"She got married young. She has two kids, a son, twenty-six and a daughter, twenty-four."

"So, she's what?"

"Forty-eight, but she doesn't look a day over thirty. Her skin is like porcelain and her hair flows down her shoulders like water flowing down a stream."

"You've got it bad for her," Rex said as he laughed.

"I just said, she's hot, that's all."

"Yeah well, I've never heard you describe a woman like that before."

"That's because I've never met such a woman before, dummy."

"If she's as rich as you say then it must be plastic surgery or something. There is nothing real about wealthy people, especially women who don't look their age."

"That's stereotype thinking. Some people do actually age gracefully."

"Whatever, anyway, what does she think about you? Does she get weird and poetic when she thinks about you the way you do her?" he teased.

I threw him a pillow which landed smack on his face. "Don't be silly." I doubted she thought of me at all, which wasn't surprising. I was her errand girl; a faceless employee.

"I hope she pays well. If you get this job you could hook me up with her rich friends."

"I doubt they'd be interested in you," I said dryly.

"Not me, my work."

He was a great artist. "Pray I get the job."

I would've loved to help him out the way he'd unfailingly helped me.

When he left, I showered and got in bed. I was out like a light the moment my head touched the pillow.

The following morning, I woke up early to go for my makeover. My dress would be delivered later on, I just needed to get the physical transformation out of the way first.

Andre was happy to see me. It was obvious he loved his job because of his enthusiasm and positive energy.

"Don't overdo it," I told him before he got started.

"I got this," he said and got to work.

He had a team of people to work with, which was comforting because it meant they would take less time. When they started, there was a lot of tweezing and hair-cutting. It got painful and uncomfortable during waxing, which almost made me leave the boutique half done but I had to remind myself of the good that would come out of this whole thing.

Andre dyed my hair into a deep chestnut color, cut it a little shorter, and used rollers and a lot of hair product to style it. They did something to my eyelashes after tweezing my eyebrows, then proceeded to a manicure and a pedicure among other things I wasn't aware I needed. At the end, I was just glad I wasn't paying the bill because I spent two and a half hours getting primped and ready.

When I saw the resulting transformation, I was beyond shocked. I recalled the embarrassing moment where I looked in the mirror, unsure of what to find, and waved to realize the stranger staring and waving back was actually, me, Olivia Williams.

I was different. Beautiful. I'd never used the word on myself, but for once I could because the woman looking back at me was without a doubt so.

"You like?" Andre asked.

I was still speechless and a little bit emotional. Andre seemed to understand that because he took my hand in his and released a squeal that deafened me.

I left shortly after and headed to the mansion. I didn't stay long because I needed to be at the venue to make sure everything was perfect and communicated with Mrs. Gallagher over the phone to keep her updated. All the guests had confirmed attendance and were ready for the big night.

Lauren's expression was priceless when she saw my

transformation. I couldn't wait to step into the gown and fully complete my new look for the party.

Time passed by pretty swiftly and before I knew it, it was nine and the guests were going to arrive anytime now. I didn't have enough money to book a room to go change into so I got my dress from the reception where I'd stored it and went to change in the ladies room.

I reapplied my make up the way Andre had taught me, put on my dress, shoes and jewelry. I'd never owned jewelry before, at least not the fancy type. Now I was wearing some pretty nice ones but it was sad to think I'd probably have to return everything once the party was over.

After my fascination with the sparkly, I did my hair and did a double take of myself in the mirror. The dress was a glamorous curve hugging gown that positively added to my physical appearance, pleasantly complimented by six-inch heels. If Rex had seen me at that moment, he wouldn't have recognized me as I barely recognized myself.

I got back to the event at the same time Amelia Gallagher and her family was arriving. The moment I saw her, I didn't notice anyone else in the room. She was absolutely breathtaking. She looked incredibly graceful in a V-necked, long black dress that exposed a little cleavage and fully accentuated her slender curves, easily making her the most magnificent creature in the room. Her hair was stylishly held up, with a few curly locks falling down her face.

Mrs. Gallagher's arm was tucked in the crook of Mr. Gallagher's arm. I'd never met him since I started working for the boss lady. In fact, I'd never even met her son or daughter. The only reason I recognized them was because I'd seen their pictures in Mrs. Gallaghers office.

There was some family resemblance but the kids looked more like their father than they did the mother. She was certainly unique. Even the daughter I'd expected to be a duplicate didn't look anything like her.

Mr. Gallagher was a good-looking man in his mid fifties. He seemed to age as gracefully as his wife. I waited for the family to disperse and quickly approached Mrs. Gallagher. She moved with the grace and elegance of a ballerina.

"Mrs. Gallagher," I said softly.

When she faced me, I thought I saw something flicker in her gaze. She was probably surprised by my unusual getup.

"Olivia, you look lovely."

The last thing I expected from her was a compliment on my appearance. The fact that she noticed made me feel confident. It also made me smile. *She noticed me.* That usually stern voice in my head screamed in joy.

"Thank you," I said, almost shyly.

I wanted to tell her she looked great too, but I didn't think it'd move her much as her compliment moved me, so I got straight to work.

Guests started arriving minutes later. In half an hour, the event was a luxurious affair, an intimate extravaganza, and one of the most enigmatic events I'd ever had the pleasure to plan and attend. The charity ball took a life of its own when people arrived and I stayed by Mrs. Gallagher's side, giving her tidbits of information on guests she needed to charm in order for them to be generous with their donations.

My photographic memory came in handy. Every face I saw, I remembered with accompanying details of the relevant information Mrs. Gallagher needed to use. People interacted with one another, ate special delicacies and drank expensive bottles of wine while I shadowed Mrs. Gallagher as she moved among the crowd, sometimes accompanied by her husband.

I kept wondering if he knew how lucky he was to be with such a woman. Every man she spoke to at the party seemed equally as awed by her presence, and mysteriously disarming charm. I noticed several men flirting with her, which slightly irked me, but she was such a lady, she handled them like a professional.

After meeting almost everybody, she went up on stage and gave a moving speech, which everyone applauded. When she stepped down, I realized Rex was right. I did have a crush on her. Something about the way she carried herself the entire night made her irresistible to me. It made her irresistible to a lot of people.

"She's good, isn't she?" Lauren said.

There was still a little hostility between us, but she'd been surprisingly nice to me that night, which I figured was because Mrs. Gallagher was there and I was practically by her side almost all evening.

"Yeah, she is," I said, almost to myself as my eyes followed the woman who everyone seemed to be enthralled by.

She had such calm and poise it was almost as though she walked on air. Everything that came out of her mouth was gold. She touched my arm a few times that night, pointing me to people she needed me to identify for her and each of those touches went straight to my heart. I was afraid my crush might have grown into infatuation.

A lot of donations were made through cheques that night and others were going to be sent throughout the week. I was certain Mrs. Gallagher had made a fortune out of the charity ball event. When people were leaving, hours later, they were each given a goody bag with personalized messages from Mrs. Gallagher herself.

She told me what to have written in the notes and I sent out word so that everyone could leave with a little piece of her. When the event was over and almost everyone had left, I was certain I'd gotten the job because there had not been any problems. I had told Lauren to make sure every possible negative scenario that could occur would be fixed before any of the guests, or worse, the boss lady, got wind of it.

At the end of the night, we exchanged notes and she told me everything I needed to know because I would have to give a detailed account to Mrs. Gallagher on Monday and that was if I was still hired.

I was outside on the balcony getting some air because I needed to absorb the overwhelming night when Mrs. Gallagher called out to me.

"Olivia."

I was going to walk over to her, but she was already approaching me when she called me. She had two glasses of wine in her hands and I was surprised when she handed one over to me. I hadn't had a sip of alcohol all night and I'd barely had anything to eat.

"You did a great job tonight," she said.

My heart started pounding. First at the compliment, then at how close she came to stand beside me. I could smell her mind-numbingly sweet perfume and it stilled my senses. I had to take a sip of wine to relax myself though it did nothing to help.

"Thank you," I said.

"To be honest, I was a bit concerned because of your lack of experience in this field, but your hardworking nature and commitment to your work gave me some faith," she said.

I wanted to tell her I'd also had some reservations, but I wasn't going to equip her with my weaknesses. I needed her to stick to that belief if I needed to keep this job.

"I was surprised at how accurate you were with details of the guests."

"I have a photographic memory. It wasn't hard for me to remember their faces, names and other relevant details," I said.

That was the longest conversation we'd ever had and I didn't know why but it felt good that she'd come see me when the event was over and tell me what she thought. I felt like she was giving me the same attention she'd given her guests while charming the money out of their wallets.

"Well, it's no surprise that I'm pleased with your work," she said, and took a sip of her wine.

Her words meant a lot to me. I'd never had a boss who actually acknowledged my work and commended me for it. This was a first. It was also the first time I was insanely attracted to an employer.

I hoped all the good things she was saying meant I'd gotten the job, but again, I really couldn't read her. Maybe this was her way of turning me down. Why else would she give me so much attention? She'd had no interest in me whatsoever. Not that I was taking it for granted, her showering me with attention made me feel like I had won a lottery.

Speaking of which, where was her family? Shouldn't she have left with them? This conversation could've taken place the following day. Had her husband left? Were we there alone? She turned to face the sky as the stars and moonlight illuminated down on us, making her face glow.

With that look, she could have seduced a god. Everything about her was so remarkable. I wanted to feel it, to touch it, just to experience a slight piece of her world. Hers, not the immensely wealthy universe I'd been thrusted into a few hours earlier.

"You're so beautiful." The words flew out of my mouth like a colony of bats out of a cave into the dark night.

She looked at me and as her blue eyes shone into me, I felt like she could see the very depths of my soul. She extracted layer after layer of my soul until I was fully exposed for her to see.

"You're the most startlingly beautiful woman I've ever seen," I said.

I couldn't believe my courage. How was I saying this? Was I under a trance? Had she hypnotized me into speaking my thoughts? She'd always made me so nervous, but now, as I stood in front of her, I felt braver than I had in years.

Then something magical happened. That invisible wall that had been between us crumbled and her face softened. It was like I could see her for the very first time and I wasn't afraid. I looked at her, quenching my sight, filling myself with her until I was full.

"Olivia," she whispered.

I took a brave step forward and put everything I'd worked so hard for on the line. I'd forever hate myself if I didn't take that chance. I'd live with regret, with what-ifs. Whatever force that was making me feel this way must've been inside her too, because why else was she still standing there? Why hadn't she walked away?

No more questions, no more thinking. I decided and dove in. I closed the space between us and covered her lips with mine. The warmth of her breath spread through me like a wild fire. The first feel of her lips touching mine was velvet smooth and intricately soft.

I wanted to absorb every moment, so when we touched, I paused for a second to take it in, then proceeded, unsure she'd kiss me back. The fear of the unknown held me captive, but I fought it and softly brushed my lips against hers.

She tasted like an exotic mix of wild flowers, champagne and her. When she gently parted her lips on my request and began to respond, I wasn't prepared for the train wreck of emotions and sensations that would overcome me.

My breathing became heavy as her lips explored mine and I carefully placed my arm over her waist, wondering if gravity had betrayed her too. A surge of excitement shot through me when she parted my lips, demanding to know me better, more intimately and I gave her access to everything that she needed, while she made true a dream I'd desired from a distance. God, I wanted this woman. I wanted her to consume me. I wanted her all to myself.

She pulled away before I could get myself together and had this look in her eyes that I couldn't interpret. I didn't know if I'd just lost a job I'd come so close to getting, or if I'd just opened the pits of hell upon my own heart.

She walked away from me with my secrets in the palm of her hand and the place she'd occupied next to me instantly filled with a cold air that accompanied an icy breeze, which snapped me back to reality.

What had I done? I kept asking myself as I left Eden plaza, heading back to my place. But something, a spark in my heart fought on. A spark that created a light no amount of self-deprecation could extinguish.

Chapter Two

When I woke up the following day, I was exhausted but my body had an alarm clock of its own and no matter how hard I tried to force myself to fall back asleep, I couldn't. It had been such a busy week. I'd hoped to rest that Sunday before I started looking for another job.

I planned on staying in bed longer but the persistent knock on my door forced me to get up. I lazily got out of bed and went to open the door.

"What time did you get home last night?" Rex asked when he walked in.

He lived about ten minutes away from my place and tended to come over on Sunday mornings with breakfast. That morning, he had coffee and bagels.

When I was about to get back in bed, I noticed how weirdly he was eyeing me and I wondered if I had drool on my face.

"You look different," he said.

Oh, the makeover and the party. I wasn't ready to let myself think about that.

"Actually, you look great. What did they do to you?"

I laughed as I took the coffee and bag of bagels from him. "Stop it," I said.

"How did it go?" he asked.

"It was a successful night."

"So, you got the job?" he asked in excitement.

"Not exactly. Actually, I have no idea. But I don't think so." I doubted after the stunt I'd pulled at the end of the night Mrs. Gallagher would ever want me anywhere near her.

"What do you mean? If the night was as successful as you say, why do you think you didn't get the job?" Rex asked.

"I screwed up and I don't know if I want to talk about it," I said.

"Come on, tell me."

I took a sip of coffee and leaned back on the pillow as the events of the previous night unfolded in my head. I told Rex what had happened without going into too much detail.

"Sounds like it went great. If she doesn't hire you, it'll have to be out of something else because it sounds to me like everyone had a good time," he said.

I avoided his gaze and took a bite.

"What did you do?" he asked.

"You were right," I said.

"I was right about what?"

"I did have a crush on Mrs. Gallagher and after the event, she kind of figured it out."

"How? Did you tell her?"

"I kissed her. And before you say anything, I just need to say this. I couldn't help myself and if I hadn't kissed her..." I trailed off.

"You would've gotten the job," he finished.

"I was going to say I would've ended up regretting it, but yeah, pretty much what you just said."

"Oh, Livvy. What the hell?"

"I know." I placed the coffee and bagel on the table beside my bed and covered my face with a pillow.

Rex got in bed beside me and placed his arm around my shoulder. "So how was it?"

I smiled at him, recalling the magical kiss. "Amazing."

"How did she react?"

"She kissed me back."

The feel of her soft silky lips running gently across mine had me reliving the moment all over again.

"Was it worth it?" he asked.

"Seeing as I might be living on the streets in a few days, the obvious answer would be no. But I don't regret it. I got to touch her and kiss her. It was like trying to reach out to an angel and having the angel reach back, embrace me and tell me it was okay to feel the way I was feeling."

"Sounds deep."

I pushed him away. "You wouldn't understand."

"Well, seeing as how you blew off a potentially great paying job for a kiss, probably not."

"Ugh. I have to start looking for another job."

"Wait, she's going to pay you for the week you worked for her, right?"

"I think so. We never really discussed the terms of payment but she doesn't look like the kind of person who'd refuse to pay an employee."

"Don't worry. You can always camp out on my couch until you get back on your feet," he offered.

I smiled at him and kissed his cheek. "Thanks, Rex. I don't know what I'd do without you."

"You can thank me by buying my artwork when you're rich. After school."

I groaned at the thought of school. I had exams coming up I hadn't studied enough for. "I don't know how long I can do this. I'm stretching myself out too thin and I'm barely covering any ground."

"You came close," Rex said.

"Not close enough. I can't think about this right now." I was already getting a migraine.

"Hey, at least you came out of it looking great. I wish I'd seen you last night. I bet you were stunning," he said.

I smiled. He knew how to lift my spirit. "Not to brag, but I kinda was."

"Kinda? Look at you. Your eyes, your face, your hair, I would've loved to see you in that dress."

I had tossed the dress on the couch, which reminded me, was I going to have to return it? It was probably the most beautiful and expensive dress I'd ever worn.

"Hey, how about we go out for a drink? My treat."

"It's ten in the morning," I said.

"So what?"

So, it was too early to drink. But then again, who was I kidding? It was probably going to be the highlight of my day.

"Okay," I said as I got out of bed.

After taking a quick shower and getting dressed, I reached for my phone right at the same time it started ringing. I looked at the screen and noticed it was a private number calling.

"Give me a minute," I told Rex and picked it up.

After a moment, an English accent spoke. Oh God, it was Francis. "Mrs. Gallagher is requesting your presence at the Gallagher mansion."

"She is?" I asked in surprise.

"You should get here as soon as possible," Francis said.

"Okay," I said as he hung up.

I didn't know why Mrs. Gallagher wanted to see me, but it made me nervous.

"Are you okay? Who was that?" Rex asked.

"Francis, the Gallagher's butler. Mrs. Gallagher wants to see me."

"Oh, that's good, right?"

"I don't know. I honestly have no idea."

"You need to go."

"I'll call you after the meeting." I kissed his cheek as we walked out and parted ways.

On my way to the Gallagher's, I kept wondering why she wanted to see me and I couldn't think of one good reason. All I could think about was the kiss. Whatever bravery that had come over me and driven me to kiss her was long gone. I was scared shitless. What if she slapped me with a sexual harassment suit? No, I wouldn't worry myself.

I would drive there and hear out what she had to say. I tried not to think about it the rest of the way. When I drove my car into parking, I took a few deep breaths and got out. I remembered the first time I'd driven there late for my interview. Gosh, it felt like ages ago. Had it only been a week?

As I headed towards the large entrance of the house, I grew more and more anxious. I pressed the doorbell and waited. Francis opened the door and let me in.

"Mrs. Gallagher's office," he said.

I looked at the intimidating stairwell and felt like David in his duel with Goliath. After the first step, I told myself it wouldn't be bad news if she'd called me there. Bad news could be delivered via phone calls so this had to be a good thing.

I confidently headed to Mrs. Gallagher's office and knocked. After the second time without a response, I walked in. There was no one in the office. Francis had probably gone to let her know I'd arrived. Good, a little time was exactly what I needed.

I'd never been in that office alone. Every time I went there, Mrs. Gallagher was always present and my gaze usually stuck to her so I never got a chance to look around the surroundings. There was a large library cabinet with quite an impressive collection of books on the entire left wall, a brown leather couch with a small table and a lamp on the opposite side, probably where she sat when she read her books. But her desk was the centre piece in the office and quite an impressive one too.

The large window behind the desk made me wonder what it faced. If my office faced a tennis court, what view did this one have? I was about to check when the door opened and Mrs. Gallagher walked in.

I grew instantly tense and waited as she walked past me and headed to her desk. That magical scent of her fragrance sweetly assaulted me again as I confidently looked up and watched her. She was casually dressed in a summer dress that looked wonderful on her. After getting used to her official outfits, I hadn't imagined she could pull off a laid back and relaxed look in such an appealing manner.

"Congratulations, your project was a success last night," she said.

"Thank you."

She sat down and summoned me to approach her throne. I walked closer as she placed an envelope on the desk right in front of me.

"Your pay for the week," she said.

My pay? This meant I wouldn't have to camp out on Rex's couch. Oh, thank goodness. However much it was, I knew it'd cover me for a while until I found another job.

"Aren't you going to take a look?" she asked.

I smiled at her and said, "I trust you." It was meant as a joke but she didn't smile and I felt stupid. "Thank you for taking a chance on me," I said before I turned to leave.

"See you tomorrow," she said.

I froze in my step. "Tomorrow?"

"You have somewhere else you need to be?" she asked.

"No, I just thought..." I trailed off.

"I would like you to continue working for me, Olivia."

I smiled, feeling a great rush of warmth overcome me. "I would be honored," I said.

"Good, see you then."

I nodded and when I turned to leave, she added, "Don't let what happened last night repeat itself."

My heart started racing at the statement as the memory of the kiss came back to mind. "I'm so sorry about that," I said, trying to sound as professional and emotionless as possible. When she failed to respond, I left her office. I couldn't believe I'd gotten the job. I was going to be working for Amelia Gallagher.

"Hey."

I stopped downstairs at the voice and turned to face Amelia's daughter.

"You must be the new girl," she said. "I'm Adrianna."

"I'm Olivia."

"Did you get the job?"

When I nodded, she smiled in what appeared to be amusement.

"No judgment on you, but don't get too comfortable. Her assistants never last."

"Oh." Was she trying to gauge my reaction? I really couldn't tell. "Good to know," I said, confident I'd last longer.

"I tried working for her as an intern…"

Oh, she wanted to chat. I wasn't sure I was supposed to fraternize with the Gallagher family.

"I couldn't handle the pressure. There is never-ending work to be done," she said.

It was better than moving from one job to the next. "That's kind of why I like the job."

"Hmm, you're weird."

No, I was broke with student loans to pay. With a consistent source of income, I could stabilize my life. I wasn't born with a silver spoon in my mouth like this pretty little princess staring back at me with soft grey eyes.

"Nice talking to you, Adrianna. I have to go," I said and walked out.

I called Rex on my way and he suggested we go out and celebrate.

Any other day I would've taken my books and started studying for my exams, but I was in a celebratory mood and I deserved a break after the busy week I'd had.

As I drove away from the Gallagher residence, I couldn't help wondering how many of Amelia Gallagher's assistants could say they had kissed the queen and lived to tell about it. What had I been thinking? And where had I gotten the guts to do such a thing?

I'd been confident all through the night, floating around the crowd beside Mrs. Gallagher, meeting so many people, hearing so many interesting stories. Stories I could only dream about but never live to see. It'd been a wonderful night and being beside Mrs. Gallagher had been a bonus.

Working for her was going to be both challenging and inspiring. Challenging because of how demanding she was as an employer, not to mention my disturbing crush on her and inspiring because of the people I'd come to meet and maybe even places I'd get to see.

Chapter Three

"Egypt?"

I was handed a first-class plane ticket and informed I was traveling to Cairo. Mrs. Gallagher was absent so the news came from Francis. He had the plane ticket waiting for me first thing Monday morning when I walked into the mansion.

I'd known travel would be part of the job but I'd not expected it so soon.

"Why I'm I going to Cairo?"

"You'll get your instructions here." Francis handed me an iPhone.

My flight was in an hour. I needed to go back home, retrieve my passport and be at the airport in due time for travel.

I hadn't signed any employment contract, so I wondered if this was another exercise by Mrs. Gallagher. Even though she'd said I'd gotten the job, the only way I was going to be absolutely sure was if I had physical proof and that meant my signature on a piece of paper.

"There is a driver waiting for you outside, ready to take you wherever you need to go," Francis said.

A driver? How convenient. I needed to get moving.

"Thank you, Francis."

A sleek blue BMW was parked outside waiting for me. A man dressed in a black suit stepped out when I approached the car.

He was a good-looking man in his early forties. He had the same serious expression as Francis. It made me wonder if I'd also get that look if I worked for Mrs. Gallagher long enough.

"Ms. Williams?"

I nodded.

"My name is James Holliday, I'm your driver."

He was polite, with a pleasant smile as he opened the back door for me.

"Thank you, Mr. Holliday."

"James will be just fine."

I nodded and sat on the soft black leather. James got in the driver's seat. As he drove out of the Gallagher residence, it felt like the car was flying. I could hardly hear the engine or the motion of the vehicle. The car must've cost an arm and a leg, but I had to admit, those Germans knew what they were doing.

"Where would you like me to take you today, Ms. Williams?" James asked.

He was looking at me through the rearview mirror while keeping an eye on the deserted Gallagher lane.

"Please call me Olivia."

"Olivia," he said.

I saw him smile with his eyes and realized he was nothing like Francis. He was warmer, definitely friendlier.

I gave him directions to my house and he nodded, paying attention to the road as I took out the iPhone to figure out what my mission to Cairo was.

As soon as I accessed the device, it pinged with an email from Mrs. Gallagher. It had specific instructions on where I was going, where I'd be staying, who I'd be meeting and his contact information.

When I opened the plane ticket to check how long my flight to Egypt would last, I found a platinum credit card. I had to admit; this was probably the best job I'd ever gotten by far.

First class plane ticket, all expenses paid for and my own personal driver. This was going to be interesting.

On my way to the airport after picking up my passport and packing a few outfits, I called Rex to let him know what was happening.

"I'm going to Egypt!" I said when he picked my call.

"What? When and Why?"

"I'm heading to the airport right now. I'm not sure yet why I'm going, I just have some contact information for when I get there. Mrs. Gallagher sent me."

"Shit, that's awesome."

"Mrs. Gallagher is full of surprises."

"How was she this morning?"

I wished I'd seen her. My sight and my being were thirsting after her. "I didn't see her."

"How long will you be in Egypt?"

"My flight is about twelve hours long, so give or take, a day or two."

"It would've been awesome were you going to stay longer so you can go sightseeing."

"Yeah, but even then I wouldn't be able to afford it. I doubt Mrs. Gallagher would take it too kindly if I spent more than I'm supposed to."

"Oh well, try and enjoy whatever free time you get. Take some pictures so I can pretend I've been there too. Have an awesome trip and call me the moment you get back," he said.

"Sure."

Rex would've loved going to Egypt. Being an artist, I was sure he would've been ecstatic to see Egyptian art in its place of origin.

I sent a quick reply to Mrs. Gallagher, wondering where she'd been that morning.

After she'd handed over my paycheck, I'd hoped I'd get to see her often but that hope was dashed now. With the traveling, I doubted we'd get to spend much time together.

She was a very busy person with countless responsibilities. I'd done my research on her and discovered she came from a family of money. Mr. Gallagher's wealth combined with her own was enough to buy several islands and happily retire for a couple of centuries if not more.

Amelia's family business was in pharmaceuticals while Mr. Gallagher's was in the manufacturing industry. Both their businesses were extremely successful and together, they were a superpower.

They owned homes in Europe and other exotic places, super yachts, jets, and technically anything money could buy.

After my research, I had goose bumps all over. I'd known the family was well off, but I hadn't imagined they were stratospherically successful.

I was more intimidated by Mrs. Gallagher than ever. The upside to her success was that my paycheck had been more than I'd expected.

I was happy because I wasn't going to be kicked out of my house for a while, and the money was enough to support my needs for now. If I managed to keep this job long enough, I'd end up paying off my student loans and perhaps even live a debt free life at some point.

Having not to constantly worry about where my next paycheck would come from and if it'd be enough to cover my expenses was reassuring. If I had to fly across North Atlantic to keep this job, then so be it.

When I stepped into first class of my flight, it felt like someone had kicked me hard in the gut. I'd only traveled a couple of times back to visit my parents in St. Paul, Minnesota since leaving home to go to school at NYU.

They'd spent every single cent of their savings to make sure I had the education I needed to succeed in life but since it wasn't enough, I'd differed on some classes to make time for work.

I couldn't visit them as often as they wished, but they understood it was hard. During my visits, I'd been in economy class and had never set foot in first class until now. The experience was similar to the first time I'd walked into the Gallagher mansion. The overwhelming feeling had me holding my breath as I was shown to my seat.

It was right next to the window with lots of privacy, plenty of legroom and space to stretch out on to. After putting away my carry-on luggage, I slid into the unbelievably comfortable chair which could easily convert itself into a bed and I noticed the wide screen beside it, for entertainment options.

The best part, much to my awe, was the bar. Though it was too early to drink, the twelve-hour flight would give me plenty of time for that later. For now, I needed to note down the information I required for Cairo.

I'd been concerned about getting a visa but it appeared I'd get it at the airport upon arrival. Before takeoff, I quickly went online to read up on Egypt and the things I wouldn't get to see, just to feel like I knew something about the country.

There was so much information online, I wished I hadn't checked because all over a sudden, it was saddening to know I'd be so close to all these beautiful, wonderful things; architectural wonders, historical buildings and holy sites, but I wouldn't get a chance to see them.

I was going to meet a man named Frank Connor, who was an original art dealer and according to the information Mrs. Gallagher had sent me, I was supposed to appraise a piece of art and sign a release form, then the parcel was going to be sent to New York.

His information was in the email, though limited, I had to go online and find out who he was and how he looked like so that I'd know him when I saw him.

My flight took off half an hour later and as we ascended, I found myself growing nervous. I didn't know why, because it was uneventful and even though I was comfortable, I was unable to relax. Later when I was arriving, I realized it was because my body was in constant work mode.

I'd never sat idle for so long without anything to do for as long as I could remember, which made it hard to close my eyes for a nap. I had a couple of drinks to relax, but I only got more anxious so when the flight landed, I couldn't wait to get to work.

There was someone at Cairo International Airport from my hotel waiting to pick me up. I spotted him the moment I walked out of the airport because he had a piece of paper with my name written on it.

The drive to my hotel didn't last long but when I alighted, I realized I was tired, probably from jetlag. The receptionist was very friendly. When I gave her my details, she had a porter take me to a suite that was a bit more extravagant than I'd expected.

It was almost six in the morning since Cairo was six hours ahead and my meeting was in five hours so I needed a shower and some rest.

I didn't have much time to enjoy the ambiance or the luxury as I was too tired to. After a nice warm shower, I got in bed and set my alarm so as not to oversleep. I'd have the experience when I woke up to fully appreciate it, not now with my sleepy and tired senses.

I met Frank Connor at the hotel lounge. He was a tall lanky man whose age I couldn't estimate because he appeared as though he was in his sixties but something told me he was younger.

I recognized him immediately, thanks to having looked him up online earlier. He was neatly dressed in a suit and was ready to get to work from the moment we met. We left the hotel, but I wasn't sure where we were headed. I was glad we were using the hotel transport because it made me feel safe.

Unfortunately, apart from a few old buildings that probably held no great story, I didn't see much on our way. Frank wasn't much of a talker so the half hour drive was a bit boring. When I asked him about the area, he had only a word or two to say.

We ended up in an old warehouse and Frank went to retrieve something. I looked around for signs of anything worthy of taking home a story, but everything in the warehouse was covered up, probably for protection from dust.

Frank came back with another man carrying an item that seemed heavy. He was holding a file in his hands next to his counterpart. I realized I was a bit eager as the man placed the object on a table some distance from where I stood.

My curiosity continued to grow when Frank slowly began to uncover the object because this was the reason I'd been sent to Egypt. The big reveal had me holding my breath.

When Frank removed the last cover, I looked at the piece placed in front of me.

"Do you know what this is?" he asked.

I looked at him, not sure how I was supposed to answer.

"It looks like a headpiece," I said.

"It is a headpiece, but do you know whose it is?"

I shook my head as I studied it closer. The headpiece featured conventional Egyptian flair with cyan colored angles of gold bead strands. The chains were long and dangling in the back and shorter in front, resembling bangs.

A lavish fabric asp with genuine gemstone eyes were attached to a band made of gold embroidery. It had to be the most magnificent headpiece I'd ever seen.

"This is Cleopatra's famous headpiece," Frank said.

My jaw dropped. "Cleopatra, as in the last pharaoh?" I'd studied the history of many world leaders and one of the female rulers had been Cleopatra so I was endowed with a little knowledge regarding the queen.

"Yes, the ruthless ruler made a great impact to the history of this country. This piece in particular continues to inspire artists, designers and everyone with creative ability."

I was completely shocked to discover I was standing right next to one of the most influential pieces of art in modern civilization.

"This is unbelievable," I said, realizing I was a little breathless.

I may not have gone on an adventurous excursion in Egypt like most tourists, but I was looking at the most breathtaking item anyone had ever seen.

"Now that you've seen it, I need you to sign here so I can have it shipped to New York," Frank said.

"New York?"

"Yes, just sign here and here." He handed me a pen and showed me where to sign.

I headed back to the hotel afterwards, leaving Frank Connor behind, and emailed Mrs. Gallagher to inform her the job had been done.

I was still completely star-struck by what I'd just witnessed and couldn't wait to get back to the hotel and call Rex to tell him all about it.

When I approached the reception desk, the receptionist I'd met earlier during arrival was still on duty. She handed me an envelope which had come in for me, and on my way up to my room, I received an email from Mrs. Gallagher.

I had to read it twice to make sure the information was accurate. She stated that my next flight was to Morocco, in the beautiful city of Marrakech and I was to leave Cairo in three and a half hours. The envelope I'd received contained my plane ticket.

I'd hoped to rest a while longer and had expected to travel back home, but I didn't mind a little more travel. I just wished her royal highness would inform me of all the other places I'd have to travel beforehand.

At this rate I could be gone for over a week and I hadn't carried enough clothes to last me that long, or maybe that was what the platinum credit card was for. The thought was appealing and made the whole thing all the more appealing.

My flight to Marrakech lasted five hours and it was nine in the evening when I arrived. Like Cairo, there was a driver from my hotel waiting for me. Whatever travel agency Mrs. Gallagher used was very efficient.

I sent her an email to inform her I had arrived as I was driven to my hotel and read through the email she'd sent me earlier to see what I was there to do.

I wished she could be more forthcoming with information but she only gave me bits and clues. I assumed I was there to do the same thing I had in Cairo and relaxed. I couldn't help wondering where she'd send me off to next.

It seemed she was fond of African countries. I hoped it'd be another exotic country with a rich history and I'd see something magnificent like Cleopatra's headpiece. The memory of it still sent chills through me.

When I'd called Rex to tell him, he hadn't believed it in the beginning. The whole thing was still unbelievable to me too, so I couldn't blame him. I'd informed him of my next stop and he'd told me to call him if I experienced pangs of loneliness, a statement I found odd because I'd never felt lonely before. Maybe it was probably because I was such a loner.

I'd had friends in St. Paul, but had lost touch with them after moving to New York. Rex was my only friend now and because of my busy lifestyle, I barely noticed the lack thereof.

I hoped one day I'd have it easier and start enjoying life, but that day didn't seem very close. The simple things in life that I should've found joy in were absent.

The kiss I'd shared with Mrs. Gallagher was by far the best experience I'd had since I'd gotten to New York four years ago. I still thought about the kiss and wondered if it ever crossed Mrs. Gallagher's mind. Probably not as often, maybe never at all, but it didn't matter because it was in my mind and my heart.

After a long relaxing warm bath, I decided to take a walk and have dinner at the hotel's restaurant. I was going to have a good time despite the lack of tourist privileges other people seemed to have.

The hotel was beautiful, just like the one I'd stayed at in Cairo. My room was a fortress, beautifully decorated and furnished.

I felt like a princess, enjoying the first-class treatment and hospitality. It put me in a league of my own and it was nice because for a while, I could pretend to be someone else; someone who didn't have any worries in the world.

After dinner, I stayed up late and read up on Cleopatra's life as the ruthless ruler of Egypt. It was an intriguing story which seemed to have inspired story tellers and playwrights all over the world.

It was fascinating how she'd conquered the hearts of Caesar and Antony, but her tragic end was befitting of a Queen who'd done everything, mostly wrong, to maintain her throne.

It wasn't her beauty that had captured the hearts of the two great men; it was her remarkable charm, her brilliance, her brash coquette and intellectual command. I wondered if I could ever be like that. Sure, I wasn't born or bred like the Gallaghers but if I possessed the confidence Cleopatra had, maybe Mrs. Gallagher would take notice of me.

It'd be so magical to watch her bathing me in her sight like a vision she needed to soak in. Her touch was probably cloud light and soft, just like the silky texture of her skin.

If a kiss had been so overwhelming it'd rendered me weak, I wondered how it'd feel accompanied by her touch, by more than a touch. I shook my head, trying to shake away the thoughts. Even though erotic thoughts of my boss were harmless, they could alter my working performance.

But for now, since I wasn't working, who would it hurt? My thoughts trailed back to Mrs. Gallagher. I imagined myself seducing her, like Cleopatra had seduced the two men.

I'd wear nothing but the golden headpiece. The image was amusing. I smiled as I thought about it longer. We'd be at a hotel, similar to one I was staying in. Unfortunately, my imagination for the finer things in life was only limited to what I'd seen because I wanted to draw from real life.

I imagined her lying on white satin sheets in a sexy red teddy exposing her beautifully toned legs and looking at me with her crystal blue eyes. The erotic thought was a turn on that stopped my fantasy because if I went any farther, I'd be unable to focus on anything else when I saw her, if ever I did so again.

Like Cairo, I met my contact at the hotel lounge and went to appraise some items. This time it was a couple of intricately ornamented traditional dresses called djellaba and kaftans. I thought it odd to come all the way to Marrakech to sign for garments-despite their uniqueness and high quality-to be shipped to New York, so I asked my contact what was so important about them.

Unfortunately, he didn't seem as informed about it as Frank so I decided to find out more about it later. When I went back to the hotel, I emailed Mrs. Gallagher and went to the restaurant for lunch.

She surprised me when she emailed back saying I could use the credit card to get whatever I needed, so I decided to tour around later and shop for a few clothes and a couple of souvenirs. I was excited until I read the next paragraph to learn where my next flight was taking me.

"South Africa?" Rex asked after I shared the news.

"Yeah, Kimberley mines."

I'd told him what I'd been sent there to do and even though Mrs. Gallagher was still not forthcoming with information, I suspected I was going to do the same thing I'd done in Cairo and Marrakech.

"Hey, get me a souvenir, will you? Something artsy. If she said you could use the credit card for expenses you can say you got it for yourself," he said.

"How is Astoria?"

I lived in Astoria, Queens. It was the only place I could afford and even the small space I lived in still felt too expensive.

"Same old, same old. Nothing interesting with you gone," he said.

"That's sweet. I miss you too."

"Any idea when you'll be back?"

"Nope, no clue. I'm enjoying the trip though. It feels easy, too easy. To be honest I much rather prefer running around carrying out impossible tasks. This feels safe, even though it's pleasant."

"You should be enjoying it. From what you've told me about Mrs. Gallagher, you can't really tell what she'll have you doing next."

He was right. I should've been enjoying it.

"So, any ideas why you're going to Kimberley mines? Do you think you're going to pick up diamonds?" His excitement and wonder was unmistakable.

"I don't know. Cleopatra's headpiece was an awesome surprise, the Moroccan attire, well, to be honest I didn't fully understand. So I can't predict what Mrs. Gallagher wants me to sign for next."

"I envy your job. I hope the paycheck will be worth it."

"It better be," I said.

We talked a while longer then hang up.

I left Marrakech in the evening and was glad for the first-class ticket because I was going to be airborne for ten hours. I was glad the flight was at night because I got a chance to sleep all through it thanks to a couple of glasses of red wine. They knocked me out and put me to sleep for most of the flight.

Chapter Four

South Africa was breathtaking. The environment was definitely different from the North African countries I'd come from. The crisp clean air, the green scenery, the clear blue sky and the lack of traffic proved I was far from home but nonetheless the entire atmosphere was beautiful.

I was taken to my hotel like the two previous locations, but unlike the rest, there were things to look at and admire. My driver was a chubby black man who was very sweet and friendly.

"Is this your first time in South Africa?" he asked.

I nodded, noticing his thick accent. "Yes, it's beautiful."

"This is a perfect place to visit for a first timer. Do you know much about it?" he asked.

I shook my head. The only thing I was aware of was that Kimberley was the largest diamond mine in the world.

"Kimberley is the capital of the Northern Cape Province of South Africa. It's also known as the Big Hole or the City that sparkles. The Big Hole was dug by humans when the mine was discovered and it's so large, its visible from space."

That was impressive. He seemed to know a lot and I was an avid learner. "Tell me more." He was the first person I'd met in the three countries who gave information voluntarily.

"If you have time, I'll love to take you around." He handed me his card and I quickly scanned it, noting his name was Lungile.

"I'm not very sure about how long my stay will last, but I'll definitely let you know."

"If you're going to be around the area, I can take you for a walk along the high platform to view The Big Hole, you can visit museums, national parks, nature reserves, hunting lodges and historic sites."

Sounded very interesting and I was certain I'd love the experience, but as I'd stated, I wasn't sure how long I'd be around. Mrs. Gallagher wasn't giving me much time to enjoy any place I visited so I doubted I'd get that chance here.

"You'll fully appreciate Kimberley if you stay overnight," he added.

He sold Kimberley to me and I wanted more than anything to stay, but the moment I arrived to my hotel, I had to email Mrs. Gallagher and inform her of my arrival and then she'd make the arrangements I needed to follow.

"I'll get back to you on that tour tomorrow." I told him when I got to my hotel. I went to the reception desk and checked in and the moment I got to my room, I stripped down and went to take a shower.

I'd run out of clothes and personal effects and needed to shop for more. I hadn't managed to shop for anything in Cairo but I'd gotten a few things in Marrakech and I planned on getting a few more in South Africa.

After some rest, I read the email from Mrs. Gallagher. This time I wasn't meeting someone. Instead, I was given a location and however I decided to get there was up to me.

She didn't mention anything about traveling to another country and that was a bit reassuring. I called Rex to inform him I'd arrived safely. Talking to him made me miss home. I'd only been gone a few days but I was starting to get nostalgic.

I found myself missing a house I resented living in and started growing concerned about school and studies and how my exams and lack of reading would affect my grade.

After worrying about it long enough, I decided I'd have to talk to Mrs. Gallagher about giving me a few hours off to do my exams. I hoped she wouldn't mind since so far I'd proven I was more than capable of handling my duties responsibly.

Later on, I decided I'd need Lungile's services after all. He'd take me to the location Mrs. Gallagher had sent, then we'd go shopping and maybe after, he could take me on a tour of the area. This was probably the only trip I was going to enjoy.

Lungile came back eight hours later after I'd rested enough.

"I see you decided to take that tour," he said.

This wasn't exactly a tour, but I couldn't tell him so. "Why do you say so?"

"Because you get to see The Big Hole after all," he said.

I wasn't quite sure what he meant, but when he parked the car and we got out, his meaning became clear.

"How big is this thing?" I asked in shock.

"The depth of the hole is 215 meters. You want a closer view?"

At the question, I imagined myself at the top of the platform and could feel my heart sinking. At that moment, it felt like I'd developed a fear of heights.

"How deep is the water?" I asked nervously.

"41 meters, come on, it's safe. There haven't been any reports of accidental falls."

The man had a poor sense of humor.

I followed after him, taking pictures with the phone because this was a sight Rex needed to see. Lungile took pictures of me as we walked along the platform and though I kept a straight face, I was terrified.

"People dug this hole?" I asked in disbelief.

"Yes, a lot of people migrated here because of work. A total of 2,722 kilograms of diamonds was produced," he said.

That bit of information was quite impressive.

"Here is a brochure with the history of the mine," he said.

I took it from him as we headed to the mining shafts. Lungile had a lot of information regarding the area. I didn't need the brochure so much as he narrated everything all throughout.

When we got to the area Mrs. Gallagher had instructed, I went to look for the person I was there to see. This time it was a woman, a pleasant looking one who took me to a vault full of genuine diamonds.

Lungile had mentioned a vault with genuine diamonds people viewed and I assumed from the room I was in, I was on the other side of that vault.

It was fascinating being in a room full of diamonds which had been dug from the very same place. Not a jewelry store or any other place I could ever find myself.

The woman took me to a red diamond I was too afraid to look at incase I blinked and it went missing and I got blamed for it. But what an exquisite diamond it was.

"These are very rare to come by," the woman said.

I could imagine.

"You need to sign here and here."

She handed me a pen and I signed.

When I rejoined Lungile, I was still overwhelmed. I wanted to call Rex immediately and tell him about it, but he was going to have to wait because now, I wanted to see everything. I'd call the hotel in an hour to find out if I had any messages or packages.

Lungile took me where I needed to go. He took me to a couple of museums and national parks, and after that we went for lunch at a gourmet restaurant where they served South African dishes.

The food was different but it was delicious. After the restaurant, he took me to historical sites and I felt like a tourist. It was a nice feeling because I was part of witnessing something many people never got to see.

I called the hotel a few times but there were still no messages for me, so I went shopping, got myself some nice clothes and got Rex some gifts and souvenirs.

By the time I got back to the hotel, I felt like I'd spent a fortune, though in American dollars, it really wasn't that much. I called Rex to tell him about my day and again, he was in awe.

I teased him a bit, informed him I wasn't sure where I was going to next and expressed my worry about school and how I feared I may have been left behind.

He promised to get me notes and anything I needed to help catch up, but I wasn't sure it'd help. I'd barely attended classes the previous week because I'd needed this job, and now I was traveling all over the place which made me miss more classes.

After our talk, I went online to check the school website to try and figure out what I was going to do. When I started berating myself on not having carried my books or my computer to study, the reception desk called to inform me I had a parcel.

I knew it was a plane ticket and much as I was enjoying traveling, I wanted to go back. I had them send someone up to my room to deliver it and fifteen minutes later, I was nervously opening it to see where my beautiful pied piper desired me to go.

The plane ticket was written New York. I was going back home. I couldn't believe it. I called Rex immediately and he was equally as excited when I told him. He even offered to come pick me up from the airport but I told him it wouldn't be necessary. I could either get a cab or James would be there waiting for me. The thought of James was pleasing.

Almost two weeks ago I'd been about to get kicked out of my house. Now I was traveling the world and seeing things I hadn't been aware were still in existence and I had a driver. It was a massive improvement.

Saturday morning, I was at the Gallagher residence at eight in the morning. I was relieved when Francis didn't hand me another plane ticket when he met me at the door. Instead, he let me in and I headed up to Mrs. Gallagher's office.

The stairs still made me feel like it was a stairway to heaven. Even though I'd been there for almost two weeks now, every time I stepped into that mansion, I still felt like an intruder.

If that was my house, it would've probably been much smaller. My family didn't need a lot of means to get by, but I doubted my older brother, Greg, would've agreed with me on that.

I didn't like thinking about him because it was depressing. In fact, I preferred not to think about home altogether. We were only two siblings and he was a great disappointment to my family, mostly to me because he'd totally failed me as an older brother and a role model.

The thought of him made me a little sad. But the thought of seeing Mrs. Gallagher again made me happy. When I approached her door, I heard two loud voices and I stopped midway from knocking.

One was clearly male, the other female. Before I had a chance to figure out who it was, Mr. Gallagher stormed out and walked right past me as though I was invisible to him. I wasn't sure if I was relieved or insulted by that.

I watched him walk down the hallway into one of the rooms and took a deep breath, wondering if I should walk in or give Mrs. Gallagher sometime to cool off because their argument had sounded heated up.

Before I could decide, the door opened and Mrs. Gallagher stepped out. She stopped when she saw me, which made me feel a little better, but her reaction totally lowered my spirits and possibly ruined the rest of my day.

"Oh, great, you're here. There are some notes on my desk. Get to work," she said.

She left me standing there, unsure of what had just happened and disappeared down the hallway to a different room.

I wasn't sure what I'd expected, but I would've been lying if I said her dismissive attitude towards me wasn't hurtful. I'd been so excited to see her. I couldn't believe she was treating me so coldly, regardless of the fact that she'd just come from fighting with her husband.

I went inside the office and her desk had notes scribbled on it. They looked more like incomplete thoughts. How was I supposed to make anything out of them? Her penmanship was quite pleasant but what she'd written was incomprehensible.

There was a name of an art gallery, but that was the only thing I could make out. I was jetlagged and fatigued but I doubted Mrs. Gallagher cared much about that. I headed back to my office and went through the contact list on the computer.

There was nothing on there about the art gallery. I went online to look it up but it wasn't listed. Mrs. Gallagher had said she was open to questions but I doubted she wanted to talk to anyone, much less me.

I needed to find this art gallery. Something told me whatever I was supposed to do was going to start from there.

My phone started ringing and I picked it up when I saw Rex's name. I didn't know why I hadn't thought of it before but Rex was an artist, so he knew most, if not all art galleries.

"Hey, I see you're back in the country," he said.

"Yeah, I got back late last night. I was tired so I went straight to sleep because I had work in the morning."

"Are you serious? You don't get any time to rest?"

He sounded more offended by the knowledge than I was.

"I don't mind, really. You know I like being active."

"You need to rest and recharge."

"I'll do that tomorrow. Hey listen, do you know an art gallery called Týsque Art?"

"It's one of the best art galleries for upcoming artists in New York, why?"

"Can you please send me the address? I need to get there as soon as possible."

"Yeah, sure, but you haven't told me why."

"I'm not quite sure. I think my next project has something to do with the gallery." I looked at the incomplete thoughts again, feeling like a detective searching for clues.

"Wait, are you sure? I'd do anything to have my stuff showcased there."

"When I find out what it is this place has to do with my next assignment, I'll let you know."

"Okay. Will you be free tomorrow or do you have to work?"

"I'll be home," I said, though I wasn't sure. I didn't work on Sundays, but with Mrs. Gallagher, I really couldn't tell.

"I'll come pick my souvenirs," he said.

I laughed and hang up.

He sent me a message a minute later with the address to the art gallery and I left the mansion. James was waiting for me when I got outside and I had to admit, a twinge of joy passed through me because I didn't have to move around in my crappy car.

"Hello James," I said.

"Ms. Olivia." He opened the door for me.

"Thank you for picking me up last night."

"No need to thank me. It's what I get paid to do," he said.

He was a nice guy and I liked that I could actually talk to him.

"I need to get to this address," I handed him the piece of paper I'd written the address on.

"You having a good day?" he asked as we headed out of the paradise that still rejected me.

"I was, but I'm not so sure anymore." I wished I was talking to Rex so I could share what had happened that morning.

"How come?"

I thought about a better answer. "I'm going to a gallery I've never heard of to figure out what my assignment is. I wish it was as easy as my boss telling me," I said, thinking about how upset she'd seemed. I'd been so shocked to see her when she'd opened the door so unexpectedly. What had they been arguing about? Were they experiencing marital problems?

"Don't worry, you'll get used to it."

I doubted it. I'd done a major project on my first week, traveled through Africa on my second and I was chasing after a lead from a gallery that may or may not have had anything to do with what I was supposed to be doing. "I hope so," I said.

James drove the car into parking half an hour later after driving through some light traffic. The gallery was located in a tall building on the twentieth floor. I stepped through the glass doors and was met by beautiful pieces of charcoal drawings, pencil drawings and oil paintings hanging delicately on the flawless white wall.

The room was actually quite large from inside and from what I could see, there were several exhibition halls. The art gallery was elegant and intimate and I could see why it'd be the perfect place to exhibit new art.

"Hello, my name is Caitlin, may I help you?" a young lovely woman said.

"I hope so, I'm Olivia Williams. I'm here on behalf of Mrs. Amelia Gallagher," I said, hoping she had an idea as to what I was talking about.

"Follow me please," she said.

I wasn't sure yet if that was a good sign since I still didn't know what I was doing there, but I followed Caitlin to an office at the back end of the gallery. The door was as white as the walls so it was camouflaged, making it look like an optical illusion because if a person was not searching for a door, they wouldn't have noticed it.

"Jaime, Olivia Williams is here on behalf of Mrs. Gallagher," she said when we walked into a well lit and beautifully furnished office with a great view of the city.

Jaime was an attractive looking woman with short dark hair and bright hazel eyes. She had an easy, pleasant smile that took no effort and she was of medium height with a petite build.

"Thanks, Caitlin," she said.

Caitlin nodded and left the room as Jaime got to her feet and approached me.

"I'm Jaime Bryce. I'm the owner of Týsque. It's nice to meet you, Olivia."

She was dressed in a beige official skirt and a white plain but feminine shirt neatly tucked in. Her coat was hanging on a rack near the door. She was sweet and pleasant and for some reason, I found myself somewhat drawn to her.

"I'm Olivia Williams, Mrs. Gallagher's personal assistant."

We shook hands and she showed me to a seat.

"I'm glad you're here. I had some ideas I was hoping to bounce off. This exhibition is a big deal because it's the first of its kind. Especially because it's hosted by someone as powerful as Mrs. Gallagher," Jaime said.

"I'm sorry, I'm not fully aware of the details. That's why I'm here, so that you can fill me in." I wasn't sure I could beat around the bush and wait for her to fully come out with details.

She sat across from me on one of her guest seats. She had long slender legs which were made even more appealing by her beautiful stiletto shoes.

"Mrs. Gallagher is endorsing the gallery for an art exhibition taking place on Friday evening next week."

"Wow, that's great," I said.

Jaime's eyes widened at my expression and I couldn't help smiling.

"It is great," she said, almost mimicking me.

"I'm sorry, I've only worked for her for a couple of weeks and I'm still learning."

"Don't apologize for being honest."

"Okay," I said.

She was looking directly at me, not past me like Mrs. Gallagher used to do. Jaime made me feel noticed and it was a nice feeling, but for some strange reason, it also made me self-conscious.

Since my make-over, I tried to look the part of Mrs. Gallagher's personal assistant because Francis had said I projected her image to the world. With my paycheck, I'd done some shopping and even though what I'd gotten had been a bit pricey, I couldn't say I regretted my choice.

I'd taken Andre's advice on how to style my hair and which products to use, so it wasn't bothering me much as before. I had curls which were freely falling down my face now, instead of a tight bun at the back of my head.

I'd also gotten some make up which I applied as directed, so I knew I looked better compared to the frail lost creature who'd walked into the Gallagher mansion late for an interview.

"I'm not quite sure what role I'm supposed to play here," I said when she didn't look away.

Her lips broke into a smile with such ease, it made my heart pick up pace.

"Well, I guess you're going to liaise with Týsque and inform Mrs. Gallagher of the progress we'll make planning the exhibition."

"We?" I asked.

"Yes, you are going to be Mrs. Gallagher's voice."

"But I know nothing about art."

"That's no problem. The gallery has gone through several pieces by several artists and we've already picked some that'll be showcased that evening. Mrs. Gallagher will provide a piece or item that's unique and artistic for all the other artists who'll be in attendance, and the guests will have something that'll inspire them to purchase the pieces exhibited."

This was something Rex needed to be part of. "How does an artist apply to be part of this whole thing?"

"I'm afraid it's a little bit too late for that. We already have some of the final pieces. We just need to add a few more from the submitted ones."

Oh, poor Rex. He was going to be so disappointed. Why hadn't he applied for this? It sounded like such a great way to kickstart his career.

"Is Mrs. Gallagher aware of the pieces your gallery has selected?"

"Some. That's why we're still looking into what we've received. We only have a few days to do this so time is of essence."

"Does Mrs. Gallagher get to pick any of the artists or pieces?"

"She does, but she's a busy person with a lot of projects so the gallery gets to do that."

"The gallery, isn't that you?"

She smiled at me again. "I appraise the pieces with several other established artists. There are certain things we look for. We don't just pick a piece. There is a process we have to follow and rules we have to abide by."

"What guarantee does Mrs. Gallagher have that you're not going to favor one artist over the other?" This was actually quite intriguing. I wanted to know more about it.

She took a moment to answer. "The fact that there is more than one of us should answer that question. But I understand what you mean. I do get the final say and I try as much as possible to be objective. I don't favor artists. I believe they all deserve an equal chance."

She was good, I had to admit. "Do you have any pieces of your own in the show?"

She paused and got to her feet, which made me wonder if I'd crossed a line.

"I have a few pieces. It wouldn't be fair to me if I didn't do any business of my own, seeing as I'm providing a platform for the other artists."

She had a point.

"Would you like to see what we've got so far?" she asked.

I knew next to nothing about art, except what Rex had taught me. So even if I did see the pieces, I wasn't going to offer any useful input. But maybe I could take some pictures and send them to Mrs. Gallagher. Whether or not she'd have time to look at them, I wouldn't leave room for error.

"Yes, please," I said.

"This way," she said and I got up and followed after her.

There was something about her that I liked but I wasn't quite sure what it was.

We went back to the gallery and she led me out. Right next door, she opened the lock and turned on the lights. It was a storage room with covered paintings on several stands, a long table with more paintings laid on top and pieces of sculptures and other types or artwork.

"As you can see, we received quite a number of submissions. We make the application process tough in order to filter out people who aren't serious. We figure if you really want this, you have to work hard enough to get yourself a spot," she said.

I walked around the stuffed room as she uncovered some of the paintings the gallery had chosen. There were all types of paintings from abstract, to photographic and landscape to still life.

"When it comes to painting, it's all about perception and representation. Everything in life has different intensity which can be represented in black, white and shades of grey," she said. "When you see a painting, most people seek to understand the things depicted and then analyze their wider cultural, religious and social meanings. Others see colors assembled on a canvas in no particular order."

That perfectly explained me. "I wish I could see more into a canvas full of paint as you seem to," I said when I noticed her intensity when she was looking at an abstract oil painting.

"Maybe I could teach you," she said.

Was she flirting with me? I wondered as she quickly concealed her smile.

"That'd be interesting, but shouldn't one first have a passion for something like this?"

"It's not as complex as you may think. A work of art seeks to hold your attention and keep it fixed: a history of art urges it onwards, bulldozing a highway through the homes of the imagination."

"That doesn't sound complex at all."

She laughed at my sarcasm. "Julian Bell, a writer and painter writes that in his book, *What is Painting*. If you seek to understand the world of painting, you must show initiative and learn about it."

Our gazes locked at her quotation and something about her made me want to learn more about art. I looked away first as my attention darted to a painting behind her.

"This looks easy. I can do this," I said.

She broke into soft laughter and said, "This is called action painting. It's closely associated with abstract expressionism where paint is spontaneously dribbled, splashed or smeared onto a canvas rather than being carefully applied."

"Do you think I can do it?"

"Sure, why not? But if you know nothing about art, how will you know what to use or how to apply it?"

"Maybe you can teach me," I said.

I wasn't sure if I was flirting back, but it was giving me a bit of a rush, especially when she responded by smiling back at me and closely studying me.

"I'd be happy to," she said.

Our back and forth reminded me of how I'd quickly and thoughtlessly acted on my feelings for Mrs. Gallagher. The difference was, Jaime was pleasantly playing along, creating a calm and easy atmosphere.

"Do you mind if I take pictures of the paintings the gallery has selected for the exhibition? I'd like to run them by Mrs. Gallagher," I said, breaking our eye contact.

"Not at all, we've put them aside together with some other types of artwork."

They were the paintings placed on the stands and the lighting was perfect. I used my phone to take images of the paintings and art works on different angles, taking my time because I didn't want to send bad quality pictures. When I was done, I sent them all to Mrs. Gallagher.

"You're a good photographer. Maybe there is an artist in you," Jaime said as we left the storage room.

We went back to her office and I spent the rest of the morning with her explaining the process of how the exhibition was going to be set up and my role in the whole matter.

I didn't have much to do except inform Mrs. Gallagher of every decision made together with how the whole thing would take place, what she needed to do and when.

Since I'd already planned one event for her, I doubted this would be quite as hard. I knew I'd have to send out invitations to her rich and powerful friends who were art lovers.

"It was nice meeting you, Olivia. I hope to see you soon," Jaime said when I was leaving.

"It was nice meeting you, Jaime." I meant it. It was great meeting her. I liked the way she looked at me and the way she spoke to me.

We exchanged our contact information and shortly after, I left the art gallery. I found James waiting for me, and he was pleasant enough to meet me with a smile.

"I hope your meeting went well," he said.

"Better than I expected."

"I'm glad to hear that." He opened the door for me. "Where to?"

"Back to the Gallagher residence."

I needed to do some research on organizing art exhibitions. Even though that wasn't part of my job, I needed to know what it involved so that if I was liable for something, I'd be aware of it. The last thing I needed was a screw up which would have Mrs. Gallagher doubting my skills and potentially even firing me.

Chapter Five

"Oh man, I can't believe I'm not going to be part of that. Isn't there anything you can do to get my stuff in there?" Rex complained.

I'd just told him about my new project. To be honest, I was very excited about this one. I didn't know if it was because I was developing a liking for art or because Jaime was part of it but something told me it was the latter.

"Rex, if I could, I would. I can try and get you invited."

"Come on, Liv, please try and see if you can do more."

"I'm telling you, Jaime told me the application process is closed. The gallery is reviewing the pieces submitted and some have already been chosen for the exhibition."

"Just great."

I could feel his disappointment but there was nothing I could do. I'd gotten into the project a little too late. "You should be grateful I brought you artistic souvenirs."

His expression changed and he leaned close and pecked my cheek. He was an affectionate guy and since we were great friends, I didn't mind his display of affection.

"I am and thank you. You know, I can't believe in just two weeks you've traveled more than you've done your entire life."

"It's amazing, isn't it?"

It was Sunday afternoon and we were having lunch together at a nice restaurant in our neighborhood. We'd just been served and were catching up as we ate. I was happy to see him because I'd missed him.

"Was Mrs. Gallagher excited to see you?"

Her reaction still made me sad. "I found her fighting with her husband. She wasn't particularly happy to see me when she walked out to find me standing at the door. I haven't seen her since and I'm not sure I want to. In fact, I think my crush might've disappeared."

"How come?"

I smiled, thinking about Jaime. I didn't have a crush on her. I just liked her because she was nice. "I met someone, the art gallery owner, Jaime Bryce."

His face lit up. "That's wonderful, how's she like?"

"She's beautiful, sweet and she has a great smile. She made me feel so at ease when we met and I think there might've been a little bit of flirting."

"Oh?"

"Yeah, I'm seeing her again tomorrow. We're meeting to further discuss the art exhibition."

"This is so great. I haven't seen you excited about dating in a long time."

"School tends to do that to a person. Speaking of which, if I do see Mrs. Gallagher tomorrow, I need to figure out how I'm going to ask her for a few hours off in order to do my exams."

"Do you think she might say no?"

"Yes, no, I'm unsure. Mrs. Gallagher is unpredictable." I was playing with the food on my plate because I lacked my usual appetite.

"I can't believe you're over her. I've never heard you talk about anyone the way you did her."

"I still find her attractive, I mean anyone would. But those other feelings have sort of faded."

"Are you sure about that?"

To be honest, I wasn't. I just thought that if I redirected my attraction towards Jaime instead, whatever I felt for Mrs. Gallagher would somehow end up fizzling out.

"I don't want to think about it right now. I want to resume studying because of the exams and I need to figure out how I'll rearrange my schedule to fit my working hours otherwise I'll be completely left behind."

"You don't want to work for Mrs. Gallagher for the rest of your life?"

His sarcasm didn't elude me.

"By the way, did she give you grief for spending during your travel?"

"No, I don't even think she cares."

"I'd like to have such a boss."

Her stunning regal features were a great bonus. "She's not as great as you think."

"She gave you a chance to work for her, you traveled through Africa on a first class plane ticket and stayed in the best hotels, spending on an expense credit card and now you have a driver and on your working hours, you get to move around in a sleek BMW. On top of that, your boss is stunning and she let you kiss her."

"Well, when you put it like that," I said.

Maybe I was being too hard on her. She'd been good to me and that day, she'd been having a bad morning. She deserved the benefit of the doubt.

"Do you think you want something more with this Jaime?"

I shook my head in uncertainty. "I don't know."

"Maybe you should find out," he said.

I laughed at the idea.

"Are you going to eat that?" he asked, pointing at my food.

I handed him the plate and he transferred all the contents to his plate.

"What? You said you weren't going to eat it," he said as he took a spoonful. "Tell me more about your exotic trips."

He was only aware of what I'd shared while traveling and now that we were together, I realized I was actually excited to talk about it in more detail. He was fascinated by the stories, as I shared what I'd seen and shown him the photos I'd managed to take.

Since South Africa had been my favorite country because I'd slightly toured through it, I talked more about it. He had so many questions but I was happy to answer them.

I was in my office when Mrs. Gallagher asked to see me the following day. I'd gotten to work on time, and was trying to figure out how I'd broach the subject of school and exams.

She wasn't seated behind her desk working as usual when I walked into her office. Instead, she was standing by the window staring into the distance.

She had an angelic aura about her that made me wonder how she managed to look so painfully gorgeous on a daily basis. I felt like it'd been too long since I'd taken a minute to bask in her presence.

I approached her desk as she slowly turned around. She was calm and composed, which made me feel like I was on familiar territory.

"Good morning, Olivia."

"Good morning, Mrs. Gallagher," I said.

"I saw the pictures you took of the paintings," she said.

"They're the paintings the gallery has chosen for the exhibition."

"They were good." She walked over to her desk and handed me her iPad. "These are the names I need you to address the invites to."

I was going to contact the company I'd used to design the invitations for the charity ball. If these kinds of events took place on a weekly basis, then the company must've made a fortune out of the business they got from the Gallaghers.

"I'll get straight on it," I said as I headed out.

"Olivia."

I turned to face her and found her leaning against her desk.

"I wanted to apologize for my behavior the other day."

Her words caught me off guard. I was under the impression that anything an employer did was somehow justified in one way or the other. I'd even decided to forget about it after my chat with Rex.

"Oh, that's okay."

"No, it wasn't right for me to treat you that way. Please accept my apology."

Wow, a full proper apology from the Queen of the Gallaghers. What a way to start a week. "Apology accepted."

I headed towards the door and slowed down, thinking this might be as good a time as any to ask for some time off to do my exams. I probably wouldn't get another chance.

"Was there anything else?"

I faced her at the question and took a few steps towards her, creating appropriate distance between us, but I could smell the fragrance of her perfume. It teased my senses, almost making me forget what I wanted to ask.

"I have a request," I said.

"Go on," she said, motioning me to keep talking.

"I'm a part-time student at NYU and I have exams coming up soon."

I was wondering if it'd be okay if I took a few hours off on the day of the exam. I'll make sure I have no pending work and will get back here as soon as I'm done."

She gave me a look I wasn't used to. "You're a student?" she asked.

"Yes," I said.

"What are you studying?"

"I'm on my fourth year of business and management studies."

"When do you get time to attend your classes?"

"In the beginning, I attended full time but eventually had to cut back because I needed to work."

"Won't that take longer for you to graduate?"

Her interest in my life was soul-stirring. "Yes, but I don't have a choice."

"When is your exam?"

"Next week on Thursday."

She appeared to be thinking about it. "That's fine," she said.

I celebrated inwardly. "Thank you."

I got back to my office and immediately called Rex.

"What's up?" he asked.

"She said yes!"

"What?"

"Mrs. Gallagher, she gave me time off for my exam."

"That's great."

"She even apologized for how she acted the other day."

"Oh, wow. Get her a best boss in the world mug."

"You know what, I just might."

I hang up and got back to work. With my mood changed, the day drastically improved. I called the printing company and had them send me sample invitation cards and shortly after, I went to Jaime's art gallery.

I was happy to see her when James dropped me off. Jaime was wearing a grey pantsuit which gave her a serious but sexy look. I'd never had a beautiful, classy woman express interest in me before.

"I'm glad you're here," she said after we exchanged greetings.

"Oh, do you need help with something?" I asked.

She shook her head, smiling at me and I realized what she meant. "Oh," I said, feeling a bit dumb. "I'm glad I'm here too."

"How was your weekend?" she asked.

I found it odd that she didn't have any paintings hanging on her office walls, but the interior décor was tasteful.

"Uneventful, how about yours?"

"It's been a busy few weeks so to relax, Caitlin and I went out."

"Oh, are you two…" I trailed off, unsure of what I was asking.

"No, no, we're just friends and associates."

I covered my lips in embarrassment. I couldn't believe how bold I was, asking about her personal life.

"Do you have someone to entertain you during weekends?" she asked, giving me that sweet smile I'd come to like.

"Rex, my best friend, he's an artist. He loves painting. You two would get along great."

"I much rather prefer spending time with you."

Her statement left me speechless. She was a good flirt.

"Okay," I said, noticing I'd suddenly grown nervous.

"How about dinner tomorrow night?"

I should've been thinking about studying for my exams. "Dinner will be great."

"I'll pick you up at eight?" she said.

"Sounds good."

We got back to work and she informed me of the progress the gallery had made so far. "You're aware of everything Mrs. Gallagher does, right?" she asked.

"I wouldn't say everything."

"She has this piece she's going to reveal on the night of the exhibition and even I don't know what it is. I did a background check on the kind of events she's hosted and I've got to say, she's one classy lady."

Classy did not begin to describe Mrs. Gallagher.

"Would you happen to know what piece she'll be unveiling?"

"No, I'm afraid I don't." Even if I did, I wasn't sure I would've told her. I owed my loyalty to Mrs. Gallagher.

"Okay, I just thought I should ask."

"Whatever it is, I'm sure it'll blow everyone away."

Maybe it was one of the things I'd gone to sign for. Maybe it was something else, Jaime piqued my curiosity and I couldn't stop thinking about it.

"Shall we get to work?" she asked a moment later and I nodded.

She gave me a portfolio of the artists whose pieces would be exhibited and their professional background. I knew Mrs. Gallagher would probably not get to read it but I went through it, thoroughly taking notes should she have questions.

Jaime gave me a lot of information which I found useful. She had a passion for her work and her projects, which I envied because unlike me, everything she was doing was for herself.

She had her own business, doing something she genuinely loved. She looked happy with her accomplishments. She had the life I one day hoped to have.

"I guess that's all for today," she said when we were done.

"Before I forget, I need you to email me a list of your guests. I'm sending out the invitations before the end of the day."

"Will do," she said.

I got to my feet. "Do you mind if I take this? I want to make Mrs. Gallagher a copy."

"You can keep it. I have another one."

"Thanks," I said.

She walked me to the door and reminded me of our date the following evening. On my way back to the office, I received the sample invitation cards and sent them to Mrs. Gallagher.

I was glad when she immediately replied and approved, because all I had to do now was send the list of names invited to the art exhibition.

When I went back to the house, Mrs. Gallagher called me to her office. It was the first time she'd requested to see me twice in one day. The knowledge had a titillating effect on me.

"Have you sent out the invitations?" she asked.

"I sent out the list of names, the invites will be sent before the end of the day."

She nodded.

I wasn't sure why she wanted to see me but since she wasn't in a hurry to tell me, I handed her the portfolio. "Jaime gave me the portfolio of the artists whose pieces will be exhibited. I thought you might like to take a look."

She placed it on the desk without a second glance.

I couldn't help wonder if I'd done something wrong. But then again, she was never quite as vocal as I wished her to be.

I still desired to know her better and didn't cower like I had when we'd first met. I looked her in the eye and she looked back at me, making me realize it wasn't such a hard thing to do.

It wasn't hard because she seemed sad. Her eyes were a darker shade of blue, her posture was more tense than relaxed and she appeared at a loss. I'd never thought I'd ever see her vulnerable.

"I'd like you to get in touch with Frank Connor. He's in town for a few days. He brought some Egyptian art which will be used at the exhibition. Collaborate with him and the gallery, then get back to me."

I was a little disappointed to know what she wanted was work-related. "Okay."

"That'll be all."

I nodded and turned to leave but hesitated at the door and faced her. Her back was turned and she was staring out the window, almost as though she was alone in the room.

"Mrs. Gallagher?"

I had no idea what I was doing. *Just turn and leave.* A voice screamed in my head. "Are you okay?" I asked.

She looked at me for a moment then smiled and I felt my heart sink. God, how could she make me feel so much with such a simple gesture?

"Have you ever been to an opera?" she asked.

Opera? This was an unusual turn. "Uh... no," I said.

"There is a show on Saturday night and I'd like you to accompany me."

I froze in place, certain I'd heard wrong. "Okay," I said.

Did she really want me to go to an opera house with her?

"I'm okay," she added.

I smiled at her, suddenly feeling a bit nervous. Maybe in time I'd get a chance to see through the cracks, but for now, I was going to settle for the slight part of herself she'd just exposed.

"I have to tell you, I don't do this often," I said the following evening.

Jaime was seated opposite from me. She'd picked a lovely little restaurant that was more romantic and intimate than I'd been prepared for.

She was looking gorgeous in a sexy turquoise dress that was just slightly above the knee, gently hugging her curves while exposing her long legs, and except for a simple but pretty pendant and a small elegant wristwatch, she wasn't wearing any jewelry.

I was slightly intimidated, dressed in a simple but pretty chiffon dress that was a little tight on top and freely falling at the bottom. It was knee-high but the heels I wore pleasantly exaggerated the length of my legs.

If I'd known she'd be taking me to such a nice restaurant or how well she'd be dressed for the date, I would've applied a lot more effort.

"Have dinner?" she asked lightly.

I smiled at her as a waiter brought us a couple of menus. She made it so easy for me to be around her. "No, go out on dates," I said.

"Really? How come?" She asked the question as though she couldn't believe it. "Someone like you," she gestured to my whole form, "I imagine would be asked out all the time."

I laughed. "I know what you're doing." She was trying to make me feel a little more at ease, which I appreciated because I didn't mind the compliments. "Keep doing it," I said.

She laughed. "So how come you don't do this often?"

We were scanning through our menus while we talked.

"Between work and school, there isn't much time left for anything else."

"What would you call this?" she asked, motioning to our situation.

I placed my menu on the table and turned my attention to her.

"Different," I said.

"Why so?" she asked, placing her own menu down.

"Because it's you," I said.

She smiled back at me then softly nodded. "That was smooth," she said.

"Did it deliver the desired effect?"

She nodded. "Yes, it did."

"Good."

Our gazes locked and I studied her beautiful features. Her hazel eyes caressed me as the tip of her manicured fingers trailed along her perfectly chiseled chin. I was tempted to lean across the table and kiss her when she ran her tongue gently over her lips.

"Have you decided what you'll have?" our waiter said, interrupting my thoughts and our moment.

"Uh, yeah." Jaime cleared her throat and gave him her order. I gave him mine as well and he left us alone once again.

"How do you manage school and work? Mrs. Gallagher looks like a very demanding employer," she said.

I was glad for the change of subject because it distracted my thoughts. We wanted to get to know each other and that was what a first date was for.

What I didn't think was a good topic of discussion was my employer, Mrs. Gallagher, because if I started talking about her, my crush would be revealed and the date would end as soon as it had started.

"I don't know, I prioritize, I guess." I didn't want to sound too serious or reveal too much. I was embarrassed I hadn't attended school in a while and studying had become a challenge because my job was taking up so much of my time.

"So most of the things you do are strategically planned?"

"Not so much. I go to work and school. My life starts and ends there. I haven't had the need to add anything on to that so I've been content with it."

"What do you like to do when you're not working or studying?"

I couldn't believe I actually had to think about that. "I like to travel." It was pathetic, since the only travel I'd done had been work-related.

"That's interesting."

"Enough about me, tell me more about yourself." I had to change the subject because I felt like soon I'd end up throwing myself under the bus and I wasn't sure why I was uncomfortable with Jaime knowing the real me.

She had everything; the education, the job and the life. She was who I wanted to be. The best part was that she was happy and willing to get out of her comfort zone and do something different.

"What would you like to know?"

"Did you always want to be an artist?"

She shook her head. "Not always. Like most people, I wanted to do something that would assure me financial success. So I went to school to study law but in the end, I realized I'd never be truly happy if I wasn't doing what I loved."

"What was that?"

"I loved painting and the more I stayed in law school the more I realized I was carving a road to a future I wasn't sure was meant for me. Half way through, I quit and applied to art school. I knew my family wouldn't understand so I kept it secret."

"You never told them you'd quit law school?"

"I couldn't afford to pay for art school myself and I knew once I told them, they'd stop supporting me."

"What happened?"

"I finished school and got a job. My father wanted me to work in his friend's firm so eventually, I had to come clean."

"How did they react?"

"How do you think?"

"He must've been pissed," I said.

"He was upset, so was my mom, but I sat them both down and told them that if they cared about my happiness, they'd let me follow my dreams."

"Did they understand?"

"No, I'd spent a lot of their money because I got accepted into a really good art school. I told them one day I'd pay it all back if it was all they were concerned about and left."

"Oh my God."

Jaime laughed softly. "Don't worry, over time we managed to work it out."

"Now that you're successful, it must be easier."

"It is, but we have our ups and downs. It keeps things interesting," she said.

"Do you have siblings?"

"Two older brothers; a lawyer and a judge."

I wanted to express my awe at her family's love for justice but I lacked in words.

"Don't say it," she said, almost as though she knew what would come next.

Our waiter came to serve us and I was glad because this time he'd be gone for a while longer. For some reason, it felt like he was interfering and I wished he'd stay away long enough for me to absorb everything this woman before me was.

We started eating our food and my curiosity about her kept on growing. I wanted to know more. "How did you meet Mrs. Gallagher?"

She looked up and a glint of light came to her eyes. I couldn't help wondering if she saw the same thing in the magnificent woman as I did.

"A friend introduced us. I hoped once I tabled the idea, she'd be interested. It took a while, but eventually she came onboard."

"You're very brave," I said.

"Why do you say so?"

"Mrs. Gallagher can be very intimidating."

"She is, but when you want something, you stomp on your insecurities and your fears and go after it."

"I wish it was as easy as saying it."

She tilted her head and studied me.

"What?" I asked.

"I don't know. You don't come across as someone who'd let anything get in the way of what you want."

She was the first person to see that from just a few days of knowing me. Unfortunately, the image I was portraying didn't take away from who I really was. "Your confidence in me is inspiring but you should know, I'm not there yet."

"Then whatever you're projecting is working out for you," she said.

"Well then, good." She kept me on my toes. Conversation never once got boring. She made me laugh, made it easy for me to talk to her, to share, but I still found it challenging to talk about myself. I didn't understand why, but maybe intimidation was playing a hand in it.

I was attracted to her and flirting back and forth was fun, but my favorite part was the manner in which she looked at me. It made me feel wanted and desired, which was something I hadn't felt in a long time.

"Have you ever been in love?" I asked.

She sipped on her red wine and met my gaze. "Once, I fell in love once."

"How was it like?"

"She was my childhood best friend. There wasn't a thing about her I didn't love. Her smile, her eyes, her soft hands, her hugs, the way she spoke, her laugh, even her tears. She was a saint and an angel to me."

Sounded intense. "Did she feel the same way?"

Jaime nodded but she wasn't voluntary with information.

"What happened?"

"She had terminal leukemia and passed away at sixteen."

"Oh God, I'm so sorry." Of all the things I'd expected her to say, I couldn't have guessed it. No wonder she wasn't overly open about it.

"It's okay."

We went silent for a while and then she brightened up and posed me the same question.

"No, I've never been in love."

"How come?"

How come? How could I explain that? "My family is very conservative and though loving and supportive, I could never come out to them. I did what I was told and focused on what needed to be done. I avoided any situation that would threaten the balance of the world I'd grown up in. When I moved here for school, I became a bit more experimental, with students." I took a breath and a sip of wine. "I never got to know anyone close enough to experience a strong bond or an affectionate relationship."

"Do you think you're open to it now?" she asked.

I didn't know how to answer her. I mean, what was love? What was the difference between loving someone and being in love? I'd read countless books that described the meaning in unbelievable detail, but ironically, I'd always thought the scattered information was wanting in nature.

"I guess so."

"You don't sound too sure," she said.

I ran my fingers through my hair, trying to think about a time I'd grown close to someone with romantic intention. Not a single moment came to mind. "I don't know, I guess, I understand desire more than I do love."

"Lust, passion and raw sexual attraction is just that, sex. Love is something deeper, something words still fail to fully capture because what one feels is too powerful, too overwhelming to be painted into anything comprehensible."

I was speechlessly intrigued. This woman had a lot to teach me. "Can you capture it in a painting?"

"Love?"

I nodded.

"It's different for everyone, you know. Some people would look at a painting and see whatever they want to see instead of what I'm trying to portray. I guess it all depends on perspective."

Somehow, our conversation drifted to the world of paintings and their distinct interpretations. I wasn't sure how long we talked about it, but our waiter came back and took our plates long after we'd finished our meals.

After settling our bill, we noticed how late it had gotten and Jaime dropped me off back home. I didn't want to invite her in when she stopped the car and walked me to the entrance of my building because I wasn't ready to show her my world.

She was pleasant enough not to push for an invitation and as we said goodnight, we both expressed how much fun we'd had and agreed to do it again. When she moved close to me, I grew a little nervous. I knew she wanted to kiss me and I wanted to kiss her back, but I was scared.

As though she understood this, she leaned forward and laid a featherlight kiss on my cheek. I was tempted to wrap my arms around her, show her just how much I liked her, but I restrained myself.

"Goodnight, Livvy," she said softly against my cheek as she pulled back.

The use of the nickname I was used to was heartwarming.

"Goodnight, Jaime."

She smiled and slowly walked back to her car. When she got inside, I waved at her and got inside my building, grinning from ear to ear.

Chapter Six

I had to admit, of all the projects I'd done since I'd started working for Mrs. Gallagher, the art exhibition was a top favorite.

Frank Connor was liaising with Jaime on the pieces Mrs. Gallagher was showcasing at the event, which was in a day, and I was excited to see how it'd turn out.

The invites had been sent out and Mrs. Gallagher's guests had responded and were all going to show up.

Jaime's guests were going to get back to her. I'd managed to get her to invite Rex, which was great because this time, I'd have a friend around to keep me company. I doubted Mrs. Gallagher wanted me to shadow her like I had during the charity ball.

I loved working for her for all the reasons she wasn't like other employers. I wasn't confined to a desk, it wasn't necessarily a typical nine-hour job, depending on the duties and responsibilities, the working hours could be more or less. And my boss, well to start, she was an incredible person.

"What's going on?"

There was some sort of construction taking place at Týsque in one of the exhibition halls. Jaime was busy coordinating with whoever was creating the noise in her art gallery when I arrived.

"You should talk to Jaime. She's not happy," Caitlin said.

The way she said it made me wonder if Jaime's unhappiness had something to do with me. I followed the ruckus and found Jaime standing safely away as a couple of men made some sort of a glass vault.

"Jaime."

She approached me, seemingly upset and asked me to follow her to her office, which was pleasantly quiet. I didn't want to speak before I knew what was going on so I waited.

We'd seen each other the day before but after our date, our meetings had been purely professional. Mrs. Gallagher understood I needed to be at Týsque, so her requests were not quite as demanding.

"This guy is drilling holes in my gallery," she said.

I had no idea who she was talking about and what it had to do with me. "Who and why if you haven't approved of it?" It was her art gallery and she had an overall say on what went on. I didn't understand how anyone would have a reason to go above that.

"Frank Connor," she said.

I wanted to speak, but the name took the power out of anything I had to say.

"After we talked, he was supposed to keep in touch, tell me which pieces he was presenting on behalf of Mrs. Gallagher, then we would plan on where to place them. They were supposed to be the centerpieces for the whole event, the reason why anyone will show up."

She was pacing back and forth and I had no idea how to appease her. This was her territory and someone was invading it. "I met Frank Connor in Egypt. He showed me the original headpiece of Cleopatra. I'm sure whatever he's constructing, it's because the security is necessary. Mrs. Gallagher goes all out, you should know that. This is the quality that keeps people around her."

She seemed to relax, which was good but she looked at me with a curiosity that made me realize I'd probably said too much.

"Wait, Cleopatra's headpiece?"

I tried to think of something smart or witty to say but she looked at me in such an earnest manner, I couldn't lie my way out of it.

"Spill," she said.

I was leaning against her desk when she stopped pacing and turned her attention to me, waiting for me to share what I knew. My loyalty was to Mrs. Gallagher, but the event was taking place in a day. She'd know as much as I did when everything was revealed.

"I've only collaborated with Frank Connor once. I had to go to Cairo to sign for a parcel that needed to be sent to New York. I had no idea about this event. Mrs. Gallagher is not very forthcoming with information."

"Did you say Frank Connor showed you Cleopatra's original headpiece?"

I remembered my own reaction when I'd seen it and smiled, knowing Jaime had not heard anything else after I'd said the very statement she'd repeated. "I'm not at liberty to say, in fact, what you just heard is not supposed to be repeated to anyone else."

Her smile was wider, more pleasant, and sweeter. Her worry faded as she approached me and somehow it was transferred into me. I was afraid she'd try and retract more information, and terrified because she'd succeed.

"You have nothing to worry about," she said.

Her voice was soft and caressing and I didn't fail to notice how close to me she came, or how quickly nervous I grew. After our date, the intimacy of what we'd shared had been put on suspended animation.

When we were around one another, there was that flirting, that warmth, but because we were connected through work, we tried to keep it professional.

I wasn't waiting for her to ask me out on another date so soon because she was occupied with the art exhibition, but I knew when it was over, we'd go out and try to get to know each other more and who knew, maybe something would happen.

That was my thought, until she gave me that look and approached me, looking at me as though I'd just revealed the most delicious secret and to my disgrace, unfortunately, I think I just had.

Cleopatra's headpiece had had an overwhelming effect on me and on an artistic level, I could understand why it'd do so for Jaime, so her reaction towards finding out why Frank Connor had people drilling holes in her office was expected.

"Are you upset?" I needed to make sure.

She shook her head and closed the distance between us. She was a beautiful woman who I was very attracted to and how I felt about her was powerful enough to shut down my motor senses when she stood so close to me.

I had thought our first kiss would take place after a second or third date, but when we stood just inches apart, her body heat calling onto mine, I wasn't so sure I was willing to wait.

The fact that I'd just given her pleasing news and it was probably why she was doing this should've stopped me, but I didn't care.

I had berated myself for not having taken the initiative to kiss her myself and if this was how our first kiss was going to take place, then I was more than willing to participate.

"Don't kiss me."

The words resounded in my head, snapping me back to reality. Not because they were said in harsh terms, but because Jaime's lips were close to mine, close enough to create something magical, but the timing was off.

"I'm sorry," I said.

She pulled back and I bit into my lower lip, unsure of what I was doing.

"I want our first kiss to be based on more than this."

She seemed to understand what *this* meant even though I didn't. What was I thinking? She was perfect and I really wanted to kiss her and hold her and feel her against me. I groaned in frustration.

"I understand," she said.

When she created distance between us, I almost reached out to tell her I'd made a mistake. But I stayed strong. If this wasn't how our first kiss was supposed to take place, then maybe I was right to stop it.

"I'm not saying for sure that Cleopatra's headpiece will be Mrs. Gallagher's masterpiece tomorrow," I said, trying to figure out the point I'd been trying to make.

Her pleased expression grew softer.

"I don't want you to get your hopes up." I needed to get out of there. The alarming speed at which I wanted to be closer to Jaime was growing dangerously out of control.

"I have a lot of things to do back at the office, I should go." I stormed out before giving her a chance to speak or myself a moment to act on my carnal instincts.

When I went back to the mansion, I gave Mrs. Gallagher an account of the progress that had been made and she gave me some last-minute errands.

My day ended around eight, after which I went out for dinner with Rex. I enjoyed spending time with him because he was such pleasant company. I'd never been that close to anyone else before so he was very special to me.

"How is it going with Jaime?"

We hadn't talked much through the week and since my life had gotten a little more interesting, he was always eager to hear about anything and everything that happened.

"It's going well." I couldn't wait to see her the following day. The event was going to start around five in the evening and I had to be there to make sure I was aware of everything Mrs. Gallagher needed to know.

"Has anything happened?"

I remembered the kiss that had almost happened and berated myself. I was being stupid trying to get a moment of romanticism considering this wasn't some sort of amatory motion picture.

"No, not yet."

"Do you want something to happen?" he asked.

Of course, I did. "Yes."

"Do you think something might happen tomorrow?"

I hadn't thought about it. "We'll be busy all evening. We'll barely have a moment to ourselves, so I doubt it."

"What about after?"

I looked right past him and imagined the possibilities. In my last event, I'd ended up kissing Mrs. Gallagher, which had been a great risk. She'd warned me not to do it again when she'd offered me the job, but it was different with Jaime.

We had chemistry, a strong electric current passed between us when we were in the same room. "I don't know, maybe. I just... I don't want to rush it. Jaime is different. She's special."

Rex's expression changed from curiosity to disturbed concern. "I know you've never done anything like this before so I think you should practice caution."

"Practice caution?"

He looked suddenly uncomfortable. "I don't want to see you get hurt."

"Hurt?"

"Yeah, be careful. Get to know Jaime better before you emotionally invest yourself."

"Emotionally invest myself?" I knew what he was talking about and I understood his concern but I'd never seen this side of him and I wanted to have a little fun.

"Yeah," he said, shifting awkwardly in his seat.

For a guy who paid such little regard for boundaries, he sure got tongue-tied when it came to talking about feelings.

"Are you afraid she'll break my heart and I'll come crying to you?"

His expression was serious until I broke into laughter and he relaxed.

"Don't worry, I know what this is and I've got it under control."

"Good," he said.

Chapter Seven

I arrived at the art gallery an hour before the show started to find Jaime in a bit of a panic. Everything was ready, waiters, wine and security. The pieces were set in their respective exhibition halls and some of the artists whose pieces were being showcased were already present.

"What is wrong with this picture?" Jaime asked.

We were standing in the exhibition hall with the vault.

"It's empty," she said.

It had been transformed into a high-tech secure vault, but it was empty.

"When will this guy get here?" she asked.

She was talking about Frank Connor and I didn't know how he worked so I wasn't sure how to pacify the situation.

"Guests will be arriving in an hour and the centerpiece is not here yet," she said.

I'd been busy all day trying to make sure everything was perfect and I hadn't seen Mrs. Gallagher even though I'd kept in touch, informing her of important details she needed to know, which wasn't much.

She hadn't responded to me, which put me in a position of my own because as much as I wanted to reassure Jaime, I wasn't sure where to start.

Jaime looked stunning in a long burgundy dress, Caitlin was lovely in a short strapless black dress and I was in the same clothes I'd been wearing all day.

I needed to change before the guests arrived and luckily, Andre was on his way to Týsque with a dress for me.

"Jaime, you're dealing with Mrs. Gallagher."

Mrs. Gallagher was one person; her husband was another. Their names combined, were an entity. Invitations had been sent out; guests had all responded. Whatever was supposed to be in that vault was going to be there. I had no doubt, fear or worry regarding the vault or what was supposed to be in it.

"I should try and remember that," Jaime said.

She was cute as she said that because she still retained that worried expression. Her hair was in soft curls, her face was bright with anticipation and her mouth… her lips.

"Jaime," I said softly.

I didn't realize how heavy my voice had become until I was standing next to her and her breath was fanning my face.

Our gazes locked, hers uneasy, mine in a state I couldn't identify and in a heated moment of panic, passion and withheld restraint, it all slowly turned into something magnetic that was pulling us both together.

"I know you're not ready…"

I stopped her halfway with a kiss.

I'd been waiting for this for a while, so when our lips touched, everything in me shut down, then almost immediately started up to concentrate on that one moment.

Jaime's lips were sweet and soft and everything I'd imagined they would be and more. When she closed her lips on mine, my response escalated and I responded, unleashing the pent up passion I'd been withholding while waiting for a perfect moment.

Jaime placed one hand on my cheek and wrapped the other around my waist, pulling me closer against her body. She parted my lips and deepened the kiss, drawing a hungry response from me.

The knock on the door drew us apart as Caitlin walked in. She paused at the door and turned her attention to me. "There's an Andre here for you, Olivia."

Oh, Andre. I'd almost forgotten I needed to get ready.

I turned my attention to Jaime and found her smiling back at me. "Do you mind if I change in here?"

She shook her head.

"Caitlin, please tell him to come in."

Caitlin nodded and left the room.

I found Jaime looking at me and I didn't have to guess to imagine what was going through her mind. I wanted to kiss her again, but Andre would interrupt us any moment.

It didn't matter though, when the event was over, we'd have more than enough time to do whatever we wanted. The thought had a titillating effect on me.

"I hope I'm not late," Andre said as he made a dramatic and flamboyant entrance.

"I'll leave you two," Jaime said.

"Beautiful lady," Andre said, making me realize I was checking her out as she left the room.

"I got your dress and make up. You're going to look fabulous tonight."

He unzipped the bag to reveal a stunning lavender gown that left my mouth wide open. "That's what I'm wearing tonight?" I asked.

"You like?" Andre asked as he pulled out a chair for me so that he could apply my makeup.

"I love."

He got to work and I drifted back to the kiss I'd shared with Jaime. I was thinking about the texture of her lips, the warmth of her touch and the desire in her eyes when Andre started styling my hair.

He finished a short while later and stepped out of the office to let me get into my dress. He had brought along a lovely pair of shoes, which I absolutely loved.

After putting on the dress, I called him back inside to zip me up and then he stood some distance away to look at me. I didn't have a mirror so I wasn't sure about my appearance but from the pleased look across Andre's face, I could tell it was all good things.

The dress was made of silk and was soft against my skin. It hung gently over my curves, exposing a figure that had been used to staying hidden in plain work clothes.

"You're stunning," he said.

I could see the joy and pride in his eyes as he was the one responsible for my transformation. "Thanks, Andre."

We walked out of the office together and I put my mind back to work mode, since that was what I was there to do. Jaime and Caitlin were busy as guests had started to arrive.

I wasn't sure what to help with until I heard commotion in one of the exhibition halls. I followed the noise and found Frank Connor and two other men in the room.

He nodded at me in acknowledgement while one of the men opened the vault. I was pleased to see the centerpiece was Cleopatra's headpiece as I'd guessed, but my jaw dropped when he revealed the rare red diamond I'd signed for in South Africa.

The vault was big enough to fit both but now I understood the need for security. One of the men with Frank Connor, dressed in a black suit was part of the security detail. It seemed fitting because the two pieces were priceless.

A moment later, Frank and the man who'd been assisting him closed the vault and left the room, leaving the black-suited man to guard the pieces.

"Are they here yet?"

I turned at Jaime's voice. I was happily going to tell her she should never doubt Mrs. Gallagher when I found her staring at me as though she was seeing me for the very first time.

"Oh my God," she said softly.

It took me a moment to remember I'd changed into my evening dress.

"You look amazing," she said.

I blushed. She sounded almost out of breath, but I took it as a compliment. "Andre is an artist," I said.

"No, this is all you," Jaime said, moving closer to me.

She reached for my hand as our gazes locked and instantly, my memory went back to the kiss in her office. I was mesmerized by her eyes. They were so intense, it felt like we'd left the gallery and were in another realm.

I wanted her to move closer and kiss me again, but before either of us could act on our attraction, Caitlin interrupted us by gasping in shock.

"Is this real?" she asked.

Neither Jaime nor I noticed her entering the room or walking past us. She was standing near the vault looking at the pieces inside.

I held onto Jaime's hand and walked her over to the vault.

"I can't believe it," she said.

I could tell she was overwhelmed as she took in the pieces and I was happy because I was there to witness how amazed she was.

My phone started ringing at that moment and I had to let go of Jaime's hand to answer it. I saw Mrs. Gallagher's name and knew she was calling to confirm if Frank had come through.

It was last minute but understandable because security was his main concern. We spoke for less than a minute before she hung up.

"Have you put your fears to rest now?" I asked Jaime when I joined her and Caitlin.

She took me in her arms and kissed me, catching me completely off guard.

I closed my eyes and slowly responded as her arms moved around my waist and I circled mine around her neck, indulging in the sensations that swirled through me from her kiss.

It was Caitlin who made us part when she cleared her throat, and we remembered we had a job to do. Jaime slowly let me go as she smiled at me.

"I need to make sure everything is in place," I said.

Caitlin was looking at us in amusement, but Jaime didn't seem to care.

"I should go make sure all my guests arrive," Jaime said.

We left the exhibition hall together and headed in two different directions. I didn't know how I was going to be able to concentrate on anything else other than her. Hopefully that kiss was a start to a pleasant evening.

Rex arrived a short while later looking handsome in a suit. I spotted him before he saw me and approached him. A lot of guests had arrived but Mrs. Gallagher was nowhere in sight. The gallery was quickly filling up, but the set up had been done so provocatively, everyone was engrossed in the artwork displayed. I had to hand it to Jaime, she knew what she was doing.

"Hey you," I said to Rex.

The surprise and wonder that covered his face was similar to that of Jaime's. I understood because he'd never seen me dressed up before.

He wrapped his arms around me. "You look so beautiful," he said.

"Thanks, you look very handsome yourself."

He continued to stare at me and I couldn't help laughing.

"I'm glad you're here," I said.

"Me too, this place is great. I haven't had a chance to take a tour but from what I see here, I have to say, I'm impressed."

"Yeah, Jaime is really good at what she does."

"Where is she?"

I scanned the room and found her talking to some guests a little distance away. Since it was her event, she was going to have a lot of talking to do and I felt for her because I knew how it was like, having witnessed Mrs. Gallagher do the same.

"Over there, in the burgundy dress." She stood out from the crowd.

"Oh, wow! She's hot," he said.

I nodded in agreement as I watched her from across the room.

"And Mrs. Gallagher, is she here?"

I shook my head, wondering what was holding her up. She was half an hour late. "She must be on her way."

"I can't wait to see her. I can finally tell if she's worth the fuss."

I almost missed his statement as I stared at Jaime.

"Take a tour, see what you could've been a part of had you applied."

He made a sad face and I kissed his cheek as he made his way to the other exhibition halls.

When Mrs. Gallagher walked in a moment later, it was like everyone noticed because there was a silence that descended in the air. She was graceful and elegantly poised, looking strikingly beautiful in a silky Versace gown.

She looked like an angel who'd been plucked from heaven and set in our presence to taunt us with her sensational appearance.

She cordially greeted her guests as she walked in, and I gave her room to chat with her friends before approaching her to find out if she needed anything.

Being the guest of honor, her arrival prompted Jaime to get everyone's attention. She gave a nice brief speech about the event, creating some suspense about the centerpiece, which left everyone eager.

Mrs. Gallagher followed with her own short but moving speech, expressing how much she enjoyed supporting artists and helping build them up to their full potential.

Afterwards, she got herself a glass of champagne and I shadowed her much like the first event, as she moved through the first exhibition hall. I'd done my homework on the artists whose works were presented, so I was set to answer any questions she might've had.

I was surprised she attended the event without her family, but I figured art probably wasn't their thing. Everyone else she'd invited was nice and warm to her, but then again, being who she was, even the president would've been humbled to be in her presence.

She didn't ask any questions, in fact, she barely spoke to me after I filled her in on what she needed to know. It was when Jaime came to talk to her that my heart started pounding.

Both women were stunning in their own unique fashion, and my heart beat for both in two different ways. Jaime's gaze washed over me after she greeted Mrs. Gallagher and I took a step back to give them some room to talk.

Much as I enjoyed being by Mrs. Gallagher's side, I wanted to be with Jaime. I loved the way she looked at me, even as she spoke to Mrs. Gallagher, every once in a while, her gaze would fall on me and my heart would pick up pace.

During their conversation, I thought I heard Jaime mention my name, but I wasn't sure. Their dialogue ended shortly after and Jaime left to go mingle with the crowd.

Whenever our gazes met from across the room, she'd smile at me and I'd smile back, wishing we could revisit our passionate encounter right before the event had started.

"Ms. Bryce seems very pleased with your work," Mrs. Gallagher said.

I turned my attention to her and wondered if she'd noticed I'd been distracted. "Oh, uh, I did my best," I said.

Mrs. Gallagher was looking at an oil painting but something told me her attention was divided. I wondered what she'd do if she knew there was more between me and Jaime but doubted she'd care.

I started talking about the painting she was studying as per the information provided in the portfolio, but she didn't seem much interested so I stopped.

"Ms. Bryce seems confident in your work so why don't you take a break and try and have a good time tonight," she said.

I thought I'd heard wrong until she looked right at me and smiled. It struck me as unusual but kind, and I did as she said before she could change her mind.

I'd seen all the artwork on display so I wasn't as intrigued with the pieces as the rest of the people in the gallery. I went in search of Rex and found him in the second exhibition hall.

"Hey, what're you doing here? I thought you'd be busy shadowing Mrs. Gallagher, who by the way, is everything you said she was and more."

"She told me to take a break," I said.

"I can see why you're so smitten."

"I'm not smitten. It's just a silly crush. It'll fade."

"She's not making it easy, is she?"

I shook my head. I wished she was a horrible boss so that it'd be easy for me to dislike her but she kept throwing me curveballs and making it impossible for my attraction towards her to fade away.

"Here," Rex took two glasses of champagne from a waiter and handed me one. "Try and have some fun."

I took the glass and took a sip. "Do you think she'd fire me if she knew there was something between me and Jaime?"

"Why would she fire you? You're more than competent with your work and your personal life has nothing to do with it."

Maybe he was right. "I get the feeling she could tell there was more with me and Jaime than we're letting on."

"So what? It hasn't interfered with your ability to perform your duties. Come on, relax. Let's try and enjoy ourselves."

I exhaled. Rex was right. I was being tense over nothing. I needed to relax and enjoy myself.

"When you get a chance, do you think you could introduce me to Jaime? It'd really help me out."

"I'll introduce you to her now," I said.

"Really?"

I nodded and laughed at his excitement. "Come on."

He followed me to where Jaime was standing talking to some rich folk and waited for her to be done. A moment later, she turned her attention to me and reached for my glass of champagne.

"I could really use a few more of these," she said.

"I'll keep them coming, at intervals though. We don't want you getting drunk on your big night," I said.

She reached for my elbow and gently massaged it.

"You're doing great," I said as she slowly lowered her hand and closed it over mine. Rex cleared his throat and I realized I'd almost forgotten he was there. "Oh, this is my best friend, Rex."

She let go of my hand and shook his as she introduced herself. "Livvy told me you're an artist," she said.

Rex nodded and shortly after, they engaged in conversation about the kind of work Rex did. Jaime was kind and sweet and as I watched her talk to Rex, I realized I could seriously develop feelings for her.

She was the complete opposite of Mrs. Gallagher and what she made me feel every time she looked at me had the capacity to chase away the crush I harbored for my boss.

"I'll give you my card and we can talk at length under more suitable circumstances," she said.

I was pleased to see how excited Rex was about the prospect of doing business with her.

"I have to go. I need to make sure the exhibition hall with the centerpiece is ready for when everyone is done with the other halls." She gently squeezed my arm and left.

"She's great, isn't she?"

"She's amazing," Rex said.

I turned to face him only to find him gawking at her as she walked away.

"Easy there tiger," I teased.

We proceeded to the next exhibition hall as we continued to talk. I was tired since I'd been on my feet all day, but it didn't bother me.

"I can't believe this is your world now."

I nodded, agreeing with Rex.

"It must be overwhelming."

"If these kinds of events took place on a daily basis, it would be."

"Any idea what Mrs. Gallagher will have you doing next?"

She hadn't hinted on anything so far, but the fact that she'd given me time off to do my exam meant whatever she'd have me working on next wouldn't be as time consuming.

"Not really," I said, then remembered her invite to the opera. It'd been an odd request since it wasn't work-related. "Actually, she did ask me for something which I thought was peculiar."

"What's that?"

"A few days ago, she asked me to accompany her to the opera, which is actually tomorrow night."

"She what?" Rex asked. "Like a date?"

I laughed, thinking it was silly. Mrs. Gallagher was a married woman who had no interest in me whatsoever. "No, it was more of a request. I didn't think it meant anything. In fact, I haven't thought about it until now."

"That's odd," he said.

"Maybe when she asked me, it was her way of making amends after the way she treated me when I found her fighting with her husband."

"But you said she apologized."

"She did, but maybe she wanted to do more. I don't know. I can't figure out how she thinks. She's the most complicated woman I've ever met."

"Heads up," Rex said and I turned to the direction he was facing.

Mrs. Gallagher was talking to a man dressed neatly in a black tuxedo. She seemed preoccupied as they talked, facing one of the paintings in the room. The man seemed completely smitten with her, which made me wonder if she'd ever cheated on her husband.

"How do you do it?" Rex asked.

"Do what?"

"Stand beside her without exploding into a tiny million pieces. She's so…"

"I know." She was an overwhelming sight.

As though she knew we were talking about her, she looked up and her gaze settled on me. I was so used to her looking past me, when she looked directly at me in a room full of people, I misread her motioning me to join her.

"I think she's calling for you," Rex said as he averted his gaze, trying to pretend he hadn't been staring at her.

"Oh shit, here." I handed him my glass and walked over to her.

"Olivia, please go get Ms. Bryce for me, I'd like to introduce her to someone," she said when I got to her.

I did as told and went in search of Jaime. When I found her, she was in a small group of people talking about how much the event was going to benefit the artists. She managed to quietly slip away when she saw me.

"Mrs. Gallagher wants to introduce you to someone," I said.

"Oh? Where is she?"

"Follow me." I lead her to Mrs. Gallagher who introduced her to the gentleman she'd been talking to. I wasn't sure if I was needed for anything else, but I stuck around just in case.

It took me a minute to realize Mrs. Gallagher had wanted to keep the man occupied so that she could get away from him. I found it amusing, as she moved along to join a couple of women who were studying an oil painting. A woman of her stature couldn't be without a few admirers.

The rest of the evening unfolded flawlessly. I noticed Caitlin was busy sticking small cards to the paintings and other types of artwork that had been sold, while Jaime with finesse, superbly handled the rich powerful guests.

When we got to the exhibition hall with the centerpiece, I noticed they'd been covered with a red silk cloth. Jaime introduced the pieces as everyone held their breath, waiting for the big reveal.

I watched Mrs. Gallagher, waiting to see if any emotion would pass across her face, but she just held on to the same expression she'd had on all evening.

When Jaime removed the cloth, I could've sworn I heard some people in the crowd gasp in surprise. I could bet of all the things they would've expected to see that evening, Cleopatra's headpiece and a rare red diamond had been the least of it.

If I had known I'd been going to three African countries to sign for these pieces to be delivered to New York, if I had known the trip would have such great impact on people, I would've traveled to any other place Mrs. Gallagher wanted to send me.

As I stood beside her, watching even the most powerful look at those pieces in awe, I couldn't believe how great an effect the whole thing had on me.

"It's overwhelming, isn't it?"

Mrs. Gallagher's voice pulled me from my thoughts. It was like she could see what was going through me and she understood. "Yes, it is."

She was probably used to this, seeing as she'd done it for so long. It must've been why it didn't seem to affect her.

"You must be used to it," I said.

"Why do you think I do it?" she asked.

I looked at her and she turned to look at me. I'd thought at that point I was used to looking her straight in the eye, but being so close to her and having her look back at me made me feel like I was transfixed. I couldn't look away.

"You just need to look at one person, see everything they feel and then it starts to mean something to you," she said.

I wasn't sure if she meant me, but I was glad she was the first to look away because that single moment of paralysis made me see her more clearly than I'd ever thought I would.

I wanted to say something, but my mind was blank so I turned my attention back to the crowd as they studied the centerpiece, all getting a closer look one at a time.

Jaime was talking to Caitlin, and I could tell she was pleased by how things were going. The event lasted five hours, and as people began to leave, I waited to see if Mrs. Gallagher would require anything else from me.

She had a chat with Jaime and left a while later, but I decided to stay behind. Rex offered to take me home, but I wanted to spend more time with Jaime, so we made plans to meet up over the weekend.

When everyone had left, Frank Connor and his two men took the pieces and left as well. I took a champagne bottle and two glasses and went to Jaime's office. She was talking to Caitlin and they both seemed satisfied with the night's outcome.

"Why don't we pick this up tomorrow," Jaime said to Caitlin, who nodded and bid us both a goodnight.

"You must be tired," I said, hiding the bottle behind me.

"Not as much as I thought I would be, actually."

"The excitement must still be coursing through you."

She nodded as she took a deep breath.

I revealed the bottle of champagne and the glasses, and she rewarded me with a smile. "Here is to hoping everything went as well as expected," I said.

She approached me and took the glasses from me as I uncorked the bottle.

"I thought you left," she said as I filled her glass.

"I couldn't leave without checking up on you."

"That's sweet."

I filled my own glass and placed the bottle on her desk. "What should we toast to?" I asked.

"To a very successful evening," she said as we clinked our glasses.

The first sip went right through me and I had to take another. Now that we were alone, I was suddenly aware of how nervous I was. "Did you manage to sell a lot of pieces?" I asked.

"Caitlin just informed me that everything was sold out and, we got orders for more."

"Oh my God, that's great news."

"It is, and I wanted to thank you because you've been of great help to me."

"You did everything, Jaime. All this was you."

"I wouldn't have been able to do it without you."

She was giving me way too much credit than I deserved.

"Now that it's over, I know I'm going to be a bit busy but I can't wait to go on that second date with you," she said.

I was glad she'd not forgotten about that. "Me too," I said.

She was smiling at me with her eyes and I could tell what she wanted to do. I wanted to meet her halfway, but I was too nervous to move. We still hadn't gotten used to one another, but after the night we both just had, it felt right that it should end the way it had began.

She seemed to share the same sentiments as she moved closer to me and reached for my face with her hand. She ran the back of her index finger over the outline of my jaw and closed the distance between us, brushing her lips softly against mine in a kiss.

We placed our glasses over her desk, and our arms circled around each other as we both deepened the kiss. I could taste the champagne from her lips and her tongue as she parted my lips and passionately whisked me from my reality and introduced me to her own.

I couldn't remember wanting someone else so much as she gently ran her hands over the soft fabric of my dress. I wanted her to take it off and explore me more thoroughly, but it was too soon.

I responded with uncontrolled lust, gently teasing her tongue with my own as she explored my mouth and an involuntary sigh escaped me when her hands cupped my breasts, exciting me further.

She broke the kiss, but didn't move away as we both panted like we'd just come from running. I understood her reasons. If we continued, it was more than likely we'd end up sleeping together.

"I should take you home," she said breathlessly against my lips.

"Yeah," I said, leaning closer to kiss her again.

She responded with a similar need and hunger and my body started acting up, sending bolts of lust and arousal to that part of me that desperately craved her touch.

This time it was me who pulled away, creating physical distance between us because we both knew what would happen if we went on like that.

"We should really leave," I said.

She nodded and took the glass of champagne she'd placed on the table and took a sip. I followed her lead, taking a sip myself and shortly after, we were heading out. She locked the gallery and we silently walked down the hallway to the elevator.

The drive home was mostly quiet. It felt as if we were afraid any talk would lead us into each other's arms again and considering the erotic condition my body was still in, I wasn't so sure it wouldn't.

Jaime dropped me home half an hour later and instead of letting her walk me to the door of my building, I stayed in the car a few minutes longer, soaking in the air that still lingered between us.

"I had fun tonight," I said.

"Me too, I'm glad it was you I got to work with."

I turned to face her and said, "Me too."

I removed my seatbelt and leaned across my seat to kiss her goodnight. I was going to peck her lips, bid her goodnight and get out of her car, but when she placed her hand over my cheek and brushed her lips against mine, I abandoned my plan and went along with hers.

This was becoming something I could quickly get used to. I loved the way her lips captured mine and explored me without a care as what her kisses seemed to do to me. She knew, and she enjoyed it, but then again so did I.

When she released me, I slowly pulled back and opened my eyes. "Goodnight," I whispered.

She smiled at me and said softly, "Goodnight."

I got out of her car and headed for the entrance of my building. When I got to the door, I turned to face her and she waved at me as she drove away.

Chapter Eight

My day started earlier than usual. Mrs. Gallagher called me an hour before I usually woke up to tell me to set up a morning meeting for her and Frank Connor.

A few minutes after she hung up, I was on the phone with Frank, who was unaware of the meeting, and had been set to travel that morning, but was forced to postpone his flight.

He wasn't very pleased, but Mrs. Gallagher practically ruled everyone who worked with her or, for her so she called all the shots. I made reservations for them at a high-end restaurant and called her back almost half an hour later to give her the details.

I was tired from the previous night, but after Mrs. Gallagher called, I couldn't go back to sleep. I woke up and prepared for work. There was a lot to follow up on after the art exhibition because Mrs. Gallagher wanted to see results from the work she'd done.

Funny enough, none of it revolved around Jaime's art gallery. I would've wanted it to because it would've given me an excuse to call her up and talk to her. But instead, I had to go to the office, get all the names and contact information of the guests who'd attended the art exhibition and send them gift bags.

I had to admit, Mrs. Gallagher was turning out to be something I'd never quite imagined she would be. The causes she took up were noble, and even though she didn't emotionally attach herself, her effort, commitment and hard work was remarkable.

I found myself looking up to her as the sort of person I would've wanted to become, had I had as much as she did. She was a role model to a lot of people and I was lucky to have a front seat into her world and into who she was.

When I left my house, I found James waiting for me outside the building. I still wasn't used to getting driven to work, and every time I stepped outside my house to find that shiny BMW waiting, with him standing outside the car ready to open the door for me, it was Mrs. Gallagher's face that came to mind.

She taunted me for reasons I made myself believe I understood. I wanted to believe that the crush I harbored for her was controllable, that the humanity I'd seen in her the previous night had been visible and necessary because the people at the event had needed to see it.

Now Jaime, she was nothing like Mrs. Gallagher. She was sweet, soft and gentle. A part of me thought that because we understood each other so well, she was that fraction in me that had always wanted to feel and experience something deeper, something meaningful.

She was my light, my passion and everything else I'd always wanted in a person. She provoked my feelings, making me want and desire more. She looked right at me, daring me to show her more than just the face I showed the rest of the world and that incitation made me want her beyond means and reasons that were lost to me.

I got to my office and had to push my thoughts of Jaime aside. I spent most of the day on the phone and when I got a few minutes to myself, I went on my computer in an attempt to study for my exams. I wasn't sure I was going to pass. I had missed a lot of classes and hadn't studied enough. The worst past was, these exams were going to count for half my grade at the end of the semester.

I'd been so busy during the last few weeks, I'd not had time to open a book to read or attend any of my classes. I was neglecting the most important thing to me; my education. It was the only way I'd ever make myself into who I wanted to become and it was the only way I'd ever make my parents proud.

Yes, I needed this job, and yes, I needed the money, but the paramount factor of this whole thing was that I graduate because it was the only way I'd ever pay back my parents.

"Ms. Williams?"

I looked up from the computer to find Francis, the butler, at the door. He had always been a bit distant, but after working for the Gallaghers for what, three weeks now, I understood his need and nature for detachment.

"Yes, Francis?"

"There is a package you need to sign for," he said.

"A package?"

I was a little confused. Why did I need to sign for it? Wasn't it a household duty? Or was it a package for Mrs. Gallagher?

Francis walked out and I followed after him. Once down the stairs, he went his own way and I headed for the door to find a delivery man with a huge wrapped package.

"Who's it from?" I asked the delivery man.

He pointed to a name on the release form.

The package read it had come from Jaime's art gallery. I assumed it was a painting Mrs. Gallagher had purchased but when I went to sign, I noticed it was addressed to me.

"Wait, it says the package is for me," I said.

"Sign here please." The delivery man couldn't be bothered.

I signed for it and picked it up, taking it upstairs to my office. When I set it down, I stared at it for a few minutes wondering if it was Jaime who'd sent it to me. I found it odd she'd sent it to the Gallagher residence rather than my house.

Deciding to open it, I carefully tore open the wrapping paper and stared at the painting in a little bit of surprise. My memory went back to the first time Jaime had taken me to her storage to show me the paintings that had been chosen for the exhibition.

I remembered joking about the only kind of painting I could do and her explaining it to me. She'd called it action painting, where paint is spontaneously smeared onto canvas.

There was a painting that had been behind her, which had fired up the whole flirting thing, and she'd ended up saying she'd be happy to teach me how to do those kinds of paintings.

I couldn't believe she remembered. I couldn't believe she'd sent me the painting. I'd call her up later on when I got home to thank her and maybe even make plans for that second date since Mrs. Gallagher hadn't confirmed about the opera.

She'd been gone all day. She usually had a busy schedule, meeting with her high society friends at their rich folk members' country club, attending business meetings and planning charitable causes among other things.

She hadn't said a word to me about the opera, so I thought she'd forgotten she'd invited me. I wasn't sure what to do. I'd never been in such a situation before. Maybe she'd invited me because there was some work-related issue she needed to deal with and my presence was necessary.

I honestly didn't know what to think. Mrs. Gallagher wasn't like anyone I'd ever come across before. I couldn't guess with her. She wasn't a straightforward type of person and it was a bit unnerving trying to figure her out. Her personality and nature were foreign to me.

I decided to go down to the kitchen to get myself a bottle of water. My afternoon wasn't as busy as the morning had been, which I appreciated because I needed the free time to study.

The house was deserted. I couldn't even find Francis to ask for directions. I'd never toured it. The only place I knew how to get to was my office, Mrs. Gallagher's office and the bathroom because those were the only places I'd been to since I'd started working there.

I was down at the foyer trying to figure out which direction the kitchen could be when someone spoke.

"Can I help you find something?"

I turned towards the side the voice had come from and froze when I met Mrs. Gallagher's son. "Uh, hi, I'm Olivia."

He slowly approached me and I grew a little nervous. He looked like a cleaner serious version of Vampire Diaries' Ian Somerhalder with dark intense eyes, short but tidy hair with a much more formal wardrobe.

"I work for your Mom." I didn't know why it felt like I'd just been caught doing something wrong.

"You're her personal assistant," he said.

"Yes."

He stretched out his arm to shake mine.

"I'm Jonah," he said.

I closed my hand over his. "I was uh," I looked around the large foyer and remembered what I'd been searching for. "I was looking for the kitchen."

He nodded, letting go of my hand as he said, "This way."

I didn't want to inconvenience him, but I didn't want to turn down offered help either. "Thank you," I said.

If I'd gone looking for the kitchen myself, I would've gotten lost because we went through a large dining room and walked past it into a very clean and very nice-looking kitchen. It seemed like no expense had been spared when building the house.

"How do you like working for my Mom?" he asked.

There was a long countertop in the middle splitting the room in two, but it left enough space for one to go around it.

One side had very modern cooking appliances, I almost didn't notice the human-sized two-door fridge until Jonah opened it because it was installed into a wall. The other side had more space with a small dining table and other kitchen paraphernalia.

There were several stools along the countertop that looked like they'd been glued to the floor, I walked over and sat on one. "I like it," I said, answering Jonah's question.

"You don't think she's a demanding boss?" he asked.

Even if she was, I couldn't tell him so. She was his mother. "No, not really." Plus, I'd worked for worse employers. Mrs. Gallagher was a peach compared to anyone I'd ever worked for.

"Are you just saying that because I'm her son?" he asked, handing me a bottle of water.

I looked at him, unsure of how to answer his question because my answer would compromise me. "I should get back to work," I said.

"Is that a yes?" he asked, seemingly amused by unsuccessful attempt to evade his question.

"No, I mean…" I trailed my thoughts back to his earlier question before the follow-ups. "Your Mom is a great boss, better than anyone I've ever worked for."

The amusement in his eyes seemed to disappear at my answer, as he made his way over to me. "I saw you a couple of weeks ago at the ball," he said.

The only part of the night I best remembered was kissing Mrs. Gallagher. The memory sent chills through me at the possibility of him having seen us.

"I think she was impressed," he said.

He was looking at me so intensely when he said that, I had to look away. "Thank you for the water," I said.

He nodded and I took a step back and turned to leave.

"Olivia," I stopped to look at him. "It was nice meeting you."

I smiled at him, surprised by how nice a guy he was. "It was nice meeting you too," I said as I left the kitchen and headed back to my office.

The hint of seriousness in Jonah reminded me of the easygoing manner in his sister, Adrianna. I had only met her once, but her personality was very different from his. He reminded me of Mrs. Gallagher.

I spent a couple of more hours at the office waiting to hear from Mrs. Gallagher about the opera, while I stole a few minutes to myself every now and then to study as I continued with my work.

When James dropped me off, I had all but given up on the opera and was looking forward to staying in and calling Jaime when he said, "Pick you up again in a couple of hours?"

I looked at him in confusion.

"Mrs. Gallagher, she told me to pick you up around seven thirty for the opera."

I nodded and got out of the car. "Thank you, James."

I headed for my building, feeling a bit miffed with Mrs. Gallagher. Why couldn't she have just called me to confirm? I'd spent the whole day wondering about it only to have it confirmed by James.

I got to my house and seriously considered calling her to cancel, or maybe I should've just stood her up. The thought brought a smile to my face.

She'd invited me a week earlier and it was starting to feel like it was last minute. I didn't even know what I'd wear. What did people wear to operas? I was probably even lucky to know it was an opera I'd been invited to considering how stingy Mrs. Gallagher was with details.

Maybe I could ask Jaime. She'd know. She'd probably attended some operas in her lifetime. I picked up the phone and dialed her number. As it rang, I paced back and forth and remembered the painting. Maybe I should've sent her flowers with a thank you note.

I stopped pacing when she picked up. Her voice was calm and composed but seemed to lack its usual warmth. "Jaime, it's me," I said.

"Hi Liv–. Olivia," she said.

Maybe I was imagining it but she didn't sound too eager to hear from me. "Is everything alright?" I asked.

She cleared her throat and said, "Yeah, yes, everything is fine."

"I wanted to thank you for the painting. It took me a little by surprise, but it was really nice of you to do that," I said.

"Olivia, what are you talking about?" she asked.

I sat down on the bed. "The painting I received today from your gallery, it was from you, wasn't it?"

"No, I'm afraid not."

Wait, if it wasn't from her and she was the only person who knew I liked it, then who could it have been from? "Who was it from then? I thought…"

"Olivia, look, it was really nice meeting you and it was great working together but I can't see you anymore," she said.

"Wait, what? What's going on?" I asked in confusion.

"I can't see you anymore, Olivia. Goodbye," she said and hung up.

I stared at my phone wondering what had just happened. Had Jaime just broken up with me? Technically, we hadn't been a couple in order for it to be a break up but still, what had just happened?

Last we'd seen each other, it had been so wonderful. We'd even talked about the possibility of a second date. How could she turn me away so out of the blue? Was it something I'd done? And if the painting wasn't from her, then who was it from?

I didn't know how long I sat there thinking, but the more I thought about it, the depressing the notion became. I'd just been dumped by a woman I'd only started dating. How pathetic was that?

I'd genuinely believed she liked me. What could have changed her mind? I was convinced she'd felt the same way, well, almost. Clearly, I'd been wrong. She'd sent me all the right signals, she'd responded to our kisses with a similar need, she'd looked at me with interest and our conversations had been so good.

What could've happened to make her change her mind about me? Since she didn't want to hear from me again, I doubted I'd ever get the answers I needed. What struck me was the fact that it hurt.

I knew I'd liked her way too soon and everything had happened fast between us, but I had never imagined she'd call it quits so soon.

I liked her but she wanted nothing to do with me. The reality sunk in with a startling and piercing realization, which left me sad.

Since it was getting late and thinking about Jaime was doing nothing but hurt me, I got up and went to take a shower. I needed a distraction and this opera had come at a more than a convenient timing.

Chapter Nine

I wasn't aware of the night's plan but when James came to pick me up in a black stretch limousine, I knew Mrs. Gallagher meant business. I was overwhelmed by the unexpected means of transport, seeing as how a mere few weeks ago I'd been almost homeless.

He opened the door for me with his usual warm smile, offering me a compliment regarding my attire. I was wearing a simple but elegant blue dress and heels but felt under dressed because I wasn't sure how people dressed to operas.

"Are we meeting Mrs. Gallagher at the venue?" I asked when James drove out of parking.

"I'm picking her up from the country club," he said.

"You must drive her to these kinds of things all the time," I said, trying not to grow nervous at the prospect of spending the evening with Mrs. Gallagher.

"She likes her operas," he said.

I fidgeted in my seat.

"It's a bit unusual though, she always goes alone."

"She probably wanted me along for some work-related issue or something."

"Like I said, she likes her operas."

Was he suggesting this had nothing to do with work?

"There is champagne and a couple of glasses back there," he said.

I met his gaze on the rearview mirror and wondered if he sensed my uneasiness. "Thanks, but I think I should stay sober."

"It's to calm your nerves."

"Still, I don't think I should drink when I'm about to go meet my boss."

"You're not on the clock, but suit yourself."

The more we talked the nervous I grew. He focused his attention on the road and the memory of Jaime ending things with me earlier came to mind. Had I not heard from her, I would've put up the snobbish pretentious attitude I assumed most people attending would be in, but I just wasn't in the mood.

I had tried to psyche myself up for the opera to no avail and knowing I was going to spend the evening with Mrs. Gallagher, probably just the two of us alone, was leaving me even more psyched out.

When James stopped the car a while later, my heart started pounding. He told me he'd be right back and got out. I looked at the champagne bottle and contemplated pouring myself a glass because my nerves were all over the place.

Almost ten minutes later, I heard footsteps approaching and braced myself. A moment later, James opened the door and I moved farther to my right to create space as Mrs. Gallagher got in.

She smelled like an expensive bottle of perfume as she took a seat beside me, and she looked gorgeous in a formal but graceful dress. "Hello Olivia," she said when she settled down on her seat and looked at me.

"Hello Mrs. Gallagher," I said nervously.

"How is your evening?"

Not so good, I wanted to say but I forced a smile and said, "Not bad."

James got back in the car and drove out of the country club.

I was so tense I didn't know what to do.

"How are your studies coming along?" she asked.

"They're coming along fine," I lied. What was I supposed to tell her, that since I'd started working for her I hadn't had a chance to study or attend classes?

I was glad when she reached for the champagne bottle and uncorked it because my throat was suddenly dry. She'd never taken any interest in me and I didn't know what this was all about but, I was going to try my best to play along.

She poured the wine in two glasses and handed me one.

"Thank you," I said.

"Have you attended an opera performance before?" she asked.

I thought it was obvious that I never had, but I smiled at her and shook my head as I said, "No, this is my first."

"Tonight's performance is one of my favorites. It's an Italian comic opera called the Elixir of Love mostly performed in Italy between 1838 and 1848," she said.

It was surprising of her to reveal something personal about herself to me. Up until then, she'd never let me see past her serious demeanor.

I didn't know how to respond. I'd never imagined the two of us in a social setting where we'd have to talk about anything other than work. "I hope I like it," I said.

"You may, or may not. Young people of today have very different uh… taste."

She appeared a little more relaxed than usual and I liked the aura surrounding her because it made me feel less tense. I took a sip from my glass and let out a breath, relaxing in my seat as the champagne trickled down my throat.

The rest of the drive to the Metropolitan Opera House was quiet. I wanted to talk to Mrs. Gallagher, get to know this side of her she was starting to show but I second-guessed every statement I thought of saying.

When we got there, we set the champagne glasses back down and got out of the limousine. James handed Mrs. Gallagher an envelope, which I assumed had the tickets and I took a deep breath and followed after her.

I assumed we had arrived on time since there was no line, but realized a few minutes later that we were going in through a different entrance. I doubted I'd ever get used to the VIP treatment as we made our way into the lobby.

There were people who had already arrived, but Mrs. Gallagher didn't seem to want to stop for a chat. Instead, she quickly showed me directions to the coatroom and washroom and led me to our sitting area, a private box with two seats.

Once seated, an usher came to hand us a program which had the synopsis conveying the plot of the performance and two opera glasses to make viewing easier.

The auditorium was huge and far more astonishing than anything I had imagined. It felt like I had stepped into another world, one that was unfamiliar but pleasingly accepting.

"This is amazing," I said, trying but failing to conceal my wonder.

Mrs. Gallagher responded with a slight nod.

I read the program to see when the intermission would take place while I looked around to see the other patrons who had attended the show.

While we waited, my excitement seemed to wear off with time as my thoughts drifted back to Jaime. I would've loved to attend something like that with her. We would've definitely had more to talk about.

"You okay?" I looked up at Mrs. Gallagher's voice.

I quickly nodded and said, "I'm fine. I'm just a little overwhelmed."

She looked at me a moment longer than I expected her to and I had to look away first because intimidation set in.

"The Italian composer Gaetano Donizetti…"

I watched her as she gave me a brief history of the original composer and wondered if she still viewed me as just a mere employee. She'd shown more interest in me than any of my former employers, but then again, that could have just been the sort of person she was.

I still found her completely irresistible and would never, for the life in me, understand how her husband could take her for granted. I blamed the slip of my tongue the night I had kissed her on alcohol, but found myself wondering where all that courage had disappeared to.

Mrs. Gallagher had given me a stern warning, but I couldn't help wonder if there was more to this opera thing.

Was this her way of extending a hand of friendship? I doubted she'd want anything from me. What could a woman who had everything in the world want from someone like me?

"It's starting," she said.

I almost didn't notice until she told me and I focused my attention to the grand stage. The lights dimmed and people started clapping. I played along and stopped when everyone else did. The orchestra started and the curtains rose as the performance began.

The performance was in its original language, but there were English supertitles projected above the stage all throughout. I followed the storyline, which caught me off guard because it was actually very good.

I could see why it was one of Mrs. Gallagher's favorites. It was funny, it had depth, the characters were extremely talented, the setting was befitting of the timing the love story had taken place and the orchestra was magnificent. I enjoyed it so much, I almost didn't notice how quickly time passed until the curtains were lowered and the lights came up, ending the first act.

"That was incredible," I said as I rose to my feet, applauding the first half of the show.

"Yes, it was," Mrs. Gallagher said.

I looked at her beautiful face to find a soft serene expression I'd never seen before, once again reaffirming she was the most stunning creature that had ever graced my sight.

"Let's go get a drink while we stretch our legs," she said.

I nodded and followed out after her. We went to a table reserved for her and after taking a seat, a chilled bottle of red wine and two glasses were brought over.

I realized James had been right. Mrs. Gallagher loved her operas. We didn't have to wait in line. I cruised along everything like it was available at the snap of a finger. Both ushers and waiters recognized Mrs. Gallagher, offering her superior service.

If I'd been there alone or with anyone else who wasn't Mrs. Gallagher, I would've had a back seat at the auditorium. I would've either been lining up at the bathroom or at the bar like everyone else seemed to do, or I would've been waiting for the intermission to end while seated at the auditorium.

At that rate, I wouldn't have been surprised to learn there were VIP bathrooms for people like her. Too bad I wasn't pressed, so I wasn't about to find out just yet, but maybe when the entire show was over.

"Are you having a good time?"

I found her looking at me at the question and nodded. "Yes, I am. Thank you for inviting me."

When I didn't think about Jaime, I found myself having a good time. Whenever I thought of her, a wave of sadness would overcome me. I'd never been dumped before. It left me feeling crappy all over again.

"Did you enjoy yourself at the art exhibition last night?" she asked.

I thought about the intimate moments I'd shared with Jaime. "Yes, it was fun. I think what you do is awesome."

"Giving back is an important part of life."

"I agree, giving back is important." I inwardly cursed myself. She must've thought I was sucking up to her.

"That boy you were with, was he one of the artists?" she asked.

"Rex? He's my best friend and an artist too, but by the time he came to learn about the art exhibition, it was too late."

"You should've told me. I would've helped."

I raised my eyebrow in surprise. "You would've allowed his pieces into the exhibition?"

"I *was* sponsoring the event so, yes."

"But Jaime said the application process had been closed."

"Ah yes, the process." She chuckled, a cute pleasant noise that drove sensations I couldn't identify through me. "The process is there to enforce the rules. The rules don't apply to me."

I felt like someone had kicked me hard in the gut. Rex was going to kill me.

"You care a lot about this... Rex," she said.

"He's the closest thing to family I have in the city. He's going to kill me when he finds out about this."

"You didn't know. He's going to understand."

She was right. I hadn't been aware I could just ask to have his pieces in the art exhibition. He'd understand. It would hurt, but he'd understand.

I looked at her and found a type of warmth in her eyes that instantly relaxed me. I smiled at her and took a sip of wine.

"So where are you from, originally?" she asked.

Her attention was still focused on me, which made it hard for me to concentrate. "Uh, St. Paul, Minnesota. I moved here for school."

"You're far from home," she said.

Her voice was low, but audible and her posture was calm and controlled. I was having a rollercoaster of emotions going through me and trying hard to keep a straight face.

"I am," I said.

"How long have you lived in New York?"

"About four years now."

"You must miss your family."

"I do."

"You visit them often?"

"Just a couple of times since I got to New York. It's not easy because of school, work and sometimes lack of funds."

She nodded as though she understood and asked, "Do you have a big family?"

"Just my parents and my older brother," I said.

I noticed people had started going back to the auditorium and took another sip from my glass, knowing we were about to head back in as well.

"It must be hard for you being in the city all by yourself," she said.

"It was, initially, when I got here and making friends wasn't easy. But I quickly got used to it." I was pleased by the fact that we were actually having a conversation, and one that didn't involve work.

"We should head back," she said.

She got to her feet and I followed suit.

"Did you like the painting?" she asked.

The painting, wait, what? I halted in my step. She was the one who had gotten me the painting? It wasn't Jaime? By the time it occurred to me to ask her these questions, she was already way ahead of me.

I caught up with her back at our sitting area and scanned the auditorium to see people getting back to their seats. "You got me the painting?" I asked when I sat beside her.

"Did you like it?" she asked, instead of answering my question.

"Yeah, a lot, actually." I started thinking about the questions I wanted to pose. "How did you—?"

The lights slowly dimmed, indicating the second act was about to start. I didn't get a chance to ask any of my questions because the performance started shortly after and I had to wait for it to end.

I was distracted throughout the beginning of the second act. I had so many questions. How had Mrs. Gallagher known to get me that particular painting? Why had she gotten it for me?

Was she responsible for Jaime ending things with me? No, no, I was getting ahead of myself. Why would she care about what happened between me and Jaime? What I did outside of work was of no concern to her. She couldn't have been responsible for Jaime's decision to cut ties with me.

As far as I was concerned, she wasn't even aware I'd been dating Jaime. Maybe she'd asked Jaime which painting I'd liked best and gotten it for me as a reward for a job well done. I shook my head, clearly, I was overthinking this.

A reaction from the audience drew my attention back to the opera. I used my opera glasses and a few minutes later, the gripping performance had all my attention.

I was shocked when during a couple of scenes toward the end, the main characters costume design matched the Moroccan attire I'd signed for in Marrakech. What had it been called, djellaba and kaftans?

Chapter Ten

"I know I already said this but thank you for inviting me to the opera. It seems to have drawn a greater reaction from me than I expected." I felt so stupid.

The ending of the opera performance had been so emotional I'd somehow ended up in tears. The most embarrassing part was that Mrs. Gallagher had seen it and had offered me her handkerchief. I felt like an idiot and just wanted to go home and live out the experience as the most humiliating moment of my life.

Mrs. Gallagher probably thought I was a cry baby who got overly emotional and to make it worse, I had apologized a couple of times and now, I was thanking her again.

"Hungry?" she asked.

I wasn't even sure I was overreacting. I still couldn't tell what she was thinking, which was infuriating. How could she make me question myself? I was sober. I knew exactly what was going on, so why was I second guessing myself? I needed to save face.

"Yes," I said.

We were in the limousine and James was driving away from the opera house. Much as the opera had affected me, I had to admit, attending had definitely been the right call. It was top of the list of my best experiences in New York. Well, a first of its kind.

James took us to an awesome restaurant. I was too distracted by my thoughts to think straight so I didn't get a chance to find out the name of the place. Plus being in the company of one of the most exquisite women I'd ever had the chance to be around, made it much easier to stay distracted.

Mrs. Gallagher wasn't just anyone. She was my boss. She was a heartbeat, actively pounding in me. If deactivated, my whole life would stop. I'd have no choice but to go back to St. Paul. Everything would be over.

I'd have to defer further on my classes until I had enough money to pay off my fees and by the time I graduated, it would probably be too late to get anywhere I'd planned to be at that stage in my life.

"Do you come here often?" I asked after we were seated.

James hadn't asked where to go next after we'd gotten back in the limousine so when he dropped us off at a restaurant, and we were taken to a table, I assumed it wasn't a coincidence.

"Not as often as I'd like," Mrs. Gallagher said.

A waiter brought us a bottle of wine and two glasses, which he made sure Mrs. Gallagher approved of, and handed us each a menu after telling us the specials. He poured the wine into our glasses and left us alone to scan through the menus.

My mind trailed back to the opera and the costume design the actors had been wearing toward the end of the show. Had Mrs. Gallagher sent me all the way to Morocco to pick out a couple of outfits for her favorite opera show? Was there any institution she did not support? It must've meant a lot for the cast and crew of the show to have her support.

The waiter came back a short while later and took our orders then left.

"I liked the costumes the performers wore toward the end of the show," I said.

Mrs. Gallagher looked at me. "You recognized them," she stated.

"They were very distinct."

"They don't usually use those kinds of costumes, but they needed something unique to add a foreign flare to the show."

"It was very nice."

"Did you enjoy the performance?"

Had she not seen my reaction when the show ended? Of course, I had enjoyed the performance. "Yes, it was amazing."

"You're not quite what I pegged you for," she said.

Curiously, I asked, "What do you mean?"

She studied me for a moment, which for some reason I found amusing, then said, "Let's just say you surprised me."

Well, that wasn't saying much but I was going to take it as a good thing. "You seem to constantly surprise me too," I said.

I wished she'd stop being so evasive and just talk to me. Would there ever come a time when she'd open up to me and let me see her for who she truly was? Or would I always be on the other side constantly trying to figure her out?

"Why were you so sad earlier?"

Her question pulled me from my musings. "Sad?"

"Yes, you seemed distressed."

Her statement was unexpectedly soft and gentle and she seemed genuinely curious but I doubted it was concern I read on her lovely features.

I couldn't tell her about Jaime. Much as I wished I had someone to talk to, I couldn't bring myself to open up to her. This was the kind of thing I would talk to Rex about; definitely not my boss.

Jaime breaking up with me had hit me hard and I was still struggling to understand it. Maybe in a day or two, it would stop being a fresh wound and I would somehow try and leave it behind me but at that moment, it still bothered me every time I thought about it.

"Something...unexpected happened today."

"You want to talk about it?"

I nervously ran my palm over the nape of my neck, wondering how I would even start. Mrs. Gallagher didn't care about me or my problems. She was probably just being nice and trying to make conversation.

"No, not really."

I was glad when the waiter brought over our meal because it gave me room to think about a change of subject. I remembered the painting and the questions that had harassed me at the knowledge that she was the one who had gotten it for me.

After setting the food on the table, I stared at Mrs. Gallagher's salad—which had been served in very little potion—then stared at the lobster on my plate.

I couldn't help wondering if that was all she was going to eat.

I took a look at my plate and the sheer size of my lobster left me a little chagrined. It was like the chef had taken the biggest in the bunch and made it for me. It looked like a meal for a small village. I liked food, but there was no way I could finish all that.

The waiter filled two glasses of water, and then refilled the wine glasses and when everything was all set, he smiled at us both and said, "Bon appétit."

I nodded, trying not to let my embarrassment show. Lobsters normally came in big sizes, and even though the one on my plate looked like a mutant, I decided to go along with it and eat what I could. It didn't even seem like Mrs. Gallagher cared.

I used my cutlery well and stole a glance at Mrs. Gallagher.

I had never seen her eat before but she was as graceful in it as she was in everything else. I couldn't help wonder how she would eat a burger. Would she use a knife and folk? The thought of it was funny.

Her mouth had probably never known the delicious taste of a beef burger. With her perfectly youthful figure, she had most likely never eaten junk food in her entire life.

I doubted she was as uptight as she appeared, though. In the few weeks I'd known her, I could tell there was more to her than met the eye. She was absolutely amazing.

I closed my eyes at the first bite to savor the moment. Last time I'd had lobster, had been back home in St. Paul. Everything about my mom, my dad, my house, my bedroom, it was somehow brought back through that single taste.

When I opened my eyes, I found Mrs. Gallagher staring at me and I blushed. She had a hint of a smile on her lips.

"Is it good?" she asked.

The lobster was incredible. "It is," I said with a little nod.

My mind trailed back to the painting. I kept getting distracted. "Can I ask you something?"

She nodded.

"Why did you get me that painting?"

"I thought you'd like it," she said.

"I do, I like it, but how did you know to get me that particular painting?"

She looked directly at me and I nervously bit my lower lip.

"Ms. Bryce was kind enough to suggest it," she said.

She was being so nonchalant about it I thought I was overreacting. Then it occurred to me to find out if she'd known anything about me and Jaime.

"Did she mention anything to you?"

"Who?"

"Jai—. Ms. Bryce," I said.

"Was there something she was supposed to mention?" she asked.

I cursed myself, knowing I'd screwed up because I hadn't asked the questions in a carefully articulated manner.

"Is there anything you want to tell me?" she asked.

She'd gotten the upper hand of the conversation, so I shook my head and took a bite of the lobster.

"You did a good job, Olivia. Give yourself a break."

I was glad she thought my questions and reaction was due to some insecurity regarding my job or some deep-rooted fear of failure, otherwise I didn't know how I would've managed to get myself out of that one.

Still, I didn't know how I felt about her getting me that painting. The only thing it would do was remind me of Jaime and I wasn't so sure I wanted that.

She should have gotten me the rare red diamond instead. At least that was extremely valuable. I would never have to work another day in my life.

"I need to talk to you about something, Olivia," she said with a hint of seriousness.

My hands trembled and I let go of my cutlery and slowly but steadily hid them under the table. I couldn't contain my sudden nervousness. I knew she'd had a reason for inviting me out.

Was this it? Had I finally reached the end of the line? Was she going to fire me? Had I violated some invisible rules I hadn't been aware of?

"You have worked for me for a few weeks now and I feel we should talk about something that is of great importance to me," she said.

I nodded.

"As you're already aware, my family leads a very private life and now that you work for me, you're bound to be exposed to some things that I shouldn't have to tell you are private.

"Your discretion is highly valued and under no circumstance must you ever reveal anything about me or my family to the media or the public."

"I would never do that," I said.

"Good, I hope you don't mind signing a confidentiality agreement," she said.

I shook my head. "No, not at all." I was a little relieved by the request.

It wasn't shocking or surprising at all. I wouldn't have been surprised if a reporter approached me to get some dirt on the family. The Gallaghers led a private life and only showed the world what they wanted to see.

If there were ever any scandals, I was sure they had people who cleaned up after them and did damage control before any of it wound up in the news.

"That's all," she said.

Steadily now, I reached for my cutlery and resumed eating my meal. I wondered if I'd somehow managed to get Mrs. Gallagher to trust me.

"The trip to Africa was amazing," I said, feeling more at ease now.

She raised her perfectly trimmed eyebrow and her eyes smiled at me. "You enjoyed yourself?"

I nodded, with a little more enthusiasm than I expected. "The countries were beautiful, but my favorite place was South Africa because I got to spend a little more time there."

"Did you visit any exotic places?"

She was showing more interest than I expected.

"This man, called Lungile, picked me up from the airport and took me around the area. He told me stories about the place and the following day we visited a couple of museums, national parks and some historical sites. It was the most amazing thing, but I think the Big Hole at Kimberly mines was the most breathtaking of them all."

I was going on and on about everything I'd seen, with the images still fresh in my mind. Mrs. Gallagher listened, every once in a while, responding or asking something and somewhere within it all, I forgot she was my boss.

I was relieved. We were communicating. I was being myself and we were both laughing as I gestured with my arms trying to describe the things I'd seen. I couldn't believe I made her laugh.

Her features were so soft and relaxed. The sound of her laugh was serenely beautiful, like something out of a movie and her posture was so calm and peaceful, I enjoyed seeing her this way.

"God, you're so beautiful." I didn't realize I'd said that out loud until she looked at me.

My memory flew back to the very first time I'd said that and the amazing kiss we'd shared replayed itself in my mind as though it was on a loop. I felt everything I had felt that night.

I recalled the wonder I had seen in her blue eyes as they had shone into me, the way my arm had covered her waist and the wonderful feel of her lips brushing against mine as she'd responded to the kiss. The memory was so powerful, I felt it fully consuming me and taking me back to that night.

The silence that had softly descended between us, the cool breeze as it passed softly caressing my skin, the accelerated thud of my heartbeat and the distant echo of the crowd of people inside the restaurant brought me back.

Quickly recalling her warning, I softly cleared my throat and said, "I'm sorry."

She surprised me when she smiled at me and said, "Don't be."

I smiled back at her and a while later, we were leaving the restaurant. On the drive back home, we didn't say much to one another, but it felt to me like we had shared something special back at the restaurant.

James dropped me off a while later and I stood watching as the limousine drove away. I smiled to myself as I walked into my building when the words Mrs. Gallagher had said to me rang in my ear. *Don't be.* I wasn't.

Chapter Eleven

"You seem so distracted, is everything okay?" Rex asked.

I was thinking about my evening with Mrs. Gallagher. The time we'd spent together had haunted me all night. I had imagined countless possibilities of there being something more between us. I felt foolish, especially because whatever I'd shared with Jaime had recently ended.

"Everything is fine," I said.

Rex and I were at a coffee shop in our neighborhood. We were supposed to be catching up but my thoughts kept trailing back to Mrs. Gallagher. I turned my attention to him as I warmed my hands on my cup of coffee.

"Jaime ended things between us," I announced.

"She what?" His surprise was evident. "I can't believe it."

"Yeah, it came as a surprise to me too but I'm trying not to dwell on it."

"Why did she break up with you?"

"To be honest, I don't know. One day we're doing really well then the next she's saying she can't see me anymore."

"You should've demanded an explanation."

I laughed at his statement. "Demanded an explanation? We went out on one date. I had no say in the matter."

"If she cared as much as she made you believe she did, don't you think she owed you one?"

He was upset, and I understood him, but I was trying hard not to think about Jaime.

"If she cared, then maybe." The thought was depressing because I'd believed we had a connection. Apparently, it had been one-sided.

"I'm sorry, I know it sucks."

Spending time with Mrs. Gallagher had impacted me in a strangely comforting way. "I'm okay."

"You sure?" The concern on his face was endearing.

I nodded. "My evening with Mrs. Gallagher was wonderful."

"Oh yeah, how did that go?"

I instantly smiled at the memory. "After the opera, we went out for dinner."

He glared at me.

"It was a little tense at first but it got easier as we talked." I recalled the soft sound of her laughter. "I made her laugh. Can you believe it?" The memory warmed my heart. I remembered my slip of tongue when I told her she was beautiful and smiled. "She has this strange hold on me. It's like a compulsion. I can't really explain it."

"You realize that nothing will ever come out of this crush you have on her, right?"

I knew that! What—did he think I actually entertained delusional thoughts of grandeur where Mrs. Gallagher and I got together and happily drove into the sunset? I wasn't stupid or... crazy. "I know my place, Rex. Speaking of which, there is something you should know," I said.

"What?"

"When we were talking, she said that if I'd told her about your work, she would've allowed it to be showcased in the exhibition."

His eyes widened in surprise.

"Don't be mad at me, I didn't know I could just ask her to do something like that." I remembered her face when she'd said it. Sure, she didn't need the rules, but why would she include me or any of my friends in something like that? "Sometimes I feel like I can see the real her and she's not uptight, cold, or distant. She's just unhappy."

Rex was shaking his head in disapproval. "Come on, Livvy, what're you doing?"

My thoughts dissipated at his question. "What's wrong with wanting to get to know her?"

"She's Amelia Gallagher and she's completely out of your league. Nothing good would ever come out of this. You know that better than anyone else."

He was right. God, what was I thinking?

"I'm not saying you're not good enough for her. This is a very precarious situation. You could get seriously hurt. It was fun when it was just a crush, but now I think you may be pushing it."

He was right, hard as his words were to hear. Maybe I wasn't okay.

Maybe Jaime ending things with me had pushed me to develop some sort of anchor as a way to protect myself.

"I'm sorry, Livvy."

"Don't ever be sorry for telling me the truth," I said distantly.

I moved my coffee from my hands as it had gotten cold and looked up when Rex's hand covered mine.

"What was that you said about my pieces being showcased in the art exhibition?"

"I thought you missed that," I said.

"How could I?"

"Are you mad at me?"

He shook his head. "I'm sure if you'd been aware of it beforehand, my pieces would've been in the show."

During the rest of our conversation, Rex mostly talked about school, encouraging me to study for my exams and suggesting evening classes seeing as working for Mrs. Gallagher was taking too much of my time.

I only half-listened as I thought about what he'd said about my crush on Mrs. Gallagher. I don't even know what I was thinking. She'd only shown interest in me once and it was to ask me to be discreet with whichever family secrets I might've come across. I needed to focus on something else; something like my studies as Rex was suggesting.

My phone started ringing half an hour before I left the house on Monday morning. I was well rested and was positive it would be a good day. I had decided to ignore what I felt for Mrs. Gallagher and focus on my work and school.

With my exams in a few days, I needed to prioritize not only my work, but also my thoughts. I had three exams in one day and I had to pass no matter what, otherwise I'd be left behind and catching up with the rest of the students while working a fulltime job wasn't easy.

"Hello," I said over the phone.

"Good morning Olivia. It's James."

"Oh, James, hi, is everything alright?" It was unusual getting a call from him.

"Just wanted to inform you that Mrs. Gallagher wants you to carry your passport. I'll pick you up in half an hour," he said and hung up.

Why did Mrs. Gallagher want me to carry my passport? Was she going to send me off again? I needed to stay in New York because of my exams. Had she forgotten?

I took the passport and put it in my purse then wondered if I needed to pack. James hadn't said anything about that, so maybe it was a short trip. Some place I could travel to and make it back before the end of the day.

My least favorite thing about working for Mrs. Gallagher was the lack of communication. Maybe this was why she had different personal assistants every other time. Who would last more than a couple of months when every week was a complete and utter surprise?

It was so frustrating. What would she have me working on now? Who would I meet? Where would I be sent off to? Did I have a say on any of this? I enjoyed my work, but sometimes she made it so hard.

I had to change my purse because I needed to carry my laptop since it had my studying material, and other essentials I would need incase I'd be sent off for another whole week.

James arrived right on time in the BMW he usually took me to work in and as usual, he was polite as he opened the door for me. Once I had thanked him and was seated in the backseat of the car as he drove away, I decided to figure out if he had any idea where I was going.

"How was your weekend?" I asked, as I checked my phone to see if Mrs. Gallagher had communicated with me. Last time this had happened, I'd met Francis at the Gallagher mansion door and he'd handed me a first-class plane ticket.

"Uneventful," he said. "How was yours?"

He had a room at the Gallagher residence because his services were constantly needed so he was more exposed to the family than I was.

"It was okay, I wish I'd studied more though because I have a feeling I may not have the time to do so before my exams," I said.

We shared small talk all the time because we saw each other often, so he knew a little about me. Mostly, he knew about school and my work because he was always polite enough to ask. I had tried getting to know him but he didn't say much about his life.

"You're smart, I'm sure you'll pass."

I smiled at him through the rearview mirror. "Thanks for your vote of confidence."

"You seem worried," he said.

"I'm a little concerned about the trip. Mrs. Gallagher didn't mention anything about it and with my exams coming up this week..."

"If you mentioned it to her, I'm sure you'll be back in time." He seemed so confident, I almost believed him.

"Would you happen to know where I'm going?"

He made a turn we'd never used before and said, "A private airport."

I was a little baffled by his statement. "Why?"

He laughed softly. "Because you'll need to fly out of here somehow."

I scoffed at his answer.

We arrived at the private airport a while later and when James opened the door for me, I stared at the private jet before me in wonder.

"Where the hell is Mrs. Gallagher sending me off to?" I uttered.

It was silly but all I could think about as I approached the jet was that I hoped she was sending me to a place with a lot of sun and sand.

First class plane tickets had been great, but this, this was freaking amazing. I had direct access to the plane and there were no long and tedious procedures like one would experience at a commercial airport.

When I got in the aircraft, a female flight attendant welcomed me inside. She spoke but I never heard a word she said as I appreciated the spotless interior. The plane was big enough to fit a dozen and a half people.

After scanning the comfortable looking white leather recliners, I chose one closest to the window.

"We're waiting for the other passenger and then we'll leave shortly," the flight attendant said.

"The other passenger?" I asked in surprise. I hadn't expected to travel with company, but this was good because now I would figure out where I was going.

"Yes, Mrs. Gallagher."

I was too shocked to speak as the flight attendant retreated. I was traveling with Mrs. Gallagher? My heart started pulsing. I was going to be on the private jet with Mrs. Gallagher?

I was in the plane for ten minutes but it felt like hours before Mrs. Gallagher arrived. I saw a limousine drive to a stop right about where James had stopped and she stepped out.

She was looking ravishing in a stunning red skirt suit that perfectly hugged her body and black stilettos.

I almost drooled at the image before I realized I was holding my breath as she approached the plane.

"Good morning, Olivia," she said when she got inside and went to seat on the row across from mine.

"Good morning, Mrs. Gallagher," I said nervously.

A moment later, the driver who'd brought Mrs. Gallagher to the airport walked in carrying her files and what looked like a laptop and an iPad. He placed them on the table facing Mrs. Gallagher and left the plane.

I was extremely curious to know where we were going but I wanted to wait for the right moment. We lifted off a short while later and when we were in the air, the pilot announced we could take off our seatbelts.

Mrs. Gallagher motioned me over to where she was seated and handed me some files.

"We're going to meet a gentleman called Alix Delacroix in Paris. He owns an organic cosmetic company I'd like to acquire," she said.

I was going to Paris?

"I want you to take a look at these."

I opened the files and the information inside regarded Alix Delacroix's cosmetic company. I didn't know what I was more excited about, going to Paris or finally working on something more business-oriented.

"If you find any irregularities, let me know."

She handed me the iPad, took the laptop and immediately got to work.

I focused on the files and tried to ignore the fact that she was seated right in front me. I could smell her glorious fragrance from the distance, but I tried to keep my mind on work.

I understood why she wanted to acquire a cosmetic company in Paris, beauty products were very lucrative, especially organic cosmetics. I'd come to learn she had a thirty percent stake of her husband's family business and was actively involved.

There was a part of me that had thought she didn't do any actual work rather than host charity events and meet up for tea with her country club friends but I'd come to learn the silly stereotype didn't apply to her.

I read through the files she'd handed me for a few hours, asking questions whenever I came across something I needed to understand better, and used the time as a learning experience.

When we took a break, the flight attendant brought us in-flight meals with water and a selection of soft drinks.

"Do you ever get used to this?" I asked through the silence.

I wasn't trying to befriend Mrs. Gallagher. After my conversation with Rex the previous day, any hope I'd had about an intimate encounter with her had been shattered.

"Used to what?" she asked.

I pushed my hair aside and met her gaze. "The luxury," I said.

Mrs. Gallagher chuckled softly. I wasn't sure I'd ever get used to that sound.

"It's relative."

"May I ask to what?" She literally had everything.

"Well," she started.

There was a part of me that wondered if it was inappropriate to ask my boss such a question, but Mrs. Gallagher didn't seem to mind.

"Imagine being unable to connect with anything that's real. Growing so accustomed to seeing things in one way, you eventually detach yourself from what truly matters."

"You don't seem to come across to me as that type of person."

"When you're born into a certain lifestyle, everything you are is dictated by that, and sometimes it's hard to see past it."

I nodded in understanding, though I doubted a lifetime of

overflowing wealth would come as a burden. With the financial ability to travel the world, see things people could only imagine and do anything I wanted sounded like a dream to me. She had the kind of privilege people could only dream of.

"What would you do?" she asked as though she'd read my mind.

"Well, off the top of my head, I'd visit exotic places like the Greek islands. I'd try cliff diving or mountain climbing, cruising, and probably a lot of sightseeing."

"And when you're done?"

At that moment I couldn't really think of anything, but I went ahead to say, "I'd make sure my family is well taken care of, try and have some sort of normalcy and somehow find a way to be happy."

She looked at me thoughtfully for a minute but failed to speak her mind.

I must've sounded silly to her expressing such shallow thoughts, but when I seriously thought about it, I realized I didn't have a proper answer to her question.

What would I do if I had all the money in the world? After buying everything I wanted, visiting every place I desired, seeing every single thing I wished, eating every type of food I liked and basically wasting the money on every single form of entertainment.

And when it felt like I'd done everything I'd been put on earth to do, would I be satisfied? Or would I die feeling like there was still a hole in me I needed to fill? Or a deep hunger I needed to satiate.

"What would you do?" She was far better suited to answer the question.

"I would live," she said.

Her answer was simple and precise and when she met my gaze, it felt like she was saying more with her eyes than her words. She looked away a moment later, immediately breaking the trance as she took a bite of her food.

She was such an enigma to me. Sometimes she seemed to say so much yet revealed so little.

After the meal, we resumed with work and several hours later, when I finished reviewing the files and had asked all relevant questions, I got up to stretch my legs.

Mrs. Gallagher had walked back and forth on the flight at intervals while I'd pretended not to look, and now I was too tired from sitting to wait for the plane to land. I went to the lavatory, which was spacious and far better in comparison to the commercial flights I'd taken and was a little proud I had something to compare it to.

When I rejoined Mrs. Gallagher, she was having a glass of champagne. Since it was around four in the afternoon, I didn't mind the glass I found waiting for me. Mrs. Gallagher was resting back on her seat as she stared out the window.

I sat quietly, thinking she didn't want to be disturbed as I counted how long we'd been traveling. We'd left around ten, so we'd been flying for six hours. We'd probably arrive in about two hours or less.

Since I'd be resting later on that night, I was glad I'd carried my laptop because it meant I'd get some time to study. I couldn't help wondering though, how long we'd have to stay in Paris. Would I get back in time for my exams? The question gave me anxiety.

"Olivia?"

I turned my attention to Mrs. Gallagher and found her still gazing out the window.

"Are you afraid of me?" she asked.

It was an unusual question but I thought she asked it because of my reaction every time I saw her. I wished I could tell her I behaved that way because I found her so exceptionally beautiful and every time I saw her she took my breath away, but I couldn't.

"I used to be, but it was only because I found you extremely intimidating." Who was I kidding, I still did.

"How come?" She looked at me now, waiting for an answer.

I cleared my throat and said, "I've never been around anyone like you before." I doubted I'd ever get used to being around her.

I took a sip of my champagne and wondered what she was thinking. What did she think of me? Had she ever looked at me as anything else other than a mere employee?

The questions reminded me of my conversation with Rex, promptly acting as a block and instantly stopped me from that line of thought.

Chapter Twelve

We landed at a private airport in Paris, and after getting my passport stamped at customs, Mrs. Gallagher and I were taken to a hotel. Knowing her, I was sure we'd stay at a nice hotel, but I wasn't prepared for how grand or extravagant it would be.

The hotel's location was appealing because it seemed to be at the center of most shopping stores, which I hoped to check out at some point. I just prayed we'd have the time.

The hotel was a huge magnificent building with a unique contemporary interior décor which I found to be breathtaking.

We approached the reception desk and Mrs. Gallagher was handed two key cards. I was glad to find out our rooms were right next to each other on the top most floor of the hotel.

When I walked into my hotel room, my jaw literally dropped. The room was enormous and glamorously decorated. It was a blend of luxury and taste. I didn't want to imagine how much it was worth but I was glad I was staying there.

I walked over to the window to see the view and realized it was a sliding terrace door. When I pulled aside the drapes, I walked out and stared in disbelief at the lit Eiffel tower.

The unbelievable view made it all the more real, making the realization hit hard, that I was truly in Paris. I took my phone from my purse and took several selfies with the Eiffel tower in the background and sent them to Rex. I had to share the amazing moment with him.

Because of the six-hour time difference, it was around midnight in Paris. I was a little fatigued from the flight but my body was still active because it was still early in New York.

Mrs. Gallagher had said we'd be meeting Mr. Alix Delacroix at ten in the morning, which gave me ample time to study. Trying hard not to let the extravagance distract me, I got my laptop and went to take a seat on the desk beside the flat screen television.

A couple of hours later, I went to the bathroom, took a long shower and when I was done, I put on an extremely comfortable white robe and got on the plush cushy bed with a mattress that felt like it'd been stuffed with feathers and almost immediately fell asleep.

The following day, I woke up on time and got ready. It was a little depressing getting back in the same clothes, but I had no choice. I met Mrs. Gallagher downstairs and wasn't surprised to find her in an elegant knee-high black dress, a white expensive looking trench coat and a stunning pair of shoes.

When we got in the car en route to the venue, Mrs. Gallagher got to work, instructing me on what to do.

"Mr. Delacroix is not entirely happy about selling his company, but he doesn't have the resources needed to run it successfully either. So, I'd like you to quickly scan through the files one more time because during the meeting, I'll ask you to quote some numbers."

I nodded and did as she asked, grateful my photographic memory was going to come into play. Half an hour later, we walked into a nice exquisite restaurant.

She recognized Mr. Alix Delacroix and approached him. After a pleasant exchange of greetings, when we were seated, a waiter came to take our order. Shortly after, Mrs. Gallagher got into character and I witnessed her transformation as she got into business mode and started speaking French.

I didn't know much of the language apart from a few basic words but Mrs. Gallagher spoke fluently, which I found fascinating.

After breakfast was served, I observed the two as they conducted business. I wasn't sure if it was going well. I wished they'd switch back to English because all I could do was observe their body language.

Mrs. Gallagher asked me to hand her some documents, which I did, and during the meeting, she gave me signals to provide statistical information regarding the market.

An hour and a half later, the meeting concluded and Mr. Delacroix didn't look too happy. I wasn't sure how to interpret that. Mrs. Gallagher waited until he left, and took a deep breath, which I also couldn't interpret.

"Is something wrong?" I asked.

"We have to stay a day longer so he can talk to his lawyers," she

said.

It seemed she'd expected things to go better, which was a bit of a relief because it meant we could still make it back in time for my exams.

"I have a few things I have to do." She stared at me for a few seconds. "Did you carry the platinum credit card I gave you?"

I nodded.

She wrote down something on a piece of paper and handed it to me.

"Go do some shopping," she said.

A little surprised by her statement, I took a look at the piece of paper and froze. She'd written down addresses for high fashion brands; Versace, Prada, Chanel and Dolce & Gabbana.

"For you?" I asked in confusion.

"For yourself; I know I didn't give you enough time to plan for the trip so get anything you want and charge it on the card. Clothes, shoes, make up, suitcase, anything."

I was speechless.

She got to her feet and said before she left, "I'll call you when I'm done. I didn't plan on us staying longer than twenty-four hours so we might as well make use of the time. Maybe we can even go sightseeing later."

I wasn't sure if she was joking about the last part of her statement, but I was excitedly looking forward to it.

"You're where?" Rex asked in shock.

"Paris!" I said in excitement as I twirled around my room in front of a mirror, admiring how good I looked in Chanel. "I sent you some pictures, didn't you see them?"

"I've been at the art studio since yesterday and you know I keep my phone on silent when I'm working."

"Mrs. Gallagher told me to shop for clothes and stuff and charge it on the platinum credit card and I'm afraid I might've overindulged." I turned around to face the bed and stared at the countless bags of clothes and shoes.

The bags had been delivered half an hour after I'd gotten back to the hotel. I hadn't thought I'd gotten so much stuff until two porters had walked in with them. Considering the shopping was original brands, I knew I'd spent a small fortune and wasn't sure how Mrs. Gallagher would feel about that.

"What if she deducts the shopping from my salary?" I said.

"She wouldn't do that. She should've given you a credit limit if she didn't want you to overdo it."

I thought about that and stared admiringly at my brand knew shoes. My feet had never been in anything so exquisitely expensive but dear Lord the shoes were stunning.

"What did you get?" Rex asked.

I looked at everything on the bed and listed them. I'd gotten several pants, tops and under garments, a few elegant dresses, a couple of leather jackets and trench coats, several pairs of shoes, scarves, handbags, make up, perfume and a couple of suitcases.

"I overindulged, didn't I?"

Rex was silent for a moment, then said, "Yeah, you kinda did."

"Maybe I should return some of them." The sentence made my heart ache. I'd tried everything and they all looked so good on me.

"Maybe you should wait and see what Mrs. Gallagher has to say about it," he suggested.

"She'll be too busy firing me." I got on the bed and inhaled the wonderful scent of high fashion and luxury and I loved it.

"Come on, stop worrying over nothing. She didn't seem to mind when you charged things on the credit card when you were going through Africa."

I sat up. He had a point.

"She never even mentioned it, right?"

"Yeah, she never did."

"So stop worrying and enjoy Paris. Go out and tour the place."

Since I hadn't heard from Mrs. Gallagher in the last few hours, I could tour the city by myself. I'd probably never get another chance to do it, so I shouldn't have been stressing over shopping. I should've been out taking a tour of the most romantic city on earth.

Paris brimmed with culture, style and romance. There were so many things I should've been doing, like going to the Eiffel tower, the Louvre museum and what was left of the Cathedral of Notre Dame.

"You know what? You're right."

"Good, take lots of pictures."

It was no wonder I loved Rex. He always had a way of making me feel better.

I took his advice and checked my phone to see if Mrs. Gallagher had been in touch. When I didn't find any messages from her, I got ready and left the hotel, leaving a message at the reception desk in case she came back and I wasn't present.

I got into a cab and told the driver where I wanted to go. I was so excited I wanted to stick my head out the window like a dog and see everything.

Paris was intimate and beautiful. The streets thronged with natives who were impeccably dressed and seemed to have an air of panache and the sidewalk cafés were a pleasant and inviting sight.

When I got to the Eiffel tower, the soaring iron construction seemed to knock the air out of my lungs. From a distance, one could imagine how huge it was, but up close, it rose high to the sky like a monolithic structure.

I was glad it wasn't a tourist time of year because there weren't a lot of people around. I got a brochure and purchased a ticket, visiting all three levels one at a time. The view was amazing from the top.

For a long while after I got up there, I stared at the stunning sight of the city in disbelief as I tried to picture where else I would've been had I never gotten a chance to work for Mrs. Gallagher. It felt like the single most important point of my life.

I wasn't sure how long I stayed there. Time seemed to stand still as I absorbed everything with every fiber of my being. It felt so surreal, how I'd woken up to go to work one morning and ended up at the Eiffel tower the following evening.

Chapter Thirteen

I got back to the hotel around six in the evening and went to the restaurant to grab something to eat because I was a little hungry. I didn't manage to go anywhere else after visiting the Eiffel tower, which was disappointing but I had to stick around the hotel incase Mrs. Gallagher needed something from me.

I was only there for fifteen minutes when Mrs. Gallagher called. I wasn't sure if someone told her I was back or if it was a coincidence. I answered the call and waited for her orders.

"Olivia, where are you?" she asked.

"Down at the restaurant," I said.

"Oh, good. A friend heard I was in town and invited me for a show. I thought you might like to join me," she said.

Her words caught me off guard because I was still trying to get used to her. Being such an unpredictable person, most things she did or said seemed to take me by surprise.

"Oh, yes, I'd like that," I said.

"Did you go shopping?" she asked.

"Yes, I did." My voice shook when I remembered everything I'd gotten myself.

"Good, we're leaving in an hour. Dress your best. I'll meet you at the hotel lounge." She hung up.

I got up and quickly headed up to my hotel room. What kind of show was Mrs. Gallagher talking about? It sounded like a social event and I was pleased she wanted me to join her.

What kind of people were going to be there? And what friend had found out she was in the country and so quickly invited her for the event. Guess I was going to find out.

When I got to my room, I took a quick shower and started preparing myself. I started off with applying my make-up, which took a bit longer than I thought because I was trying to match Andre's aptitude and finesse, but when I was done, I wasn't disappointed.

I was excited about dressing up and tried in and out of almost all the social event outfits I'd gotten, but I finally settled on a gorgeous little red dress that elaborately hugged my body and nicely exposed my cleavage. I chose a pair of black Prada heels that matched the look.

I wasn't sure what to do with my hair, but since Andre had taught me how to fix it, it was less unruly and easily agreeable to many styles of choice. When I was done, I applied some perfume and looked at myself on the mirror and smiled, thinking Andre would've been proud of me.

I got down to the lounge on time as Mrs. Gallagher approached me looking ravishing in her usual stunning getup. I didn't know why but every time I saw her my heart began to race.

When she got to where I was, she looked me up and down as I waited for her verdict on my choice of clothing for the evening and I was relieved when she smiled and said, "You have good taste."

I bobbed my head and smiled as I followed her out of the hotel. There was a black stretch limousine waiting for us outside. When the driver opened the door for Mrs. Gallagher, I wondered if I'd ever get used to such a lifestyle.

I got in after her and trembled when I accidentally brushed up against her. When I was settled down beside her, I closed my hands over my legs and tried to loosen up.

"How was your day?" she asked.

I wanted to tell her everything, but I was too tense. She always seemed to have that effect on me every time we met or were in close proximity. "It was lovely."

"What did you do?" she asked.

I looked at her and found her looking at me, which made my heart pick up pace and my hands tremble. "Um, I went shopping as you suggested and then went to see the Eiffel tower."

I thought she'd comment on the shopping or rather, how much money I'd spent, but she seemed more interested in my satisfaction of what I'd gotten and what I'd thought of the Eiffel tower, which put me more at ease.

"Are you happy with what you got yourself?" she asked.

"Yes," I said, feeling guilty for the sizable amount I'd spent. "But I think I might've overdone it and I can take some of it back." I could never have gotten away with spending so much money.

"Why would you do that if you're happy with what you got?" she asked.

I bit my lower lip and averted my gaze from her. "I got carried away and overspent."

"And you're worried I might do what...?"

I cleared my throat, feeling like a child reporting myself to a parent over a wrongdoing. "Let me go as your employee, deduct the money from my salary—which I will fully understand," I said.

She was silent for a while, which made my heartbeat pound loudly in my chest. I thought she was going to tell me to go back to the hotel, pack my bags and head back to New York, but she softly said, "I'm not letting you go."

I looked at her in amazement and tried to conceal my joy as she looked back at me with a bit of warmth in her eyes. I'd never seen her look at me that way before. As her words reverberated in my head, I wondered if there was a deeper underlying meaning to her words other than what we'd just been discussing.

A slow rush of heat vibrated through my being and I tore my gaze from hers, realizing I was getting aroused. I unconsciously crossed my legs and thought I saw her sneak a peek, which made my hands feel clammy.

I must've imagined it because there was no possible way Mrs. Gallagher could've been attracted to me. She was a married woman with children. She was high society. She was someone who would never look at me twice in a room full of people and remember my face.

I took a deep breath and repelled the self-deprecating thoughts, which helped with my arousal situation, but lowered my spirit.

"What did you think of the Eiffel tower?" she asked.

"It was incredible," I said, lacking words to describe the emotions I'd experienced. "I honestly don't know how else to explain it."

"I think your expression says it all," she said.

My gaze fell on her and that hunger I was restraining within myself came alive again. I struggled to look away, wondering if she was experiencing any of the motions going through me.

God, could she see it? Could she feel my desire for her? Could she sense how much I was fighting myself to conceal how she made me feel? The fear of her having any knowledge of how she made me feel broke the trance.

When the car came to a slow stop, I wanted to jump out and get some air, but her hand fell on mine and she said, "I think I have something that will compliment your outfit."

My heart instantly started pacing at her soft touch, fearing it would burst. I was glad when she broke the physical contact and placed her hand inside her purse. She retrieved a stunning rose gold pendant necklace and motioned me to turn.

When I did, she slowly placed the necklace around my neck as the scent of her delicious perfume teased my nostrils. Her hand gently moved the tendrils of hair falling over the back of my neck, which created goosebumps all over my body. I unconsciously exhaled as I closed my eyes, trying hard to hold it together.

When she fastened the necklace, I let out a faltering sigh and placed my fingers over the pendant, feeling as though my heart had stopped throughout the whole time she'd been putting on the necklace.

I turned to face her, avoiding her gaze because I didn't want her to see what her touch or our closeness did to me.

"Much better," she said.

I smiled at her compliment and the door opened before I had a chance to respond. I stepped out in dignified poise, trying to pretend the few minutes hadn't rattled me and was met by flashing, blinding lights.

It took me a moment to realize I was standing on a red carpet in front of photographers.

"Just smile and slowly walk along," Mrs. Gallagher said beside me.

When she'd said we were going to a show, she hadn't specified the nature of the event. I realized shortly after I was able to adjust my sight to the flashing lights, that it was a Paris haute couture fashion show.

I followed slowly behind her as photographers took individual pictures of us. The moment was so bizarre, I thought I was dreaming.

After what felt like forever, I was ushered away from the photographers and inside the venue.

I tried to control my excitement when I saw familiar faces of celebrities, who all seemed to recognize Mrs. Gallagher in one way or another. She introduced me to some of them, which was great and even though I was starstruck, I maintained my cool.

I spoke to a few, expressing a contained appreciation for them and their work. I would've given anything to take pictures with some of the celebrities but I was too scared to do so because I didn't want to look like an idiot or to embarrass Mrs. Gallagher.

She seemed to float through the crowd with that poise she commanded, provoking a similar curiosity from others as they provoked from me. I could sense the insurmountable amount of admiration for her from others, as I had from past similar situations. She was a woman in her own league.

She spoke to some of her friends while I mingled with some of the celebrities and other important figures and when the time came, we were all taken to the room where the fashion show was going to take place.

I assumed the fashion show had taken weeks or even months to plan and execute and last-minute tickets like Mrs. Gallagher's was going to get us back seats, but I was once again surprised when we were taken to the first row of seats.

When I saw my full name written on a chair reserved for me, I looked at Mrs. Gallagher and found her smiling at me. I smiled back and took my seat beside her, wondering what she was thinking.

The runway was long, raised high above our seats and very well constructed. From the surrounding, the people attending and the photographers at the very end of the runway, I could tell the designers showcasing their work were renowned.

Almost half an hour later when everyone was settled, a male host introduced the event announcing names of designers whose work was going to be shown as the lights dimmed in the room except for the runway.

As I had guessed, it was the famous ones; Giorgio Armani, Oscar de la Renta, Carolina Herrera and Reem Alasadi.

A live performance by Pink almost had me at my feet when she emerged to introduce the first designer by singing a song from her latest album.

If I wasn't already, it felt like I'd just fallen in love with Mrs. Gallagher for making me her plus one to the show.

Pink was singing right in front of me and I was on a front row seat to see her perform. For a while, long after the models had started walking down the runway, I just gawked in disbelief. She was gorgeous in person and her voice was magnificent. I loved her music as lyrics flawlessly rolled out of her mouth.

If this was the life Mrs. Gallagher was used to, how did she manage to be so humble amidst the overwhelming wonder of it all?

I stared at her in admiration and something more, something that seemed to materialize all at once, sparked. It was like my heart expanded, creating room for something she seemed to draw from me, something I couldn't name.

Chapter Fourteen

After the fashion show, Mrs. Gallagher went backstage. I was almost sure she was going to talk to one of the designers, if not all. The fashion show had been something out of The Devil Wears Prada movie.

Both male and female models had been flawless on the runway and Pink had been joined by a couple of other artists on stage for the live performance. It had been so surreal because my reality still felt like an expensive illusion.

The designers were unbelievably talented and the crowd seemed to have loved what they'd seen.

Mrs. Gallagher joined me a few minutes later and told me we were going for an after party for a couple of hours. I was more than excited to go with her because I'd get to have a little fun around other people.

"What did you think of the show?" she asked when we were in the limousine leaving.

I liked how she was starting to express interest in my opinions. I knew they didn't mean much, but having her ask and watching her pay attention as I answered made me feel good.

"I enjoyed Pink's performance. I've loved her music throughout her entire career. The fashion show was a grand new experience. I loved it. Thank you so much for inviting me," I said, fighting to contain my excitement.

It was proving hard being around her because I was always battling something within me. If it wasn't an untimely arousal, it was my excitement for something else.

I didn't know what image I wanted her to have of me, but I knew it wasn't one of a babbling idiot. I wanted her to like me.

We got to the after party a while later and it had more people than I expected. It was at a large mansion and had people partying on all three levels of the building. Mrs. Gallagher seemed to know exactly where to go as I followed her to the third floor, where the people were more composed and sophisticated.

The first floor had the crazy lot of party animals with a lot of energy, alcohol and loud music, the second floor had a calmer environment with people who were more controlled and the third floor had to be accessed with a pass, which Mrs. Gallagher had. I had to admit, I loved seeing her world firsthand.

If I hadn't been with her, I was certain I would've enjoyed the party taking place on the first floor. I loved to see how crazy people could get and it had been a while since I'd attended such a party. The third-floor party felt more like a formal party, but the crowd of people present was a bit more mature.

I got a glass of champagne and moved along the crowd to mingle with the people. I doubted Mrs. Gallagher wanted me to shadow her wherever she went and I didn't want to burden her with having to introduce me to every single one of her friends.

She probably wanted to let off some steam and the last thing she needed was for me to get in her way. I didn't know anyone at the party other than her, but the people seemed friendly.

I went outside the terrace to watch the party taking place on the first floor, which had migrated to the poolside area. The group was loud, which was refreshing to me because I felt a little less out of place.

"You should go down there."

I turned towards the direction the voice had come from and met a handsome smiling face.

"Excuse me?" I said.

"Looks more like the sort of party you'd enjoy," he said.

It must've been because I'd been observing. "I'm good here," I said.

"I'm Jonathan," he said, extending his hand.

He must've been around thirty. He was well dressed in a tailored black suit and had a short neat beard.

"Olivia," I said, closing my hand over his.

I thought it'd be nice to know someone, anyone else other than Mrs. Gallagher.

"Are you enjoying the party, Olivia?" he asked.

"I just got here, but so far so good."

"I saw you walk in with Amelia Gallagher," he said.

I nodded, unwilling to volunteer information.

"Are you her new pet?"

I was taken aback by his odd question. "Excuse me?"

"You know, are you her new form of entertainment?" He had a cynical smile as he asked the question.

"Um, I'm not sure how to answer that."

"Young, beautiful and ripe for the picking," he said softly as he moved closer.

I took a step back in discomfort, unsure of what exactly was happening.

"Jon, give her a break," a female voice said from behind me.

I slightly turned to find a tall, slender, gorgeous woman looking at Jonathan in amusement.

"Don't mind him. He's always had a thing for Amelia but she's never given him a second glance. He doesn't take it well when people reject his advances," she said.

I wasn't sure what I was stuck in the middle of, but I was curious.

"I'm Zola," she said. She looked vaguely familiar.

"This is Olivia," Jonathan chimed in.

We shook hands as she came to stand beside me.

"Are you two friends?" I asked her.

They looked at each other and laughed as though sharing an inside joke. "If that's what you'd call it, sure," Zola said.

"What did you mean when you asked if I was Amelia's new pet?" I asked.

"Ignore Jon, he tends to be a little dramatic," Zola said.

I couldn't help wondering if there'd been more to his question.

"Why don't you get us some drinks, Jon?" Zola said and Jonathan rolled his eyes and left.

When we were alone, she leaned over the railing of the balcony and stared at the poolside.

"I hope he didn't bother you much," she said.

"He didn't."

"You don't seem like you're from around here," she said as she turned her attention back to me.

"I'm not."

"Where are you from?" she asked.

"New York." I didn't see any reason to withhold harmless information that didn't involve Mrs. Gallagher.

"What're you doing in France?"

"Work." I took a sip of my champagne.

"Must be one hell of a job, partying on a Tuesday night."

"It is."

She responded with a smile.

"Where are you from?" I asked.

"Florence," she said.

She was Italian? Her English didn't have a hint of an accent.

"I've never been there, how's it like?"

"Magical, romantic, unbelievably beautiful," she said.

I didn't know anything about Florence, but I believed her.

"Are you here for work too?"

She nodded and I smiled back at her, wondering what she did for a living then it occurred to me why she looked so familiar. "Oh my God, you're one of the runway models from tonight's fashion show."

She didn't respond but from the look in her eyes, I could tell I was right. Jonathan must've been a model too. He'd probably been on the runway as well.

"When I was a kid, I used to steal my Mom's clothes and make up. I'd dress up and catwalk in front of her mirror. I'd mess up her room and she'd get so upset," I said as I recalled my childhood.

"You would've made a lovely model," she said.

"No, I was too conservative and my dad would never have allowed it."

"I was a rebellious child," Zola said.

"What did you used to do?"

She stood up straight and looked at me as though she was contemplating sharing. "I went against everything I was supposed to do just to piss off my parents."

"They must've been displeased," I said.

"They sent me off to live with my grandmother. She was a dear old soul. I drove her crazy, but she never gave up on me."

"She sounds great."

"She was," Zola said.

Jonathan joined us a minute later and handed us each a glass of champagne. "What are you two talking about?" he asked.

I scanned the room for Mrs. Gallagher but couldn't find her. There were a lot of people there and the place was huge so she could've been anywhere.

"Nothing that would interest you. Where are Zach and Amy?" Zola said.

"Last I saw them they were headed to the first floor," Jonathan said.

"Hey, you want to check it out?" she asked me.

I shook my head, unsure I should leave with them.

"It's just downstairs and we won't stay long," Zola said.

I wondered if Mrs. Gallagher would mind.

"It's a party, let's have some fun," Jonathan said.

"I can't," I said.

Zola tucked her arm around mine and dragged me along with her. She was surprisingly sweet and I liked her. I wasn't so sure about Jonathan though. He'd come on a bit too strongly for my liking.

The music downstairs was so loud I couldn't hear a word anyone was saying. We met up with Zola's friends, Zach and Amy and headed outside to the poolside where it was less noisy.

Everyone in attendance looked like they came from money. It was like a secret club for rich people. They looked great all dressed up in their fancy outfits, they seemed educated and all behaved with a certain kind of aura.

We joined a few other people who appeared a little drunk and I assumed they were friends of Zola's. They were a bit unruly as they danced, talked and laughed. I would've been a lot more comfortable if my boss hadn't been somewhere within the location.

"Who's your friend?" Zach asked Zola.

Amy and Jonathan were dancing together as they inappropriately groped each other. I wasn't a prude, but I didn't feel like Mrs. Gallagher would be pleased to see me in that company.

"Olivia," Zola said.

She took my hand and pulled me some distance away from him.

"Let's dance," she said.

I wasn't much of a dancer, but she was already swaying herself around me. I was a little tense and awkward, and she seemed to sense it.

"Come on, loosen up. You're at a party."

"I don't dance," I said.

She moved her arm around my waist and pulled me closer to her. I was too sober to act as carelessly or inappropriately as her friends.

"Try and move your hips to the rhythm," she said.

I couldn't. If it had been a frat party, maybe I would have, but I just couldn't. I didn't have it in me. "I'm sorry, I can't do this," I said.

I placed my glass down and left. I didn't feel like going back to the third floor so I went through the house and headed back where Mrs. Gallagher's driver had packed the limo.

He was inside the car when I got there. I knocked twice on the window and he quickly got out and opened the door for me. I got inside and told him to wait for Mrs. Gallagher since I couldn't leave without her.

I thought about what had just happened and felt like an idiot. Zola had been nice to me and all she'd wanted to do was dance. Why had I behaved that way? Her group of friends had seemed fun and outgoing. I would've had fun with them, but I'd been so uptight.

Maybe I should've gone back and apologized. At the thought, I tapped the driver's shoulder and told him I was stepping out for a minute. I got out of the car and headed back to the house.

I'd just turned a corner to head to the entrance when I stopped on my heels at the sight of Zola and Mrs. Gallagher. They seemed to be talking about something. At first, I thought Zola might've been telling Mrs. Gallagher where I'd disappeared to, then it occurred to me that Mrs. Gallagher hadn't known I'd been with Zola.

I watched them for a few minutes and when their conversation ended, Mrs. Gallagher started heading towards me. She didn't see me because I rushed back to the limo and by the time the driver was opening the door for her, I was calmly seated, pretending nothing had happened.

"Did you have a good time?" she asked when the limo was pulling out of parking.

"Yes," I said, trying to figure out what was happening. I wasn't trying to make up a conspiracy but something told me there was something going on that I wasn't aware of.

"Why did you leave?"

"I was tired," I said.

The rest of the drive to the hotel was silent. All sorts of things went through my head and for the life in me I couldn't figure out what was going on. Had Mrs. Gallagher asked Zola to befriend me? Had there been more to it than just keeping me company at a party I was a stranger to?

"Are you okay?" Mrs. Gallagher asked when we were in the elevator heading up to our floor.

I nodded as questions rummaged through my mind.

I calmly bid her goodnight when she got to her room and I proceeded over to mine. When I got inside, I gently rubbed my temple with my fingertips, trying to make myself believe I was being paranoid.

I replayed the evening in my head from the moment I'd met Jonathan. His questions had been unusual and his behavior towards me had been odd. Zola had joined us, quickly befriended me and then invited me to join her friends.

I poured myself a glass of wine and headed out to the terrace. The air was pleasantly cool and the Eiffel tower looked wonderful in the night. I stared out into the night as my thoughts trailed back to the last couple of hours.

When Zach, Zola's friend had asked who I was, Zola had pulled me away and started dancing with me. I hadn't thought it much at the time, but now it almost felt like she hadn't wanted him to talk to me.

I'd been too tense to dance with her, especially when her friends had been groping each other. But she'd gently nudged me to dance along, and I'd walked off.

It didn't seem like Mrs. Gallagher would've had anything to do with such a situation. I'd walked myself right into it. No one had forced me to do anything I hadn't wanted to do. But then, why had Mrs. Gallagher been talking to Zola? Was it a coincidence or was there something more going on?

When I finished my glass of wine, I gently massaged my neck and my hand fell on the pendant necklace Mrs. Gallagher had given me. I walked back to the room, went over to the mirror and looked at it. It fell on the valley between my breasts, complementing my cleavage.

I remembered her gentle touch as she'd put it around my neck and sensations she'd provoked in me. Her touch was as powerful as her presence.

Shaking away the thoughts, I took a closer look at the pendant. It looked expensive and I doubted Mrs. Gallagher had given it to me for keeping. I took it off, deciding to return it now that the evening was over.

I didn't really think about it, but I should've because once the thought crossed my mind I left my room and went to knock on her door. It was then that I realized I should've probably waited till morning. What if she'd gotten into bed? And how inappropriate was it of me to knock on her door so late at night?

Wait, what time was it? The door opened and an overwhelming wave of nervousness overcame me. I wanted to apologize and head back but it was too late.

She was standing on the other side of the door in a robe. Her hair was freely falling over her shoulders and she was holding a glass of red wine in her hand. It was a seductive image I hadn't prepared myself for.

"Olivia, come in," she said, leaving the door open for me as she retreated back to the room.

"I'm sorry to disturb you, I know it's late," I said as I closed the door behind me and turned around to find her watching me.

"How can I help you?" she asked.

Think. I commanded myself, successfully managing to tear my gaze away from her. "I uh, wanted to return this," I said, showing her the pendant necklace on the palm of my hand.

She placed her glass of wine down and slowly approached me. She stopped right in front of me and I struggled to keep still as those untimely sensations started coming awake.

She slowly ran her index finger over the pendant and deliberately touched my palm, rousing awake every dormant desire I tried to keep buried within me.

"Do you like it?" she asked softly.

Whether she was asking about her touch or the necklace, I wasn't sure. She withdrew her hand and looked at me, waiting for an answer.

"I do but–."

"Then keep it."

"Mrs. Gallagher, I can't."

"Why not?"

I tried to think of a plausible excuse. "It looks really expensive," I said.

"So?" She seemed undeterred by my reason.

"Mrs. Gallagher," I wanted to remind her of the shopping I'd charged on the credit card and all the other things she seemed willing to pay for, but when she took another step closer to me, every thought flew out of my head.

"It looks good on you, and I'm giving it to you as a gift. Why wouldn't you want to keep it?" she asked in a low tone of voice, which made me tremble.

I wasn't sure if she noticed the effect she had on me, but it didn't seem to stop her. I felt like I was drowning and I needed a lifeboat so I said the first thing that crossed my mind. "Did you ask Zola to befriend me at the party tonight?"

"Yes," she said.

She didn't even flinch or pause at the question. "Why?" I asked.

"I was testing you."

I was slightly glad I hadn't been paranoid, but surprised she wasn't going to any length to conceal the knowledge from me. "Why?"

"I wanted to see how you'd behave under the circumstances."

I was a little baffled and was trying to understand, which was hard because she was so calm and she was still standing really close to me. I took a few steps away from her, creating distance between us so I could think clearly.

"Are you upset?" she asked.

"Yes, no, I mean–." I was confused.

"Olivia, I need to know that I can trust you."

"Trust me with what exactly? I feel like I'm constantly jumping through hoops for you trying to prove myself and now you're what–playing games with me?" I might've been a little upset.

"I don't play games," she said.

I was frustrated with myself for being so damned attracted to her. What had she used Zola to test me on? And what if I'd played into Zola's hands? What would Mrs. Gallagher have done?

"Did I pass?" I asked, trying but failing to conceal my anger.

"Olivia," she said.

I remembered the first night I'd kissed her, how daringly brave I'd been. I'd risked everything for a kiss. And now, I was confronting her. What was I thinking? Did I want to risk losing my job?

I walked up to her in resignation and held out the necklace. If I wanted to keep working for her, I needed to be stronger. I needed to push down everything I felt and remember she was my boss.

She opened her palm and I dropped the necklace on her hand. When she closed her fingers around it, I headed for the door, but she closed her free hand around my wrist, stopping me on my tracks.

I turned to face her and she moved closer to me. I held my breath as her presence absorbed me. I couldn't think or speak. I didn't know what she was doing but my body was fully under her command.

All those things I was trying not to feel came back alive. The attraction I fought to conceal was now visible and the sensations her magical touch had on me left me completely bare.

I deeply inhaled, trying to contain the heat burning me up inside as her gaze held me captive. She released my wrist and gently placed her hand over my waist, causing every strand of hair on my skin to rise.

With a deliberate slow speed, she trailed her hand up from my waist to my ribs and I exhaled in desire as more heat spread through my body. She intently stared into my eyes as though she was enjoying the effect she had on me.

Our lips were inches apart. I wanted to lean in and kiss her, but she'd warned me against it. She was in control of the situation. I couldn't do anything other than continue to melt as she tortured me. I wanted to beg her to just kiss me and end my suffering, but I couldn't expose such degree of weakness.

Her blue eyes grew darker and I realized through my weak state that if she was holding me that close, something I felt for her had to be reciprocated. When I felt her delicious warmth merging with mine, I stopped caring about the repercussions and closed the space between us in a fiery kiss.

She responded to the passion in kind, crushing my lips with her own and my lust for her burned through me as it increased. She allowed me to taste her once more in a moment I'd never thought would occur again and just when I was starting to enjoy it, she broke the kiss, but didn't pull away.

I wondered if she was deliberately torturing me as I stared at her in desperation. She must've known what she was doing to me. She must've known how desperately I wanted her.

She trailed her other hand over my cheek, as she leaned forward and captured my lips in another kiss. With incredible restraint, I slowly responded at her pace as she gently brushed her velvet lips against mine.

I was completely turned on and was dying to run my hands all over her perfect body. I felt like I was kissing a goddess and I could never quench my yearning for her. I wanted to feel her hands skimming all over my body, to feel her touch underneath my dress, and all that need and passion drove me insane. I was longing for so much, but she was offering so little.

She slowly broke the kiss and pulled away, this time fully letting go of me and I deeply inhaled as I struggled to regain my composure. I felt like I was still under her spell as she turned her back to me and took a few steps away from me.

Knowing that was my cue to leave, I placed my hand over my heart in an attempt to calm it down because it was beating loudly out of control and shakily left her room. I weakly leaned against her door when I was outside and replayed the scene of what had just happened between us in my head.

I could still feel her on me, her scent, her warmth and her kiss. She had kissed me! She'd looked into my eyes and seen everything I felt for her and she hadn't pushed me away. I had no idea what any of it meant. I just knew something had changed.

When I went back to my room, I was still trembling. No one had ever had that kind of effect on me. It was a little terrifying and the fact that my body was still stuck in an animated mode of arousal didn't help.

I undressed and stepped into the bathroom. I turned the knob and stood under the nozzle as the cold water ran down my body, nicely cooling me off.

Chapter Fifteen

The shower helped during the duration of time I was in the bathroom, but the rest of the night was filled with erotic dreams of every other possible way my night could've ended with Mrs. Gallagher.

I woke up the following morning as I'd fallen asleep, hot and bothered. I couldn't get the previous night out of my mind. Mrs. Gallagher had kissed me. I wanted to focus on the erotic part, because it was fun and I'd dreamt about it so many times, but my stupid brain kept dragging me back to the questions I didn't want to dwell on.

Had any of what had happened between us meant anything? Did the fact that she had initiated the whole thing mean that she liked me? Did anything have to change between us? And they kept on going to the point where I thought I'd go crazy.

Finally, I got out of bed around seven in the morning and forced myself to study. It was Wednesday and my exam was taking place the following day. I was almost certain Mrs. Gallagher had forgotten until she called me an hour later.

"Good morning, Olivia," her voice sounded casual.

I was glad we were talking on the phone because if it had been in person I wouldn't have been able to conceal my growing desire for her. "Good morning, Mrs. Gallagher."

I wasn't sure if she was in the next room or if she'd left already but I walked over to the wall separating us and leaned against it as we spoke.

"Some business has come up and I have to stay in Paris a while longer, there'll be a car waiting for you at ten after you check out to take you back to the airport."

I wasn't sure what to say. I was happy to know I'd travel back to New York, but sad to know I'd be traveling alone. Plus, as far as I was concerned, our work hadn't come to a conclusion yet. "What about Mr. Delacroix? Weren't we supposed to meet up with him again today?" I asked.

"He called me this morning, the deal went through," she said.

"Oh, that's great."

"It is. You can take the day off tomorrow. I'll see you on Friday," she said.

I wanted to protest because a greater part of me wanted to stay, but with my exams coming up, it was compulsory I go back to New York.

I tried to force myself to study long after the phone call had ended, but thoughts of Mrs. Gallagher kissing me and touching me kept taking over me. It was like she'd left a part of herself inside of me.

Several minutes before my check out time, I was at the front desk. I couldn't help wonder if Mrs. Gallagher would continue staying at the hotel for the next few days she'd be in Paris.

After checking out of the hotel, I was handed a package and shown to the car that'd take me back to the airport.

During the drive, I distantly looked at the beautiful city as memories from the last couple of days replayed themselves in my mind. It all felt like a dream I was just about to wake up from.

I'd never intended to show Mrs. Gallagher how I felt about her, but she'd practically charmed it out of me. I'd never desired anyone else with the intense passion I desired her. I had no idea how her knowledge of my attraction to her would impact our working relationship, but I hoped it wouldn't end up costing me my job.

A few hours later when I was in the air heading back home, I decided to study further for my exams. I was reaching for my laptop when the package I'd gotten from the reception desk fell from my bag.

I thought it was a random gift the hotel gave to visitors who stayed at their hotels. I opened it in curiosity and my jaw dropped when I found the pendant necklace Mrs. Gallagher had offered me the previous night.

I stared at it for a long time in disbelief. I'd already rejected it and wasn't sure if it'd seem rude to reject it again. Mrs. Gallagher was a generous woman but I wasn't sure where she stood on giving personal gifts to her employees.

I didn't want to overthink it. Maybe she'd given me the necklace simply because it had complimented my outfit. It didn't have to have a hidden meaning behind it. I placed it back in the bag and took out my laptop. I needed to prepare for my exams.

Thursday was a long and mentally draining day. I managed to do all three exams, but at the end of the day, I didn't feel like I'd done the best that was expected of me. I didn't feel like I had passed.

I'd been so busy during the last few weeks, I'd missed coursework, essays, and group work, fully relying on studying which I hadn't done enough of. Before leaving the school, I went to the administration to enquire about evening classes.

Now that I had a job and was confident in myself, it was time I made a schedule for school. I worked eight hours a day. I could attend evening classes from seven to eleven. I just needed to figure out how I'd make it work what with all the traveling.

Since it was still early, I went to Rex's art studio. He was renting out a small amount of space from an old building a few blocks from his place. I'd been there a few times before and more often than not, felt like it wasn't a safe place but it was the cheapest he could afford.

I was driving my car, which I was planning on selling because I didn't need it to get to work. I was getting used to moving around in a sleek BMW and every time I saw my car I was reminded of the poor state of my finances.

After parking it near the entrance of the building, I headed to the art studio which was situated at the very end of the second floor. I could hear a soft buzz coming from the room when I got to the door.

I knocked twice and opened. Rex was wearing an apron and protective gear; a pair of glasses and headphones. He was making a sculpture using hard limestone and the area around where he was working was covered with paper to collect the dirt.

He didn't store finished pieces in the studio because of theft. Two finished pieces of paintings had been stolen from the studio before, which was a mistake he was unwilling to repeat.

I wished he could afford a safer neighborhood for the studio so that he could store his pieces. Instead he stored them either at his place or mine and neither one of us had enough room, which slowed his work.

He stopped working when he saw me and removed his gear. He was always happy to see me, which gave me a warm feeling. He approached me and raised his arms in an attempt to hug me when I stopped him because his apron was covered in dirt.

"Are you kidding me?" I asked him.

"C'mon, I've missed you," he teased.

"We saw each other four days ago and we've spoken on the phone every day since," I said.

He lowered his arms and offered me a seat on the couch he slept on when he spent nights working at the studio, which was placed some distance away from his working area.

Apart from the couch, a small fridge, his equipment and the pieces of art he was working on, there wasn't much else in the room. The art studio was small and bordering on filthy but he'd done some work to make it presentable, and I was proud of him because he took his work very seriously.

"What are you working on?" I asked.

He took a bottle of water from the fridge and handed it to me, then walked over to his masterpiece and turned it to face me.

"That's…" I wasn't quite sure what to say. The piece he was working on appeared to be the upper body of a man screaming as he tried to escape from a frame and there were arms grabbing at him, almost pulling him back inside. "Dark," I said.

The sculpture was far from done but he'd done a great job because the representation was so clear.

"When I'm done you'll be able to see the articulation more clearly," he said.

"You must be drawing your inspiration from a very disturbing place."

The sculpture was a little terrifying.

He smiled at me as he came to take a seat beside me. "How was Paris?" he asked.

I was dying to tell him about my amazing encounter with Mrs. Gallagher but I didn't want him to reproach me and remind me of everything I was risking by doing exactly what he'd warned me against.

"Paris was amazing, I didn't manage to do much but I visited the Eiffel tower, which was a humbling experience."

"Don't be modest, I want to hear everything."

I recounted the events, but didn't mention anything about my kiss with Mrs. Gallagher.

"I envy you," he said.

"If I were you, I'd envy me too," I said.

"Private jet, expensive hotel room, in the most romantic city on earth and with the woman of your dreams, must've felt like a dream."

I remembered her sweet scent, the amazing kiss and her hands trailing up my body and exhaled.

"That amazing, huh?" he asked.

I nodded, unwilling to reveal more.

"What did she say about the shopping?" he asked.

"She didn't care." I remembered her interest had been more on my satisfaction.

"There is something you're not telling me," he said, closely studying me.

I hated how well he knew me. I got up to conceal my expression and his hand closed on my wrist as he turned me to face him.

"Something happened between you two, didn't it?" he asked as though he could read my mind.

"I want to tell you but I'm afraid you're going to reproach me."

His gaze softened as he moved closer to me, gently squeezing my hand. "I haven't been hard on you on purpose," he said softly. "I just don't want you to get hurt, that's all."

I groaned and leaned my forehead against his shoulder. "Maybe I don't want to tell you because you're going to ask the same questions I'm trying to avoid asking myself."

"I won't ask anything if you don't want me to," he said, softly pecking my forehead.

I pulled away and approached his sculpture but my mind was back in Paris, in Mrs. Gallagher's hotel room. I told him the details I'd left out and when I was through, I turned to face him.

"Why do you seem so sad when everything that happened would've made you jump to the clouds a week ago?" he asked.

"I'm happy and every time I remember, my hands tremble and my body reacts as though I'm standing right in front of her but I'm so confused."

"Why?"

"I don't know. What does this mean? Is it supposed to mean anything? I have all these questions and they're driving me crazy."

"You shouldn't overthink it. Can't you just focus your thoughts on the fact that it happened? That she initiated it?"

I was embarrassed to tell him the very thought of the memory left me extremely turned on. "I'm going back to work tomorrow and I don't know how I'll face her."

"If she knows how you feel about her then I don't think it should be a problem."

"*It is* a problem. I won't know how to conceal it and even if I try, we'll both be aware of it."

"You're looking at this whole thing the wrong way," he said as he took my hand and led me back to the couch.

"Have you considered how she might be feeling? Has it occurred to you that she might be into you and may be thinking about the same thing you are?"

I hadn't thought about that.

"When you go to work tomorrow, you'll play everything by ear. Just follow what she does. Don't put so much pressure on yourself."

I looked at him, realizing that he was right. "You know what? I don't give you enough credit. You're incredibly intelligent," I said.

He flashed me his biggest smile.

"And your sculpture is terrifying," I added.

"It's a school project. I hope the art teacher sees the same thing you do."

"How long have you been working on it?"

"A little over a week now, oh by the way, how were the exams?"

I groaned again. "I'm not very confident the results will be good."

"You think you failed?"

I nodded and leaned back against the couch. "I enrolled for evening classes."

"That's great. You won't have to fully rely on just studying."

"I'm a little worried because of all the traveling."

"But you need the job, and the traveling, if you ask me is a huge bonus."

I laughed at his enthusiasm.

We talked a while longer then I left. On my way back home, I picked up some take out for dinner. I spent the rest of the evening going through the syllabus, as I prayed that Mrs. Gallagher would be a bit more transparent with information regarding the work she was going to assign me.

Chapter Sixteen

"Did you make it back on time for your exams?" James asked the following morning as he drove me to work.

"Yes," I said as I smiled at him.

"And how was the trip?"

"It was great. I had a good time."

I knew James had worked for Mrs. Gallagher for a long time, so he knew her better than any one of her employees. I also knew that he respected her deeply.

"Can I ask you something, James?"

"Sure, go ahead," he said.

It was easy forging a friendship with him because he was easy to talk to. "How many personal assistants has Mrs. Gallagher had?"

His gaze met mine over the rearview mirror. "Several," he said.

I expected him to give me a more articulate answer, but he didn't seem willing to reveal any more information. I wasn't surprised to hit another roadblock in my attempt to know my boss better.

"She had a long-term personal assistant whose name was Michelle Fields, but she resigned when she got married because she wanted to start a family and the job was a bit too demanding for her," he said.

The unexpected information surprised me.

"After she left, no one could really fill her shoes. The chemistry wasn't right with most of the employees and the job was too much for others."

"How long did the best last?"

"A couple of months, but even then it was a bit of a struggle. Mrs. Gallagher likes people who take initiative when she's absent."

"Take initiative?"

"Yeah, like knowing what you need to do without her necessarily having to tell you."

That explained why she wasn't voluntary with details.

"I like you, Olivia. I think you're the best for this job and I think Mrs. Gallagher thinks so too," he said.

His words were comforting.

"Thanks, James."

When I got to the mansion, I went directly to my office and stopped short when I found Mrs. Gallagher there waiting for me. She was seated on my chair going through the laptop when I walked in.

"Oh Gosh, I'm I late?" I asked nervously as I checked the time on my wristwatch.

"No, you're on time," she said calmly, leaning back against my chair as her gaze moved up, down, then up again, scanning me.

I nervously approached the desk and was inwardly delighted she was in my chair because it would be filled with her magical scent. "Good morning," I said.

"Good morning." She stood up and casually came around my desk.

She looked absolutely gorgeous in an official purple dress that femininely hugged her body, and the sight of her made me squirm in my controlled but thriving hunger for her. Memories of our time together were alarmingly alive in me, but I tried hard to conceal it because I didn't want her to see it.

She leaned against my desk and crossed her arms over her chest where some cleavage was exposed and I looked away in an attempt to hide my desire for her. God, at this rate I was going to have a hard time having a face to face conversation with her.

"How were your exams?" How did she manage to be so calm?

One of my favorite qualities about her was her growing concern for me, or at least that was what I thought it was. It was titillating to know that she cared.

"They were okay."

I couldn't bring myself to tell her I was afraid I might've failed.

"You don't look too certain."

"I did my best," I said, concealing the uncertainty with a smile.

She studied me for a moment then dropped her hand over an iPad on my desk. "This iPad contains my schedule, most of the projects I'm currently working on and a very important contact list of clients and business associates. I've giving it to you because I trust you."

My heart started racing as I wondered if this had anything to do with my confrontation with her in Paris.

"You'll be in charge of my time and most of what I do and you'll be required to keep it updated. I need you to thoroughly go through it and learn everything because when I'm unable to take some meetings, you'll take them, which is why I need you to be completely knowledgeable."

I couldn't believe what I was hearing.

"This is going to be the most challenging part of your job."

She handed me the iPad and my hands shook at the responsibility I was taking on.

"Some of the stuff in here is very complicated but I'll assign you someone to help you with whatever you're unable to understand."

She had to be the best boss in the world. I couldn't believe she was going to have someone teaching me on the job. This was going to build my resume for when I was done with school.

"Do you have any questions?" she asked.

I shook my head. "Not at the moment," I said.

I was too excited thinking about all the possibilities.

She straightened up and approached me. "Do you think you'll be able to handle it?" she asked.

I wanted to appear confident so I met her gaze and tried not to let my stance falter. "Yes, I can handle it."

She smiled at me and said softly, "Good, because from this point forward, you're going to be an extension of me Olivia."

The words left me breathless. I knew it was a work-related statement but I wished it had a deeper meaning. My gaze followed her to the door and I remembered the pendant necklace she'd given me. "Mrs. Gallagher," I said.

When she turned to face me, I almost forgot what I wanted to say. "Yes," she said.

"Thank you for the pendant," I said.

She didn't say anything. She just smiled and left my office.

My knees were a bit weak from forcing my leg muscles to hold still. Soon as she walked out, I weakly went around the desk and sat down.

I was a little disappointed she hadn't broached the subject of what had happened between us in Paris. She'd behaved like it'd never happened at all. I'd been fighting my nerves and she'd completely held it together.

Where did she find the strength? Who was this woman? How could she conceal her emotions so well? I'd known her for weeks now and I still had no clue who she really was.

I took a deep breath and my senses were overwhelmed by the rich scent she'd left behind. I wanted to pretend it didn't affect me but somehow, it made me even hotter for her.

Trying to focus my mind back on the project she'd just handed me, I opened the iPad and began my work.

Chapter Seventeen

BOOK TWO: AMELIA

At the age of eighteen when most young women were starting to discover who they were, I was stuck in a life I wished I could get away from. Most people would've thought me stupid, after all my family did own one of the most successful pharmaceutical companies in the world. But I wanted out.

My father was an extremely ambitious man and inherited the business from his father who inherited it from my great grandfather.

My mother was a socialite when they met but shortly after getting married, she quickly grew to be his ally and business associate. Together they ruled and made the business an even greater success.

I figured that was how they managed to stay together and in love.

From the moment I was born, I wasn't meant to have a childhood. I was forced to grow up quickly and had tutors from the minute I could talk. By the time I was five, I could speak multiple languages and was on my way to becoming the hybrid child of two people who loved nothing more in the world than money and success.

All I ever wanted was to make my parents proud, so I did what was needed to make sure I'd be everything they wanted me to be. But woe unto me, they barely took notice. All they saw was mixed DNA of themselves; a product of two brilliant people who'd continue the lineage of the family business.

I had a cousin from my mother's side. I resented him. He was a mean sonofabitch who was always in competition with me. He somehow managed to make my mother like him more than me. He was devilishly charming and cunning as a fox.

I was given a better education, maybe even a better life before my mother took him in and started raising him. She wasn't any more affectionate with him, but he was always desperate to please her.

My father didn't like him. In fact, if anything, he was nicer to me. This made Eric, my cousin, very hateful. We went to different schools because my father felt I deserved the best education money could buy.

I was just glad I didn't have to be around Eric.

He was a couple of years older than me and his resentment towards me grew when I skipped several grades because I was too smart for even some of my teachers. When I graduated a year earlier than him, I had to admit, I was a little proud.

My father couldn't be happier. My mother didn't care.

I graduated high school at fifteen and immediately went to campus. I never got to make friends. My parents thought making friends at such a young age was a waste of time.

By the time I was eighteen, my father had already given me a position in the company and Eric was furious. He went through four years of college, but I finished earlier and moved further up the ladder. It was amusing to know I was beating him at everything without even having to try.

Halfway through my first year at the company, my father died in a plane crash. It was by a stroke of luck my mother wasn't in the plane with him since they worked so closely together.

At the funeral, there were hundreds of people. Faces I couldn't recognize. My mother was inconsolable. I thought his death would somehow bring us closer, but I was wrong.

I didn't mourn much for my father. I barely really knew him. Just like my mother, he was a stranger to me. But I did feel his absence and thought since my mother undoubtedly experienced it too, we could somehow build something from there.

Instead, she sent me to run one of our companies in Europe, creating as much distance between us as possible.

I grew resentful towards her and the world for being so cold to me. I resented myself for feeling lonely because it was a weakness that wasn't in my genes and focused on work.

Within two years, my work spoke for itself. I was based in Germany, and managed to make it the main headquarters for all our European branches of Winston Enterprises. Since it was a privately-owned company, everyone wanted a piece of it but we managed to keep it in the family.

My mother started noticing me then because I was single-handedly making profits beyond my parents' imagination.

I was a billionaire and should've been happy my mother had finally started reaching out, but I wasn't content. I hated my life.

Due to how driven I was, I didn't care about having a personal life. I had countless suitors from the wealthiest men in the world to some of the most powerful leaders. I knew being young, beautiful and brilliant was appealing to them, but I had no interest.

My mother came to Germany to visit me. I didn't know much about what was going on in her personal life and to be honest I didn't care. I should've been emotionally starved but instead, I was empty. There was nothing but a void where my heart should've been.

To me, the heart was just an organ that pumped blood through the rest of my body and the idea of love was nothing but all nonsense.

I'd met some of the most handsome men in the world, but none of them ever evoked any type of emotion in me.

The magazines said I was incredibly intelligent. They described me as a quiet person who didn't say much. Most people thought I was shy and tried to take advantage of me, but to be honest, I found it easier to read people from observing them and listening.

It was a technique I'd learned from my father. I could tell the type of person anyone was from just one look. It infuriated most men when I rejected them, and because I led a private life, which was due to the fact that I had no personal life, I was called a lesbian.

I didn't mind. I didn't care. Women also come on to me and I rejected them as well. At some point I thought I was asexual. I had no sexual desire. Nothing turned me on.

I was a robot. The perfect machine my parents had created. I was ruthless because my feelings didn't alter my judgment or get in the way of business. I'd somehow managed to eradicate all sorts of weaknesses.

The first time I saw my mother after my father died was when she came to visit me in Germany. I was a younger replica of her with my father's intelligent blue eyes.

It was awkward and we treated each other like business associates. She'd never been much of a mother to me; I failed to see any reason why I should fake affection for her.

I offered to let her stay in my apartment, but was relieved when she told me she'd booked a hotel. A day after resting, I gave her a tour of the mother ship I ran, introduced her so some of my employees and gave her a detailed report of how the companies in other European countries were doing.

I didn't expect much from her so there was no disappointment when she failed to react.

I was a little surprised though, when she asked me to go back to America with her. The reasons stated were the company wasn't doing well and she needed me to do something to change that.

Being the obedient child, and knowing my father would expect this of me, I packed up the life I'd built, and took the company jet back to America.

My mother insisted I live with her in a five-bedroom mansion she'd bought herself, but I turned her down and got myself a three-bedroom penthouse. I didn't need much space and knew I wouldn't spend any time in the penthouse anyway since I was always going to be working and traveling.

I didn't like that she was applying more effort trying to reach out to me. Weirdly enough, it made me uncomfortable. I assumed that was how she'd felt when I'd tried to build a relationship with her.

It troubled me that I'd somehow turned into her and promised myself I'd change. I didn't know how, but I was determined to turn out different.

When I started working at the American headquarters in New York, I thought I'd take over from her, but she insisted on being in charge. Our company occupied all the office space in the fifty story building and on the top most floor, there were only two unbelievably large offices where several floors lower, the space hosted at least ten offices and continued to increase in number as one descended down.

There were several private elevators, but only she and I had the key to the only private elevator that led to the top floors. I didn't understand her obsession with space.

Personally, I preferred working around employees in order to establish a better relationship with them, so instead of taking the office she'd kept for me, I took one on a lower floor, where I was able to deal with most of the people I needed to help raise the company back to its original standard.

I could tell she wasn't pleased but she needed my help and there was nothing she could do about it. She'd pushed me away all her life, so she could continue enjoying the isolation on the top floor all on her own.

I knew I was extraordinary. Most people who met me were instantly intimidated. My body said twenty but my brain had the intelligence and knowledge of a man the age of my father, had he still lived.

I got to work immediately, racing from factories to offices all over the world in countless company jets, trying to save this enormous empire my great grandfather had created.

I wasn't shocked to meet chauvinistic men who believed I had no business running such a huge company, but I'd gotten used to it and it didn't bother me as long as we concluded our business.

My responsibilities were countless but I was a gladiator, always ready to go to war. I was sharp and had unbelievable problem-solving skills. Being a Winston demanded it from me.

Winston Enterprises was a giant snake with countless heads and I was riding that snake like a wild mustang, kicking ass and being awesome in every aspect of the word.

I was severally featured in Time and Forbes magazine as one of the most successful women in the world. They said I was a ruthless business tycoon, a fashion icon, a role model for young women all over the world and every other thing they could come up with but during all this, I was busy traveling from North to South America, Asia to Europe to Africa.

I was untouchable, until I met her.

Isabel Price.

Chapter Eighteen

She was absolutely brilliant, unbelievably stunning and extremely wealthy. At twenty-five, she was an heiress to a powerful oil dynasty.

My mother was hosting a party for some influential business associates. She'd always been very good at that sort of thing. I never attended the events because I never saw the need but on that particular one, she insisted on my presence.

I hated the parties because they bordered more on socialization rather than business. But I did what I always did, I put on a mask. During these kinds of parties, there were always hyenas gathering around trying unsuccessfully to attract my attention in attempts to court me, which was also why I never attended the parties.

On my mother's insistence, I showed up. I conducted myself the way I always did, flawlessly. Halfway through, I noticed an odd thing about my mother. She kept introducing me to young eligible bachelors.

I wasn't sure what her intention was, but I didn't like it. Our relationship was very clear-cut, which was why we got along and also why I did everything she asked. What I wasn't going to stand for was her trying to find me a suitor.

Out of courtesy and respect, I played along several times, but I was getting frustrated and my patience was running out. I'd never liked anyone trying to force something on me and while in the past I could never really have a say with my mother, times had changed and so had I.

I left halfway through the party and didn't bother to inform her. I knew she'd be upset, but to be honest, I didn't care. In the elevator on my way down, I heard someone clear their throat and turned around.

That was when I saw her.

Through the years, I'd met a lot of people but nothing and no one quite as strikingly beautiful as the woman standing behind me.

"Why are you running away?" she asked.

Her question startled me. How did she know I was running?

She came to stand beside me and stared at me with her catlike eyes which had the darkest shade I'd ever seen. She had long, black as ebony hair that flowed effortlessly down her shoulders to her back, a small and perfectly symmetrical nose and a pair of full pink lips.

She was my height with the body of a goddess and everything about her was working together to create something that shook me for the very first time in my life.

"What, you don't speak to strangers?" she teased.

I couldn't take my eyes off her.

"I don't know how to answer your question," I said.

"Your mother is a very charming woman. She's got all the men up there eating out of the palm of her hand, even my father."

"She's very uh…, gifted," I said, for lack of a better word.

"Very gifted indeed, I wonder if you share that quality," she said.

I looked at her, unsure of what she meant then she smiled, exposing a perfect set of white teeth.

"I'm Isabel, Isabel Price." She stretched out her hand in greeting.

"Amelia, Amelia Winston." I closed my hand in hers.

"Why are you leaving your own party, Amelia Winston?" she asked.

I looked at her hand, where she was still holding onto mine and cleared my throat, a little uncomfortable from the physical contact. "It's not my party."

"With all those bachelors your mother invited to meet you in search of a suitable partner for you?"

I pulled my hand away. I wanted to get away from her. She was a bit nosy and I didn't like people who liked to pry.

"Have I made you uncomfortable?" she asked.

She had an amused look across her face.

"No, not at all," I said, forcing myself to smile.

When she didn't speak, I wondered what she'd been doing at the party and why she was leaving. "Why were you there? Was your father looking for a suitor for you?" I asked.

"My reasons are purely work-related, though I have to say, it was entertaining watching you turn down all those poor saps."

"You were watching me," I said.

"Everyone was. You must be used to that kind of attention," she

said.

"No, not at all."

"I have a business proposal for you," she said.

Her statement managed to get my attention.

"I know your American company is uh… struggling."

She looked at me as though she was waiting for me to deny it. When I failed to respond, she went on.

"I'm stuck in the family business and I want out."

"What do you want from me?" I asked.

"I'd like to hire you."

"Hire me?" I almost laughed.

"Yes, I'd like to hire you for consultation services."

"What would I be consulting on?"

"Business, of course."

The elevator finally stopped and we stepped out.

"I'll be very generous. You can use the money to help your struggling company."

I didn't have a response for her. Did she seriously think I needed her help saving my company? I was a billionaire. I didn't need pocket change.

"Here is my card, you can take some time to think about it," she said.

"I don't need to. I have an answer for you right now."

We stopped outside the building as the valet went to get our cars.

"No," I said.

She smiled at me and I couldn't understand why she was so amused. I was running a company that demanded all my time and attention, even if I wanted to, I couldn't take on a side job that wouldn't be beneficial to me.

"Why don't you take a little more time to think about it? Our parents are very close. I'm sure they'd be very supportive."

I didn't know anything about my mother being close to her father and frankly, I didn't care. Using my mother as bait to get me to work for her was working completely against her.

Before I could respond, a silver Porsche that wasn't even on the market yet stopped right in front of us and she winked at me as she went, got in and quickly drove away.

I had a driver because my mother had insisted I use a limousine so my exit didn't match hers.

On my way back to the penthouse, my mother called to ask where I'd disappeared to and I made up some excuse. I could tell she was upset as I'd suspected she would be and it gave me some joy to make her life slightly uncomfortable.

The next few weeks progressed quickly. I avoided seeing my mother and traveled purposely because I didn't want a repeat of what had happened at the party.

After my encounter with Isabel, I didn't think much about her after we parted ways. She left a lasting impression, but being who I was, I barely had time to dwell on her or her proposal.

Unfortunately, the case wasn't so for her. She insisted on having a meeting with me, but I managed to avoid both her and her calls. I wasn't quite so lucky because she used my mother to get to me.

I went to dinner with my mother and she happened to be there. The second time I saw her, the effect was similar to our first encounter. I wasn't even sure I had words to describe it.

I tightly smiled at her, trying to conceal my disdain and sat between her and my mother. My mother as usual, was her charming self. Halfway through our meals, Isabel brought up the business proposal.

Since she got along so well with my mother, she was more descriptive with her ideas and didn't fail to mention that she needed my help. Funny enough, she didn't use my struggling company as a tool of persuasion.

I watched her, thinking about how exploitive and conceited she was but didn't say anything, which I knew annoyed her because I was certain she wanted to hear my thoughts.

She wrote down a number of the amount of money she was willing to pay for a couple of weeks for the services rendered and handed it to my mother, whose love for money always betrayed her.

They tried to engage me in conversation, but I didn't say much, which to my amusement, frustrated both women. When dinner was over, I made up some excuse and left.

The following day, my mother came to my office and talked me into accepting the job. She claimed it wouldn't take much of my time and that consultation was easy, but I knew she was only interested in the money.

"Its twenty million dollars for just expressing your thoughts on the matter," she said.

I didn't want to argue with her and I knew she'd still somehow manage to talk me into accepting the proposal so I said, "I'll think about it."

The following day at eight in the morning, I was in Isabel's office.

I resented how beautiful she was. I resented how she always seemed amused whenever we were in the same room but mostly, I resented that she had forced my hand at doing something I wasn't interested in.

"That was a low blow," I said.

"You gave me no choice," she said.

"There are countless people out there who are more than qualified to do this for far much less pay."

"I wanted you."

Her statement failed to deliver the intended effect.

"What do you really want from me?" I asked.

"Your consultation services," she said, batting her eyebrows.

"You get two weeks and I never hear from you again," I said.

She walked over to me and stopped so close it was like she didn't care for personal space. "Welcome to Price Industries," she said, stretching out her arm to shake mine.

"Send me everything you have on the project before tomorrow," I said and walked out of her office.

She infuriated me, which was odd because I never let such trivial afflictions affect me. I spent the day clearing some time from my busy schedule so that I could work on her project and in the afternoon when I was on the phone talking to some contacts in Japan, Eric made his way into my office.

"I'm sorry Ms. Winston, I tried to stop him," my secretary said, walking in after him.

"Go on, tell her who I am," he said.

I dismissed my secretary and replaced the receiver.

"How can I help you?" I asked.

He slowly walked around my office, taking in the expensive interior décor and then approached my vintage mahogany desk and ran his index finger over the perfect outline of the edge.

"I heard you were back, so I came to see for myself. After all, we're family."

He was a junior executive and it'd take him years to get where I was in my career. The fact that he wasn't a Winston guaranteed that he'd never run the company and I knew that knowledge caused him a lot of rage.

"Unfortunately," I said dryly.

I'd never tried to conceal my contempt and he knew exactly how I felt about him.

"So why did Kathy bring you back here? I thought she was done with you when she dumped you in Europe," he said, referring to my mother. When he was around her, she was his beloved Aunt Kathy but around me she was plain old Kathy.

Nothing he could say had ever gotten to me. Not in the past and certainly not now. He wasn't worth my time or effort so I let him rumble on until he was satisfied.

"The only reason you've come this far is because your daddy made it happen. We both know I deserve this more than you," he said.

I didn't understand his logic. He wanted to believe we were equals and therefore deserved equal treatment and opportunity but the simple fact was, I was a Winston and I was exceptionally brilliant and he was neither.

"I've seen what they say about you, what they think. They call you a heartless cold bitch and you know what, they're right."

He was trying to provoke me, and the fact that it wasn't working was making him agitated and frustrated. He came to stand in front of my desk and tried to match my cold stare.

"Are you done? Can I get back to my call now?" I asked.

He slightly flinched and retreated, then laughed audibly as he made his way out of my office. He was a maniacal sociopath who believed the world owed him for picking me over him.

Undeterred, I got back to my call. When I was done, my mother requested to see me in her office.

I wasn't surprised she wanted to talk about the Price project. She seemed almost pleased I'd met up with Isabel and accepted the job.

"The family is extremely wealthy and I think we could benefit from this greatly," she said.

I didn't know what this we talk was about. As far as I was concerned, I was the one doing the project and it was a side job that had absolutely nothing to do with Winston Enterprises.

"Our ties to the family will come very much in handy in the future."

Isabel had said she felt stuck in the family business and wanted to venture out. I doubted her father would be pleased with the idea and I doubted my mother would've been so supportive had she known she might have been crossing Mr. Price by asking me to help his daughter.

I considered telling her, but decided to keep the knowledge to myself.

"Keep me updated?" she said.

I nodded and left her office.

Before the end of the day, I received the information I'd requested from Isabel. She wanted to venture into healthcare. I had expected other business ideas but all she sent me were scraps of information on one particular business venture.

I had my secretary get in touch with her and a few minutes later, she was on the phone.

"I don't understand," I said.

"What don't you understand?" she asked.

I tightened my hold on the phone, trying hard to avoid thinking about how attractive she was and that annoying look of amusement on her face. "If you want to venture into healthcare, what exactly do you need me for?"

"Two weeks for twenty million dollars was quite costly, so I decided it'd be more beneficial to me if you knew where my interests lie and we can proceed from there."

"How much do you know about healthcare as a business venture?"

"I wouldn't get into it if I didn't know anything about it, now would I? Anyway, I just need you to find out if it's a good business to get into."

"Are you sure about this?" I asked.

There were plenty of other types of businesses she could have gotten into, why was she interested in healthcare?

"Do it," she said.

Long after the conversation ended, I found myself admiring her. I wondered if I'd ever try to venture out of my family business. Every part of me had grown up learning the ins and outs of the entire operation. Would I ever risk trying out something new, something so different from what I'd been brought up in?

Isabel was an heiress. She had a legacy to uphold. If her father was anything like mine had been, this business venture of hers was going to be shut down before she could do anything about it.

Something about it made me want to help her, if only just to see how it'd all unfold. If she was paying me twenty million dollars, then she must've had more than enough financial backing.

Chapter Nineteen

After several days of doing intense research and consulting experts in the field, I compiled a list of names and companies. Working in the pharmaceuticals industry gave me extensive knowledge about healthcare so the project was easy. I talked to Isabel often on the phone because she requested daily updates, but I didn't mind.

We met up in her office during the end of my first week working for her and I met Mr. Price. He was coming out of her office just as I was going in. He seemed pleased to see me, which was the same reaction my mother had when she saw Isabel.

I wondered if there was more to their friendship. My mother had been single for two years now and no one could blame her for wanting to move on with her life. I just failed to understand what the secrecy was all about.

When I walked into Isabel's office, she was standing by the large window overlooking Manhattan. She almost didn't notice me walking in until she turned around to pick something from her desk.

I noticed the teary troubled expression across her face and stopped. She seemed surprised to see me. It was like she'd forgotten we had a meeting.

Something stirred in me when I saw her like that, something alien and it made me uncomfortable.

"We can postpone the meeting if this isn't a good time," I said.

I didn't know how to offer comfort so her current state disturbed me because I wasn't sure how to reach out and I wasn't sure I wanted to.

"No, no, this is a good time."

She quickly dubbed a tissue over her eyes and dried the unshed tears.

"What, the iron lady has never seen a woman cry?" she asked.

I wasn't sure how to answer her. I was still at the door debating on whether or not I should leave and come back when she was a little more composed. "I uh… try to avoid the situations," I said.

She laughed softly and a strange feeling moved through me at the sound.

"My father and I don't see eye to eye on a lot of things so we have these moments a little more often than I'd like. It's tough being an only child, you understand, right?"

When I was a child, I could've fully related to the situation but years of being programmed to be someone who had no capacity for emotions had changed me. I wasn't designed to deal with emotional situations or people. I used logic and lacked the ability to empathize with an emotional situation.

"Come closer, I'm not going to infect you with my tears," she said.

I reluctantly approached her desk. "I'm not very good at this kind of thing," I said, gesturing to the situation.

"I kinda gathered," she said, coming around the desk to where I was standing.

"Can we start?" I wanted to get as far away from there as possible.

"In a minute, I'd like to ask you something," she said.

I nodded, trying to conceal my discomfort and busied myself by placing the files on her desk and spreading them across to show her I wasn't there for chitchat.

"Don't you ever get tired of wearing this mask of composure?"

She was leaning back against her desk now.

I stood upright and looked at her. "Mask of composure?"

"Yeah, doesn't anything get to you?"

You're getting to me, I wanted to say but instead asked, "What does that have to do with our work?"

Isabel's dark catlike eyes were unwavering. It was like she was trying to pry me open and see the contents inside my head.

I prided myself in knowing people but every time I thought I was getting a clear sense of the type of person she was, she changed on me. That unnerved me.

She stood upright and moved closer to me, again rudely disregarding my personal space and before I could take a step back, she closed her hand on mine as though stopping me from trying to escape.

"What are you doing?" I asked, frowning in fright.

"You completely fascinate me," she said.

I wanted to pull back but she was transferring her warmth into my hand, slowly softening her touch so that her fingers were trailing themselves against mine.

The touch sent strange and unusual vibrations all through me, spreading around my body in a manner I'd never experienced before. I took a wary step back, uncertain of what had just happened.

"Isabel." My voice sounded strange.

This was a brain thing. I was aware of what people experienced when they found other people appealing. It was simple science. I was human, not a complete robot after all.

"You don't like being touched," she said.

I pursed my lips together and shook my head.

I'd never experienced any sort of intimacy with another human being but I'd been in physical contact with people, like when we shook hands or when a situation required a hug or when a gentleman pecked one's cheek.

I tried to think of something to say because she had a look in her eyes that I didn't trust, but my brain was shutting down.

"I want to touch you, Amelia," she said.

I should've turned around and left, but instead, my curiosity was accompanied by a strong sense of intrigue.

She touched my hand again.

This time the earlier sensation felt like it had magnified. When she moved too close, I found myself holding my breath, unable to fully comprehend what was happening.

"I can't," I managed to say.

"You can't what?"

How could she have this kind of effect on me? It was like she was slowly turning a key to open a portal of sensations I'd never been aware existed.

"I can't move," I said, deeply inhaling and unconsciously filling my senses with the scent of her sweet perfume.

Her hand moved to my face, and she slowly trailed her fingers over the outline of my jaw, down to my chin. Her face was inches away from mine and my body was experiencing an epiphany of sensations that were too much for me to bear.

My hands trembled as her breath gently fanned my face. My being was stuck and unable to move and my insides were in a state of havoc and confusion.

She closed the space between us and gently pressed her lips against mine. On impact, my eyes automatically closed as a rush of heat violently spread through my body. She brushed her lips against mine, gently parting them, and something happened in my stomach as my temperature rose.

Isabel's lips were as soft as petals and her touch was far too overwhelming. Why was I feeling this way? I was stronger than this. This was a weakness. I wasn't built for weaknesses.

When she was about to deepen the kiss, I managed to regain my strength and pulled away from her, creating distance between us. My hands were shaking, this time visibly for her to see. I tightened my jaw and took a deep breath, staring at her with anger spewing from my eyes like boiling lava.

"If this is how you're going to conduct yourself, our business is done. I can't afford any distractions. It's either we work together or end this right here, right now." I'd never been so angry in my life.

"I'm sorry, I–. I… uh, work, of course, work together," she said.

I ran my tongue over my lips, tasting her soft lips on mine and averted my gaze to the files across her desk. "Go through the files and we'll pick this up tomorrow."

I couldn't stay another second in her office. I needed to understand what had just happened.

When I walked out, I quickly headed to the elevator and tried to slow my racing heart. There was a small part of me thinking, that was my first kiss. I'd never focused on my sexual side before and I was a little disappointed to learn I possessed one.

I couldn't believe it was Isabel who evoked it. I was twenty years old and had just discovered my wiring was the same as everyone else's. It wasn't something I was prepared to deal with. If Isabel couldn't control herself, then my business with her was compromised.

I had postponed a trip I'd been supposed to take to Switzerland to work on her project. Now, after what had happened, I wasn't so sure I wanted to see her quite so soon. She'd understand my reasons. She'd have no choice but to.

I spoke to my secretary over the phone and told her to put the plans back on. Two hours later, I was on a plane to Switzerland. I put everything that had happened out of my head and put my game face back on.

My trip lasted a couple of days longer than I expected and by the time I got back, I had countless messages from Isabel.

I was more than willing to give back the money she'd paid in advance but after spending a few days away and being completely unable to get our encounter in her office out of my mind, I wanted to see her again.

I didn't want a repetition of what had happened. I wanted to prove to myself that my weakness had subsided. Her eyes and her kiss had mercilessly haunted me, and every moment I'd had to myself had been filled with thoughts of her, but this was just another hurdle I had to overcome.

I couldn't understand what was happening to me. I'd never felt this way before. Most people who'd ever come on to me had always been forgotten the moment they exited the room, but not Isabel.

I found messages from my mother requesting to see me in her office and went to see her immediately when I arrived. She was bombarded with work, but she'd gotten used to that lifestyle.

"Oh, good, you're back. I need to talk to you," she said.

"What's the matter?" I asked, noticing a hint of anxiety.

"The Price project, I'd like you to drop it."

She was looking at some documents spread across her desk as she said this.

"Why?" I asked.

I knew the reason. She'd found out Mr. Price was against Isabel's venture.

"Because I've asked you to," she said.

She failed to make eye contact, which slightly got to me because I felt I deserved a reason rather than an order. I failed to respond and headed for the exit.

"Are you going to drop it?" she asked me at the door.

Without turning to face her, I said, "No," and walked out.

"Amelia," she called after me.

Apart from her secretary, there was no one else in the large office space.

I stopped as she approached me. "Yes," I said politely.

"Mr. Price doesn't approve of his daughter's ideals with this project. I don't want to jeopardize our business ties to him."

"You asked me to undertake this project after I'd turned it down. I've worked halfway through it and put my own work aside to focus on it. Don't tell me I wasted my time."

"You didn't, Mr. Price approves of the advance payment Isabel put forward."

I'd never seen her like this before, but then again, maybe it was because I was starting to see the type of person she truly was.

"This is business. I started a project. I must finish it. If it causes you strain with Mr. Price, that is too bad. I will not drop this project because you asked me to."

I headed for the elevator.

"Amelia, you don't understand."

"I understand perfectly," I said and got in the elevator, leaving her with a surprised look across her face.

I had business principles I had to adhere to, but to be honest, it was satisfying to see my mother in a huff. That was probably why I refused to drop the project, well, that and the fact that I was now determined to help Isabel succeed.

If her life was anything like mine, she must've been dismally miserable. I wasn't going to get in the way of her dreams and the fact that her father thought it was ridiculous for her to want to do something else rather than work for his oil company, let's just say it drove me to want to help her even more.

Maybe it was because if she could do this and succeed, there'd be hope for me too. I could get out from under my mother's thumb. I could live without the ghost of my father's influence.

I got in touch with Isabel the moment I got back to my office and we agreed to meet up for lunch. I knew she'd be upset with me but I understood. If the pressure had come down on my mother, I couldn't imagine how rough it was on her.

We met at a beautiful Italian restaurant and both arrived at the same time. Like I had suspected, she was furious with me and didn't care to hide it.

"How could you go off and leave when you knew how much I was depending on you?" she asked.

That look of amusement was gone, now replaced by a serious expression.

I still couldn't get past how beautiful she was, even now when she was angry.

"I know I upset you, but you didn't have to run off on me," she said.

I remembered my anger after she'd kissed me. It felt so trivial now. Her world was falling apart and she had no one to help her.

"My father is threatening to take away everything I have if I don't stop this."

What had she expected would happen? Both our fathers had been torn from the same cloth. We weren't the kind of people who were allowed to have dreams of being anything else other than what we'd been born into. That was fact.

"Are you going to stop it?"

"It's a ridiculous dream. What was I thinking?"

"I don't know," I said.

"Of course, you don't. You're a robot. You don't feel anything."

Her words delivered an unexpected sting.

"I am, Isabel. I'm a robot. I don't know what you're expecting from me. I don't think in the same way that you do." I wasn't saying that to hurt her, I said it because there was a deep part of me that believed it. "You practically forced me to undertake this project and what, now you want to quit?"

She raised her eyebrow.

"Stop wasting my time, I have other important things to do," I said. "You set out to do this project believing it'd be possible. It only stops when you say it stops."

She searched my face for something I couldn't understand. "Will you help me?" she asked.

"I still have a week. A lot can be done in that amount of time," I said.

"What about my father?"

"What about him?" I asked.

She smiled at me then asked, "Have you ever wanted to get out from under your parents' shadow?"

I hesitated. I'd entertained thoughts of leaving and going far away where no one knew me, but I wasn't brave enough to do it. I didn't even know how to interact with people. "No," I said.

"So it's all just black and white to you?"

There were shades of grey but I wasn't about to confide in her. "Let's get to work, Isabel," I said.

"Can we at least eat first?" she asked.

I'd even forgotten we were at a restaurant. When she summoned a waiter, I got to my feet and said, "I have another meeting in ten minutes. Why don't you drop by my office later and we can continue with your project."

She looked pleased and disappointed at the same time. The real reason why I was leaving was because I didn't want to spend any more time with her than was necessary and having a meal with her would force conversation and so far it hadn't gone too good.

Chapter Twenty

During the next one week, my services went further than the required consultation services Isabel had paid for. I was determined to see her succeed and didn't care if it took time away from my own work.

We spent a lot of time together and I came to learn more about her. She was worldly and insightful. She had more people skills than I did and she had a sense of humor, though I hadn't decided if it was good or bad.

For some reason, even though we were so different, we understood each other. She didn't complain about her father, but I was sure it was because I'd shown her I had no interest in her personal life.

She had a knack for provoking me, but I maintained my cool. I wasn't going to give her the satisfaction of knowing how much she got under my skin. I didn't like how well she was getting to know me either. I'd never spent enough time with anyone to give them a clear picture of who I was and Isabel was getting too comfortable around me.

I wasn't intimidating to her. She, like the rest of the world however, still believed I was an ice-cold bitch because I hadn't given her any reason to think otherwise and I wanted to keep things that way.

I didn't like that I was starting to enjoy spending time with her. It rattled me. I'd never liked anyone.

"So, what do you like?" she asked on a Friday afternoon.

"Excuse me?"

"What's your type?"

"Type of what?"

"The kind of person you want to be with," she said.

"How do you manage to turn most of our business conversations into personal questions?" I asked.

"I'm just trying to get to know you," she said.

"There is nothing to know. What you see is what you get. Besides, I have no interest in you whatsoever and I think you should exercise the same principle."

"I would, but I'm not a robot. I like getting to know people."

She could be stubborn too, one of my least favorite qualities about her. Not that she had any qualities I liked. "Isabel, we've got work to do, let's focus on that."

"Why did you get so angry when I kissed you?"

I shot my head up at her question. I thought about that kiss every time I saw her.

"Did you hate it?" she asked.

She looked so innocent as she asked, I thought we were carrying out two different conversations. "Isabel, please."

That look of amusement colored her face. I knew she was trying to get to me and I couldn't believe it was working.

"Fine, I'll drop it."

"We have the final markings and you've got all the information you need. We've identified healthcare companies you can invest in or acquire. All you have to do now is get the ball rolling. Just know that this isn't going to be easy and there's a great possibility you might end up failing," I said.

"Wow, great pep talk," she said.

"I'm giving you facts, Isabel. If you want me to lie to you, I can do that too."

"Don't, it's what I like most about you."

Was she flirting with me? "Now, our business has concluded," I said in relief.

"Thank you, I really appreciate all you've done for me."

I nodded and stood up to stretch my legs. Now I could go back to my life and forget she'd ever existed. "When we started this, our agreement was that once our business had concluded, I'd never hear from you again," I said, hoping she hadn't forgotten.

"Would it really be so bad? Have I been such horrible company?" she asked.

I knew she was teasing and I wasn't going to indulge her.

"I understand you need to be like this in order to stay focused, but don't you get tired of being so stiff and uptight all the time?" she asked.

I leaned against my desk and watched her as she packed up. I couldn't wait for her to walk out of my office and out of my life. "We may have come from a similar background, but you and I are not the same."

"Clearly," she said, turning to face me.

"I don't expect you or anyone else to understand. This is who I am. I can't change myself to suit other people."

"You shouldn't have to, but maybe you should learn to relax a bit. Maybe have a little fun. You're about to turn twenty-one and you're in charge of an empire. Do you know what people your age are doing right now?" she asked.

I couldn't help being curious. The reason I wanted to get out of my world and get away so bad was because I wanted to be ordinary. I wanted to be those people she was talking about. "What?"

"They're partying, having fun, sex and enjoying life. You're young and incredibly beautiful. Anyone would be lucky to have you, but your attitude is off-putting."

I didn't think I cared enough to let what she was saying get to me. "I wasn't born to be like other people," I said.

"A robot can be reprogrammed," she said.

I could tell this was one of her jokes but it wasn't funny to me.

"I've met a lot of women, but never one quite like you," she said.

"If my lifestyle is so unbearable to you, you should be happy you're leaving."

"On the contrary," she said as she approached me.

"Isabel, don't."

"What are you so afraid of?"

"I'm not afraid of anything."

I was standing between her and my desk and a wave of nervousness was slowly crawling up my spine.

"Like you said, our business has concluded," she said.

"And you should be walking out the door," I said.

She placed her arm around my waist, moving unbearably close to me and I closed my eyes, taking a deep breath to calm my nerves.

"I know what I do to you, Amelia. You do the same thing to me. I know that's why you can't wait for me to get out of your life."

"Isabel," I was barely audible.

Her face was so close to mine and all those sensations were starting to take over again. There was a strange excitement forming between my legs and I didn't know why but I wanted something I couldn't even understand from her.

"I want you, Amelia. I've thought about you every day from the very first moment I saw you," she whispered against my lips. "I want to make love to you, over and over and over again. I want to see you lose control," she continued.

I tried to pull away but she wouldn't let go. When I tried to protest, she crushed my lips with her own and awoke a savage animal in me that had been lying dormant waiting for someone brave enough to provoke it.

She wasn't soft or gentle like the first time she'd kissed me. She was angry and impatient and demanding and I found myself responding to her in a similar manner. I was lost in her domineering passion, drowning in it and my body was begging me to let her do everything she wanted to do to me.

"Please stop, Isabel," I said hungrily against her lips.

I'd never experienced sexual desire or passion before. I'd never thought about its depth or degree. What Isabel was creating in me was a chemical reaction that was going to destroy me. This was too intense for me, too disastrously delicious. Couldn't she feel it?

As though she'd heard my thoughts, she slightly pulled away and broke the kiss while her arms stayed in place around my waist, but my body wasn't paying attention to my brain. It was in a state of pleasurable turmoil. I crushed her lips as a fire burned inside me, threatening to wreck me.

"Stop it," I moaned against her mouth.

I wanted her to stop the dizzying frenzy of sensations. I wanted her to stop the current flow of excitement running amok through my veins. It was like some aroused monster had been unleashed in me. I had no control.

She broke the kiss and trailed her lips over my jaw then slowly down to the curve of my neck, sending bolts of lightning pleasure directly to that spot between my legs. I stifled a moan as I opened my eyes wide in shock.

Every part of my being was awake and craving her touch and something more, something primal and dangerous. How anybody could drive such desperate yearning through another person was beyond me.

I shouldn't have given into the kiss. I shouldn't have given into her. I shouldn't have let her touch me. I couldn't deal with this. I wasn't familiar with it.

"I don't want to stop, Amelia. I never want to stop," she said.

How could she say that when she knew she was on the verge of erupting a volcano in me? "I can't do this, it's too much."

"That's exactly why you should do it," she said, her lips never breaking contact with my flesh.

I wanted to feel her hands on my skin. I wanted to know the extent of how far these sensations could go, but I was too afraid.

A moan escaped my lips when she kissed the curve between my neck and shoulder and my nails dug into her flesh. It was a good thing my hands were over her clothes.

"Isabel."

She silenced me with a kiss and I automatically responded as though my body was already in sync with hers. God, she was so good at this. I never wanted her to stop either. But this wasn't who I was.

She came to a slow gentle stop and met my aroused gaze. I was panting for breath as I tried to regain my composure.

"You're so desirable, Amelia."

I didn't know how, but I managed to pry myself out of her arms. My body was in an extreme state of arousal and I didn't know how to stop it. It was like I was high on some drug.

"I'm going to make you mine one day, Amelia," she said as she slowly but steadily picked up her things and left my office.

I walked over to my chair and slumped myself onto it. I rubbed my temple with my fingertips and tightly crossed my legs in an attempt to rid myself of the heat that had accumulated down there.

It was impossible because my mind was still stuck on what had just happened. I could still feel Isabel's hands on me, her lips hot and hungry on mine and all those million sensations traveling all over my body and somehow settling on that damp core.

The door flew open and Eric walked in. I groaned in frustration because he was the last person I wanted to see or talk to.

"I don't have the patience to deal with you right now, Eric," I said.

"Kathy sent me," he said.

I took a deep breath and looked at him, and somehow his presence had the ability to take away my arousal. I must've resented him more than I even knew.

"What is it?" I asked.

"She wants me to be in charge of the factory in Belize," he said.

I shot up to my feet. "You're not qualified for the position."

He smiled, clearly amused by the disturbed state the news had delivered. He'd come to rub it in and I was letting him get to me. "You were controlling every branch in Europe when you were eighteen."

I didn't know how that was supposed to make his point but he sounded like an idiot to me. I might've been young but I'd known exactly what I was doing. "Age is not a factor."

I didn't even know why I was talking to him. I needed to have this conversation with my mother.

"Don't worry. I actually care about this business."

"If it was up to you, you'd run it to the ground." I walked past him and headed to the elevator. When the private elevator to my mother's office opened, I walked in and Eric followed.

"What do you think you're doing?" I asked him.

"You think I'm going to stay behind and let you bad mouth me?" he asked.

I groaned, taking a step further from him. I couldn't stand being in the same room with him so the elevator felt claustrophobic.

My mother was on the phone when I walked into her office. I had a feeling she'd promoted Eric to get back at me for helping Isabel because she knew as well as I did that Eric didn't deserve that promotion.

"Hi, Aunt Kathy?" he said, turning into the blood-sucking parasite that he was.

"Do you mind explaining to me what promotion he's talking about?" I demanded.

"Last time I checked, I was the boss around here and I can promote or demote anyone I please," she said.

Eric scoffed at me as he walked over to her side when she stood up.

It took me a moment to realize I was overreacting and this was exactly what she wanted. She was an intelligent woman and she knew sending Eric to Belize was a mistake.

Talking to her wasn't going to accomplish anything and telling her that her decision was ill-advised was only going to equip her with armor. She was testing me, searching for weaknesses.

"Okay, if that's your decision," I said.

I didn't stick around to watch her reaction but if she wanted to go to war with me, she was going to lose. I had every bit of her wit, intelligence and more.

Chapter Twenty-One

It was my birthday. I was turning twenty-one. My mother had thrown me an extravaganza for a party. Every important person she knew was present and so was every successful eligible bachelor in New York.

I'd wanted a small intimate party, but she'd said I was coming of age and therefore deserved the best of everything the world had to offer.

It was three weeks after our little spat and she'd sent Eric off to Belize, though according to the reports I'd received, I knew she was regretting her decision.

She was affectionate that night and it greatly disturbed me because it was all for show. She wanted every one of her guests to see what a good mother she was. She wanted them to think it was her hard work and effort that had molded me into who I was.

This was supposed to be my party, but for some reason, it was more about her than it was about me. I didn't mind though because I didn't like the attention, but that didn't stop people from coming over to chat with me.

I was charming, just like my mother, polite and kind because these people were important and in one way or the other, my work was related to theirs.

The party was being hosted at the Plaza and my mother hadn't spared any expense. She must've spent several million dollars to bring that night to life. It was overflowing with expensive bottles of champagne and all sorts of foreign cuisine.

She'd hired a band, one of her favorites of course, so the music was pleasant. The setting of the room was magnificent. I had to hand it to her, she knew how to throw a party.

I was a little embarrassed because I was dressed in a knee-high Christian Dior dress that my mother had picked out for me. I'd changed at her penthouse and since I didn't store any of my things there, I'd had no choice since we'd been running late.

During the drive to the Plaza, we'd been silent all the way. Now, the dress which accentuated my curves a bit too well was drawing men to me like bees. The Prada heels I was wearing were exaggerating the length of my exposed legs making the whole situation a bit ridiculous.

But I wasn't going to complain. I wasn't going to reveal my discomfort. I was a lady and I was going to behave exactly like one. I had a couple of glasses of champagne to calm my nerves and was able to maintain my calm through most of the night.

Everyone wanted to talk to me, to wish me a happy birthday. I'd received countless gifts from people I'd never even heard of. There were celebrities present and a couple of rock stars who hit on me, which I found amusing.

My mother didn't fail to request my presence whenever she met someone she needed to make an impression on and I played my role flawlessly. Mr. Price's presence was a bit of a surprise, which made me wonder if Isabel was there with him.

I hadn't seen or spoken to her since we'd parted ways and there wasn't a day that went by that I didn't think of her. I wondered if she thought of me, but when those moments came, I rebuked myself.

I thought about everything she'd made me feel and sometimes it was so intense, I'd feel it all over again as though she was there with me. I detested those moments.

There were reporters at the party as well. My mother had to make sure the media would share the news with the public of my coming of age grand party she'd thrown in the honor of my twenty first birthday. How vain.

Around midnight, the party started heating up and my mother forced me to stay by her side so I wouldn't disappear like I had at the previous party she'd hosted.

I didn't expect Eric to show up, but when he snuck around me and wrapped his arms around my waist, I cringed. His touch made my skin crawl.

"Careful, there are people present," he said, noticing my disgust.

"What are you doing here?" I asked.

"I'm family. I had to show up to show my support."

A photographer blinded me with his camera when he took a picture of us with Eric's arm around my shoulder.

"If you touch me again, I'm going to cut off your arms," I said through gritted teeth and he cautiously retreated.

"Happy birthday," he said, leaning in to peck my cheek but I pulled away right on time.

"Why don't you go suck up to my mother," I said, moving away from him.

I preferred entertaining anyone else in the room over spending another second with him.

At around one, I was so bored out of my mind I wanted to blow my brains out. I never got a second to myself. I never got a moment to breathe. It was so annoying, I thought my jaw would get stuck in the permanent position with the smile I'd forced on my face all night.

I needed to get out of there but everyone was hovering around me like predators on prey. When I decided to excuse myself, I was fed up with the over showering of attention.

I left the room and immediately headed for the elevator, anxiously waiting for it to open before anyone discovered I'd ditched my own birthday party. When the doors opened, I got in and held my breath and when they closed, I exhaled in relief.

"We have to stop meeting like this," she said.

I knew her voice before I even turned to face her.

"I didn't think you'd come," I said, failing to turn around to look at her because I could already sense an incoming storm.

"I wasn't sure you wanted to see me."

I felt her moving closer to me and held my breath.

"You look so good, Amelia," she said breathlessly as her hand moved gently and slowly along the curve of my waist.

She took a step closer to me and I could feel the warmth of her body fusing with mine and it made me tremble in restrained desire. She flattened her palm over my stomach and a strange unexpected sigh escaped my lips.

She was infecting me like a virus and taking full control of my body. She used her other free hand to move my hair aside, leaned close and softly kissed my neck. All sorts of goosebumps crawled up my skin, making every strand of hair on my body to rise in anticipation. I was so hot for her and she was barely doing much to draw such a reaction from me.

"Isabel," I moaned.

It was my birthday and my mother had said I deserved everything the world had to offer and I knew exactly what I wanted.

"Yes," she said, planting another kiss on my neck as she breathed into my ear, sending shivers of intense arousal through me.

"Get me out of here," I said.

In one swift motion, she turned me around, pinned me against the wall and crushed my lips with hers. She demanded entrance with her tongue, and I readily granted it.

Her hands were on my stomach, on my waist, on my hips, they were all over and I loved it. She lured my tongue into her mouth and I sought after treasures I never knew I desired.

There was a deep dangerous longing growing inside me with such violence, it frightened me. I'd never wanted anything or anyone so bad. I wanted her to undress me and make love to me right there against the elevator wall but before we could go any further, the doors opened and we pulled apart.

Luckily, there was no one outside the elevator. Isabel closed her hand around mine and stepped out. I obediently followed after her which was completely out of character for me.

When we got to the exit, she gave the valet her ticket and turned to face me while we waited for her car. The air outside was cold but my body was still hot from what Isabel had done to me in the elevator.

I could see the lust in her eyes. I could read her mind because everything going through her was the same thing going through me. We were an extension of each other.

She moved closer to me and I realized that if it wasn't for the powerful engine of the black Aston Martin that came to stop where we were, I would've been willing to let her do anything she wanted to me right there.

"You want to drive," she offered, handing me the keys to the car.

My father had been a collector so I loved automobiles. I took the keys from her hand and slid the door open, taking a seat on the extremely comfortable driver's seat.

When she got on the passenger seat and buckled up, she asked, "You like it?"

I stepped on the gas just to hear the powerful roar of the engine once more and my heart started racing because of the adrenaline pump. "I love it."

"Good, because it's your birthday present."

I looked at her in shock. "Are you serious?"

When she nodded, I squealed in a cocktail of arousal, joy and excitement.

"This is the side of you I wanted to see," she said.

It was a side I never knew I had, but I kinda liked it. "Thank you," I said, referring to the car right before I punched the gas and flew out of parking.

I glanced at her for a second then stepped on the gas, driving faster than the traffic rules allowed, and used my quick reflexes to navigate through the light traffic. In ten minutes, I was parking the car outside my building.

"You're a good driver," she said as we got out.

"I was around a lot of cars growing up. Wrecked a few too," I said, revealing the first detail about my past to her. "Come on." I took her hand as we approached the doorman at the entrance. He nodded politely as we walked past him and entered my building. We passed the reception area and headed to the elevators.

"Great place," she said.

"Thanks."

When we were in the elevator heading up to the penthouse, she pulled me back in her arms and kissed me senseless. I lost control again. It seemed to be an often occurrence whenever she kissed me.

The moment the elevator doors opened into my penthouse, I knew my whole world was about to change. We parted momentarily and made our way inside.

Now that we were there, alone, I was suddenly starting to grow nervous. I had no idea what I was doing and I didn't really know if I was ready for whatever was about to happen between us.

I pulled away from her and went to stand in the middle of the living room. My heart was racing in a mixture of anticipation and arousal.

She seemed to have that effect on me and I wasn't sure how I felt about it.

I could see the lust in her eyes and it was as primal and dangerous as the fire brewing in the pits of my core. I wasn't so sure if this was a good idea after all. Was I rushing into something I wasn't ready for?

Isabel swiftly made her way over to me and the moment her arms came around my waist, she cleared me of all doubt.

"Kiss me, Amelia," she said.

It had always been her making the first move, her initiating every kiss and now, she wanted me to do it. The intoxicating heat coming off her body drew me to her. I leaned in and closed my lips over hers and the moment she responded, that savage need in me came awake again.

She expertly removed my dress and I kicked off my shoes and a moment later we were making our way to my bedroom while I undressed her.

She laid me back on the bed and broke the kiss, pulling back to look at me. "God, Amelia, you're so damn beautiful," she said.

I didn't know if I felt so considering how exposed I felt in my black matching bra and panties.

"I've thought about you like this," she said, trailing her hand over my cleavage, drawing out the hunger in me.

When she laid herself on top of me and our bodies gently grinded against one another, the friction made me so hot I pulled her in for a fiery kiss. She stroked my skin with her fingers, leaving a warm tingling feeling wherever she touched.

I'd never had sex with anyone in my life and even when I'd tried to imagine it in the past, it had felt like an alien thought and had left me feeling weird and abnormal. This feeling had left me with little to no interest in sex.

Compared to what I was feeling at that moment, it felt like I had split into two different people. My fingers fumbled with Isabel's bra and when I finally managed to unhook it, she took it off to reveal a pair of firm ample breasts.

I'd never thought breasts would turn me on before, but looking at her made me feel like there was too much blood rushing to my head.

"Are you okay?" she asked.

She must've noticed my reaction. "I've never been with a woman before." I didn't want to reveal that I'd never actually had sex.

"I promise to make it worth your while," she said, drawing a smile from me as she kissed me.

I ran my hands over her naked back, enjoying the soft feel of her skin against my fingers and she gasped against my lips, making me realize she liked my touch. It was both empowering and encouraging so I did it again, this time moving my hands to cover her breasts.

She almost bit my lower lip. "That is too distracting," she whispered against my mouth as she placed my hands over the top of my head and effortlessly removed my bra. She gently ran her body against mine, making me moan from the pleasure of the friction of our bodies coming together.

She ran her hand over my bare breast and both my nipples stiffened in response. I breathed heavily, trying to control the sensations moving through my body and Isabel lowered her head and gently nibbled on my earlobe while her hand stroked my breast, making me involuntary jerk my leg at the unexpected sensations that went to settle at the moist lips between my legs.

She cupped both my breasts and I unconsciously thrusted my lower body upwards, moaning against her mouth when she met my lips for a kiss.

She trailed her lips down my neck and ran her index finger over the valley between my breasts right before she covered one nipple with her mouth, making me writhe beneath her.

The pleasure was too much for me to bear. Every feel and every kiss was new to me. My body was getting an introductory lesson to lovemaking from someone who knew far too well what she was doing and it was all too overwhelming.

I was grabbing at the white satin sheets spread across my bed trying to find an anchor and every time one sensation passed, another more powerful than the last took its place and then they would all merge and flow down my body to go meet at the wet spot starved for Isabel's attention.

"I want you, Isabel," I moaned.

I wanted her to touch me down there and put out the fire but she didn't seem to be in a hurry. In fact, my words excited her so much, she slowed her pace. She turned her attention to the other nipple and gently flicked it with her tongue right before she suckled on it, sending me closer to the edge.

She lowered her hand while her mouth continued shattering me with stirrings of pleasure I'd never known I'd come to love and using her forefingers, slowly rubbed the protruding bud that hungered for her attention.

The moment she came into contact with that part of me, everything intensified. My moans grew louder, the sensations magnified and the intense heat reverberating between us turned scorching hot.

Isabel must've noticed that I couldn't take it anymore because she slid the panties off my legs and returned her attention back down there. She had full and direct access to the one part of me no one had ever gotten close enough to touch and she was worth the wait.

I cried out in pleasure when her fingers motioned back and forth against the pink bud and when I couldn't take it anymore, she slid lower and slipped inside me.

I was aroused beyond despair and right when I thought this was the most powerful sensation I'd ever live to experience, she started stroking the upper walls of my moist source of pleasure and my body shuddered.

I was ready to reach climax and she knew it, but she pulled back momentarily sending my body into a state of frustrated agony then she slipped two fingers inside me and used her thumb to apply pressure on the sensitive bud still eager for her touch.

She slowly began thrusting while her thumb stimulated the pink erect nub and my breathing became quick and shallow as the pleasure ricocheted back and forth between the two sensitive spots, driving me closer and closer to ecstasy.

When I finally couldn't take it anymore, I unbuckled under her and spasms took refuge in me creating a shuddering mess of climatic bliss. She gently slipped out but my body continued to spasm in an uncontrollable manner.

I pulled away from her and curled into a ball, involuntarily moaning as my body shook and shuddered, reliving and recreating those sensations.

When I finally calmed down, I felt Isabel's hand snaking over my belly as her lips touched the back of my shoulder.

"Happy birthday," she said and we both broke into a fit of laughter.

I turned around to face her and ran my fingers over her cheek.

I felt so vulnerable and exposed, I wanted to put my mask back on.

"You're extraordinary," she whispered and pressed her lips against mine.

"So are you, Isabel."

"This was your first time ever, wasn't it?" she asked.

I took a deep breath and turned away from her, staring at the ceiling. What did she expect me to say?

"It's okay, Amelia. It makes it even more special."

She kissed my chest and moved closer so that our gazes were locked. There was an intimate silent communication between us, then a thought occurred to me.

"What were you doing in the elevator?"

"I was coming to your party."

"That late?"

"I didn't want to have to compete for your attention like everyone else and…"

"And what?"

"I didn't want to watch as all those people tried to win you over." She buried her face in the crook of my neck and a tingling sensation moved through me when her lips connected with my shoulder.

"Why did you leave?" she asked.

"My mother put me in a short dress and invited every successful eligible bachelor in New York, why do you think?"

"She's still trying to find you a suitor?"

I nodded.

She kissed my cheek and touched my chin, turning me to face her. "How come you've never been with anyone?" she asked.

I turned to look away, immediately put off by the pillow talk. I wasn't used to people asking me personal questions. Just because we'd slept together didn't mean she could start.

"I have to go to the bathroom," I said as I got out of bed, wrapping a satin sheet around myself to cover my nudity.

"Amelia, please don't push me away. I'm just trying to get to know you," Isabel said from the bed.

She didn't care to cover herself so her upper body was bare but she was still wearing her panties. She looked incredibly seductive.

"Well, stop." I didn't want to be vulnerable and if I gave her access into my life, she was going to have power over me. The sex had been great and maybe we could do that, but that was as far as it could go.

"Why are you so guarded?" she asked, getting out of bed now.

"I don't want to have this conversation," I said and left the room.

I locked myself in the bathroom and took a deep breath. I walked over to the mirror and stared at the reflection looking back. I ran my fingers through my hair and turned the knob, splashing some water over my face.

I didn't know how I was feeling. So much had happened that night, it felt like my feelings had been reshuffled. I'd never had any intimate human contact. I had no idea what to do now that it had happened.

Was I supposed to pour out my feelings now? Share my life? Bond? I couldn't do that. That part of me was missing. I'd never had to bond before. I had no idea how. I'd always kept people at an arm's length. The concept was completely foreign to me.

Maybe if I explained this to Isabel she'd understand. I wasn't trying to hurt her, this was just who I was. I wiped my face on a towel and walked out of the bathroom. When I went back to the bedroom, there was no trace of her. She'd left. I wasn't sure if that made me sad or relieved.

Chapter Twenty-Two

The untidy bed spoke of what had just taken place between us moments ago. I was pretty sure it was all I'd ever think of whenever I walked into the bedroom. Somehow, the room still retained Isabel's scent.

My stomach growled and I left the room in resignation, going to search my fridge for food. I'd not had a chance to eat at the party because I'd not had a moment to myself.

"I hope you don't mind, I helped myself to one of your robes," Isabel said from the couch.

I was stunned she was still there. "Uh, no, not at all," I said, almost tripping over the shoes I'd carelessly tossed off earlier.

"Are you hungry?" she asked and I noticed she was eating pizza. Where had she gotten pizza from?

"Starving," I said as I went to sit beside her. "Where'd you get this?"

"Your fridge," she said, handing me a plate with a large slice.

"I didn't know I had pizza in my fridge." I was hardly ever at home, but I had a housekeeper who came to clean and restock my fridge. It was pepperoni and cheese and it was delicious.

"It's good, huh?" Isabel said, watching as I ate.

"Great."

"Hey."

I looked at her soft features as I enjoyed the bite of pizza.

"I'm sorry if I came on to you a bit too strong. I know you're not used to this kind of thing so whenever I go a bit off rail, how about you tell me instead of running off to the bathroom."

I was taken aback by her statement. I didn't expect her to step up and take responsibility for something she wasn't to blame for.

She leaned forward and pressed her lips against mine and I responded. When she pulled back, I slowly opened my eyes, trying to fight off the growing need in me for her.

"I don't know what I'm hungrier for, the pizza or you," I said.

"Pick," she said.

I instantly placed the plate on the table and practically jumped her. That yearning in me arose as I devoured her lips, enjoying the thrill of being the one in control.

I laid her down on the couch and stretched myself on top of her as I disrobed her. She removed the sheet around my nudity and our bodies merged. Our heat came together to create a powerful ball of sexual energy.

When she went to turn me over, I broke the kiss and pulled back to look at her. I wanted to know her body. I wanted to kiss and touch every inch of her and I wanted to see her surrender herself to me.

Through a silent communication, she rested back on the couch and I moved my body against her, loving the friction of the rise of her breasts against mine. I gently kissed her lips, parting them slowly with my tongue and requested access.

When she conceded, I teased her tongue with mine and went further to tease the roof of her intoxicating mouth. She sighed against my lips as I kissed her in the same intense manner she'd kissed me then broke the kiss to follow a trail down her neck.

Her skin was smooth and soft. She was an incarnation of the perfect woman and the fact that I was the one giving her pleasure, and making her writhe beneath me in desire gave me immense joy.

I kissed and touched every inch of her with a hunger for knowledge of what she liked, and how she reacted to it. It was the most amazing thing I've ever done.

Her body was hot under mine as I learned the contours of her skin with my lips. I covered her aroused nipple with my mouth, loving the soft velvet taste and she sighed under me.

I was completely aroused by her reaction to me, but I was determined to drive her as wild as she'd driven me. She parted her legs when I turned my attention to the other nipple and noticed she was still in her panties.

No worry, there was no rush. I thought, smiling to myself as I ran my hands over her upper body, cupping her breasts as I mercilessly played with her nipples.

She moaned softly, thrusting her lower body against me. I kissed my way down, positioning myself perfectly along her body as her chest heaved in an up and down motion.

I pressed my tongue in her inverted navel and her hands moved over my head, with her fingers moving through my hair. I was extremely turned on at this point, but I proceeded in my quest to give her pleasure.

When I got to her lower abdomen, I pulled down her panties and gently ran my index finger over the pink erect nub, at first in curiosity at what it would do to Isabel when I touched her then at fascination at the reaction it drew.

She moved her lower body up to reach for my touch and I looked up to watch her face as I gently stroked her. She looked like she was in a world of her own and I was the one who had taken her there.

Curious to know more, I wondered how the soft nub tasted like and closed my mouth over it, gently running the tip of my tongue against it. Isabel moaned and pulled her hands over her face.

I did it again a couple of more times, loving the soft taste of her in my mouth then focused on the glistening moisture on her entrance.

"Stop teasing me, Amelia," she said.

I ran my finger along the outline of her outer folds, gently exploring this new intriguing object of my obsession.

"Amelia, please," Isabel begged.

At her request, I slipped a finger inside her and was amazed by the hot, moist welcoming embrace. I stroked her back and forth then slid in another finger when she thrusted her pelvis forward, matching my rhythm.

Isabel was moaning freely now. I placed my free arm around her waist to hold her in place and thrusted harder but carefully, running my forefingers in a come-hither motion against the walls of her vagina.

I was completely mesmerized by how amazing it felt and the exhilaration was making my own groin throb in need. Isabel's walls started closing around my fingers and she threw her head back as a violent orgasm shook her body.

I withdrew from her and examined the dew on my fingers. When her gaze met mine, I placed both fingers in my mouth and licked off the juice. Her eyes widened in surprise and I smiled at her, loving the delicious taste of her.

I crawled back up on top of her and kissed her lips, allowing her to have a little taste of herself. It didn't escape my mind that this was the wildest thing I'd ever done or the fact that I liked it immensely.

"I want this, whatever it is," Isabel said later after we'd gotten back to bed. "It doesn't have to involve conversation that makes you uncomfortable, we don't even have to talk at all as long as we do this and I get to be around you."

"Really?" I asked.

I felt her nod.

We were spooning and her arms were warmly and intimately wrapped around my neck and my waist.

"I may not give you everything you want," I said.

What if she started seeking a deeper connection that I couldn't offer her? What then? Would she leave? Would she stay? Was it fair to her?

"If this is the only way I can have you, then it's everything that I need," she said.

I wanted to be selfish with her and if this was what she wanted, then it was more than enough for me.

"Don't you think an Aston Martin is too extravagant a gift to give?" I asked, wanting to change the subject incase it progressed deeper than I was willing it to go.

"You can't put a price on happiness," she said.

"I assume your father hasn't taken everything from you then?"

"He tried."

"Really? What did you do?"

"I can't tell you, it's a bit embarrassing," she said.

That made me even more curious. "I want to know. Come on, tell me."

"I ratted him out to my mother," she said.

She'd never mentioned her mother before so I was a bit surprised to find out she was still in the picture.

"They're one of those bitterly divorced parents who can't stand each other but they love me. I had dinner with my mother and mentioned the idea to her, just to gauge her reaction and she was a little more supportive than I expected so I told her what my father thought about it and what he was doing and she said she'd take care of it."

"What did she do?"

"I don't know, but my father has backed off and somehow, our relationship is still intact."

"I'm glad everything worked out for you," I said, wishing my parents had been as loving to me as hers seemed to be.

"It's been a bit of a struggle, headbutting with board members and associates."

"It'll take a while to establish yourself. By the time you start making any real impact you'll probably be tired and just about ready to give up."

"Are you serious? That is how you encourage me?"

I was so used to working with facts and numbers it didn't occur to me to offer a word of encouragement. This was why I wasn't very good with people on a personal level. My mind worked with facts, not luck.

"I'm sorry, I'm terrible at this."

She planted a kiss on my shoulder blade.

"I'd never be brave enough to do what you're doing," I said.

"I read about you on the Time Magazine. You took over your father's European company at eighteen and made it a major success."

"That's because I was my father. Everyone who worked for me knew they had no choice but to do their work and follow my leadership. There was no room for doubt or error."

"How is that so different from what I'm doing?"

"You invested in a large company. By the time you got there the rules had already been set. It's you who gets to adapt. If you don't like the way things are, find a way to purchase more stock and be the majority shareholder. Everyone else will have to answer to you. Just make sure you know what you're doing."

I didn't know how the conversation had drifted to business, but we were both tired and shortly after, we fell asleep.

Chapter Twenty-Three

"Here is a full report of the progress so far." I handed my mother the files.

"Amelia, sit down I want to talk to you for a moment," she said, getting to her feet as she came to offer me a seat on the black leather couch across her desk.

I had a feeling whatever was coming wasn't going to be good but I sat down and braced myself.

"Whatever it is that is going on with you, I want you to know that you can share it with me," she started as she sat down beside me.

I tensed up in surprise. What was this all about?

"I know things have been a little tense between us, but it's not something we can't work through."

"What are you talking about?" I asked in confusion.

"It's humiliating to host a party for my daughter, who is the guest of honor, and then she disappears halfway through. It leaves people with a very bad image. It makes them think you don't respect me," she said.

I didn't know what to say or even where to start. "And it's not humiliating for you to try and set me up with someone every time you insist on my presence for these parties?" I asked.

"Amelia, you just turned twenty-one. It's time for you to start thinking about finding someone," she said.

"Don't you think that should be my choice to make?"

"Why have you become so rebellious?" she asked.

Rebellious? Just because I wasn't going along to whatever plans she was making for me before even informing me? Was she serious?

"Our relationship has always been very simple. We both do our jobs and stay out of each other's lives." I got to my feet.

"Stay out of each other's lives? You're my daughter." She was calm and composed.

"I'm not acting out, Mother. This is who I've always been. You'd know that if you'd taken the time to get to know me."

"I'm trying, but you won't give me a chance." She got to her feet and walked over to me.

I took a step away from her and said, "What you're trying to do is find a suitor for me. What you're trying to do is find a way to control me."

"Amelia," she said.

"Stop, Mother. Please."

I didn't understand. I'd become what she'd carefully molded. If there were faults in the product she'd created, that was on her.

"I have to get back to work," I said as I left her office.

A couple of days had passed since my birthday, since my night with Isabel. She'd gone back to work, as had I, but before parting ways we'd thoroughly and tirelessly relived our night of passion.

We'd not made any plans since we both had very demanding careers and I wasn't sure if or when we were going to see each other again. I thought about her more often than I desired because I found it distracting.

When I got back to my office, I received a troubling call from Germany. One of the drugs we manufactured was receiving negative reports due to some lethal side effects to users when ingested and one of the people who'd been affected by this was suing Winston Enterprises.

I called my lawyers from Germany and shortly after made traveling arrangements. I needed to be there personally to take care of this. The drugs the company manufactured went through thorough testing and if the side effects were lethal, we discontinued the drug or redesigned it.

There had never been any reports of lethal side effects for this particular drug and it had been in the market for almost a year now so I didn't understand where this was coming from. Someone had made a mistake and I needed to go figure out where things had gone wrong and fix it.

I was about to leave the office when my phone rang. I saw Isabel's number and stopped to look at it. This was terrible timing because I had to go put out a fire.

"Hi Isabel, I'm afraid this is bad timing. I can't talk right now," I said.

"What's wrong?" she asked.

"I have to be in a flight to Germany in an hour."

"I haven't been to Germany in a while," she said.

I was about to respond when a thought crossed my mind. "If you're not too busy, maybe you can accompany me." I was almost certain being with her would calm me down.

"Uh, it's a bit crazy around here but let me see what I can do," she said.

I wasn't sure if I was disappointed, but I tried not to focus on such trivial feelings.

"Okay, I have to go." I hang up before she responded and left the office, notifying my secretary to inform my mother I was leaving for Germany.

Impromptu traveling always messed with my schedule so I had to postpone meetings with lawyers, bankers and important business associates and as for the ones I was unable to get out of, I had to inform some of my representatives to attend in my place. Others I could handle via calls.

When I was done, I headed to the airport. I never really needed to pack for some of the trips because I had an on call personal shopper who made sure I had everything I required whenever I was in a country.

I preferred traveling in some of the smaller company jets but in recent years, the company had upgraded some of the planes to bigger, better modern jets but one of my favorites was a customized luxurious converted Boeing 737.

It was a hundred-seat airliner with a redesigned interior to accommodate only twenty passengers. This Boeing flaunted a spacious lounge with a television, a large bedroom with a king-sized bed and a private bathroom with a hot shower, a kitchen with convection and microwave oven, a refrigerator and a wine cooler and a marble-paneled dining room. This flying luxury apartment was one of a fleet of ten planes.

"Are we ready for takeoff?" I asked the pilot when I got inside and found a flight attendant preparing the lounge.

"Yes, Ma'am," he said.

I nodded at him and went to take a seat.

"I like what you've done with the place," Isabel's voice came from the back and I turned to watch her approach me.

I was surprised to see her, especially because she'd sounded unsure about accompanying me on the trip. "What are you doing here? I thought you were busy," I said, uncomfortably aware of how glad I was to see her.

"I told you, I haven't been to Germany in a while," she said as she came to take a seat right next to me.

"How did you manage to get here so fast?"

"I have my ways," she said.

I smiled at her and put on my seatbelt.

"So, what's in Germany?" she asked as we prepared for liftoff.

"A problem that needs fixing."

Isabel bit her thumbnail while she half-smiled at me then shook her head.

"What?" I asked.

She was wearing a snow-white knee-high trench coat that made her eyes and her hair look even darker. Her pink shade of lipstick made her mouth look very desirable.

"You look great," she said.

I smiled at her, oddly pleased by her compliment.

The plane taxied down the runway and shortly after started its ascent.

When we were on the air, Isabel got to her feet and went to the wine cooler in the kitchen. She came back with a bottle of white wine and two glasses.

I watched her in wonder as she came over to me, pecked my lips and walked past me, heading to the back of the plane where she'd come from when I'd arrived.

I got to my feet and followed her, wondering what she was up to. I was pleasantly surprised when I walked into the bedroom to find a trail of her shoes and trench coat on the floor.

"You thirsty?" she asked and my jaw dropped.

She was wearing a seductively sexy lacy red teddy. The sight of her made my throat go dry and I couldn't find the words to answer her as I lustfully stared.

"Well?" She had a smile across her face as she held out a glass of wine for me.

I could feel the pace of my heartbeat increasing as I summoned my feet to move forward. My eyes hungrily moved over her sexy frame and I swallowed a ball of air as I stretched out my arm and reached for the wine.

She tilted her head, slowly stuck the tip of her tongue out one side of her mouth and slightly squinted her eyes as she moved the wine glass over to her lips then paused, watching me.

I unconsciously took a sip of the wine and coughed a bit because of the dryness in my throat.

"You okay there?" she asked, taking a step closer to me.

I nodded, fully aware of how painfully attracted I was to her.

"Nice um…outfit." My brain had shut down. I couldn't think. Had I just stuttered?

"Glad you like it."

She took the glass of wine from my hand, placed it on the bedside table and slowly got on the bed, posing seductively.

"Want to join me?" she asked.

I didn't know why my body wasn't operating the way it should've been. My speech was impaired, my brain wasn't functioning properly and my feet were weak and couldn't move.

I somehow managed to approach the bed and she gave me that amused look I'd initially resented. I think she could tell I was having trouble because she sat up from the bed and stood up to help me.

She moved her arms around my body, deliberately pulling me closer to her and her wonderful scent filled my nostrils. Her lips were so close to mine, but I knew her mission was to torture me as she slowly reached for the zipper on the back of my dress and slowly lowered it.

I released a shaky breath as her fingers touched the exposed flesh on my back, moving back up my shoulders to ease my dress off. She was killing me inside, moving so delicately slow.

She pulled my dress down and I summoned my strength to assist her because her speed and deliberate touches were driving me crazy.

When I pulled my arms free from the dress, she lowered it down my chest, to my waist and then to my hips, pausing down there to place a light kiss over my panties.

I kicked off my shoes and completely freed myself from the dress and she held me in place, laying soft moist kisses along my stomach while her hands moved gently over my thighs and hips.

She slightly parted my legs and trailed kisses down my lower abdomen and I inhaled deeply as I closed my eyes, knowing the last of my strength was just about to leave me.

Her hands moved over my waistline and her fingers lowered my panties down my legs, making me gasp in anticipation. I couldn't believe how much power she had over me, commanding my body as though she'd enslaved it.

"On my way over, I couldn't stop thinking about how much I wanted to kiss you," she said.

Kiss me? I thought, just as her warm moist mouth covered my hot slick sex.

My feet unbuckled at contact and she laid me back on the bed. She didn't pause as her mouth quickly reunited with my core centre and she continued to fervently explore me, making me go utterly out of my mind.

I moaned and squirmed under her while her tongue teased the now extremely sensitive part of me, sending countless waves of sensations all through my body. I cried out in pleasure, thrusting my pelvis forward and she applied more pressure with her tongue then gently slipped inside me. Shortly after that, she sent me plunging into a fit of orgasmic spasms.

I hated how good she was at giving me pleasure because that little fact made her exceptionally unique and no one had ever done that to me.

She got on top of me and I ran my hands over the sexy lacy garment she was wearing. I couldn't believe that little outfit had rendered me absolutely powerless.

Things between us progressed really fast from there. When we got to Germany, Isabel kept herself busy though she wouldn't tell me what she was doing. I got into work mode, visited the factory and had the drugs that were causing problems tested.

Turned out they had a foreign contaminant so they had to be pulled from the market. A new batch was carefully made and tested to replace the contaminated ones and the person suing was anonymously offered a more than generous settlement.

Isabel was called back a day after we arrived so she didn't stay long but we made most of the period of time we spent together. She brought out a new side of me. She made me laugh. She made me soft. But weirdly enough, I liked it.

My stay in Germany lasted three days. After I fixed the problem and was certain careful measures had been taken to make sure there wouldn't be a repeat of what had happened, I went back to New York.

I found Isabel in my apartment waiting for me and something about it made my heart beat. It was like the first time my heart had ever palpitated. She'd made dinner and set it presentably on the dining table. We sat indulging in the surprisingly delicious meal, aware that I was experiencing something new, something foreign but I didn't let it shake me.

Chapter Twenty-Four

We occupied most of our conversational gaps with work talk. Isabel filled me in on most of what was going on in her business and I did the same with mine.

I found her fascinating. She had great dreams. Healthcare wasn't just a business venture to her as I came to learn, it was a passion.

She took my advice, purchased more stock and bought out most of the shareholders, then hired the best minds in the business quickly becoming a healthcare magnate.

During that period, we tried to see each other as often as possible, but it proved hard because our careers were far too demanding.

After three months of an intense love affair, Isabel grew impossibly busy. We were always in two different continents or countries. We tried to communicate as often as possible, but since I was incapable of an emotional relationship, it became a bit strained.

When she wanted reassurance, I was unable to offer it because I believed she knew I was with her in a manner I'd never been with anyone else and that should've said what I couldn't.

When she wanted companionship and I was too busy, I thought she understood because we'd never let what we shared get in the way of our work life. So in a way, it was complicated but I thought we both understood each other.

I was too afraid to step out of my world and live the life that dared me to want more, because I thought and believed I already had everything.

My mother eased up on her attempts to reach out to me, which I liked. We were finally on the same page. She respected me as a business woman and I respected her in the same capacity. She didn't use Eric to get to me but his struggle in Belize was still amusing to me.

I could've helped, but he thought he deserved the position and the added responsibility so I stayed out of his way.

During my fifth month with Isabel, I believed things were going to work out in every aspect of my life. I was willing to try and explore the possibility of giving her what she needed from me. I wasn't quite sure I knew what that was, but she made me daring enough to want to give it a chance.

A couple of days later, I received a troubling call from Mr. Price.

Isabel was in the hospital.

She was critically ill.

Apparently, she'd had lung cancer all along and during the last few months, it had spread to other vital organs and there was nothing doctors could do for her.

I refused to go see her. I couldn't believe the news. There were these sharply disturbing pangs of pain with every beat of my heart every moment I thought about it.

Why would Isabel let me get close to her, let me trust her, having known she had a terminal illness? Would she really be that cruel?

I thought about it for days.

When I couldn't function, I decided to go see her. It was out of anger and frustration rather than responsibility and concern. I wanted her to see just how pissed off I was. But the moment I walked into her hospital room, all that rage disappeared.

Seeing her so pale and weak awakened something in me. Sympathy.

I was seated next to her bed, terribly afraid of what I was about to lose.

"You hate me, don't you?" she asked.

I wanted to say no, but she knew I'd be lying. "Yes, I hate you."

"I'm sorry, Amelia. I want to explain something to you, if you'll let me," she said.

I watched her for a moment then nodded.

"If it was up to me, I'd spend my every waking moment with you."

"No... no, Isabel. You don't get to say that." My heart was breaking and I wasn't even aware of it.

"I love you, Amelia. I don't know if you understand what that means, but you've become one of the most important people in my life."

"No, don't say anymore. I don't want to hear it," I said as I got to my feet and took a few steps away from her.

"For some stupid reason, I genuinely believed this would be easy on you. I didn't think it'd hurt you. That's why I never said anything. It made it easy to be with you."

I looked at her as though she'd just slapped me hard across the face.

"Because I don't feel anything?" I asked, trying to contain the rage brewing inside.

"Not to the extent that other people do, and it's okay," she said.

Uncontrollable tears started streaming down my face. There was a painful ball in my throat and those pangs in my heart were intensifying.

"I got into the healthcare business because I thought with enough time and research, we could develop a cure. Getting into this, I knew I wouldn't have enough time and I'd already made my peace with that. I did all I could to stay healthy, in the end, all I wanted was to be happy. "

When I didn't respond, she asked, "What would someone who has all the money in the world do if they knew their life is just about to end?"

Well, she couldn't exactly buy life. But she could buy a business that dealt with saving lives, which explained her passion for the healthcare business.

"What would they do?" I asked, unsure of my answer.

She was struggling to speak while I was inwardly struggling to control myself.

"I chose to live, Amelia. I chose to love. I chose you."

Her words broke me and nothing had ever broken me before. "You can't do this to me, Isabel. You can't let me…" I tried to gesture with my hands in an effort to express myself, but I didn't know what I was trying to say.

It was all happening too soon and it felt like someone had punctured a hole in my heart and I was helplessly bleeding out.

"It's not my choice."

"It was your choice. You could've told me."

"And then what? Would you have stayed with me?" she asked.

She knew I couldn't lie. There was a part of me that wanted to tell her I would have, but we both knew the truth. Before I could come up with a suitable answer, the machines started beeping.

Nurses and doctors flooded into the room, quickly asking me to leave but I watched in horror as her doctors tried to work on her until the nurses managed to get me out, and locked the doors.

I'd never seen anything like it.

My hands were shaking out of dreaded fear. My heart was experiencing some sort of disconnect, almost like something inside me was breaking and I couldn't ... I couldn't move.

An hour later, I was standing at the waiting room with Isabel's parents when her doctor came and gave us the news.

Isabel was gone.

I remember her parents embracing, crying in helplessness, in desperation.

I was numb.

I never attended her funeral.

Three weeks later, I was summoned by her lawyer. I needed to be present in the reading of her will. She'd invested over half a billion dollars in the healthcare industry and she left it all to me.

Chapter Twenty-Five

BOOK THREE: OLIVIA AND AMELIA

"You'll not believe this!"

"What? What's going on?" I asked, a little surprised by the enthusiasm.

"Some art promoter guy came across my work and wants a few of my pieces showcased in an art gala. You see, every year he chooses a random art student from different campuses. Somehow, he came across my work and he liked it," Rex said.

"Oh, my goodness! That's amazing!"

I jumped into his arms.

"Some of the most prominent artists of our time are going to be there, Olivia."

I pulled back to look at him. "Hey, this is your big break. You get to show the world just how talented you are," I said.

"I just– I didn't expect this. It came out of nowhere."

"You should focus on the fact that it has happened."

"I know, but…"

I wrapped my arms around him. I could tell this was a huge deal for him.

"I hope I'm your plus one," I said.

"Of course, you are," he said. "I got the news today. I had to tell you first."

"That's sweet, Rex."

His family supported his art, but lived in Alberta, Canada. The only difference between us was that his parents continued financially supporting his studies while I supported myself.

"They told me on short notice. The art gala is tomorrow night."

"Tomorrow is Friday."

"I know. The promoter guy called me last night."

I'd spent a whole week in the Gallagher mansion. I needed a break.

Every single day had been spent in the office trying to learn and get myself accustomed to Mrs. Gallagher's work life. I loved my job, and I thoroughly enjoyed working for her, but I didn't like being in the office all the time. It made me feel like I was in prison.

I think the worst part was that I never got to see her and our communication was very limited. When I asked her to assign me someone for assistance, I had to email her, leave a note on her desk and leave a voicemail on her phone.

When she did assign me someone, she sent me a guy called Colin Peterson. He was good, in fact, he was great. He made me wonder why she was still letting me work for her.

She had a large group of established employees. I was a single, probably faint shadow unnoticeably orbiting around her, but for some reason she'd chosen me. That should've made me feel good but it made me feel unqualified.

So, did I need to take a break and go to an art gala with my best friend? I think so.

When Rex picked me up, I was wearing one of the elegant outfits I'd bought myself in Paris. It had only been a week but I was still experiencing pangs of guilt for overindulging in Mrs. Gallagher's wealth.

Even wearing one of the amazing outfits I'd bought myself made me feel bad, but when I wore the pendant Mrs. Gallagher had given me, I felt less guilty.

"Oh wow!"

"What? I'm I overdressed?" I asked when I opened the door for Rex the following evening. He was dressed in a pinstripe suit and a nice tie. He looked great, as he stared back at me in awe.

"You're ravishing," he said.

I smiled. "You don't look too bad yourself."

He leaned forward and gave me a light hug and peck on the cheek, then stood back to look at me again.

"Okay, stop that," I said.

"Oh, trust me, I'm trying," he said playfully as he extended his arm.

"I hope you don't mind us taking your car," he said.

I rolled my eyes and laughed.

"What? You're making more money than me," he teased.

I had received my first monthly paycheck from Mrs. Gallagher, which had taken care of most of my immediate bills and expenses so I was going to be okay for a while.

"I need a miracle to get out of my financial situation."

"With this job, you just might get a miracle," he said.

I pecked his cheek as we headed downstairs.

"So how many pieces were chosen?" I asked.

"Two paintings and two sculptures," he said.

We headed to the venue in Manhattan using my crappy car and in forty-five minutes, he was driving into parking.

I was a little tired from work because I'd been confined to my office all week, but I was eager to see the night unfold.

"This art promoter guy, do you know his name?" I asked.

"I'm sure he told me, but I got so excited from the news, I forgot. He sent someone this morning to come pick up the pieces."

"How do you know he's legit?"

"I asked around school, plus the guys he sent to pick up the pieces came with some documents for me to sign."

It shouldn't have bothered me that all this had taken place in just a couple of days, but it did. I didn't want to express my concern in case I was wrong.

"That's the venue, right there," he said, pointing to the building.

There were fine cars driving by, stopping at the entrance and dropping people off. There were also a couple of valets by the entrance. The event appeared to have an elite list of guests.

"I knew the gala was a big deal, but I didn't think there'd be so many fancy people," Rex said.

Me neither. "Don't be nervous, you're going to be great."

"You hosted this kind of thing a few weeks ago, what should I do?"

I was very aware that we were still in my car parked some distance away. "Well, I noticed the artists would move slowly through the crowd talking to potential buyers. When someone viewed a piece, the artist would approach them and talk about it."

"Great, thanks."

"We should probably go inside now."

"Yeah," he said.

He took a deep breath and we both got out of the car.

We headed for the entrance and he handed over the invitation cards. When we walked inside, I was a little surprised to find out it was actually a big event.

"Oh, my God," he said.

"Hey, don't worry. It's going to be a great night," I said, squeezing his hand.

He nodded, even though he still looked nervous.

"Okay, let's get some wine and find this promoter guy so that we can figure out where your pieces are," I said.

The gala reminded me of Jaime's art gallery. The difference was that it had only two large halls with ample space for guests to move about and the art display was carefully placed and well spaced.

There were a few people present, but the gala was going to start in about an hour so I assumed the rest of the guests would've shown up by then.

Rex took two glasses of champagne from a waiter who was moving around the room and handed me one. I was about to take a sip when he emptied his glass in one long swig.

"Hey, these are snotty rich people. You need to act like you're one of these established artists and not a struggling artist from Queens," I said.

"I'm sorry," he said.

I smiled at him and pulled him aside. At this rate he wasn't going to be able to function properly. He was far too nervous.

"Alright, listen. You're an incredibly talented artist. All you have to do is move around the room, take a look at the other pieces of art and get to know your audience. It's that simple and you're going to be great."

He relaxed and smiled at me.

"You're the best, Liv," he said, lightly pecking my cheek.

I got him another glass of champagne and he took a proper sip.

We started moving around the room slowly observing the pieces.

I didn't have that artistic perception, but the pieces were eye catching.

"Wow, these guys are really good," Rex said.

Intimidatingly so, but then so was he.

"I'll go look for the promoter," he said.

I moved along the room, observing the large paintings hanging on the walls and the sculptures on display.

More people had arrived and the soft music playing in the background was accompanied by the humming sound of the guests discussing the art pieces.

"Olivia?" A familiar feminine voice said my name and I turned around in surprise, wondering who had recognized me.

When my gaze met Jaime's, I froze.

"Olivia, what're you doing here?" she asked.

"Uhm... my friend Rex," I said, trying to think.

"Oh, yeah, I remember him."

"His pieces were chosen for the gala by an art promoter so..." Why was she talking to me as though she'd forgotten what had happened between us?

"Oh, I didn't know they endorsed students. But that's great for Rex, he must be very excited," she said.

She looked great but standing next to her carrying out a casual conversation felt a little weird. "He is," I said.

"Listen, I'm sorry for the way I left things off. It's just that–"

"You don't have to do that," I said.

"Do what?"

"Explain," I said.

She looked at me as though she wanted to tell me something then slowly nodded.

"You look good, Livvy," she said, her gaze softening.

I was glad when Rex chose that moment to join us.

"I found him," he said.

"Hi Rex," Jaime said.

Rex stared at her with a bit of hostility and said, "Hi," he turned to me and added, "Come on, Livvy." He placed his arm over my shoulder and took me away.

"Are you okay?" he asked.

"I think so."

I was a little confused. I'd liked her so much and seeing her was a bit of a surprise but there was no hurt or anger in me towards her.

"I didn't know she'd be here tonight," he said.

I took a deep breath and turned to face him. "You couldn't have known. It's okay. I'm fine."

"You sure?"

"Surprisingly, yes."

"Okay, you want me to introduce you to the promoter? He showed me where my pieces are, we can head there after you meet him. The display is amazing. It makes my work merge in with the rest," he said.

"Sure, let's go."

We went to the second hall which had quite a number of art pieces on display.

"Over there."

I followed Rex to his promoter and froze for the second time that night when he said, "Excuse me, Mr. Connor?"

Frank Connor turned around and his gaze widened in what appeared to be recognition.

"Olivia, how nice to see you," he said.

"Nice to see you too," I said.

I should've known I'd run into Jaime or Frank. They were both in the art world and the gala was a big event. Now the only person missing was Mrs. Gallagher. At the thought, my heart skipped a beat. Was it possible? Could she be present?

"Your friend here is quite gifted," Frank Connor said.

"Yes, he is," I said.

"Thank you, Mr. Connor. Come on, Livvy," Rex said.

He closed his hand around mine and led me away from Frank Connor.

"How do you two know each other?" he asked.

"He works for Mrs. Gallagher. Remember Cleopatra's headpiece?"

He quickly nodded. "No wonder I thought he looked familiar."

"This night keeps getting more and more interesting," I said.

He took me to where his pieces were displayed.

"This is amazing," I said, noticing the same thing he had.

The display was perfectly merged with the rest of the pieces in the hall. "Congratulations, you're in the big league now," I said, gently patting his shoulder.

I was so excited for him. He'd always been so committed to his art and it was finally paying off. This gala was going to expose his work to the world of art lovers.

"Now that you know where my pieces are, why don't you go mingle with the crowd and check out the rest of the art," Rex said.

"Are you going to be okay?"

"Yeah, I want to see the art too. When I spot someone checking out my work, I'll just come over and see what they think."

"Okay," I said.

I watched him proudly as he walked away to view the other art pieces. I studied his pieces for a while then moved on, silently listening to what people were saying about the pieces they were viewing.

They might as well have been speaking Latin. It felt like we were looking at two different works of art. When I looked at an abstract painting, I saw a mix of colors merged together on canvas.

I continued along, listening to what a couple of women were saying about a sculpture. It was an abstract sculpture. I walked away from them sadly reaffirming I was not an artistic person.

Rex made abstract art sometimes, but for some reason, I seemed to understand his. But it was easy because he always explained them to me.

An hour and a half later, I was on my third glass of wine. I assumed all the guests had arrived because the halls were a bit crowded, but not enough to be annoying. Rex had disappeared, but I wasn't looking for him because I knew he was working.

After exhausting the artwork in the second hall, I went back to the first since I'd not had much of a chance to check them out. It was less crowded there and easier to spot a person.

Rex found me half an hour later and he seemed ecstatic. I laughed at his enthusiasm and asked, "What's going on?"

"All my pieces have been bought," he said.

"What?" I wrapped my arms around him.

"Yeah, can you believe it?"

We pulled apart. "Who bought them? Do you know?"

"No, it was an anonymous buyer," he said.

"Wow, that was fast," I said.

"Yeah, Mr. Connor said he's interested in being my agent so we're going to meet on Monday morning to discuss it."

"That's amazing!"

"I know. I can't believe it myself," he said.

I was about to respond when my gaze settled on an image across the room. I could hear Rex talking but I wasn't listening to him anymore.

She was there.

She wasn't directly facing me but from the angle at which we stood, it was clear enough for me to see her face. God, she was sensational. I hadn't seen her all week. I couldn't believe how much I'd missed her.

"Liv, are you listening to me?"

I looked at him as I tried to shake Mrs. Gallagher's image out of my mind. For a moment, I thought I'd imagined her presence. "Sorry, what?" I asked.

He followed the direction my gaze had been fixated on and a smile rose on his lips. "I didn't know she'd be here," he said.

I followed his gaze and watched Mrs. Gallagher from a distance. She was talking to Frank Connor. "Neither did I," I said.

"You want to go say hello?" he asked.

"Should I? Would that be appropriate?" I was suddenly nervous.

"I think it's appropriate," he said, but the smile on his face was misleading.

Frank walked away from her and then she turned. Somehow, across the room our gazes met and locked.

"Go to her. It would be rude at this point not to," Rex said as he left me alone.

The rest of the room fell silent and as though by magic, a pathway to her cleared. I was so uneasy I couldn't bring myself to take that first step, then as though by some pull, I started walking over to her.

Chapter Twenty-Six

"Hello Mrs. Gallagher, I didn't expect to run into you," I said.

I would've stretched out my hand to shake hers in greeting, but I was afraid if I touched her in any way, I'd want to do more.

"Hello Olivia, it's lovely to see you," she said.

I was enchanted by her words and had to force my brain to function in order to carry out a conversation with her. "My friend…uh– Rex, I think I've mentioned him before…" With her busy lifestyle, I doubted she'd recall any personal information I'd shared. "He's an artist. Frank Connor sought him out as an art promoter." I studied her beautiful ageless face.

"Oh, I see," she said.

I didn't realize until that moment that she might've had something to do with Rex's art having been chosen by Frank Connor. The thought was absurd, but having spent enough time with Mrs. Gallagher to know her, especially after the stunt she'd pulled in Paris, I couldn't be sure.

"Mrs. Gallagher, did you ask Frank to talk to Rex?" I asked, knowing I could be wrong but braving it.

She calmly looked at me and said, "No."

I exhaled in relief.

"I asked him to take a look at his work," she said.

I wasn't sure if it was her brutal honesty or her statement that struck me most.

A second before I could respond, a couple joined us. They politely greeted Mrs. Gallagher and dubiously extended their greetings to me, ignoring me while carrying out a conversation with her.

The thing was though, they didn't bother me. It was what Mrs. Gallagher had said that did. Was she endorsing Rex through Frank? Why would she do something like that?

The art gala was clearly an event for popular modern artists. And I remembered Jaime saying she didn't know they endorsed students. So, was this one of Mrs. Gallagher's ploys? And if so, what was her goal?

I cleared my throat and excused myself as they talked, while thoughts swirled through my head.

Why was Mrs. Gallagher reaching out to my best friend? What was she trying to accomplish? Yes, Rex was a great artist and he more than anyone deserved this opportunity, but at what cost did it come?

"Olivia."

I was outside the building getting some air and trying to assemble my thoughts. Since all the guests had already arrived, I was out there by myself.

I thought about going home but Rex had the keys to the car. I figured a taxi would do when I heard Mrs. Gallagher's voice.

I turned to look at her, wondering why she had followed me outside. She was a Gallagher, a queen in her own right. Why would she care to know what I thought, or how I felt?

To be honest I would've been much happier if I hadn't found out she was responsible for Rex's work being displayed at the gala. It made me doubt her intention and made me worry because I had a feeling Rex would be unhappy to learn the truth.

It felt like she was manipulating me. But was it really manipulation if it turned out she didn't want anything from me or my best friend?

"I didn't–" I stopped, trying to remind myself that this woman was my boss and I wasn't trying to get myself fired. "Mrs. Gallagher, did you ask Frank Connor to endorse Rex for the gala?"

Mrs. Gallagher slowly walked up to me. I tried to read her but her face gave nothing away. We were standing out there alone and it was quiet, with dimmed security light illuminating the surroundings.

"Yes," she said.

Again, her honesty was unexpected.

"Frank acting like an art promoter was all your idea?" I asked.

"He is an art promoter, but I brought your friend's work to his attention."

I took a step back. "Why would you do that? You don't know Rex. He doesn't matter to you," I argued.

"He matters to you," she said softly.

I speechlessly stared at her.

"You said if you'd had a chance to tell him about the previous art event, you would have," she said.

"So you sent your art guy to go and recruit him?"

I tried to match her calm poise but I was upset. I didn't want to lose my cool and Mrs. Gallagher was being such a lady as she spoke, she was like a mother soothing a child, which inwardly annoyed me. I wanted to break that façade but she was an impenetrable iceberg.

"Olivia, you expressed you wanted your friend to be in an art event."

I recalled the conversation. "Yes, I did. But I only said that because if he'd known about that particular event, he would've applied."

"I don't understand why you're upset. I was trying to help."

The sad thing was, she was right. She'd done this in an attempt to help. I should've been grateful, but Rex was probably going to be upset with me. He preferred to earn things through merit.

"Are you the one who purchased his pieces?" I asked.

"No," she said then added, "Olivia, if you don't want Frank to pursue this, all you have to do is say so but you should know, he believes in your friend's ability and thinks he can help."

That was Rex's decision to make but I wasn't sure I could tell him. What if he got upset and ended up resenting me? He was so happy about all that was going on.

"I'm sorry for overreacting," I said.

"It's fine," she said.

I was a little bit embarrassed. Sure Mrs. Gallagher taking a step to help Rex was a little suspicious and I was well within my right to doubt her intention but maybe I should've been more grateful instead. She'd always had a giving heart.

"Are you going back inside?" she asked.

I wasn't sure I could face Rex just yet. He was having a great night and I was afraid I wouldn't be able to conceal the truth from him. I needed time to absorb it.

"I think I'll just head home," I said.

"Do you want a ride? I was thinking of leaving too."

Since I'd been considering taking a taxi, I didn't see any reason to turn down a free ride. "That'll be great, thank you."

She nodded and retrieved her phone from her purse.

I retrieved my own phone and text messaged Rex so he wouldn't worry or look for me. A few minutes later, Mrs. Gallagher's car came to stop where we were standing.

Suddenly, I was very aware I was going to be taken home by Mrs. Gallagher. She had dropped me off once before, but back then things had been different between us.

James came to open the door for us and said hello to me. I said hello back and got in after Mrs. Gallagher. When we were seated, I ran my hand over the nape of my neck, unconsciously trailing my fingers over the pendant and a few minutes later, we were on the road.

I couldn't believe I was still so tense around this woman. What did she do to me? Would I ever get used to her? She didn't make it easy since she was always so aloof. Maybe it was me who needed to change.

Mrs. Gallagher had been this way from the very first day I'd met her. Maybe it was me who needed to adapt to her. I was so deep in thought I almost missed her question.

"How are you and Colin getting along?" she asked.

I cleared my throat and bravely turned to look at her. "Very well, thank you."

She nodded and asked, "Any problems or difficulties so far?"

Her hair was held back, exposing her perfect symmetrical facial features.

"No, not at all," I said.

Her gaze slowly trailed over me and settled on the pendant. I dropped my hand to my lap and breathed out.

"I'm glad you're wearing it," she said softly.

I looked away at last, a little proud of myself for my show of confidence and leaned back against the seat. "I don't want to go home anymore, Mrs. Gallagher," I said.

What am I doing? A voice screamed in my head. Was I crazy? Had I lost my mind?

"Where would you like to go?" she asked.

I should've probably said I wanted to go back to the art gala or maybe told her to drop me off wherever we were, but it was like something else was driving me. "Anywhere, so long as you'll be there."

There was a prolonged silence during which I felt like my life was hanging in the balance. I couldn't believe I was the one speaking those words. The thoughts going through my head drove me to paranoia. I'm going to get fired. She's going to ask James to stop the car and tell me to get out.

By the time she spoke my heart was pounding so loudly in my chest, I thought I'd go into cardiac arrest.

"Okay," she said.

I slowly exhaled, hoping she didn't notice how tense I'd grown waiting for her answer. I watched her say something to James who just kept on driving.

I had no idea where we were going, but I was eager and anxious. Mrs. Gallagher always seemed to surprise me. I doubted this time would be any different.

I resented how nervous I always grew whenever I was around her. This uneasiness should've passed by now. I should've gotten used to the unusual aura she gave off. I doubted it was her intention to come off seeming so distant.

People seemed to like her and fear her at the same time. It was a little odd because I'd never heard or read anything negative about her. I wished she'd open up to me and let me get to know her better.

I didn't want to cross the line but I wasn't very sure where that line was. I was almost too afraid to speak my thoughts out loud. "Mrs. Gallagher," I said.

I could feel her gaze settle on me.

"God, I get so nervous around you."

I didn't think she thought about placing her hand over mine on my knee until the physical contact occurred. "Don't worry, I don't bite," she said and retreated.

"You have a very strange effect on me and every single time it takes a different form. I don't think I've ever felt this way around anyone else before," I said.

"What way is that?"

I met her gaze and tried to think about the appropriate words to use. "Sometimes it's a blend of excitement and uneasiness. Other times, it's pure fascination and admiration."

"And you don't like feeling this way," she said.

It was more of a statement than a question. "There is a helplessness that accompanies it. A lack of control, if you may."

She nodded, but failed to respond.

"I'd like to take some of that control back," I said.

"Okay," she said.

"I'd like to get to know you better, Mrs. Gallagher."

I thought I saw her tense up, but I wasn't sure.

"I think about you...more often than I should. I wonder...about you, the things that have happened between us in the past..." I couldn't say anymore. I was revealing far too much. I was going to get myself into trouble and she probably didn't even care about how I felt. "I'm sorry," I said.

The car came to a stop just when I thought she was going to respond.

"James, could you give us a minute?" she said.

James stepped out of the car and Mrs. Gallagher turned to me.

I didn't know what to expect. I'd just said things that were probably better off left unsaid. Mrs. Gallagher was always so guarded, there was no way she'd ever express any type of vulnerability.

"Olivia," she said.

I turned to face her. My hands were trembling and my heart was racing.

She slowly raised her hand and gently placed it over my cheek. Her thumb trailed the outline of my jaw, stopping to rest on my chin. "You remind me so much of someone I used to know." Her voice had never been softer.

I had seen her in many forms but this side of her was new and utterly mesmerizing. It was almost as though she was wounded. I wanted to know more about this person she spoke of with such tenderness, but I knew I'd have to be patient until she'd voluntarily tell me on her own.

She broke the physical contact, but instead of pulling away, she rested the back of her forefingers on my chin. Her eyes were a startling ocean blue. They were so deep and enchanting I'd never have pulled away from her had I even been offered a million dollars.

She leaned close to me and I closed my eyes as her lips softly brushed against mine. I responded at her pace, a little afraid she'd pull away if I did more. She moved her hand from my chin and gently ran it through my hair and I inwardly fought to control my body's sexual reaction to her.

She pulled me closer and deepened the kiss and I unconsciously inhaled in controlled desire. I was fighting a raw carnal hunger. Didn't she feel how much I wanted her? I was dying for her touch. I was dying for her to do more.

The kiss came to a slow gentle stop. I slowly opened my eyes and met her gaze then she smiled and pulled away. She could've said anything, but the kiss was far much better than words.

"How about a drink?" she asked.

I hesitated, still trapped in the moment that had just occurred and said, "A drink sounds good."

I looked out the tinted window to figure out where we were as I opened the door. James rushed to my side to help me out, shortly doing the same with Mrs. Gallagher.

Chapter Twenty-Seven

I shouldn't have been encouraging Olivia. I shouldn't have been seated next to her having a glass of wine.

My intention had been to drop her off, but when she'd said she didn't want to go home, she'd looked so nervous and vulnerable all I'd wanted to do was indulge her.

But this was exactly what I shouldn't have been doing. I had crossed the line in Paris and greatly reprimanded myself and just a short while ago, I'd crossed that line again.

I should've followed through with my original plan. The first day she'd walked into my office, I'd urgently needed to hire someone to carry out the charity ball event.

I could tell she was inexperienced and could stand to be a little more enlightened, so after the project, I'd planned on replacing her but during that first week she'd surprised me.

I'd considered keeping her on as my personal assistant, until the charity ball event had ended and she'd thrusted me back to a world I'd painfully bid farewell to.

It had been the most unexpected thing-having this lovely young woman-look at me and so boldly state what was on her mind and then go a bit further and express it in a kiss.

To this day I still didn't know how in God's name I'd responded to that kiss.

I'd planned on paying her for the week she'd worked for me and dismissing her, but after thinking about how brave she'd been to actually get that close to me and say those things, it had felt like she was challenging me.

I wasn't disappointed in her work. In fact, she was very good. She diligently performed her duties as she was supposed to, at times going even further, which I silently commended.

"I've never seen Rex so excited before," she said now, pulling me from my musings.

We'd just taken our seats at the counter. She was playing with the rim of her glass as her gaze rose and settled on mine. She had beautiful emerald-green eyes.

Whenever she was nervous, she always avoided my gaze. But when she was happy or upset, she faced me head-on, which I found oddly titillating.

When those few moments of bravery occurred, I could sense her courage was laced in fear. I couldn't remember a time when someone, anyone, stood up to me. But Olivia did.

Then there were those moments when she was happy or excited and she'd carry out a conversation with me without being nervous or afraid. During those moments when she looked at me, the shade of her green eyes deepened and I found myself enthralled.

"Are you happy for his success?" I asked.

I had a feeling the boy liked Olivia. I'd observed them a bit earlier that evening and if he hadn't been touching or hugging her, he'd been kissing her cheek. There was also a way that he looked at her.

"Of course, I am. He's been waiting for this for a long time," she said.

She smiled at me then looked away.

I didn't think she was shy, but there were moments when she appeared to be.

"I'll make sure Frank does everything he can to help him."

I didn't know why I was helping. To be honest, I didn't know why I did some of the things I did for Olivia.

"You said you're helping him because he matters to me," she said.

I nodded, taking a sip of my wine.

"Why do you care about what matters to me?"

The hint of diffidence was in the corners of her eyes.

I didn't know which answer she expected. This was a question I asked myself all the time. "You're my employee, Olivia."

I didn't know if my answer was satisfactory but she looked down at her drink and slowly exhaled, almost sadly. She bit one side of her lower lip and a memory flashed through my mind.

I remembered running my fingers over her lovely face and leaning forward to kiss her. I could feel how much she fought to restrain herself. I'd felt it back in Paris and I'd felt it again that night.

There was something about her. She reminded me so much of…

"I like working for you," she said.

Her gaze was distant, as though she was thinking about something.

"I can't help wondering how Rex will feel when I tell him you're responsible for tonight," she said.

"How do you think he'll feel?"

"He'll be upset at first; at me, you then me again. After some time, he'll come to the same conclusion I did."

"What conclusion is that?"

She massaged the back of her neck then slightly tilted her head. "You had only the best intention at heart," she said.

Her statement delivered an unexpected and unknown wave of emotion over me. "You seem to know him well," I said, trying to ignore it.

"Do you have a best friend, Mrs. Gallagher?" She sat up straight and crossed one leg over the other and her dress fell back a bit, exposing her well-toned thighs.

I turned my attention to the bar and ran her question through my head again. It was probably time for me to go. I wasn't sure how comfortable I was with her new line of questioning.

"No, I don't," I said.

"Do you think you'd ever be friends with someone like me?"

I struggled with the question and answer because in my world, I'd never usually meet someone like her and if I did, I doubted I'd invest any of my time or effort in creating a friendship.

Most of the friends I had made through the years were business acquaintances. No one really knew me the way Olivia seemed to know the boy.

"You don't have to answer that. It's a silly question," she said.

"I'd like to try." Maybe this was my chance to draw the line. I'd never befriended any one of my employees and so far this was proving to be a bad idea. "In my world, you don't get to make a lot of friends. Most people I consider such are business associates. We're not as familiar with each other as you seem to be with your friend."

My socializing skills were still wanting, but over the years I'd grown better at it. I'd never wanted my children to grow up thinking I didn't love them so I'd done all I could to fill those spaces that had run empty for so long.

"You're a little familiar with me," she said.

I wanted to respond, but I didn't know what to say because I wasn't sure what she meant.

"I'm an open book to you, Mrs. Gallagher. You know everything you need to know about me. You know how I–how I…feel," she hesitated, then resumed. "But I don't know anything about you. You're a…"

Robot.

"Closed book," she said.

A robot can be reprogrammed. A memory flashed through my head and I shifted uncomfortably in my seat.

"I'm I making you uncomfortable?"

I shook my head, looking at this young woman who dared provoke me so.

We came from such diverse universes; it was a wonder we were seated there chatting. She had an unmatched power to bring back sensations that had long over time faded out of existence. Feelings I'd thought I'd never live to experience again.

She was brave, bold and strong. She could speak her mind when calm and be daring enough to confront me when she felt wronged. Most profound of all, sometimes when I was close to her, I felt like I was twenty-one again.

But I wasn't twenty-one. Circumstances had forced me to grow up.

"You look… sad. Was it something I said?"

I shook away my thoughts and smiled at Olivia. "No," I said.

She finished her glass of wine and a waiter immediately came to refill it.

For some reason, I didn't mind talking to her. She was like a touch of ice on a scorching hot desert. She intrigued me. I didn't know how, but she did. I'd met every type of person in the world, but no one quite like her.

"How does it feel when you do all these wonderful and generous things for people?" she asked.

I placed my right arm over the counter and held my glass with the other hand, slowly moving it over to my lips as I pondered her question. I took a sip, emptying my glass and a second later, a waiter came to refill it.

"When I give back to society, I don't do it because of how it makes me feel. I do it because it's my duty."

"Why do you think it's your duty?"

My mind took me back in time. "I've been in a situation where I couldn't help... I guess I never want to feel that way again."

"Is that why you went into healthcare? Because you wanted to help people?"

I remembered being in the hospital. Isabel's frail features that had been so bright, beautiful and healthy a couple of weeks earlier were contorting in pain as machines beeped and a moment later, the room filled with doctors and nurses.

A sharp prick of pain went through me like a bolt of lightning. After all these years, Isabel was still buried somewhere within me. "I didn't go into healthcare. Someone I used to know did," I said.

"What happened?"

I looked up at the question. I'd never shared that part of my life with anyone. "I can't talk about it."

"I'm sorry," Olivia said.

I met her soft gaze. Her eyes had that dark shade of green in them. I felt like she was staring deep into my soul and it was a little terrifying. I broke the gaze and a moment later, I felt her hand lightly moving over mine on the counter.

I wanted to break the physical contact, but she started to pull away before I could, stopping to rest the tips of her fingers over mine. It was a very simple gesture, but it was as comforting as it was unsettling.

"How can you give so much to the world and not allow yourself to experience the joy that comes with it?" she asked.

It was something I'd gotten used to doing, so I never experienced anything profound. But when I did something for her, there was a way that she looked at me and that made me feel strangely good.

"I haven't given enough," I said.

There was nothing I could give to the world that would ever bring Isabel back, but when I helped people, I knew it was what she would've wanted.

Strangely enough, when I helped Olivia, it felt like it was something I was doing for myself.

"You're the most generous person I've ever met. Probably the most amazing person I'll ever know," she said.

Then there was that thing that stirred in me when she said things like that. "You haven't met enough people," I said, fully aware that her fingers were still touching mine.

She laughed at my statement and I wondered what I'd said that was funny. The sound of her laughter managed to draw a small smile from me.

"Maybe, but even if I ever get the chance to do so, I doubt anyone will ever compare to you."

I cautiously pulled my hand away at that point, feeling as though we were drifting off topic. She said a lot of lovely things but at some point, I had to draw the line. She wasn't my friend, she was my employee.

"I think we should get going," I said.

A serious expression came across her face and she nodded and said, "I think I'll get a cab. I don't want to put you out."

I smiled at her reassuringly. "You're not putting me out."

She smiled back and got to her feet.

The drive to her place was mostly quiet.

She seemed to have gone back to her shell.

I liked talking to her but I needed to draw some boundaries. It may have probably been a little too late, seeing as I had crossed those boundaries myself, but it was something that needed doing.

I couldn't keep encouraging her and leading her on when in the end I knew she'd end up getting hurt. So to protect her, and maybe myself, it was only safe to keep a distance.

When we got to her place, James parked the car and stepped out. I thought Olivia would say goodnight, open the door and leave, but she hesitated in her seat.

She nervously turned to face me and I looked at her, waiting to hear what she wanted to say.

"Thank you for what you're doing for Rex," she said. "No matter how he takes it when he finds out, I just want you to know that it made me happy."

Her words caught me off guard and momentarily lowered my defenses. When she leaned forward and captured my lips in a kiss, an overwhelming sensation moved through me.

I placed my hand over her cheek, intent on pulling away at the unexpected effect the kiss had on me, but Olivia gently brushed her lips against mine luring me, and I slowly started to respond to her.

The heat coming off of her body seemed to merge with mine, drawing a surprising response from me, and I pulled her closer and deepened the kiss. She sighed softly against my mouth and I ran my fingers through her hair.

She always seemed to draw such a powerful and baffling reaction from me. She wasn't the type I'd usually go for. Not because she wasn't beautiful or anything, but because she was as much an alien in my world as I probably was to hers. She was also too young for me.

I think though, what disturbed me the most was the fact that she was the second woman I'd ever kissed who provoked such strong sexual yearning from me. I'd never thought I'd meet anyone who made me feel anything close to what Isabel had once made me feel.

It was similar but extremely different. Isabel had taken me on a journey of sexual discovery but Olivia was reminding me of needs I'd long buried, needs that had gone far too long forgotten. She was starting to make me feel... alive.

She broke the kiss, but didn't pull away. She was panting and surprisingly, so was I. How was she doing this to me?

In Paris when we'd kissed, she'd lit a fire in me. That fire had grown when I'd taken her in my arms and kissed her again.

I had hoped some time and distance would help clear my head because I thought I'd gone a little insane to do something so uncharacteristic, but I was coming to realize that fire had never fully gone out and kissing Olivia again only continued to intensify it.

"We can't keep doing this, Olivia," I said.

"Why not?"

"Because it's blurring the lines, I'm your boss."

"Are you going to fire me?"

I didn't want to have to. "If circumstances force me to, yes."

"Then before those circumstances present themselves, can you do just one thing for me?"

I took a deep breath and nodded. "What?"

"Can you touch me?"

Her request came as a surprise. I met her gaze and could see her desire. I could always sense when she was fighting to restrain herself, but that night she wasn't. If anything, she seemed vulnerable, innocent but completely sensational.

"Olivia, if I touch you, I'll be opening a portal to something we can never come back from," I said, gently running my fingers over her cheek.

I wanted to touch her. I had wanted to touch her from the very first day she'd kissed me, but I'd put it out of my mind and pretended that night had never existed.

She closed her hand over mine and drew it closer to her lips. I closed my eyes at the tender effect of her lips caressing the palm of my hand and tantalizing sensations continued to spread through me.

I held my breath when she pulled my hand from her lips and moved it over her knee, slowly trailing it up her thigh. I drew in a sharp breath as her unwavering gaze stayed on mine.

Then as though something was pulling us back together, our lips recaptured in a passionate kiss and she pulled away her hand, leaving it to me to decide if I wanted to continue with the quest she'd entrusted me with.

Apart from Isabel, I had never really felt intimately connected to another woman or another soul so I was too afraid to take this journey. But there was a deep contained thirst in me begging to be quenched.

Olivia's skin was soft, smooth and warm as I hesitantly trailed my hand under her dress. I was desperately seeking to know her more intimately but I wasn't ready and I wasn't confident I could actually go through with it. I couldn't do this. I was getting everything mixed up again.

I almost continued when she moaned against my lips, but I summoned my inner strength and stopped touching her. It was harder trying to stop myself from kissing her because her lips were so soft and wonderful against mine, but somehow, I managed.

I moved back on my seat, creating some distance because the erotic heat reverberating between us was making the situation too hard to resist.

Olivia took a deep breath and a moment later, she wordlessly opened the door. James offered his hand and helped her out. The second the door closed, I leaned back against my seat and exhaled.

I had settled into a life of calm, but Olivia was starting to create some turbulence which was unwelcome. This wasn't something I wanted to explore. I couldn't go down this road again. I had lived it once and while it had been completely fulfilling, it had ended up damaging me.

Isabel's death had affected me more than I'd ever wanted to admit. Because of it, my work had suffered and my mother, being the predator she was, had seen the weakness in me and deviously exploited it.

I'd not had the will to fight her at the time so in six months, I'd been engaged to a suitor of her choice. His name was Patrick Gallagher, my husband and father of my children.

Chapter Twenty-Eight

When I asked her to touch me, I didn't really think she would. She had too much control, too many rules and yes… for a second, I did consider the possibility of her firing me. But I didn't care, because her touch was the drug I craved for, to death and back.

Maybe a little bit of wine had something to do with this surge of confidence, but all my life, I'd never had the courage to do anything so bold. So when I asked her to touch me, I put everything on the line.

I was terrified, but courageous enough to see it through. That was why I made the first move by taking her hand, placing a tender kiss on it and gently resting it over my leg.

I figured she already knew how I felt. She had voluntarily kissed me once before that night. Why not go a step further and seek the one thing I craved from her most, her touch.

The soft feel of her lips against mine when we kissed arose my sexual hunger for her. God, I wanted her so bad and whether or not I'd ever have her, the touch, her touch, was golden.

When she ran her fingers through my hair and deepened our kiss, every part of my being went entirely under her spell. Her mouth was like the sweetest thing I'd ever tasted. When I kissed her and she kissed me back, it felt like I was in a sacred place where my dreams grew bigger and came alive.

She made me feel like a whole new person, like I could do just about anything, but those dreams as I was coming to learn, were short-lived.

Despite it all, her touch, no matter how minimal, was worth everything. She was worth everything.

"Olivia?"

I looked up at the insistent voice to find Colin Peterson blankly staring at me.

"Where were you?" he asked.

"Uh…" I couldn't come up with a plausible excuse.

He retained a serious expression.

"I'm sorry. I'm a little distracted."

"You've been distracted all week," he complained.

All week? Oh yeah, it was Friday. "I'm just a little bit tired," I said.

"This whole week your mind has been elsewhere, you need to focus. What I'm teaching you is important if you want to keep this job."

"I know, Colin. I'm sorry. I don't mean to waste your time."

"You're not wasting my time, Olivia. I get paid to do this, remember?"

He slumped himself onto the seat facing my desk.

I liked him. He was a good guy. We didn't know each other well, but we got along and he kept the learning experience professional.

"What's going on?" he asked.

Amelia Gallagher.

I thought about her every day, all the time. I thought about that Friday night every second of every minute. It wasn't just about our intimate encounter... okay, mostly it was. But also, I thought about our talk.

She wasn't open, but she made an attempt to be. It was a poor attempt but at least she tried. I must have appeared like a nervous wreck to her. God, I hoped she didn't see me that way.

"Nothing, just a little bit of stress," I said.

My evening classes were going to start the following week and I wasn't prepared, I had managed to avoid Rex all week and seeing his calls made me feel even worse and to top it off, I couldn't think about anything else other than my boss.

"Why don't you go out tonight and blow off some steam?" Colin suggested.

Maybe that was exactly what I needed.

"A friend of mine is having a party. You can come with me if you want."

Colin was sweet, but I missed Rex.

I was sure he suspected something was amiss. But I still wasn't sure I could face him just yet. I was trying to prolong the moment where he'd learn the truth and get mad at me, but maybe I should've just ripped the band aid and gotten it over and done with.

"Sounds great," I said.

Colin peered over his wristwatch and got to his feet. "I think we've covered enough for the day." He put his things together and picked up his jacket.

"What's the hurry?" I asked.

It was past five so we were free to leave.

"I have a few errands to run. I'll call you around seven?"

I nodded. I should've probably been getting ready to leave too.

I hadn't seen Mrs. Gallagher all week but I wasn't surprised, I'd come to learn she was an extremely busy person. Every single minute of her time was booked. Even when she was in her office, she was always constantly working.

"Hey," Colin said at the door, pulling me back to the present.

"What's up?" I said.

"Are you okay?" he asked.

I got up and walked over to the door where he stood watching me with what appeared to be concern on his face.

"I will be," I said, opening the door for him.

He placed his hand over my shoulder, lightly squeezing it and a second later, Mrs. Gallagher's office door opened and she stepped out looking as enormously stunning as always.

"I'll see you tonight," Colin said to me, then silently acknowledged Mrs. Gallagher as he walked away.

Since she opened the door, my gaze didn't leave hers. I'd worked with Colin for two weeks now and since we'd started, Mrs. Gallagher had been so preoccupied we barely saw each other.

Seeing her at Rex's art gala and spending time with her had been a real treat, but since then, we'd hardly spoken during the week.

Now I was standing right in front of her and I was at a complete loss for words. What did you say to a person as deeply complex as she? I didn't have to wonder for long because she broke our gaze and walked right past me.

You're my employee, Olivia. Her words echoed in my mind as her scent lingered long after she was gone.

I constantly wondered if she meant those things she'd said that night, but I was in denial. There was a part of her—it didn't matter how small—that cared for me. Why else would she do anything she'd done for me? Why would she go to any trouble to help out my friend?

When I got home that evening, I was more exhausted than I'd thought I would be. I called Colin to inform him I wouldn't go to his friend's party and instead settled down with my school work to study.

The following day, I was drained. I didn't think I could take another week of spending all day at the office but I was a quick study and Colin was almost done. He looked a little more tired than me when he showed up, but his exhaustion was attributed to his night out partying.

When the day was over, I was elated to go home but my high spirit was shot down when I found Rex at my door waiting for me.

"If I didn't know any better, I'd say you were avoiding me," he said as he wrapped his arms around me.

I hugged him back, letting the calming effect of our friendship embrace me. When we pulled apart, his soft gaze met mine and his lips curved up in a smile. He placed the palm of his hand over my chin and leaned forward to peck my forehead.

"Whatever it is that I've done, I'm sorry," he said.

My heart broke at his words.

"You haven't done anything, Rex."

I opened the door and we got inside. I placed the bag I used for work over my bed and turned around to find him watching me.

"You want to tell me what's going on then?"

My approach may not have been subtle, but I couldn't have been able to face him knowing whenever he found out the truth he'd get upset with me.

"I never saw or heard from you again after the art gala. I was worried. Did something happen with Mrs. Gallagher? Did she do something to you?"

His concern for me was endearing. "No, I mean…" So much had happened that night. "Why don't you take a seat," I said.

His expression grew more concerned as he sat down and faced me.

"I hate lying to you, Rex." I went to sit beside him and closed my hand over his.

"Liv, you're scaring me," he said.

"No, don't worry, it's not like that." I took a breath and slowly resumed, "When I talked to Mrs. Gallagher that night, I found out she was responsible for Frank Connor seeking you out."

He looked at me in confusion.

"She asked him to take a look at your work. She was the reason your pieces were at the art gala," I said.

He pulled away from me and got to his feet. "I don't understand. Mrs. Gallagher doesn't even know me, why would she..." he slowly turned to face me. "Did you ask her to do it?"

I shook my head. "I found out that night when we went outside to talk."

"Then why would she help me?"

I recalled our conversation. Mrs. Gallagher claiming she'd only helped Rex because he mattered to me. "She said it was because I'd once mentioned to her how much you would've loved to have your work showcased at an art event. She was trying to help."

He paced a couple of times then stopped and turned to face me. I couldn't read him quite yet. "Is she trying to buy off your friends now?" he asked.

"Rex, she's not trying to buy anyone off," I said as I got to my feet.

"Think about it, Liv. Every single artist at the art gala was established except for me. I'm an amateur. I did not deserve to be there. She used her power and influence to do this and she did it for you."

"You're not an amateur, Rex. She admitted to having asked Frank to take a look at your work but she told me that he thought you were good."

He peered at me. "Liv, if you believed I deserved the opportunity to be there, you wouldn't have kept this information from me all week. You would've told me the moment you found out."

"I do believe you deserved the opportunity. I just didn't want you to get upset with me."

He silently observed me.

"She did this for you Liv, but I doubt her reasons are as innocent as you think."

He walked over to the door.

"Rex, please."

"I'm leaving tomorrow. I've been trying to get in touch with you all week to tell you so."

"What?"

He turned and looked at me. "I think she did this to get me away from you," he said.

He didn't make sense. "What do you mean and why do you say you're leaving? Where are you going?"

"When the time comes and whatever it is that's going on between you two comes to an end, I'm more than certain Mrs. Gallagher's reasons for doing everything she's doing will become clear to you." He walked out.

"Rex!" I called after him before he slammed the door.

I wanted to go after him but I didn't think I'd accomplish anything. He was far much more upset than I'd thought he'd be. He seemed to harbor some distress for something far much deeper than I'd expected.

What had he meant Mrs. Gallagher had helped him to get him away from me? Was she responsible for his going away? Where was he going? How long would he be gone for?

I was so dependent on him as a friend. Who was I going to talk to? Why would he leave without telling me where he was going or the purpose of his departure?

Suddenly I wished I'd kept in touch with him during the week because I would've been aware of everything that had happened and what was going on.

Chapter Twenty-Nine

I couldn't stop thinking about what Rex had said. Our entire conversation kept replaying itself in my head. I had a lot of questions, but he wasn't available to answer them.

On Sunday morning, I went by his apartment and art studio, but he was gone. I tried calling him on his cell, but all my calls went straight to voicemail. I didn't know what to do.

Maybe I deserved the silent treatment because I'd done the same to him the week before, but at least he'd known I was fine and he'd known where to find me. With him gone, I felt like someone had disturbed my sense of direction.

Why did he think Mrs. Gallagher had anything to do with him having to leave? And why would he say she was trying to keep him away from me? What reason would she have to do so?

He was my best friend and I trusted him, but his anger towards me for not coming clean about the art gala must have driven him to say those things. I believed Mrs. Gallagher's intention had been good, but then why couldn't I stop thinking about it?

This whole situation was a little absurd. Rex was a fulltime student, so his travel was going to get in the way of his school work. He would never put his studies on the line. So whatever reason he had for leaving, it had to be a damn good one.

Did Frank have anything to do with it? Had Mrs. Gallagher played a role in it? Was that why Rex thought she was trying to keep us apart? And if so, why would Mrs. Gallagher want Rex to stay away from me when she knew for a fact that he was my best friend? The questions left me in distress.

When I went to work on Monday, I had tired myself thinking about Rex and at the end, his analogy managed to cast a shadow of doubt on Mrs. Gallagher.

Sure, most of the time I couldn't understand some of the things she did or why she did them, but I always chose to blindly trust her because I believed in her good intentions. Now, I was questioning myself about her too.

She summoned me to her office shortly after I arrived. My feelings for her had developed but I always struggled to hide them from her at work even though she was fully aware of it. I didn't want to create an uncomfortable working environment and I still badly needed this job.

I went to her office and found her leaning back against her desk as she swiped her iPad with her perfectly manicured index finger.

"Good morning, Olivia," she said.

"Good morning, Mrs. Gallagher."

Colin hadn't showed up to work. I wondered if I had learned all she'd needed me to learn to fully perform my duties as her personal assistant.

"How was your weekend?" she asked.

With Rex gone and me stressing about starting my classes later on in the evening, I didn't have anything happy to report.

"It was fine," I said.

She turned her attention to me. "Is something wrong?" she asked.

I doubt her reasons are as innocent as you think. Rex's words echoed in my head. "Uh, no." I pulled my mind back to the present and put on my professional suit. "What can I do for you?" Maybe I needed to take a step back from my feelings to see if there was any truth in what Rex had said.

Mrs. Gallagher seemed to be studying me, and then said, "I have a couple of meetings I'd like you to attend in my place today. I've forwarded the information to your iPad."

Did she really think I was ready? I couldn't do what she'd done in Paris.

"Olivia, what you've learned is just a small part of what I do. There are things that cannot be taught in an office. From today, some of your added duties and responsibilities will be to attend meetings I cannot take. You'll have to learn these things on the job. I'll provide you with all the information you require so that you'll know exactly what to do."

I nodded, trying to conceal my nervousness.

"I need you to be confident in your skills. You're intelligent, you know how to read people and you have the ability to retain information. I need you to use this to your advantage. It's going to be challenging, some of the people you meet will not want to meet with you in my place, so you need to be creative and prove to me that you can do this because from this point forward, you're going to be my right-hand man. Do you understand?"

"Yes, I understand." I may have been nervous but I was excited. I wouldn't have to be confined to my desk. I was going to meet important people to discuss important issues. I was going to be a mini Mrs. Gallagher.

"You're my protégé," she said.

My entire being vibrated from the powerful effect of her words. Did she really mean that? Did she want me to be just like her?

"Your evening classes start tonight, right?" she asked.

I hesitated, wondering if I had mentioned this to her earlier. "Uh, yes." How did she know?

"I need you to be sharp and alert. You cannot let anything get in the way of your work so I'll need to know if this becomes somewhat of a struggle for you."

"I'll not let anything get in the way of my work," I said.

"What if you need to travel? You'll miss out on your studies," she said.

I had thought about that and had figured when the time came, I'd find a way to deal with it. "My work comes first," I said because at the moment, I needed the job more in order to pay my debts.

"It shouldn't have to. Your studies are just as important as your work."

I hesitated in my response.

"If you lost your job after putting in so much of your time and effort, wouldn't your studies suffer?"

"Yes, but I'd find a way to catch up."

"You'd have accumulated debt, you'd be left behind, it'd take you years to graduate and finding another job would not be easy." She stood upright and went around her desk.

Why was she stating my fears? Didn't she think I stressed about it enough? Where was she going with this conversation?

"I want you to succeed, Olivia."

I met her gaze, which had grown softer. Why would Rex suggest she was after anything when she only seemed to want the best for me?

"I don't want you to get distracted."

Wait, what? She didn't want me to get distracted? Did that have anything to do with Rex?

"I need your studies to work around your work schedule and you may not be able to juggle it all because it's going to be a lot of responsibility."

I was torn. What did she want me to do? I couldn't quit school and from what she was saying, it didn't sound like she wanted me to quit either.

"I've hired you several professors who are going to pay their undivided attention to your studies. They'll work with you around your schedule and should you travel, you'll correspond through video. This way, your studies won't interfere with your work."

I stared back at her in shock. "Mrs. Gallagher, I can't–I can't afford these professors."

"I'm paying for it," she stated.

"I can't ask you to do that."

"You're not."

"I uh–I don't know what to say."

Did her generosity know no bounds? Why would she do this for me? I would never be able to pay her back.

"You can say thank you," she said with a bit of amusement in her eyes.

My hands were trembling. "Thank you, thank you so much." I couldn't begin to explain my elation.

"There are a couple of things I'd like you to add to your syllabus."

I looked at her in curiosity.

"Languages and healthcare management. I've already assigned you the appropriate professors. I just need to know you're going to give it your all."

I nodded, growing more uncertain about her reasons for doing this.

"You're about to become very busy, Olivia. Do not disappoint me."

She wasn't leaving any chance for me to do so. "I won't. I promise."

"One more thing," she said.

I held my breath.

"I need you to live in a convenient location, somewhere in the city. The company has furnished apartments for some of the employees. I'd like you to take up residence in one of them. Does that sound like something you can do?"

"Yes." How could I possibly say no to a new apartment in the city?

Mrs. Gallagher watched me intently, almost as though she was contemplating the decisions she had made. I knew she was putting a lot of faith in me so a little doubt wasn't an alien possibility.

I was determined not to fail her. "Mrs. Gallagher, I will not let you down."

"I know." She said it with so much conviction I wondered if she saw something in me that I failed to see in myself. Why would she put so much trust in me? "I'm investing in you, Olivia. I'm investing in your future. You have no choice but to succeed."

"Why are you doing this for me, Mrs. Gallagher?"

She'd said she wanted me to succeed, but she had to be motivated by something else, something greater. No one could be so selfless in their giving. Did she have any ulterior motives? I was going to owe her everything, was it going to come at a price?

"Do I need to have a reason?" she asked.

Yes, I wanted to say. But I didn't want to reveal my doubt in what she was doing. "No, I guess not," I said.

"Olivia, you need to resign yourself to the fact that you may not always understand everything I do. But I need you to know that I never make mistakes."

She was starting to sound cryptic. But if she was willing to do all these things for me, I needed to trust her. "Okay," I said.

"Good, you start immediately. You'll move before the end of the day, attend the meetings I mentioned and find an appropriate place for where you'll be meeting with your professors. Is that clear?"

"Yes," I said.

She nodded, showing me she was done. I headed for the door as I fought to restrain my excitement. I wanted to scream in order to let it out as my whole body trembled.

"Olivia," Mrs. Gallagher said when I was at the door.

I turned around and found a small smile on her face.

"Good luck," she said.

I smiled back at her and opened the door, hoping the unpredictable turn of events meant great things were about to happen.

Chapter Thirty

I went through the file a third time. I had quickly scanned through it once and placed it in my desk drawer, only having read what at the time I thought was important.

The private investigator I'd hired to look into Olivia's background had done an extremely thorough job. The file consisted of everything I needed to know about Olivia.

I had requested the background check to verify the accuracy of the information she'd put forward while applying for the job.

My private investigator had gone a step further and included drug tests, education, employment and medical records, financial information, and personal information regarding her past, her relationships and details about her family.

The second time I'd gone through the file was to confirm the decisions I'd made regarding Olivia's future.

She was doing a Masters in Business Administration and should've finished by now, but being a part-time student with countless temporary jobs had greatly slowed her down.

She excelled in her studies and really tried to keep up with the rest of the students but she'd missed out on a lot of classes during the time period she'd worked for me.

The last exam she'd done during the time I'd given her a day off, she'd gone past the average mark though she could've done better considering how bright she was and how well she'd performed in the past. I attributed this decline to the time-consuming work she did for me.

Her parents had paid her tuition during the beginning of her studies but had eventually run out of money, which had forced her to seek employment. She struggled with her student loan debt, but worked hard in attempts to pay it.

Past employers credited her work, saying she was had working, driven and committed to her duties.

She'd never experimented with recreational drugs and was in good health.

She had an older brother named Gregory Williams. He lived with their parents and did not have a steady source of income and according to the file, he had a child and a girlfriend who lived with him in his parents' house.

I was going through the file a third time now, uncomfortably aware that I was invading Olivia's privacy but I told myself it was of paramount importance that I learn as much about her as possible because of the responsibility I had entrusted her with a couple of days earlier.

What was stopping me was the fact that what I was about to read now revolved around Olivia's personal life. I opened the page where I had left off and read on.

Gregory, Olivia's older brother, was thirty-two years old. He was a slacker and mostly relied on his parents' income to support himself, his child and his girlfriend.

He was so different from Olivia. It was like one of them had been adopted.

I opened the last page and went on to read up on Olivia's personal life. The only person she had ties to in New York was Brexton Phillips, whose nickname was Rex and he was Olivia's best friend.

The report went further to say that Olivia had never been involved in a long-term relationship with anyone, but had encountered sexual activities with women. I closed the file and put it back in my desk drawer.

I'd read enough. The surplus information wasn't necessary, though it did manage to shed light on Olivia's personality.

By now, she must've settled in her new apartment. I'd personally chosen it for her, but I didn't want her to know that because I didn't want her to think I had any personal motive for doing this. I wanted her to focus on work and school without outside interference.

She had all of her professors contact information and had chosen a public library close to her new place to carry out her private studies. So far, she was keeping up with the pace.

I wasn't disappointed with the meetings she'd attended. I'd purposely set them up as a test to see how she'd conduct herself and from the report I had received, apart from a little self-confidence, she'd been well-informed, had properly handled the meeting and had professionally conducted herself.

The knock on the door interrupted my flow of thought.

"Come in," I said.

My son, Jonah, walked in. He had grown into a handsome young man and strived to be more like me, which I disapproved of because my life wasn't as fulfilling as people thought it was.

Unlike the way I'd been brought up, I'd made sure my children had a somewhat normal upbringing. They had a childhood and had attended school at a normal pace as compared to my rushed one.

Jonah was loyal, hardworking and ambitious. He had finished his studies and was working in a financial managerial position for the pharmaceutical company.

"Hey Mom," he said as he took a seat across my desk.

"Hey honey."

It had been a personal choice to work from home because I had wanted to be closer to my children, but now that they were both grown up, I was considering going back to the office.

I was the Chairman and CEO of Winston Enterprises. My mother, who was just a member of the board now, had handed over control of the company six years after she'd married me off.

My cousin, Eric, still ran the company in Belize. He'd managed to find a balance and settle down and was now married with four kids; three girls and a boy.

I still couldn't stand him, but if there was one thing I was grateful for, it was the fact that my mother had sent him away, which ironically, I had initially disapproved of.

"Grandma and I have been talking," Jonah said.

Whenever a sentence started off that way, I always somehow went into shutdown mode. That woman still managed to make my life difficult. She was well into her late sixties but did not look a day over fifty.

After I'd gotten married to Patrick, I had cut her off from my life and that of my children. When she'd handed over control of the company to me six years later, fully relinquishing her control, I'd let her meet her grandchildren.

It had been her punishment for forcing me into a life I hadn't been prepared for. I loved both my children but my life was still far from perfect.

"When are you planning on merging Price Healthcare with Winston Enterprises?" he asked.

I'd had the same discussion with Kathy and Patrick for years, which on a number of occasions had ended up in unpleasant arguments. I couldn't believe I was now having the same conversation with my son.

I had a thirty percent stake at Gallagher Manufacturing Industries, but no one said anything about that. But when it came to Price Healthcare, something that didn't belong to the family, everyone seemed to have a say in it.

"You've run the businesses as two different entities for so long."

He was my son and I loved him, but he would never know or understand the significance of Price Healthcare. "Jonah, did your grandma tell you how I came to acquire Price Healthcare?" I asked.

"I thought it was part of the family business."

Kathy seemed to have conveniently left out that part during their talk. "How about you go do some research, and then we can talk."

He looked at me in confusion.

Twenty-seven years ago, it had been all over the widespread media. Everyone had known I'd acquired the business from Isabel Price shortly after her passing. Details over how I came to acquire the business had been entirely based on speculation.

I didn't blame Jonah for thinking Price Healthcare was a family business. It had been a long time and no one spoke about it anymore. If Jonah made the effort to actually try and figure it out, maybe I'd share my reasons for keeping the two businesses apart.

"Was there something else?" I asked.

"You're so secretive, Mom. Can't you just tell me?" he asked.

"No," I said.

He smiled at me and got to his feet. "See you at dinner," he said.

When he left, I picked up my phone and dialed Kathy's number. I kept my distance, but she still couldn't keep her nose out of my business.

I allowed her to maintain a relationship with my kids under certain circumstances but sometimes she overstepped and forgot her place, and I was forced to remind her.

I wasn't sure if it was age or the presence of the kids, but over time, it seemed a softer side of her had developed. Nonetheless, our relationship was more strained than ever.

She'd thought Patrick would somehow manage to control me, but he'd never even come close to succeeding. It must've been why she was reaching out to Jonah now.

"Hello Kathy," I said when she picked up.

"Amelia, how pleasant to hear from you," she said.

"Have you been talking to Jonah?" I asked.

"Oh yes, we had lunch the other day."

"During this lunch, did Price Healthcare come up as a conversation piece?"

She hesitated. "Ah, yes. He asked about it."

"I need you to stay out of my business, Kathy. Just because you failed to get your way through Patrick doesn't mean you'll succeed using Jonah."

"Amelia, he was just asking–"

"I don't want to hear it. If I learn you've been talking to him about this again, I'll not be quite so lenient with you. Do you understand?"

She was silent for a while.

"I understand," she said.

I hang up the phone. Her weaknesses were more exposed now, so she couldn't have her way with everything like she had when I'd been younger. She was older now, and alone. She needed to feel like she was part of a family, my family.

She should've expressed more interest in Eric's family. If they were anything like him, I was certain they would've doted on her, falsely or not.

I got back to my duties and somehow, my mind flew back to Olivia. For some reason, I thought of her more often than I should have. I had my motives for helping her, but they would be revealed in time.

I didn't want anything from her, but that fact did not sway my mind from the memories of our intimate encounters during the time we'd spent together. She made me feel more alive than I'd felt in my entire marriage.

I'd met Patrick during a luxury cruise vacation with my mother. She'd forced me to take some time off from work because I'd been unable to function after Isabel had passed away.

I was almost certain she'd known the true nature of our relationship, which had been her keen motivation for rushing me into a marriage I had not desired.

The first time I met Patrick, I thought he was a nuisance. Sure, he was tall, handsome and came from a good successful family but like every other time before that, I couldn't stand the fact that Kathy was trying to find me a suitor.

Unfortunately, I couldn't run as I had during previous similar situations because I was in the middle of the Indian Ocean. Patrick was traveling with his family who were old friends of Kathy's.

He kept trying to force conversation, in spite of me expressing my lack of interest but in the end, I realized the cruise was equally as miserable for him as it was for me because he was traveling with his parents and did not have anyone else around his age to hang out with apart from me.

I made an attempt to be friendly to him because I thought it'd make the trip lighter on both our parts, but I had no idea he'd fall in love with me. He always said the sadness in my eyes had drawn him to me because he'd wondered how it'd be like to see me smile or laugh.

I came to learn he was kind and sweet because he was constantly trying to cheer me up in an attempt to win me over. When Kathy saw that I was actually paying attention to him, she started plotting.

Being idle drove me crazy because I didn't know how to relax, but Patrick found ways to entertain and distract me.

"I know you like your comfort zone and don't like to talk much but I think I might've found a way to change all that," he said one afternoon.

I was sunbathing when he joined me. "What way is that?" I asked.

He held out his hands to reveal two expensive bottles of wine.

"One is for you and one is for me. We're going to get drunk and make our parents miserable for a change."

The last part of his statement was appealing to me, but I didn't see how getting drunk would make our parents miserable. Nonetheless, being stuck on a ship with absolutely nothing to do played a big role in me wanting to have a drink.

"Where are the glasses?" I asked.

He lowered his sunglasses, meeting my inquisitive gaze and dramatically said, "No need to be a lady today, we're breaking all the rules." He uncorked his bottle and took a sip.

I was slightly amused, but I didn't show it. He uncorked my bottle and handed it over to me. I followed his lead and took a sip from the bottle. "Where'd you get this?" It was really good wine.

"I stole it," he said.

I almost gave back the bottle. "You stole it? Why would you do that?"

"My father manipulated me into coming on this cruise. I just want to give him a little taste of his own medicine," he said.

I took another sip.

"What makes you happy, Amelia?" he asked.

His question prompted me to remember Isabel, which drove me to take another sip. "Nothing," I said.

"There has to be something."

"Can we drink without talking?" I asked.

Back then, he thought it was amusing whenever I barricaded myself. He thought somehow over time, he'd manage to get me to open up.

"You're a beautiful girl, don't you have someone special waiting for you back home?" he insisted.

I looked at him, wondering why Isabel and I had never gone on a cruise. We'd have had such a lovely time. We would've probably spent most of it in our room making love and we would've enjoyed every minute of it.

"Amelia?"

The look of concern on his face pulled me back to the present. He moved closer to me and stretched out his arm, slowly reaching for my face and wiped a tear from my cheek.

I didn't know I'd been crying. I didn't cry. It wasn't in me. Embarrassed by my show of weakness, I got to my feet and walked away from him. He didn't follow after me. It was like he knew I needed time to myself.

Later on, in the evening, I was taking a walk along the deck when I saw him standing at the edge of the ship. He was still drinking, but he had a different bottle.

"What are you doing?" I asked when I approached him.

"Amelia, my current favorite person in the world." He was drunk.

I took the bottle from him and took a sip. "Did you steal this one too?"

"No," he shook his head. "I charged it on my father's credit card."

His anger towards his father made me curious. "I know your father manipulated you into coming along on the cruise, but is that the only reason why you're so angry with him?"

"If I tell you, will you tell me why you're so sad?"

I didn't answer him.

"You have to trust somebody, Amelia," he said.

"You wouldn't understand."

"Try me," he said.

I took another sip. "You first," I said.

"Right before I agreed to come on the cruise, he promised me a great position in the company. I've done the work, put in the time and effort so I knew the job was mine. After we boarded the ship, I called the office to confirm everything was in order and came to learn that he'd offered the position to someone else. So not only did he use the position to bait me, he managed to screw me over," he explained.

I handed him the bottle and he took a sip. It was the first thing he said that made me feel like I could relate to him. My mother had used the company to manipulate me on several occasions, so I understood how he felt.

"Your turn," he said.

I took a deep breath and said, "I lost a close friend."

"Oh, shit. I'm so sorry."

We spent the rest of the evening talking and somewhere through it all, I got drunk as well. The following morning, I woke up in his bed.

I was surprised to find him sleeping on the floor because I'd never known any man to be such a gentleman.

He was my first friend after Isabel, but my relationship with him from my side was purely platonic. After the cruise, we went back to our normal lives and two weeks later, he called me to tell me his father had promoted him to an even better position.

We went out to celebrate and when my mother found out, she couldn't stop talking about him or making plans for us to spend more time together.

Somewhere along the second month, he finally worked up the courage to confess his feelings for me. It was a little tense and awkward since I didn't feel the same way and when I told him so, he decided that he couldn't be just friends with me and ended it.

It was saddening, but I didn't want to lead him on just to hurt him in the end. It must've been over three months before my mother reunited us again. She hosted a party and invited Patrick. I had no idea he'd be there when I attended, but I was pleased to see him.

We started seeing each other again, spending more and more time together. I knew his feelings for me hadn't changed but I needed a friend and at the time, he was the only one available.

"Patrick is a good young man. I don't see why you don't want to give him a chance. You need companionship, Amelia. Patrick is willing to give you everything. He's smitten with you." Kathy's sermons became part of a daily routine.

Leave me alone. I wanted to scream. Couldn't she see I needed Patrick as a friend because I was hurting over someone else? What was her obsession with wanting to marry me off? Was she doing it for me or for herself?

"I think Patrick is serious about wanting to spend his life with you. Wouldn't that be lovely?" she said.

What about me and what I wanted? What kind of world had I been born into that what I wanted for myself didn't matter?

"Your father would approve of this union. He'd want you to be with Patrick. He's such a gentleman. Any woman would be lucky to have him," she continued.

Then let any other woman have him. I would respond in my head.

"Listen honey, I know since Isabel passed, things haven't been easy for you. I understand you two were close, but the only way you can feel better is by having someone you trust by your side."

I didn't know what made her use Isabel to make her point, but her words got to me. She was sweet and soothing and didn't use her usual nagging tone. She touched my face, tucked my hair over my ear and spoke to me like a mother to a child.

I should've known it was her way of getting what she wanted, but I was too in need to care. Once she knew what my weakness was, she started exploiting it. She would use Isabel to make me feel like I needed Patrick.

When he proposed, both our families were seated at the dining table at Patrick's house having dinner. During dessert, he went down on one knee and declared his undying love for me right before he popped the question.

I couldn't remember saying yes to him because my mother squealed in joy and everyone got caught up in the excitement. My mother must've been celebrating because finally she'd succeeded in her attempts to find me a perfect suitor.

She planned the wedding, making it a bigger extravaganza than my twenty-first birthday, and a month after the proposal, I was no longer Amelia Winston. I was Amelia Gallagher.

Chapter Thirty-One

I knew it wouldn't be easy juggling my work and my studies but having professors teach me on my own time sure made things a whole lot easier. I loved being busy, it kept me active.

During the day, I attended meetings and learned more about Mrs. Gallagher's job and healthcare business and in the evening, I got home, showered, changed, had dinner then went out to meet with my professors.

I got back to the apartment sometime around midnight and after reviewing my day, I retired to bed in exhaustion. The following days ran on a loop in a similar manner.

It wasn't until I'd step back into the apartment that I'd remember my whole life had taken a complete turn. The two-bedroom apartment was large and it was fully and elegantly furnished.

It would've probably taken me a decade to afford such luxury. It felt like I was living in an expensive hotel room.

Apart from food and some shopping for clothes, shoes and handbags, I wasn't spending much money. I had free transport, accommodation and Mrs. Gallagher was generous enough to pay for my professors.

I thought about Rex all the time and I missed him terribly. I imagined how happy and supportive he'd be to learn how much my life had improved from that girl who'd been about to lose everything just a few months back.

It had been a week since he'd left, but it felt like years and for some reason, I still couldn't reach him.

I still thought about his allegations, and sometimes I thought he might have been right but I wasn't brave enough to confront Mrs. Gallagher on this one, not after all she was doing for me.

I couldn't help being suspicious, though. I wanted to understand her reasons behind her motivation for doing so much for me. I wanted to know if this was something she did for her other employees.

The wondering came at night right before I fell asleep, then somewhere along it all, my thoughts would take an erotic turn.

I imagined Mrs. Gallagher in the large comfortable bed with me, sliding between those cozy satin sheets. I pictured her eyes dark and full of desire, her lips trembling in want and anticipation and her skin hot and soft under my touch.

Dreams of her haunted me in my sleep and more often than not, I woke up hot, panting and sweaty with my fingers twitching to touch her. My feelings for her were growing stronger everyday and I had no idea how to stop them.

I wondered if she had any feelings for me. Did she think about me as often as I thought of her? Did she think about our intimate encounters? Did she desire to revisit them as I did?

Usually at this point my thoughts grew depressing so I tried to occupy my mind with other things like my studies or my work. I wanted to pick up a book and study for a while before I fell asleep when the doorbell rang.

I didn't know anyone who knew where I lived so I assumed it was someone from the front desk at the reception area of the apartment building, coming to probably check on something so I went and opened the door.

My jaw dropped when I saw Rex.

"Oh, my God!" I said in shock.

He didn't speak. He just took a step forward and wrapped his arms around me.

It was the most overwhelming thing I'd ever felt. "What? Where? How?" I didn't know what to ask first.

"I've missed you so much, just let me hug you for a minute," he said.

I exhaled and let it be. I hugged him back, tightly. Like a bear coming out of hibernation, I embraced him like he was my summer. God, I couldn't believe how much I'd missed him.

When we pulled apart, he looked at me and awkwardly dropped his arms to his sides. "I feel so stupid, I had to come here in person," he said.

"What are you talking about?" I asked.

He scratched the nape of his neck and I realized he was nervous. I stepped aside and let him in.

"This is a great place," he said.

I cared more about him, than the apartment and I just wanted to know where he'd been and if he was okay. "Where have you been, Rex?"

He looked at me in sadness and remorsefulness. "I'm sorry, Liv."

What was he sorry for? Last I checked, I was the one who'd hurt him.

"They wouldn't allow us access to our phones. I wanted to talk to you the moment I got there."

"Rex, I don't know what you mean," I said.

"When you told me about Mrs. Gallagher having something to do with the whole art gala thing, I freaked out. I didn't understand at the time, which was why I accused her of sending me away."

I watched him as he struggled to find words to explain.

"Liv, the whole time I've been away, I was at an art workshop. I had the best, most talented artists in the industry teaching me everything I needed to know. I had no idea and to be honest, I wasn't prepared for it. When Frank said I needed a little time off from school and went as far as to make it happen, I thought Mrs. Gallagher was trying to create distance between us."

"Wait... wait a minute, what?" I was having a hard time trying to process everything he was saying.

"I was on a luxurious yacht trip full of talented artistic students from different schools and different parts of the world. I saw, heard, felt, smelled and tasted everything. I experienced art in its utmost form with every single sense of my being. When I was done, the only person I wanted to share this with was you, because I knew you'd understand but most importantly, because none of his would've happened without you."

I absorbed everything Rex was saying, but only one thing stood out for me. "Are you saying that you're not mad at me anymore?" He was my best friend and I'd missed him. I just wanted everything to be okay between us.

"I know I was upset about the whole art gala thing but after I left, I wanted to call you... every day, tell you where I was, what I was doing, what was happening but one of the rules were no access to our phones. I should've known that you'd never do anything to hurt me. I should've trusted you. I'm sorry, I screwed up."

A wave of relief washed over me as everything else started making sense and I walked up to him and wrapped my arms around him.

A moment after we pulled apart, his face lit up in a beautiful genuine smile. "When I was gone, I thought about your passion and your desire for Mrs. Gallagher."

The change of subject was an unexpected turn.

"I thought about how you felt about her and everything that's happened between you two, how discouraging the situation is considering her status is society and her family and at the same time, how she's doing so much to try and make you happy and I found the whole thing inspiring."

Had he smoked something during his trip back? "Rex, you're saying so much. I'm not sure I understand where you're going with this."

"Let me get to the point," he said.

I took a breath and nodded.

"She knows I'm your best friend. I think that's why she had Frank do everything he did, including giving me your new address."

I wanted to speak, but I didn't know what to say. At least his statement explained how he'd known where to find me.

"Livvy, everything she's done, it's been to make you happy. I think this is her way of showing you how she feels. She's a generous person and she gives back a lot to society but she's used this persona as a veil to express herself to you without exactly having to say it. Why else would she reach out to me if she didn't know it'd please you?"

Finally, he was making sense. What he was saying in a way, was answering some of the questions in my head. Like why would Mrs. Gallagher do anything at all for me if I was just a mere employee? Why would she help my best friend? Why would she pay for my education?

I was aware of the rush of adrenaline pulsing through me, but I didn't know what to do. How did acquiring this knowledge change anything? She was still a married woman with grown children.

If this was her way of expressing what she felt for me, then it also meant it would never go further than this. Our relationship would never develop into anything more than what it was.

"Rex, I don't think…" I took a breath to calm my beating heart. "I don't think that means anything."

"I think it means everything," he said, walking over to me. He touched my chin and our gazes locked. "Be headstrong Livvy, and risk it all otherwise you're always going to be stuck in this stasis wondering if things will ever change. I think the change should begin with you."

"Are you sure this was an art workshop you were on?" I asked.

He laughed softly and pulled me into his arms. "I've missed you. I had a completely clear state of mind where I thought about everything and this is the conclusion I arrived at."

"I was worried about you," I said.

"I know. I'm sorry. I was worried about you too, but I see that I shouldn't have been." He let go and walked around my living room. "Did you get a promotion or something?" he asked, turning to look at me.

I folded my arms and shrugged my shoulders. "Something," I said.

"I know it's late, so do you want me to come back tomorrow and we can catch up?"

"I think this is the best time because tomorrow night there's a corporate gala dinner I have to attend." I walked over to him, took his hand and led him to the couch.

When we sat down, he looked at me and said, "Explain this …something."

It was a little past midnight and I didn't want to go to bed just to end up thinking about Mrs. Gallagher. I had missed Rex and I wanted to spend time with him. I wanted to know everything that had happened to him while he'd been gone.

"I'm not sure how to explain Mrs. Gallagher's recent behavior. She told me she wants me to be her protégé so my work, my duties and responsibilities have shifted." Maybe talking to someone was going to help me understand her.

"What do you mean?"

"I'm working more and more on her healthcare business, meeting people, attending meetings and she's added healthcare and languages into my curricula. I'm not just her personal assistant anymore. I think she's building me to be something more like her."

Rex gently massaged my knee. "Is that a bad thing?" he asked.

"I don't know."

"What else has she done?"

"She paid professors to teach me at my convenience because the new responsibilities are demanding more of my time, and she had one of her companies give me this apartment."

Rex had a blank look on his face. "It sounds like a dream come true, Liv. Why is it bothering you?"

"Because." I got to my feet and started pacing. "It feels too good to be true. Have you ever heard of anyone else doing something like this for someone?"

He gave me an obvious look. "I told you, she likes you too. That is why she's doing all these things for you. She's trying to make you happy. I mean, clearly she's taken the time to get to know you and she's using that to help you."

"It scares me," I admitted.

"What about it scares you?"

"Is she drawing me in so that it'll be impossible for me to get out? Is there a price I'll have to pay for all of these in the end?" I said, gesturing with my hands.

"I think you're over-thinking it."

I groaned and sat back down beside him. "Maybe, but what you said last time we met left an impact. I can't help being suspicious about her motives."

"I was speaking out of anger. Look, I'm back, aren't I?"

I reached for his hand and calmly and slowly nodded, further confused my Mrs. Gallagher's actions.

"Tell me about your trip," I said, leaning back against the couch and watched as his eyes lit up.

Chapter Thirty-Two

I was wearing an elegant grey evening gown with a short lace train and white stiletto heels. I had silver teardrop earrings with a matching necklace and bracelet, and I was carrying a clutch purse matching my outfit.

I'd visited Andre earlier that evening to get my hair done and it now freely cascaded down my back in luscious curls, and after several online make-up tutorials, I'd perfectly learned to apply my make-up.

When James opened the car door for me and I stepped out, I felt like Cinderella heading to a ball. These were some of the rare moments that made me love and appreciate my job.

The gala was sponsored by Price Healthcare, and was a gathering of some of the partners, employees, current and prospective clients. The goal was to create an atmosphere of networking for both staff and clients and to build on new and existing relationships.

It also served as a reward for employees for work well done and, in a way, it was meant to encourage all the others to reach set goals in order to be part of such extravagant future events.

The venue was at a large hotel ballroom and the gala's program indicated there would be live entertainment such as poetry readings, singing and stage shows. I couldn't wait to get inside since this was my first corporate gala event.

There was a VIP entrance with a red carpet that enhanced the experience for me. I was led to the elevator where I found several people in wait and I assumed we were headed to the same place. I was a little nervous since I didn't know anyone at the gala.

I personally worked for Mrs. Gallagher and had never set foot at Price Healthcare offices therefore all the faces I saw were new. I stepped inside with a confidence I didn't possess and played along like I had every right to be there.

Since one of the goals was to mingle and network, I had a feeling I wasn't going to be the only nervous attendee. When we got to the floor hosting the gala, the red carpet continued to the main entrance leading to a large ballroom. I couldn't help staring in awe at the grandness of the venue.

The stunning décor offered a sophisticated ambiance and the outstanding color and lighting added a taste of glamour. The countless round tables had a black and white theme and were beautifully adorned to match the event with several bottles of champagne in an ice bucket as a centerpiece.

There was a dimmed stage with a podium on one side of the ballroom which made me eager for the night's entertainment.

I handed in my invitation and was given a place card for my table. A number of people had arrived and as I looked around, I wondered if my boss would be in attendance.

I was glad to be a guest in the event instead of playing a background role like in the past. I found my table in the middle of the room and was surprised to hear someone recognize me.

"Olivia? Is that you?"

I turned to face the familiar voice and was relieved to find Colin Peterson walking over to me.

"Wow, look at you. You look absolutely gorgeous," he said as he lightly hugged me and planted a kiss on my cheek.

"It's so good to see you, Colin. I was afraid I wouldn't know anyone here," I said.

He was handsomely dressed in a black tuxedo and a bowtie. I'd been used to seeing him in official clothing during our time working together, but the tux made him look great.

"It's good to see you too," he said. "I see we have the same table. How awesome, right?"

I nodded, greatly pleased I'd be seated next to someone I knew.

"Have you attended a gala dinner before?" I asked.

A waiter serving champagne walked over to us and Colin took one glass and handed it to me and then took one for himself. "Once, last year. It's a little nerve-wracking for a newbie but once you get the gist it gets easier. It was easy for me since I work at Price Healthcare offices and I know some of the staff."

It was going to be challenging for me since I was isolated from the other employees.

"You shouldn't worry, you'll attract more attention than you think, granted it won't be for all the proper reasons but you can use that to your advantage."

I met his gaze, wondering what he meant. "What're you talking about?"

He gave me a slow flirtatious once-over, indicating his meaning and I couldn't help laughing as I playfully slapped his shoulder.

"Did Mrs. Gallagher attend last year?" I asked, masking my interest by sipping some champagne.

"I think so. Yeah, she attended, but only briefly, you know, just to make an appearance."

"Who makes the keynote speech?"

"One of the other two partners," he said. "Mrs. Gallagher does most of the heavy lifting and generates a great deal of profit for Price Healthcare. The other two partners are old guys who refused to sell their shares during the acquisition and usually just follow her lead because they've greatly benefited under her leadership. At this point, a speech is more in their department," Colin explained.

Wow, she definitely was a force to be reckoned with.

"How are you doing as her personal assistant?"

"Not bad, it's a challenging position but I'm having fun," I said in enthusiasm.

"Having fun? She's a bit of a slave driver, how do you manage to have fun?"

"I find my ways." I loved working for Mrs. Gallagher. I loved being around her and talking to her. I hated days when time passed without me seeing her and with my added responsibilities and crazy time schedule, it was happening a little more often than I desired.

"How long have you worked for her?"

"Going on four months now, I think. Why?"

"I've worked for Price Healthcare for almost five years and I got my first invite last year. You must've made quite an impression."

I cleared my throat and scanned the room. A lot of people had arrived but not nearly enough to fill up the tables. "How long do these things last?" I asked.

"About four hours, though sometimes they can go past midnight. Let's mingle. Just join a group, listen to what they're talking about, express your opinion and if it's interesting enough, you'll get their attention and then you can introduce yourself. We'll meet back here when everyone is present and ready for dinner."

I nodded and looked around. There were a lot of people in groups, both men and women. They were all elegantly dressed in gowns and suits and made me feel like an extra in an episode of Revenge during one of Victoria Grayson's lush parties.

I joined the group of five people who were standing closest to me and tried to conduct myself the way Mrs. Gallagher would, with confidence and charisma. There were four men and one woman and they were talking about female empowerment in the modern business world.

I didn't have any particular opinion in the matter, but I had a feeling I'd joined the wrong group because there was only one woman present and I knew she expected me to express my thoughts in support of what she was saying.

Some of the men were forward-thinkers and agreed with her but one particular guy challenged her, stating that women best expressed their strength in controlled environments and while they were capable of competing with men, masculinity would always win out.

I didn't think I cared about the subject, until I heard myself speak. "So, I guess women like Ginni Rometty, Abigail Johnson, Oprah Winfrey, not to mention your boss Amelia Gallagher have only succeeded in getting where they are today because they expressed their strength in controlled environments...or has there been some form of masculine intervention we're unaware of?"

Everyone was speechlessly staring at me. I had to rerun what I'd just said in my head to make sure I'd not crossed anyone. A second later, everyone except the guy I had challenged laughed and one by one, they all introduced themselves, stating their positions in Price Healthcare.

When I introduced myself, everyone, including the male chauvinist, wanted to hear more from me. It was encouraging and a bit overwhelming, but I was more interested in networking and identifying people who I could make some use out of in the future if and when the need occurred.

After that, it was easy to move among the groups and talk to different people. My confidence didn't waver and for the most part, I sounded like one of them, which was nice.

I spent over an hour meeting and talking to strangers and while it was a little weird, I found the experience pleasant and educational, except for those several occasions when I met some people who were more interested in me than the reason why we were there.

"How did it go?" Colin asked when we took our seats for dinner.

"Better than I expected," I said.

"I'm glad to hear that."

The night's entertainment was introduced when dinner was served and over the hour and half long duration of a three-course meal, light conversation resonated over the table.

People continued to express interest in me, which I figured was because they'd somehow learned I worked closest to Mrs. Gallagher. While it was a privilege, I found it a little exhausting because my goal in communicating seemed to conflict theirs.

I kept searching the room for Mrs. Gallagher but I never saw her. My invitation had been delivered via mail as everyone else, I assumed. One would think I'd know if she'd be in attendance but I was only aware of her time schedule during working hours. After that, I never knew what she did, where she went or who she met up with.

I turned my attention to the stage while I ate and watched one of the night's talents; an amusing stage show. I was entertained and enjoyed the shows which followed. The food was delicious and as the night went on, I found that with enough confidence, I could initiate a conversation with anyone in the room.

After dinner and entertainment, a man in his mid seventies was introduced to give the keynote speech and from what Colin had told me earlier, I figured he was one of the partners in Price Healthcare.

I made a mental note to research the background of the company from how it had started to where it now was, because all indication showed Mrs. Gallagher wanted me to learn about the business. Why else would she add Healthcare to my curricula? And why would I be invited to that particular gala dinner?

When the speech was over, people got back to their feet again and continued mingling. It became odd for me because I had people coming up to me instead of me going to them. They didn't ask any direct questions about Mrs. Gallagher. Most of them just wanted to know how she was like in person.

A few months ago, I'd been an outsider, a dreamer who hoped to one day join that prestigious part of the world and now, I was at the centre of it. Mrs. Gallagher was an intrigue, a mystery to them just as she had been to me before I'd gotten to know her.

I felt lucky and special to have gotten as close to her as I had, considering all these people had more knowledge and experience in their field of expertise than I'd had in my job when I'd started out.

Around eleven thirty, when I was a little tired of the attention, Colin came and rescued me from one of the groups.

"Thank you, I needed a break," I said when he managed to pull me away.

"Dance with me, it'll keep people away from you for a while," he said.

"I don't dance," I said.

"You're gonna have to," he said, motioning to the people watching us.

There were others dancing already so it wasn't a big deal, but I still didn't want to embarrass myself. "Seriously, I can't dance," I said.

"I'll lead," he said, carefully moving his arms around me to hold me in place. Shortly after, I was being swayed to the music and somehow, I was dancing.

"You're popular tonight," he said when I got the hang of the dancing moves.

"It's not me, it's the position," I said dryly.

"I doubt that. Any guy in this place tonight would use the most apparent reason or excuse to get a chance to talk to you," he said.

I looked at him inquisitively.

"You're hot," he stated.

I broke into laughter.

"Do you know how many guys wish they were in my shoes right now?" he asked.

"I don't want to know," I said, suddenly uncomfortable.

"It's okay, they're not animals. They just want your attention. It's harmless."

I had never been a popular girl but knowing people were watching me made me a little bit uneasy but somehow empowered. I imagined it being a thousand times more magnified for Mrs. Gallagher and recalled how she carried herself like a lady. Would I ever reach such status?

"You know, Price Healthcare tends to book rooms for some of the employees who get too intoxicated to drive and some people just use them for the fun of it..." he said.

I looked at him. "Are you inviting me to go up to one of the rooms with you?"

He shrugged his shoulders, asking, "Is it such a foreign idea?"

I couldn't help laughing. "Flattered as I am, I'll have to say no."

"It was worth a shot," he said, laughing along with me.

He was a nice guy and we got along well, so I wasn't offended by what he said. Whether he was playing or not, he still managed to conduct himself like a gentleman and I liked that about him.

While we were dancing, I thought about everything that had taken place that night and my mind somehow drifted back to my last conversation with Rex. I thought about what he'd said regarding my relationship with Mrs. Gallagher and I pictured the image all the people I'd met that night had of me.

Be headstrong Livvy, and risk it all otherwise you're always going to be stuck in this stasis wondering if things will ever change. Rex's words resonated in my mind.

The gala dinner was my debut into the corporate world. I'd been strong and confident and people were going to remember me for being more than just Mrs. Gallagher's personal assistant.

Did that mean I was strong or confident enough to face her and promote this change Rex had talked about? Be headstrong Livvy, and risk it all. Could I? What if I risked it all just to lose it?

I lightly shook away the thoughts. I was already losing by letting my mind go in that direction.

"Are you okay?" Colin asked.

I stopped the dance and looked at him. "I'm a little tired, I think

I'm just gonna go home," I said as I let go of him.

"You want me to drop you off?" he asked.

I quickly shook my head. "No, I'm fine. Thanks though, for everything."

He nodded and I headed for the exit as I reached for my phone and called James to come pick me up. It was almost midnight, so the event was almost over. I was certain a lot of people were going to stay behind and continue having fun since it was Saturday night.

I didn't know what I was doing, but I was determined to make an attempt to follow Rex's advice. Risk it all. I wasn't sure I had the nerve, but with my new found confidence, I could do just about anything.

By the time James picked me up, I was a nervous wreck. What I was planning to do was stupid.

"Did you enjoy yourself?" James asked as he drove.

"Yeah, a lot actually," I said.

He was still the easiest person who worked for Mrs. Gallagher I could talk to. "James, would you happen to know where Mrs. Gallagher is tonight?" I asked.

I'd not seen her at the gala, so she was probably at home with her husband and kids, but then again with the large number of attendees, it was possible she might have been present.

"Uhm, yeah, she has a penthouse in the city. Sometimes when she's had a long busy day she spends the night there," he said.

"Do you think you could take me there? There is something I need to discuss with her." I was finally taking the initiative, but I had no idea where it would lead me.

"Sure," he said.

Are you going to fire me? I recalled my dialogue with her. *If circumstances force me to, yes.* Oh, God. What if this was one of those circumstances that would force her to fire me?

Little by little, I continued to lose my nerve. Could I really risk losing my job over an illusion of confidence and Rex's few words of encouragement? "James?" I gave in.

"We're almost there, don't worry," he said.

My hands shook as my heart pounded in my chest. God, I was

going to have a heart attack and I wasn't even there yet. What would happen when I got the chance to stand right in front of her?

Be headstrong Livvy. Rex's words reminded me of those few occasions where I'd made an attempt to be headstrong. The memories of my intimate encounters with Mrs. Gallagher replayed themselves in my head. They were impassioned and powerful and had all started with one bold move.

"We're here, Olivia," James said.

The building was one of those old apartment buildings in the city that retained a classical and affluent look. I knew for a fact that such a building didn't just house anyone so I had no idea how I'd be allowed in. This was a stupid impulsive thing for me to do.

"They know me here because I drop off Mrs. Gallagher all the time so if you want, I could take you in, talk to the front desk for you," James said.

"Yeah, that—that'd be great." Did I just stammer?

James got out of the car and came and opened the door for me. I followed him past the security guard outside the door to the front desk. The closer I got the more scared I grew and the more stupid I continued to believe I was.

The nametag on the uniformed guy we found at the front desk read Samuel Wilkins. James took the lead and talked to him.

"I just have to make a call to Mrs. Gallagher, please give me a second," Samuel said.

At that very moment, I wanted the earth to open up and swallow me.

"What'd you say your name was?" he asked.

I wanted to dismiss the whole thing, but James stated both my names before I could talk.

"Olivia Williams," he said.

My nervousness escalated a hundred thousand times higher. I'd have looked like an idiot at that point if I had run.

Samuel spoke into the phone, giving my name.

At that point, all possible scenarios started running through my head. What if Mrs. Gallagher was there with her husband? What if she was there with someone else?

Panic struck me into paralysis as the pause on Samuel Wilkins' end stretched out to eternity. He finally hang up, but I wasn't sure if his answer was positive or negative until he returned his attention to me and handed me a key to Mrs. Gallagher's penthouse.

"Call me when you need me," James said and walked out before I recovered from my paralysis to thank him.

"The elevator is right over there," Samuel said.

It took me a few seconds to recover before I absorbed his words and followed the direction he had pointed out. I could hear my heart pounding loudly in my chest and my pulse racing. I could feel every physical form of motion taking place within my body and I wanted to turn and run, but I'd come this far. I couldn't cower away now.

I got into the elevator and inserted the key. I forced myself to stop thinking and took a deep breath as I counted the floors in a therapeutic manner to calm myself. The elevator finally stopped on the twentieth floor and dinged open and my eyes grew wide in utter shock.

Chapter Thirty-Three

A dimmed corridor welcomed me to the penthouse, but what held my attention was the feminine silhouette standing at the end of the hallway. I took a deep breath, retrieved the key and stepped out of the elevator.

"What are you doing here, Olivia?" Mrs. Gallagher's voice was low and sultry, but I doubted that was intentional.

I was overwhelmed, but every part of me that was experiencing fear or doubt immediately and completely shut down because I desperately wanted, no. Needed, this moment.

"I thought you'd be at the gala dinner tonight," I said, taking a step forward.

She took her time to answer, and when she did, she said, "I was."

"I didn't see you," I said.

I could imagine how exquisite she'd looked. God, even her silhouette was desirable.

"I saw you…" she said in that low voice.

"You did?"

The ballroom had been full of people, how could she have possibly seen me when I hadn't seen her?

"You were…" She trailed off.

I could barely make out her face in the dark lighting.

"…are exceptionally lovely," she said, finishing her statement.

I was flattered she thought so, but I didn't care much for how I had looked at the gala dinner. At that moment, my bravery had driven me so far, there was little I was thinking about except seeing her face.

I took slow steps forward and she disappeared into the room directly facing the short hallway and I followed after her, walking into a large furnished living room which was also dimly lit. I looked around and when my gaze finally settled on her being, my jaw literally dropped.

The dark lighting was working in her favor as she wore a sensual lavender mid-thigh satin robe and a matching gown underneath. I felt like I'd walked right into one of my fantasies.

"You shouldn't be here," she said softly.

"I know," I agreed with her. Hadn't I argued with myself all the way there?

"Why did you come?" she asked.

I lustfully gazed at her alluring image in the robe and gown and my fingers twitched in longing. God, I wanted to touch her. "I wanted to see you," I said.

She silently watched me for a while before she asked, "Why?"

I slowly made my way over to her and stopped. I couldn't believe how much restraint I was exercising at that moment. "To be honest…" I said, meeting her dark blue gaze and daring myself to be brave enough to change the course of our relationship. "I hate going a long period of time without seeing you and I don't know how long I can keep fighting for self-restraint when I'm around you."

She slowly stretched out her hand and gently ran her fingers over my cheek. Her touch was soft, silken and instantly arousing. Her thumb rested on the corner of my lips, then lowered diagonally to my jaw.

It felt like she'd put a spell on me because all sensations of arousal came awake and all I wanted to do was touch her, feel her skin against mine and fully fill my senses with her scent.

She dropped her hand and for a second I was terribly afraid she'd turn me away, but instead, she closed the distance between us and kissed me, slowly, gently but before I could respond, she pulled away.

I opened my eyes and met hers. I still couldn't read her, which was frustrating. I wanted to know what she was thinking but before I could wonder for long, she closed her hand over mine and my body's movement instantly synchronized with hers.

Like an enchanted puppet, I followed her out of the living room, down the hallway to another room. When she turned on the lights, the spell broke and my heart restarted, but I was no longer afraid.

She came and stood close to me. Her image was so irresistible I wanted to reach for her and crush her lips with mine, but I had a feeling she was enjoying watching how tortured I was by the effect of being so close to her, and being unable to do anything about it.

When she finally closed the distance, it felt like I'd been frozen in time and my heart had just started beating again. She leaned in and lightly kissed my lips. When I went to respond, she pulled away again.

She was teasing me and it was making me want to implode because I was fighting to maintain my self-control. I wanted to wrap my arms around her and hold her closer. I wanted to feel the warmth of her body against mine.

She lightly caressed my cheek with her fingers and lowered her hand to my waist. She leaned forward and I closed my eyes as she planted a kiss on my neck. I released an involuntary sigh and drew in a ragged breath as intense arousal rampaged through my body.

When her lips met mine again, I could barely contain myself. I was starving and I desperately needed to feed. I kissed her with a savage passion and she responded, but only briefly.

"Easy," she whispered against my lips and I opened my eyes and slightly pulled back to find her smiling at me.

"I don't know if I have the strength to control myself," I confessed.

When she took a step away from me, I was afraid I scared her off, but she moved behind me and I felt her hands move along the curve of my waist. I didn't know what she wanted to do but I was holding my breath, waiting in anticipation.

She slowly trailed her hands up to my ribs and when her warm hands made contact with my skin, I drew in a sharp breath. She moved my hair over my shoulder and planted a kiss on the nape of my neck.

I bit into the fleshy part of my lower lip and my toes curled at the arousing effect. She seemed determined to drive me insane. Her hands rested on the back of my dress and a second later, she lowered the zipper.

The dress slowly fell to my waist and I closed my eyes and took a deep breath when her hands caressed my skin over the black strapless bra then moved up to my neck and unhooked the necklace. She came back to face me, closed her hand over mine and led me towards the bed.

When we stopped, she pulled me closer and placed one arm around my waist as the other one softly skimmed over my flat stomach in an upward motion towards my ribs. She was so intricately sensual, that I was willing to let her do anything she pleased to me.

Her gaze was dark and blazing with desire when she recaptured my lips, and her mouth was firm but slow. I responded in a similar manner, taming the monster within me fighting to be unleashed as I finally wrapped my arms around her slender waist.

She lowered my dress from my waist and it fell to the floor as we got on the bed. I kicked off my shoes and she gently climbed on top of me. It all felt so magical and surreal I could have sworn I was in a dream, except it was truly happening.

I ran my fingers through her hair and a strong sense of freedom washed over me because she was finally letting me touch her and express myself in the way I'd been dying to, since the very first day we'd met.

I eased her robe off her shoulders and she broke the kiss and pulled back to look at me as she dropped the robe on the side of the bed. I was in her bed in nothing but a bra and panties and she was looking at me the same way I'd always looked at her whenever we got too close.

"You're beautiful," she said, softly running her thumb over my cheek.

At that moment, with the intense way she was looking at me, I felt beautiful. "So are you," I said softly.

She smiled and lowered herself down so that her body was intimately pressed against mine. She planted a kiss over my neck and slowly followed a trail down to my chest.

My body involuntarily squirmed under hers as it burned in desperate need. She kissed me across my torso and one of her hands skimmed over my belly. I was so turned on, my toes were curling while my feet trembled.

I grabbed a fistful of the sheets beneath me as her hand trailed up from my belly to my ribs and over my breast. I could feel my nipples hardening over my bra at her touch as sweet sensations traveled all over my body.

She moved her hand to my back and unhooked my bra as her lips kissed the rise of my breasts and my chest rose to meet her halfway. She slowly pulled away the bra and her lips closed around one nipple, drawing a shuddering effect from me.

Her mouth moved sensually around my nipple as her tongue coaxed it and I nearly reached climax. She diverted her attention to the other nipple and a moan escaped my lips.

I surrendered to the sweet torture as both her hands now cupped my breasts, rhythmically stroking my nipples with her thumbs and index fingers while her lips kissed the valley in between.

At that point, my whole body was so overwhelmed, all the sensations fled to the damp spot between my legs, making me convulse in an unexpected but amazing orgasm. I was unconcerned about concealing my moans as they filled the room synchronizing with the pleasure ricocheting back and forth within my body.

She stopped momentarily to allow me to calm down and when I did, I bit my lower lip and looked down to find her watching me with a pleased smile across her face. I thought she'd stop, but instead, she lowered her hand down and moved it under my panties.

Her fingers circled over my slickness and she groaned, then suddenly she got to her knees and removed my undies, carelessly tossing them on the floor. She got back on top of me and recaptured my lips in a passionate kiss as her fingers moved over my clitoris and I moaned in pleasure.

God, she was good at this and my body was so responsive to her. The excitement coursing through me felt like I'd been shot up with ecstasy.

She parted my legs with her knee and slid inside me, drawing a cry of extraordinary pleasure from my lips while she rained kisses over my neck. My body rocked to the rhythm of her steady thrusts as my cries filled the room and before long, my muscles tightened around her fingers, giving way to another mind-blowing orgasm.

My body continued to spasm in pleasure as I tried to control my heavy breathing and my pulse raced. She rested her forehead over mine and kissed me as she shifted her   weight off of me.

A while later, I flickered my eyes open when my body relaxed and found her soft gaze on me. I smiled at her in unbelievable delight and leaned in to kiss her. When she responded, I moved my hand over her cheek and deepened the kiss.

I wanted to make love to her and get to know her as intimately as she'd just gotten to know me, so I trailed slow light kisses along her ear, down her neck and moved on top of her, gently running my hand over her body and sliding against the satin gown she still had on.

Her skin was smooth and warm and she smelled like heaven. She quivered beneath me and my arousal awoke again in response to her. I laid soft kisses across her torso, not letting the gown concealing her nudity stop me.

I moved my hands over her breasts and covered one of her erect nipples with my mouth over the satin gown. When she sighed under me, another wave of arousal swayed through me and I fought to restrain myself from being consumed by my desire for her.

I kissed my way down her body and stopped at her waist, reaching for the hem of her gown over her hip. I slowly pulled it up and my eyes widened as I hungrily absorbed the erotic image of her.

I lowered my body and planted a kiss on her inner thigh, then followed a trail up over the lacy fabric of her red undies as I continued to reveal bit after bit of flawless flesh.

I laid feather light kisses across her belly and paused to dip my tongue in her inverted navel, which caused her to release a moan. When I finally pulled the gown over her breasts, I pulled back to look at her.

She had the body of a goddess. The sight of her lying on the bed exposed for me made me growl in lust. I pulled the gown over her head and my lips sought hers in a fierce kiss.

It was extremely gratifying to finally be able to express myself in ways I'd only dreamed of. The smooth friction of her nudity against mine nearly drove me to climax and I had to break the kiss to calm myself.

I continued with my intimate exploration, loving the movement of her body under mine and the moans and sighs that escaped her lips. I could make love to her all day everyday for the rest of my life.

I playfully teased one of her nipples with my tongue while my fingers played with the other one, and she arched up her lower abdomen. I kissed my way down her body, painting the erotic image of her sexy body in my mind because I never wanted to forget that moment.

Every inch of her tasted wonderful and her sweet scent was now deeply ingrained in me. The sexy sounds escaping her mouth were music to my ears, and the feel of her silken skin against my touch was divine.

I planted soft kisses over the lacy fabric and her body continued to shudder beneath me. I wanted to make her lose control. I wanted to please her in an unmatched manner so that no one else would ever be good enough for her. I wanted to make her mine and I needed her to feel it. Feel it so deeply and intensely, she'd never forget me even if she tried.

I eased the undies off her long slender legs and slowly ran my fingers over the outline of her femininity, softly following the trail with my lips and her body responded by slowly arching up to meet my touch.

I ran the tip of my tongue over the small protruding pink bud, gently teasing it before I closed my mouth over her and kissed her, finally learning her exquisite taste. The sound of her cries fueled my desire for her as I slid my tongue inside her, slithering back and forth in a relentless motion.

I went crazy for her, knowing that I was falling deeper and deeper into the abyss of my feelings for her, but I didn't care. I lived for that moment with her as she groaned in excruciating delight.

The uncontrollable spastic movements of her hips told me I had succeeded in making her lose control as her muscles tightened and her body convulsed in a violent orgasm.

I rested my head on her lower abdomen and she placed her hand over my head as I waited for my beating heart to return to its normal rate. After a moment, I pulled myself up and went to rest my head on her chest and I drifted off to sleep listening to the beautiful sound of her heartbeat.

Chapter Thirty-Four

I woke up the following morning to find myself alone in a large comfortable bed and looked around the room to realize I hadn't noticed its mass size, luxurious furnishings and tasteful décor.

I replayed the scenes from the previous night and my heart started racing. I couldn't believe I'd spent the night making love to Mrs. Gallagher. My body felt glorious as the memories reawakened my sexual yearning.

I remembered her making love to me, kissing me, touching me and reaching climax from the initial intensity of it all and my cheeks turned scarlet. I remembered her losing control while exploring her and a rush of heat overwhelmed my body.

Where was she? I wondered as I got out of bed and reached for the robe she'd been wearing the previous night. I put it over my nose, deeply inhaling her rich delicious scent then put it on and walked out of the bedroom. I walked down the corridor, following the faint sound of her voice to the living room.

She looked absolutely seductive in a black robe and gown while she spoke on the phone. When she saw me, she gave me a small smile and I decided to let her finish her phone call as I looked around the room.

My sight had been compromised the previous night and I hadn't seen much but now that it was daytime, I could clearly see what I'd been unable to. One side of the living room wall was made of sliding glass doors. On closer inspection, I noticed the large balcony with several chairs and a table.

I made my way over and looked out into the city. The view was a magnificent sight because of the location of the building. I stood there enjoying it for a while and when I could no longer hear Mrs. Gallagher's voice, I turned to find her standing right behind me.

She planted a kiss on my shoulder blade and a warm feeling moved through me. I turned to face her and she leaned in and captured my lips in a kiss. When we pulled apart, she softly asked, "Would you like some coffee?"

"Yes," I said.

She went to the kitchen which was separated from the living room by a large partitioned marble countertop and I sat down on one of the stools spaciously built along the kitchen island, watching her as she poured the coffee in to two mugs.

"Did you enjoy the gala dinner last night?" she asked.

"Yes, it was nice being around everyone." I was desperately hoping our night of passion had opened other channels between us and we could now be more than just employer-employee. "How about you?" I asked.

She handed me a steaming mug and I closed my hands around it as she came to sit beside me.

"I was only there briefly."

I took a sip of the coffee, loving the taste and burning sensation on my tongue. Being so close to her after the passionate night we'd shared was overwhelming, but I wasn't going to let it put me back in my shell.

I faced her in order to share my thoughts about our amazing night together and found her staring at me. Specifically, my exposed cleavage since I wasn't wearing anything underneath the robe.

I was pleased to learn she found me attractive. When her gaze rose and met mine, she got to her feet and closed the distance between us. I held my breath when she placed her hand over my thigh, slowly trailed it down to my knee then parted my legs.

She occupied the space between my legs so that our bodies were almost touching, and leaned forward. She blew softly in my ear and my body shuddered awake in desire.

She slowly ran her hands over my body against the soft satin and planted a light kiss on my throat. I tried to harness my growing excitement and closed my eyes when her hands parted the robe and made physical contact.

When her lips met mine, she was soft but passionate. I responded to her in need and moaned against her mouth when her hands covered my breasts and her fingers gently glided against my nipples.

She deepened the kiss, coaxing my tongue with hers and the effect created a magnitude of sensations that all went to concentrate on my sex. Just when I thought I couldn't take it anymore, she broke the kiss and followed a trail down to my breasts with her lips.

She tenderly teased my nipples with her tongue while her hands explored my back, my stomach and my thighs. Then her lips slowly moved back up my neck and met my lips. After a moment, she pulled away to look at me.

I was panting in arousal and desire. I wanted her so badly it hurt and I knew she could tell because when her hand closed over my sex, the evidence was there.

She moved her left arm around my waist, pulling me closer and used her fingers to explore my slickness. I groaned at the wonderful effect of her touch and squeezed my eyes shut.

I wanted to feel her inside me but she was teasing the protruding bud with such ease, it appeared she was in no rush. I couldn't speak for myself because what she was doing to me was driving me closer and closer over the cliff.

When she stopped, I inhaled deeply in an attempt to calm myself and opened my eyes as I wrapped my arms around her neck. Her fingers slowly resumed their sweet torture and shortly after, she slipped them gently inside me all the while watching me, gauging my reaction. I loved what she was doing to me.

She recaptured my lips but I could barely respond to the kiss because my body was in agonizing bliss as she took me higher, driving me closer and closer to the edge until I couldn't take the sweet torment anymore. I cried out in pleasure as she continued with her firm gentle thrusts and a powerful orgasm seized my body, leaving me in a shuddering mess in her arms.

I rested my forehead on her shoulder. When I recovered, she lifted up my chin and softly kissed me. I couldn't believe how gentle a lover she was.

"Let's go back to bed," she said against my lips and I eagerly nodded.

We spent the rest of morning hours making love. I couldn't get enough of her. She was a dream I'd desired so much from afar and now that I had a chance to touch that dream, to feel it and continuously relive it, I couldn't stop.

Every time one of us reached sexual peak, we'd take a moment to catch our breath and before we knew it, we'd start kissing, which led to touching and shortly after, we'd be at it again.

It was the best time of my life. I got to explore Mrs. Gallagher's body in a slow intimate manner and kissed every inch of her skin, binding her image to my heart and mind for all of eternity.

Finally, when we grew tired, we both fell back asleep. I didn't know how long I was out but when I woke up, I felt absolutely wonderful. I stretched out my arm to feel for her but the space she'd been occupying was empty.

I got up and went to search for her, thinking she was in the living room like earlier before, but she was nowhere in sight. She was gone.

I didn't know how to interpret the situation; if there was anything to interpret at all. What was clear though was the fact that she'd left me alone in her penthouse. I was confused. I didn't know what to think. We'd had such a wonderful time together. Why would she leave without a word?

I understood if she'd needed to go. It was Sunday. Maybe she was used to spending the day with her family. I got that, but why not say anything or maybe even leave a note?

When I got back to the bedroom, I went to the bathroom and took a shower. I wanted to focus on the pleasant part of my time with Mrs. Gallagher instead of the disturbing questions that lingered.

After the shower, I got back into my dress and called a cab to take me home. I found a different man at the front desk and for a moment, I seriously considered taking Mrs. Gallagher's penthouse key with me, but decided to give it back.

I found my cab outside the building waiting for me and headed home to find Rex at my door. I was happy to see him.

"Are you just getting back?" he asked as he wrapped his arms around me.

"Yeah," I said.

I should've been tired from the exertion of my night and morning with Mrs. Gallagher, but I was surprisingly well rested.

"Must have been one hell of a gala dinner. You look great," he remarked as we got inside.

I wondered what he'd say if I told him that not only had I followed his advice, but it had also worked in my favor. It was selfish of me to keep the amazing encounter to myself, but I wasn't ready to share what had happened just yet.

I trusted Rex and I knew whatever I told him would stay between us, but I wanted to know where Mrs. Gallagher stood with everything before I got ahead of myself.

"Thank you, and it was," I said.

"What happened?" he asked as he flopped himself on one of the seats.

I went to the kitchen, got myself a bottle of water and went back to join him as I downed it. "I met a lot of people who work for Mrs. Gallagher. It was more of a mixer than anything else really."

"Was Mrs. Gallagher there?"

"I didn't see her, but yeah, I'm pretty sure she was. We were like over a hundred people."

"Did anything interesting happen?"

Scenes from my passionate night with Mrs. Gallagher flashed through my mind. I shook my head, "No, not really, but when people found out I was Mrs. Gallagher's personal assistant, I became pretty popular."

"Is that so?"

I nodded.

"So, where'd you spend the night?"

I found him looking at me and knew if I wasn't careful with my answer, he'd know I was lying and would demand the truth. "I was tired so I stayed in one of the rooms Price Healthcare books for employees who get too intoxicated to drive."

He watched me for a while, then sat up and said, "Let's go out for lunch. I'm starving."

I smiled at him, thinking I could use some food myself. I'd only had a sip or two of coffee for breakfast. "I'll go change," I said.

We went to a nice Mexican restaurant and halfway through our meal, we started talking about his work.

"You didn't tell me what you're going to be doing next after your adventurous cruise. Has Frank planned anything else for you?"

"He has identified some art galleries which would be good for my work, but I need to finish up with school first. I need to graduate and I just have a few months remaining so there's no need to rush into anything."

"Just a few months? Oh, I envy you."

"You shouldn't, with the professors efficiently working with you, you should graduate within a year or less." He reached for my hand over the table and I looked up to meet his gaze. "You have a great job and practically no bills to pay. In no time, you'll have paid all your student loans and finally have some control over your life."

He was right. I had no complaints. I finally had a future I could look forward to. Everything was working together in my favor. "Your uncanny ability to make me feel better is unmatched," I said.

"I should hope so. I'm your best friend."

I laughed and resumed eating. "I want to start sending home some money. I'm sure my parents could use it. I doubt my brother helps out," I said.

"I'm sure they'll appreciate it. It'll be comforting to know you're doing well."

"Yeah."

"Have you thought about visiting them?"

"Yeah, but unfortunately, now that I have the means I don't have the time."

"Sad that you can't have it all," he said.

"What about you? Do you plan on going home anytime soon?"

"Maybe when I graduate, but I talk to my parents all the time. I wouldn't want them to come here and surprise me because I failed to keep in touch."

I couldn't remember the last time I'd phoned home. I missed my parents. Maybe I should've made a little more effort to reach out to them. I knew they wouldn't care much for the money and chances were, they could reject it, but I was certain hearing from me would make them happy.

"You're a very model son."

He grinned. "I try."

We spent the rest of the afternoon together just hanging out and it felt great because it had been a long time since we'd done that. Rex somehow always reminded me of what was truly important in life.

Chapter Thirty-Five

"Mom, did you hear me?" Adrianna asked.

We were in the dining room having dinner together. Both Jonah and Adrianna were present but Patrick, as usual was unavailable.

"What?" My thoughts kept trailing away and it was happening more often than I desired.

"I said it's good that dad's not here tonight. We can talk about his birthday. I was thinking we could throw him a party at the country club," she said.

"Sure," I said.

"You could show a little more enthusiasm." She sounded frustrated.

"Don't you get tired of pretending we're one big happy family?" Jonah asked.

"I'm making an effort to unite this family," she said.

"Anna, if you want to throw your father a party, go right ahead," I said.

"He's never here. Doesn't that bother either one of you?" She was clearly upset.

"If you miss him so much, why don't you go find him," Jonah said.

"Come on, Jonah. Anna, you know how busy your father is," I said.

She got up in a huff and brusquely left the room.

"She's twenty-four. When is she going to realize he's got another life out there?"

"Doesn't it bother you?" I asked.

He looked at me as he played with his folk on the plateful of food. "It'd bother me if it was hurting you, but it doesn't seem to."

"You shouldn't base what you feel about him on me."

"You two have been unhappy for years. You barely even get along anymore. If dad isn't here, it's because he doesn't want to be. Anna needs to get that." He got to his feet and left the room.

I looked at my untouched food and leaned back against my chair. Patrick was a good man. He was a good father and I had no doubt that he loved both Jonah and Adrianna.

My relationship with him was complicated. It had been for a long, long time. I couldn't remember a time when a conversation hadn't escalated into an argument. Over the years, we'd learned the easiest way to get along was to avoid each other.

We worked well together and he trusted me when it came to business, but there was nothing more there. My fondness for him had never developed into anything substantial.

After we got married, he was wonderful and patient with me. Unfortunately, he was only human and therefore prone to weakness and his patience eventually ran out. A few kisses here and there were not enough for him and soon we had to consummate our union.

The first time we slept together, I told myself it was just sex and in time, I'd get used to it. He was sweet and gentle and had I reciprocated his feelings, I was certain I would've enjoyed it. Unfortunately, that part of me still somehow belonged to Isabel. Soon, our sexual encounters became a meaningless physical act for me that was a necessity for the marriage.

A few months into it, I discovered I was pregnant with Jonah. Patrick was ecstatic. I was a bit in shock but as Jonah grew in my belly, I came to learn how to love. When he was delivered, Patrick and I couldn't be happier.

It was the first time I felt like a part of something important. I ended my relationship with my mother because I didn't want to raise Jonah under her toxic influence and I wanted him to have some semblance of a normal life.

Jonah was a wonderful, playful kid and I was happy being a mother. I separated my duties and managed my time between my family and my work and for a while, it worked.

Patrick eventually started demanding more from me emotionally. He'd never questioned my feelings for him before, which I believed was out of fear of learning that I didn't love him in the same way he loved me.

He wanted me to stop working and stay home. My work had never affected my relationship with my son so I didn't see why it was suddenly a problem for him. We argued severally about this, and it must've been a real problem for him because he sought out my mother for help.

He never told me. I figured it out on my own because his approach changed. He argued that if I could merge Price Healthcare and Winston Enterprises, I'd spend less time at work and more time with him and Jonah.

I heard my mother in his words and resentment took root in me. Every time the subject came up again, I'd walk out on him and leave the room. Price Healthcare was all I had left of Isabel and I was never going to let any greedy person near it.

I withdrew from him and distanced myself and for a while, we were like two people who had nothing but a son in common.

"Don't you feel anything?" he asked one drunken night.

I couldn't talk to him in that state so I went to leave the room but he stopped me.

"I love you. Can't you see that? I just want to be with you. I hate the way things are between us. I'm sorry, Amelia." He looked so broken, I pitied him.

"I just want to be with you," he said, wrapping his arms around me, repeatedly saying it. "I just want to be with you, I just want to be with you." He broke down. "I just want to be with you."

"It's okay," I said.

It took a while for me to know what I meant, but later on that evening, I realized my saying it was okay made me learn he felt neglected.

He was a wonderful man, and he deserved better. So I did my very best. I tried to be as affectionate with him as I knew how and he seemed happy for a while and before long, I was pregnant with Adrianna; my beautiful little, Anna.

Things were good between us. Patrick and I were no longer fighting. I was doing everything I could to make sure everyone was happy and content.

When my mother tried to reach out after Adrianna's birth, I realized how much I had changed. I was suddenly someone whose job was to constantly please others.

In an act of anger and rebellion, I fully cut my ties to her hoping I could reclaim an ounce of the person I'd once been, but I grew so busy juggling my career and motherhood, it wasn't long before Patrick started up again.

He grew impatient and frustrated and I grew tired. I had two kids and two extremely demanding businesses that needed my attention. I couldn't handle another responsibility. Eventually, he stopped nagging me and an impromptu meeting to his office one afternoon explained why, when I found him having sex with his secretary on his desk in his office.

"Amelia. Oh my God! What—what are you doing here?" he asked as he got off his secretary.

I watched her stumbling to cover up her nudity and after quickly absorbing the situation, I approached his desk and dropped some documents he needed to sign.

"I can explain, this is not—"

"You must've forgotten I was supposed to pass by and drop this off," I interrupted him. "I apologize for the intrusion." I turned around and walked out of his office.

I should've been hurt or at least experienced some sort of betrayal, but to be completely truthful, I understood him and his desire to search for what I couldn't offer him outside our marriage.

When we saw each other again that night, he was profusely apologetic. "I'm so sorry, Amelia. I swear that was the first time I've done this," he said.

"Patrick, it's okay. I don't blame you."

"You don't?" he asked in what appeared to be surprise.

"No," I said.

He watched me, waiting for a deeper explanation but I didn't have anything more to say. He grew upset because I failed to express myself and since I didn't seem to have the reaction he wanted or expected, he lashed out at me.

"Don't you care if I sleep with other women? Doesn't it hurt you?" he asked.

Calmly, I looked at him and asked, "Is that what you were trying to do? Hurt me?"

He shook his head in what appeared to be frustration. "No, of course not."

"I understand you're not getting what you need from this marriage, Patrick. I'm not going to take some self-righteous stand and condemn you for seeking it elsewhere."

He watched me in bewilderment, and then asked, "Does that mean we're okay?"

I got to my feet. "Yes, but you and I will never share the same bed again," I said before I left the room.

Things between us changed drastically after that. I could tell he was sorry because he tried to make up for cheating by buying me ridiculously expensive jewelry and offering to take me on luxurious trips, but I didn't see the point because his affair didn't matter to me. To be honest, I was relieved because I could now focus on what was important to me; my children and my work.

When he realized there was no situation to appease, our lives continued but our relationship took a backseat as we both focused on our kids and careers.

Patrick grew bitter, resentful and distant. I wasn't blind to the fact that he continued to have a string of affairs but I commended him for being discreet about it.

As time went on, I started paying more attention to Price Healthcare in order to make it grow and created more distance from my mother. I wanted to own the entire company, but two stubborn stockholders refused to sell their twenty percent share. It didn't matter, with my eighty percent I could do just about anything.

During my mid thirties, I started to feel like I'd accomplished everything I'd set out to, but the knowledge came with a bit of emptiness. I had everything, yet there was something missing.

I took some time off from work and traveled around the world. I felt like I was searching for something, but I didn't know what that was. One day, during a short stay in the leading resort on the French Riviera, Nice, I was having a late dinner by myself at the restaurant in the hotel I was staying at.

There was a woman on the table next to mine who kept staring at me and every time I looked at her, she'd look away. She was beautiful and appeared to be in her late twenties or early thirties, I couldn't be sure.

"I'm sorry for staring," she said.

I could tell she was French from her thick accent. "It's fine," I said. "You can join me if you want." I wasn't sure why I invited her over to my table; it usually wasn't in my nature.

She smiled and came to join me.

I summoned a waiter for her and she ordered a glass of wine. Since I was done with my food anyway, I had the table cleared and got myself a glass of wine as well.

"Are you staying in the resort?" I asked.

"No, my cousin was supposed to meet me here about an hour ago but he's caught up somewhere," she said.

We didn't have much in common and didn't talk much either but somewhere along it all, we ended up in my room.

It was the first time I slept with another woman and for a few hours, it was exhilarating but the following morning when I woke up, I was met by a familiar emptiness.

We got together a couple of more times before I left Nice and those few moments of exhilaration gave me a little bit of what I was searching for. I continued with my travel and when I realized I couldn't get what I needed from it, I went back to work.

I kept myself busy and occupied, but at times I couldn't help thinking about my encounter in Nice. It wasn't so much the woman as it was the experience. I wanted to try it again, but I was home now. I had a family to think of and a reputation to uphold. This wasn't a random thing I could do with just anyone.

I tried to suppress the need, but eventually, I caved. In a moment of desperation and identity crisis, I tried being with another man, thinking maybe the reason why it had never been great with Patrick was because I'd always seen him as more of a friend, but after a try or two I gave up, once again forcing myself to smother any desire I had to be with anyone.

Then one day on a business trip, I met another woman. She was lovely, interesting and we got along well. On a whim, I ended up sleeping with her and reawakened that hungry part of me.

Again, it wasn't the woman so much as it was the experience but that was when I discovered what I was looking for. I wanted to experience something similar to what I had felt when I'd been with Isabel.

The realization was depressing because I knew it was an impossible desire so I gave up altogether and refocused on my family and work. I ignored the emptiness growing deeper inside me and after a long time of pretending it wasn't there, I stopped feeling it.

I made myself forget Isabel and everything she'd ever made me feel and made peace with her untimely passing. I didn't want to feel anything anymore and after a long time, I finally became the person I had once been until Olivia Williams walked into my life.

Chapter Thirty-Six

A knock at the door interrupted my work. A moment later, Olivia stepped inside. "I'm sorry, I know you're busy. I just wanted to let you know the meeting went well," she said.

She'd started taking some of my meetings and had gotten much better at it. "Good, that's good to know."

It was on a Friday afternoon, six days since she'd shown up at my penthouse. We still hadn't talked about what had happened between us but I knew we needed to do so sooner rather than later. It was still fresh in my mind and the memories were a bit too distracting and could be overwhelming at times.

"I should also remind you that you have another appointment in two hours."

I was pleased by her professionalism because what had happened between us hadn't affected her working performance. "With who?"

"Your husband, Patrick Gallagher."

I met her steady gaze but before I could respond, Adrianna walked in.

"Mom, can we talk about dad's party tonight?" she asked.

Olivia excused herself but before she could leave, Adrianna stopped her.

"Hey, are you busy tonight?" she asked.

I didn't think it was a good idea for my daughter to invite Olivia to my husband's birthday party, but I couldn't express the thought.

"I uhm—," Olivia looked at me. "I have classes," she said.

"Classes?"

Olivia nodded. "I attend evening classes after work."

"Oh, okay," Adrianna said and Olivia stepped out.

When she turned her attention back to me, she approached my desk and took a seat.

"Why would you invite her to the party?" I asked out of curiosity.

"Some of dad's work colleagues will be there so I thought I could invite some of yours."

"That was thoughtful of you," I said, even though I was relieved

Olivia wouldn't be attending. "What did you want to talk about?"

"It's a surprise party so you're going to have to keep him occupied until around seven then casually bring him by the country club," she said.

"I'm seeing him in a short while. I'll figure out how to keep him busy."

"Good, I also have a request to make." She leaned over the desk and made a pleading face. "Can you try and be less tense around each other? All my friends will be there and I don't want them to think my parents hate each other."

"We don't hate each other."

"Yeah right," she said as she stood up.

"Anna, things may be complicated between us but it doesn't mean we hate each other."

"I know," she groaned. "I just wish he'd be home more."

I got to my feet and approached her. She had a very close relationship with her father so I understood if she felt neglected. "I know, honey. Come here."

She walked into my arms and I pecked her forehead.

"I have to go finish up the final preparations," she said.

When she left, I went and sat back down and despite my best effort, my thoughts traveled to Olivia and our night together.

I could still remember the soft feel of her skin against my touch, the sweet taste of her lips, the intoxicating scent of her body and her echoes, oh those glorious echoes.

I closed my eyes and let the moment replay itself in my head. It felt like something within me had been tampered with. That thing I'd sought after for so long, the unquenchable desire I'd ignored and ceased out of my existence, Olivia seemed to have tapped into it and the exhilaration I'd experienced with her remained awake and alert.

Her relentless pursuit of whatever had been between us had led her to my doorstep and I'd taken the daring step to meet her half way and that simple act had been my undoing.

I didn't regret what had happened between us. I'd enjoyed every breath, every sigh, every touch and every orgasm. Olivia had reawakened a part of me no one had ever been able to since Isabel.

The only thing I regretted was the fact that she was my personal assistant. All the plans I had for her future were now in jeopardy and our working relationship was forever changed.

She worked way too close to me, to my family and that made our situation a bit dangerous. By encouraging her or making her think there was more between us, I was failing to foster the proper working environment.

We needed to talk about what had happened and I needed to let her understand how inappropriate it was, no matter how good it had been. I also had to remind myself that I wasn't single or in my twenties anymore. I had a family and a reputation to protect.

What had happened that night and the morning after was everything I'd been searching for. But I found it in the wrong person.

"Olivia, could you please come into my office," I said over the intercom.

I needed to stop thinking about that night, about her. I needed to refocus on what was important. I needed to be me again. I took a deep breath, got to my feet and went around my desk just as Olivia entered my office.

I leaned against the desk as she came and stood right in front of me. Since she'd started working for me, I'd noticed her drastic transformation from a timid, self-conscious person to a self-assured and strong-willed woman.

Whereas she'd been shy, almost frightened to meet my gaze, now she stood upright and boldly looked me in the eye. Her sense of fashion had greatly improved and her full and complete makeover both physical and psychological was remarkable and commendable.

"Olivia, I think we need to address what happened at the penthouse," I said.

She pursed her lips and nodded.

"You're an exceptional employee, Olivia. What we did—." I'd never had this kind of conversation with anyone before so I wasn't sure how to approach it. "It was out of control. I have a family I need to protect and they come first for me. I know it may seem hypocritical—."

"Mrs. Gallagher, I understand," she said.

I was a little taken aback, but greatly relieved. "You do?"

"I do, but——." She took a step closer to me, leaving appropriate distance between us. "What happened was something that has been building up between us since the day I first kissed you. Yes, it was out of control and I know you have a family to protect. I understand all of that."

From the deep intense look in her eyes and the way she was talking, it was more than obvious I'd somehow created a situation that wasn't going to be easy to get out of.

"When something unplanned and out of control happens in a world that has permanent order and operates like a well-oiled machine, it can be frightening. But if you ask me, your world could use a little bit of chaos," she said.

She was right. What had happened was frightening. It was a weakness. Exposing vulnerability was the first step to destruction. My experience with Isabel had taught me that.

I silently studied her for a moment, recalling those times I'd sought after the impossible only to end up feeling emptier than before. That emptiness was now gone and an overflowing mass of lust and desire had taken its place.

"If you want me to pretend that I'm not attracted to you, that I don't feel anything for you or that our time together didn't have any impact on me——," she moved closer, pushing the limits.

I stood upright. *She's my employee. Even if I give her preferential treatment, she's just like any other person I have working for me.* I told myself.

"I can try and do that." She finished her statement.

I tried to keep still but she was standing so close to me, I could almost feel the smooth texture of her skin against my hands.

She'd always been so intimidated by me. I couldn't believe how well she'd taken control of the situation. A little part of me was proud but the other part was weighing the danger of the situation.

"At this moment though, I'm finding that particularly hard to do," she said.

I couldn't help it; the flirting, though simple in nature, managed to draw a small smile from me. She must've taken that as encouragement because the next second, she closed the gap between us and planted a kiss on my lips.

I moved my hand over her cheek to stop her, but my other arm—as though it had a mind of its own—moved around her waist. The feel of her lips against mine made me linger, making her deepen the kiss which created unexpected longing in me.

I'd always been the one in control, the one taking charge but at that moment, she was the one leading the kiss, brushing her soft lips against mine and making me feel like I was being swayed away from reality into a magical place I'd never known existed.

I didn't know when I started to respond, but I unconsciously pulled her closer in sudden need to satisfy that hungry part of me that she seemed to know how to please.

She sighed softly against me when I parted her lips and explored her intoxicating mouth. The moment everything in me went silent and rose to welcome the intense arousing sensations the kiss drew from me, I knew I was doomed.

The intensity of the kiss and how temptingly easy it was for me to lose myself in it had me pulling away. I forced my thoughts back to order, released her and opened my eyes.

Olivia's emerald eyes slowly opened and settled on mine. She had the most tauntingly beautiful eyes I'd ever seen. Her lower lip quivered and I had the urge to pull her back in my arms and continue the kiss, but the warning bells going off in my head stopped me.

"We can't do this here," I said as I regained my composure.

"I'm sorry. I don't want to do anything that could hurt you," she said.

It was sweet that she was concerned about me, but it was also clear that the message I'd been trying to get across had been wrongly interpreted. "This is a bad idea," I ended up saying because the urge to touch her was becoming increasingly incessant.

"I don't want to have come this far just to stop when I know there's a chance you may feel the same way I do," she said.

I didn't know how I felt. I'd always been terrible at identifying feelings that were unfamiliar to me and at this stage in my life, I wasn't sure I was entitled to feel anything at all when I had so much counting on me.

When it came to feelings, I could openly admit that was the one department I'd experienced colossal failure in, and it wasn't something I was eager to try again.

"I don't want to go back to what we were," Olivia said.

I wanted what we shared because it was different from anything I'd ever experienced, but thinking about how negatively it could affect my life was scary enough to make me want to stick to what I was used to.

When I went to speak, Olivia took a step forward and closed her hand over mine. She gently leaned forward and laid a light kiss over the side of my neck—which sent tingling sensations all over me—and then slowly let go of my hand, locking her pinky finger over mine.

"Tomorrow night," I said, fully aware she was going to be an addictive weakness.

She rewarded me with a pleased smile and slowly let go of my pinky as she pulled away, turned and walked out of my office.

I exhaled and instinctively placed my hand over my chest to notice how strong my heartbeat had grown.

I had no idea what was happening to me. The way I felt; my body's unexpectedly eager response, my excessive thoughts, unbelievably arousing sensations, the lingering longing and disastrous desire in me, it was all new.

It wasn't an old memory that had been reawakened. It felt more like a portal had been opened to a whole new dimension because of the newness and intensity of everything I was experiencing.

The frightening part was, the last time I'd started to feel something new, it had ended with tragic results.

Chapter Thirty-Seven

The very idea of thinking there was a chance I may never get to be with Mrs. Gallagher again drove me crazy all through the week. I had to be professional, she was my boss but every time I was around her, I couldn't help wondering if she thought about our weekend together because there wasn't a second that went by that I didn't think about it.

When she called me to her office and finally said she wanted to talk about what had happened between us, I was absolutely terrified. I knew she'd renounce everything, probably transfer me to some far away office or maybe even make an attempt to fire me.

But something deep within me rejected that. I knew what she'd say and I expected it because I'd obsessively thought about it all week, but I didn't know how I'd respond until I stood in front of her.

I told myself I was going to be brave enough to look her straight in the eye, take what was coming and respond as I was supposed to. But when I was standing in front of her, when she started talking, everything I'd thought of, everything I'd planned to do, all of it just vanished.

At that moment, I didn't see her as my boss. I saw her as a woman I'd desired for far too long, a woman I'd shared something special with and all I wanted to do was remind her of what she was about to throw away.

So I flirted, partly because I was curious to see if she'd respond but mostly because I desperately missed her and wanted her again. When she took me in her arms and kissed me back, I lost whatever power I'd been trying to exercise.

God, she was such a good kisser and her amazingly soft lips provoked such arousal in me. I almost expected her to push me away when I kissed her, but she didn't and that changed everything for me.

I couldn't believe she was holding me in her arms. I would've been willing to do anything she desired of me at that moment but when we parted and she expressed her concern, it all came back to me. We were in her office, at her home. Anyone could've walked in on us.

I didn't know what to expect from that point forward, but again, I refused to give her full control of the situation. I needed her to know exactly where I stood and what I wanted. I was taking total shots in the dark, but I was brave and confident and that might've been what won out in the end.

I headed home with a broad smile that day. I couldn't stop thinking about what would happen between us the following evening. I wished I could fast forward the hours to that moment.

I couldn't wait to lose myself in Mrs. Gallagher's kisses. Our previous encounter was still glued to my mind. I dreamt about her touching me again, over and over, every single night since she'd left me at her penthouse.

Sometimes at night I woke up writhing in bed from dreams of her making love to me. Other times I'd stay up and thoughts of her touching me and kissing me would make my body burn in desire. It was so much torture, I was almost tempted to touch myself but the fact that it wouldn't be the same put me off.

Her exquisite taste still strongly lingered in me because it was something I never wanted to forget. It had the ability to intensify in depth whenever I remembered how passionately she'd responded to me.

I tried to chase away the thoughts now because I was getting turned on and headed up to my apartment when James dropped me off.

My routine hadn't changed and Rex was graceful enough not to complain about my time-consuming schedule because it barely left enough time for us to spend together.

I found a male form standing at my door with his back turned and slowed my speed along the corridor. He must've heard me approaching because he turned around to face me. When our gazes met, I cursed under my breath.

"Hey Liv," Greg said.

"What're you doing here?" I asked, slowly walking up to him.

"Is that any way to greet your older brother?" he said.

"You know there's a reason why people have cell phones, right?" I said.

"I wanted to surprise you."

"How did you even know where I live?" I opened the door and he followed me inside.

"Quite a place you got here," he said, admiringly looking around the apartment.

I placed my bag and keys on a table next to the door and turned to face him as I waited for an answer.

"When you sent home the money, I thought it'd be a good idea to come check up on you. Mom and dad were very supportive of the idea," he said, slowly making his way over to me.

"How are they?" I asked.

"Mom's okay but dad has been a bit unwell."

"What do you mean he's been unwell? What's wrong with him? Has he seen a doctor? Is he on medication? Is he going to be okay?" I asked in concern.

"Slow down, it's nothing serious, probably just a cold or something. Mom's taking care of him."

I took my phone from my bag to call home.

"What're you doing? It's late. They're probably sleeping. Call tomorrow," he said.

"Are you sure it's nothing to worry about?"

He nodded, then smiled and stretched out his hand to run his fingers over the outline of my trench coat. "You seem to be doing well," he said.

I smacked his hand away. "What're you really doing here, Greg?" I knew him well enough to know it was money that had brought him there.

I'd sent my parents some money hoping to finally start helping out but I hadn't expected it to lead my brother to my doorstep. I didn't want him anywhere near me. He was lazy and greedy, an ironic combination that no one else possessed in the family.

"Told you, wanted to see how you are. So tell me, good job or loaded boyfriend?" he asked with a smirk on his face.

My family didn't know I liked women. It wasn't something I would've wanted Greg to find out because I was sure he'd somehow find a way to exploit it and use it against me. "None of your business," I said.

"Must be the latter because all your school loans have been cleared, you're living in what appears to be a very pricey apartment and dressing up like a pampered little princess..." he ran his finger over the pendant necklace I was wearing and I smacked away his hand again.

"My school loans have been..." I was yet to pay for the school loans so he must've been mistaken.

"What's the name of this rich boyfriend?" he asked.

We'd never had a close relationship because of the extreme differences on the manner in which we'd both chosen to grow up. We had the same background and had been afforded the same opportunities.

I couldn't get how a grown man who was capable of looking after himself and his family was still relying on his parents for so much. One would think his family would motivate him to make an attempt to work hard, but it didn't.

I had always been ambitious, but my ambition had never been driven by greed. I wanted a comfortable life and I wanted it through my own hard work. I couldn't say the same for him. He'd single-handedly managed to screw up every chance he'd ever gotten to build himself a better life.

"I don't owe you any explanations," I said.

"Fair enough," he said as he went to the kitchen, opened the fridge and got himself a soda.

"Where are you staying?" He'd only been there shortly and I was already bothered by his presence.

"I got a rental parked downstairs." He went to my living room and sat down.

"That doesn't answer the question," I said.

He reached for the remote, turned on the TV and put his feet up on my coffee table. I was so irritated I wanted to throw him out.

"You don't expect me to sleep in my car, do you?" he asked.

"Greg, you're not staying here."

"Why not? You've got plenty of space."

"I didn't ask you to come to New York."

"Come on, Sis. What? Does your boyfriend have a problem with me staying with you?"

"There's no—." I groaned and walked over to him. I took the remote from his hand, turned off the TV and kicked his feet off my coffee table.

"Your brother travels all the way from Minnesota to come see you and you kick him out. How do you think mom and dad will feel about that?" he asked.

Was he seriously trying to manipulate me? "I'll take you to a hotel," I said.

"No, I like this place much better."

"Look, I'm barely ever here. I work from morning 'til late and attend classes afterwards. I don't have time for your visit."

"Doesn't seem like I'll get in your way," he said.

I needed to start getting ready for my classes. I couldn't get into a long tedious argument with him. I'd let him spend the night then tomorrow after work, I'd look for another place for him to stay. "How long are you planning on staying?"

"A few days. I want to see if I'll have the same luck as you," he said.

"By the same luck you mean, get yourself a rich boyfriend?" I asked in amusement and his serious but annoyed expression pleased me. "I have to get ready for my classes. You can spend the night, but tomorrow we're going to find you another place to stay," I said as I left the living room and headed to my bedroom to get ready to go meet my professor.

Chapter Thirty-Eight

"You look beautiful."

"You look wonderful."

"Gorgeous, as always."

"Stunning as the first time I met you."

Compliments went on and on from people I'd met at different stages of my life and the smile I'd learned to force upon my lips came naturally and automatically. I'd done this so much, I didn't even know if it was real or not anymore.

I would've been flattered and happy if I hadn't been used to it but I'd spent decades hearing the same thing over and over again and somehow over time, it had become countless voices offering different compliments which had all merged into one.

My arm was securely tucked into Patrick's. We'd attended enough events together to know how to play the role of a happily married couple. He was a very handsome man in his mid fifties and looked like a replica of a younger Richard Gere in any one of his amorous leading roles.

It was no wonder he had so many young women after him. He was extremely successful, looked way too good for his age and he was in an unhappy marriage. I knew him well enough to know exactly what was happening when he was away from home.

Unfortunately, his absence was the main reason for Adrianna's pining, which was why I was playing along to this surprise birthday party.

We'd grown so far apart that we led two completely different lives now. I'd met up with him earlier in the evening for business reasons. We were supposed to be living in the same house but, our lives had taken such different paths we had to put our meetings on a schedule.

"You know what you were supposed to do," Patrick said ten minutes into our meeting.

We were at a high-end restaurant and I'd just informed him of the progress I'd made on the Alix Delacroix meeting in Paris. Everything had gone smoothly but it was taking a little bit longer than expected, which was why I was closely monitoring him.

All the necessary terms and conditions had been negotiated but it had been brought to my attention that he was stalling for a reason. I had people looking into what he was working on and was aware he had another similar business that one of his investors wanted to fully acquire with him as a partner, which was illegal per our contract.

I knew what I was doing, but Patrick's blatant accuse almost made me lose my temper. I'd put up with him for so long, I had no patience for him anymore. He knew how good I was at my job. He'd practically begged me to invest in his company, an industry I'd had no knowledge of whatsoever, and not only had I stepped in, ready and eager to learn, I'd thrived in it.

So I wasn't willing to let him make me feel any less worthy than I was because I'd stepped in and helped raise his family business to its former glory when it'd been on the verge of bankruptcy. I understood his resentment, but I wasn't going to take his insolence.

"Anna has planned a surprise birthday party for you tonight at the country club," I said.

His eyebrows rose and his face seemed to relax a bit. "She has?" he asked.

I nodded, sipping my red wine. The last thing I wanted was to disappoint Anna so I was determined to do everything possible to make sure the night would be a success, and most importantly, to make sure my kids were happy.

"I don't want to fight tonight." It was supposed to be a surprise party, but in order to make the time easier, he needed to be aware of the information. "We're supposed to be there at seven. If you have somewhere else you want to be, you can go. I just need you to know her only request was for us to act like a family."

He went silent and was distant for a while as he took a sip of his scotch. He loved Adrianna. I had no doubt, so I knew he wouldn't let her down considering how much effort she'd probably put into the night.

"Did you ever think things would turn out this way?" he asked.

I met his gaze. His eyes were a deeper shade and his expression was softer. I hadn't seen this side of him in a long time.

"To be honest," I shook my head. "No, but we've raised two beautiful wonderful children."

"I mean between us, Amelia." He reached for my hand over the table.

My automatic reaction was to pull away, but I faltered. This man was the father of my children. I had caused him pain and unhappiness. This day was his birthday, the least I could give him were my sentiments on the matter.

"I know we married young," he said, pulling away his hand. "But I was so in love with you." He took another sip of his scotch.

"Patrick."

"You never said yes," he said in a slow sad voice.

I had no idea what he was talking about. "Patrick, we've had a good life together. We have a beautiful family."

"Amelia, when I proposed to you, you never actually said yes."

I raised my eyebrows in bewilderment and a bit of surprise.

"I didn't realize it until years later. I was so happy and in love it never really occurred to me. When it did, we'd already had Jonah and Anna. I was so happy. I just assumed your answer had been yes. But when I look back, I don't recall hearing you say it."

Come to think of it, he was right. I'd never said yes. I'd never expected him to propose to me that night and when he did, my mother took over and shortly after, everything happened so fast, it never really crossed my mind.

"Oh my, God." I shouldn't have been shocked. This was Kathy.

"It made more sense to me years later after I realized this. You were never in love with me. That was why we were never able to be a conventional married couple."

"Patrick, it's your birthday. Do you really want to talk about this right now?" I was unsure of how else to respond.

"I'm tired of being cold and distant. I'm tired of acting like I don't care about you." He reached for my hand again, interlocking our fingers. I wasn't sure if he was drunk or just being different. It just felt like he was someone I wasn't sure I knew.

"What are you saying?" I asked.

He took a deep breath and relaxed his fingers on mine. "I'm saying that I'm sorry. You were the absolute best thing that ever happened to me. I had chances to leave, to walk away and I'm pretty sure you did too. But you stuck by my side and we raised two great kids." He released a soft laugh. "I know at times I've been a sanctimonious idiot, but I just want you to know that you did a great job with Jonah and Anna," he said.

I was baffled. He hadn't paid me a compliment in years. As a matter of fact, I'd never heard him speak that way about anything else other than our kids and work.

"I'll be at the country club by seven. We'll walk in together," he said and left before I could protest.

I felt guilty for some reason that I couldn't bring myself to understand. I cared deeply about Patrick. He'd been a part of my life for a very long time and even though it hadn't always been great, he'd given me something no one else would ever have been able to; my children, Jonah and Adrianna.

I knew our relationship was strained, but I didn't understand why he took off just when he'd made an attempt to make himself heard.

We'd both led different lives for a long period of time, but despite that, he'd always played a very important role in my life both personally and professionally.

Since we'd gotten married, men had grown more respectful towards me and best of all, through him Kathy had learned to keep a polite amount of distance from me, which had led to me keeping her away altogether. So we had a lot to appreciate about one another.

Perhaps our only downside was the fact that I'd never really truly loved him, which I'd always regretted. But to now learn on top of that, that I'd never said yes to his proposal, it made the whole matter sad.

The most prominent thing I remembered about that period of my life was losing Isabel. Everything else had been a blur except for the wedding and the birth of Jonah. It made me wonder about my mother and her motives during that period when I'd been grieving.

Without a second thought, I called James and told him to bring the car around. I got up a few minutes later and walked out. I found the car waiting for me, got inside when he opened the door and gave him Kathy's address.

I'd never willingly visited Kathy but I'd been to her house before. She had an extremely large estate, but then again, she'd always had a thing for space. Her place was only twenty minutes away from the country club so I got there in no time. I had no idea what I was going to say until I knocked on the door and she opened.

The look of surprise on her face did little to affect my being there.

"Amelia, oh how wonderful to see you."

I walked past her and replayed Patrick's words in my head.

"You know I was just thinking about how nice it'd be—,"

"Stop!" I couldn't think with her yammering about. "I'm not here for you," I said firmly.

She stood upright, surprised by my belligerence. Though physically she still appeared fit and strong for a woman in her seventies, I could tell she was tired and on the verge of surrender. I hadn't seen her in years, but her state wasn't going to deter me from what had brought me to her doorstep.

"What—. What's going on?" she asked.

She was one of the guests at her son-in-law's birthday party and while it was still early, I could tell she'd just started to prepare for it.

"You knew, didn't you?" The look of confusion on her face did nothing to appease me. "You knew about the nature of my relationship with Isabel," I said.

"Amelia, why are you bringing this up now? It's half a lifetime away," she said dismissively.

"Not for me!" I didn't mean to come off sounding so upset but there were emotions going through me that I hadn't prepared myself for. "You knew about us. You knew it wasn't just business or friendship."

She watched me for a while then exhaled, turned and walked away. "I don't see what purpose this serves now," she said.

"It doesn't have to serve a purpose. I just need to know the truth."

"You were young, Amelia. You didn't know what you were doing. It was my job as your mother to guide you. I had to make sure you made the right decisions."

The ironic thing was, there was a part of me that was actually surprised to hear her say that. "You knew my heart was breaking," I

said.

She turned to face me, her expression softer. "I did," she said.

My heart constricted in my chest. Kathy had broken my heart plenty of times, but there was something about this particular one that felt different. "So you orchestrated the whole thing with Patrick."

She helplessly watched me, then nodded and said, "He was humble, sweet, kind and patient, just like her."

I could almost feel my heart dislodging itself from my chest. I forced myself to breathe. "He was nothing like her." My voice came out sounding harsher than I intended it. "I can't believe this." How was it possible? How could I not have seen it?

"You've had a good life, Amelia. Everything worked out for everyone," she said.

I looked at her in consternation. "For everyone except me," I said.

"You have two amazing kids, a good husband and a great business. I don't understand how you choose to see only the negative."

I walked up to her so fast, I was tempted to scream.

Her eyes widened in shock and what seemed like fear. Then it occurred to me. "Did you know she was dying?" I asked, trying hard to be strong but knowing her answer would destroy me.

"Not in the beginning," she said, then went ahead to explain. "When you two started working together, I had no idea. When her father threatened to take everything away from her, her mother told him about the illness and he shared the information with me, so we both backed off."

My heart was pounding so hard, my whole body was shaking. "So you knew she was going to die."

Kathy met my gaze and nodded.

I couldn't believe it. It felt like I couldn't breathe. There wasn't enough air circulating to my lungs. "Why didn't you tell me?" I asked. "How could you not tell me?" I took a few steps away from her. I'd never had a panic attack, but it felt like one was occurring.

"I thought you knew," she said.

I pulled away my arm when she tried to reach out to me. "I'd never cared about anyone else in my life."

"Amelia," the concern in her voice was evident.

"You're a monster," I said in between gasps of air.

"I was trying to protect you. Please understand. Your father and I worked so hard for your future. I was only trying to make sure you had everything," she said.

Suddenly, everything went quiet. I calmed my physical form and repeated a therapeutic mantra in my head as my breathing slowed. I was reeling, but I needed to regain my self control. When my breathing came back to normal, I stood upright, slowly opened my eyes and met Kathy's gaze.

She'd always been one step ahead of me. She was old now. There was nothing I could do to get back at her.

Isabel was gone and my anger towards her and the illness had greatly declined over the years, so there was nothing I could do about that either. There was nothing left. Kathy had failed to help ease my pain and had instead opted to exploit it.

At that point, I was more than certain she'd picked out Patrick for me way before Isabel had died. She'd held all the cards. She'd gotten her way. She'd won and all this time, I'd thought I was the one in control.

"My father worked hard, like his father before him. You were just a pretty face by his side. Everything I have, it came from him. Everything I am, it came from him. You've made no contribution to who I've become," I said. "I'm never going to let you take any credit when it comes to my life, my kids or my work. You were never a mother, a friend or a mentor to me." I'd never really thought I'd ever have to say these words out loud. "You were weak then and you're weak now."

I wasn't trying to hurt her. I was speaking the truth. She was a horrible excuse of a human being, manipulating my entire life and exploiting my pain to serve herself.

When I left, there was a lot going through me. I'd never been able to tell if Kathy hurting me was intentional and at that point, I was done trying to figure it out.

I was still thinking about her when James informed me Patrick had arrived. I put myself together and got out of the car to meet him. He looked a little more like himself, though there was still something different.

After my conversation with Kathy, I was too worn out to wonder about it so I tucked my arm around his and headed towards the entrance of the country club. He acted surprised, as he was meant to and Adrianna couldn't be happier.

My natural social poise carried me through the night even though I was breaking inside. I'd never had to deal with these kinds of emotions before, but they all accumulated at once and were on the verge of pouring out and destroying me.

Chapter Thirty-Nine

Patrick and I parted ways after the party while the kids stayed behind with their friends after the older crowd dispersed.

I was a little tired from spending so much time around people while pretending to be happy and I just wanted to be alone so I headed to my penthouse.

I had managed to silence my thoughts all through the party but now, when I was alone, they were slowly starting to find their way back.

My earlier conversations with both Patrick and Kathy replayed themselves in my head as my past with Isabel came alive with a breathless effect that weakened me.

I remembered our time together. Over the years I'd grown accustomed to feeling different things which I could now identify and somehow manage to comprehend, so I was able to tell how I had felt about her.

It had been powerful and overwhelming. I remembered her asking if I would've stayed with her had I known she was gravely ill.

At the time, I hadn't known how I felt about her, but now I knew my heart and at that period of my life, it had been breaking for the person it had loved. The sad part was, she had never known. Maybe the knowledge would've given her peace.

If Kathy hadn't rushed my grieving period and gotten me married so fast when the wounds were still fresh, I probably would've dealt with Isabel's passing a long time ago.

I wouldn't have to experience flashes of her every time I desired to feel the way she'd made me feel. She'd be a lovely memory that I fondly remembered instead of a phantom of loss and pain.

The thoughts drowned me in a pit of distress. When I got to the penthouse, I poured myself a glass of red wine and went to my bedroom. I undressed and went to the bathroom to prepare a bath as I wondered how I would've turned out had I never met Isabel.

Would I have ever experienced anything close to what I'd shared with her? Would I have ever noticed something was missing? Or would I have lived my entire life never knowing there was more to it other than work?

The questions went on and on as I got into the bathtub. I took a deep calming breath and submerged myself under the flowery scented foam. When the water started to cover my face, I closed my eyes and relaxed.

I'd never thought about Isabel so much or so consistently. The unexpected appearance of Olivia had awakened her in me. My thoughts and feelings about her were not in a chaotic manner anymore. They were clear and in order.

For the first time in my life, I understood myself better than I ever had before and through it, I lifted my head up from the tub and took my first breath of freedom. It was time to let Isabel go, time to let her rest.

I wasn't sure how long I spent in the bathtub, drinking my wine, letting go of all the cares of the world, but when I got out, I felt somehow lighter. It was a nice feeling.

When I was done dressing, I went to refill my glass of wine as the memories of the evening took over. Adrianna had been pleased because the party had been a success and Jonah, well, he'd been his usual self.

There was a great part of me that had wished the person standing by my side, holding my hand had been someone who made me happy. Someone I cared about in a deeply passionate way.

I knew it was too late for me to get what most people had gotten in their late twenties or early thirties, but it didn't make me want it any less.

It was strange though, because when I was in a room full of people and Olivia happened to be there, I'd notice her and some strange motion would take place in me. I didn't entirely understand it, but I wanted to believe it was purely driven by my attraction towards her.

We'd made plans to meet up the following evening and I'd had half a mind to cancel but there was something I was craving that only she could offer. Your world could use a little bit of chaos. Her words echoed in my head.

I had denied myself so much over the years. My kids were grown,

I'd done all I could for the businesses, and Patrick was leading his own life. Where was I? What did I have to show?

I wasn't seeking some sort of reward, but didn't I deserve a little bit of excitement? I knew Olivia was the wrong person to seek it in. She was half my age; she was my employee and she was my protégé.

I took a breath at the unsettling thoughts and went outside the balcony of my living room for some fresh air.

It was a warm night and the skyline of New York was stunning. The countless stars in the sky were casting down a white glow that met the bright lights of New York skyscrapers halfway.

I took in the view and slowly, my mind went back to Olivia. My unsuccessful attempts to resist thoughts of her were tasking so I just went with the flow.

Her confidence was becoming more and more appealing. She could move closer to me, touch me and kiss me without fear in her eyes.

Her touch was always so unsettlingly gentle. It always felt like her softness was a response to the intimidating way I presented myself and instead of pulling away, I always lingered, which allowed her to melt my icy exterior.

She presented herself to me in a non-threatening manner, which I always somehow found myself responding to. She'd taken the time to study me and get a glimpse into what I responded to.

She was also incredibly brave. During those first encounters, I'd always threatened to fire her. She'd had everything to lose and she'd constantly put it on the line. She'd never stopped and for what? A kiss, a touch?

It was an admirable trait which I believed she invested in the wrong thing.

I thought I heard the elevator open but I wasn't expecting anyone. The penthouse was my escape and no one bothered me when I was there.

The front desk always informed me whenever I had a guest so I dismissed it and turned my attention back to the beautiful view before my eyes.

"Mrs. Gallagher?" Her voice was soft and gentle so it didn't startle me.

I turned slowly and found her standing in my living room, looking right at me. She was wearing a nice casual dress and a pair of heels. Her hair was falling on one side of her face giving her a lovely innocent look.

She had a couple of books in her hands and was carrying a small bag over her shoulder which I assumed had her laptop. I couldn't help notice it was way past midnight. Was this how late she finished her studies?

"I know our plans were for tomorrow night," she said nervously.

It almost felt like my mind had projected my thoughts of her into reality.

"My brother showed up at my place uninvited today." Her voice was low as she spoke. "Being around him is a bit stressful, so I just thought…" she trailed off.

I placed my wine glass over the railing and slowly made my way over to her. When we were standing just a few inches apart, I stopped.

Her eyes moved over my physical frame and settled on my face. She had that intense look of desire and restraint.

When most people looked at me, it was with a kind of poorly concealed lewdness that over time I'd come to ignore.

When Olivia looked at me, she had the power to make me feel like the most beautiful creature in the world. Her gaze was always accompanied by so much more.

When she looked at me the way she was looking at me at that moment, it felt like she wanted to tear off my clothes and make love to me right there and the odd thing was, I had no intention of stopping her.

"To be honest Mrs. Gallagher, I couldn't stop thinking about you."

I wanted to reach out and touch her, but I couldn't because I could see there was more in her eyes, more than what her words portrayed and that slightly frightened me.

"Olivia, there can't be anything more between us other than this. You understand that, right?" I asked.

"I know, and I understand. But that's not going to stop me from developing feelings for you."

How could she be so confident? "It should, Olivia, because you're only going to get hurt."

"I don't think you want to hurt me," she said.

I turned and walked away from her. "I don't, but circumstances have a way of doing so. Look," I faced her, "I need you to understand that what we have, here and now, it's all it's ever going to be. I'll never be able to give you more than this."

She placed her books and bag down and took a step towards me. "Here and now, you're not my boss and I'm not your employee. Here and now, we're two people who are attracted to each other. Here and now...," she placed her arms around my waist. "We get to have equal say." Her voice grew unbelievably soft. "Here and now, Mrs. Gallagher, you're mine and I'm yours."

She stared deeply into my eyes as her words took effect. Her confidence was so sexy I couldn't help being swayed by her passionate words.

I closed the space between us and kissed her, she softly responded, holding me closer, more intimately and my heart seemed to expand in my chest. This was what I'd been craving to feel all night.

I shouldn't have let the words or the moment mean so much to me, but every time I tried to put up a wall of resistance, Olivia always knew how to work her way past it. It was like she had a manual written about me. I would've given anything to get my hands on it.

I broke the kiss and slightly pulled back. I touched her face and lightly ran my fingers over her lovely features. Her green eyes were always filled with so much life and so much light. I enjoyed looking into them.

"You want to sit down and tell me more about your brother?" I asked, feeling the need to want to know her better.

She smiled at me. "Can we go to the balcony? It looks so beautiful out there," she said.

"Why don't you go make yourself comfortable while I get you a glass and some more wine?"

She pecked my lips and slowly released me. I watched her as she made her way out to the balcony and the turbulence of emotions going through me calmed.

When I joined her, the night seemed to have grown even more beautiful. I couldn't explain it. Olivia was standing where I had been earlier on, with her chin high and her eyes closed.

I silently watched her before she knew I was there and took in how her presence seemed to have changed everything around me.

"So your brother showed up uninvited, huh?" I said, trying not to let myself get sucked in by the moment.

She turned to face me and nodded. I handed her the glass, uncorked the bottle and poured her some wine. After placing the bottle down, I reached for my glass and took a sip, then silently exhaled.

"His name is Greg. We're very different," she said.

I was already aware of everything I needed to know about him, about her family, but I wanted to hear Olivia's thoughts. I wanted to know how she felt.

"Sometimes I think one of us was adopted." She laughed softly as she looked into the horizon. The starlight was illuminating her face and giving her an angelic glow. I couldn't take my eyes off of her.

"He has a girlfriend and a kid and they're all living with my parents. He can't keep a job so my parents, who are already struggling, support his family. I started helping them out and he found out where I lived, so when I went home, I found him at my door."

I could already tell he was going to be trouble. Olivia was working so hard. His presence was only going to disrupt her life. "What does he want?" I asked.

She shrugged her shoulders. "He says he came to check up on me, but I'm pretty sure the cheque I sent home is what brought him here."

"He's here for money?"

"He's my brother and I know him. So I think, yes. He's going to find an angle and he's going to exploit it regardless of whether or not I get hurt."

I tightened my jaw in aggravation at the thought. "Why don't you ask him to leave?"

"I love my parents. I wouldn't want them to think that I kicked him out after he came all this way to see me."

"Don't they know the kind of person he is?"

"They have an idea, but they always choose to see the best in him."

"So what are you going to do?" This was a family problem that I couldn't get involved in. It was up to Olivia to deal with it.

"Well, tomorrow I'm going to find him another place to stay. He said he wants to try out his luck in New York, which is silly because I've been here for years and he's only been here for a day."

"Is he unlikely to cause you trouble then?"

She shook her head. "I don't know."

"Olivia," I reached for her hand and turned her to face me. She'd shown so much strength, I would've been disappointed to think she'd let her brother take advantage of her. "You're not who you were a few months ago. You've changed and you've grown, far much more and in such little time. I'd hate to see you show weakness when it comes to your brother, someone you know will hurt you at any opportunity he gets."

"I'm doing all I can right now," she said.

"It's not enough."

Her eyes grew a bit wider as her pupils dilated.

"You can't let him get in the way of what you want. You need to stand up to him. You need to stand up to your parents. You cannot let anyone have so much power over you," I said. "You're not weak anymore, Olivia."

She straightened up.

"You have the power to do anything and everything you want right here," I closed my hand around hers. "You need to exercise that power, couple it up with your strong will. The results will amaze you."

I was trying to empower her and for the most part, I thought it was working because her stance grew bolder and more defined, but when she closed the distance between us and kissed me, I realized what she'd been projecting on.

Her arms slowly came around me and I found myself automatically responding to her. She was sweet and slow but ravenous and passionate.

I wrapped my arms around her and responded in kind, but just when it was about to create a dangerous flare, she broke the kiss and pulled away.

I could still feel her lips on mine when I opened my eyes. I found her looking at me with an acuteness I'd never seen before, which froze my entire being.

I'd always known how to read people, but once again, this was a quality in Olivia that was new to me. She seemed to always know how to surprise me.

She ran her index finger over the neckline of her dress and slowly went to settle on her throat, then moved down to her chest.

Her finger slowly trailed the buttons, which somehow seductively came undone. It was the sexiest move I'd ever lived to see, as I tried hard to swallow a ball of air in my throat.

My sexual yearning was at the peak. I wanted to reach out and kiss her senseless, but what she was doing was drawing such an insanely intense carnal reaction from me, I was too eager to see what she'd do next.

I felt silly to think I'd been prepared for it, but when she pulled down her dress and stepped out of it to reveal a seductive pair of a sexy red bra and a matching g-string, I closed my eyes and inhaled because the sight of her was irresistible.

She took a few steps back and went to sit on one of the lounge chairs and leaned back. She had the body of the Greek goddess Cytherea. Her eyes were looking at me with that familiar lust, her arms were laid right above her head and her lean sexy body was lying on the lounge in that alluring two-piece that made my insides hurt.

I did what any other red-blooded human being would have done, because I was drawn to her like a moth to a flame. I went to her.

She welcomed me with a smile and wrapped her arms around my neck and our lips met in a kiss. It was odd that the tables had turned and I was the one trying to restrain my desire for her.

I trailed my hands over her body relearning the contours of her flesh against my fingers and deepened the kiss. Her mouth tasted of wine and something else, something stronger that merged with mine and made me lose myself in a kaleidoscope of confusion that extracted some form of self discovery.

I was no longer, Amelia Gallagher or Amelia Winston. I was someone who was learning what it was like to feel something for the very first time; without restraint, without doubt, without fear and without responsibility. I was, Amelia.

"Mrs. Gallagher," Olivia said hoarsely in between our kiss.

"Amelia," I breathed.

I could tell from the look in her eyes that she was surprised.

"When we're here, when we're together…" I took a deep breath to fill my lungs. I'd never given anyone else the personal privilege to address me by my first name. "I want you to call me, Amelia."

She kissed me so fiercely when I said that, I felt everything she felt for me in that single moment and it was more than I was prepared to feel, so I pulled back in a battle to fight myself, to fight her and then she said my name for the very first time.

"Amelia."

I lost the battle.

Chapter Forty

"Where are you going?"

My first sneak out attempt and I was barely out of bed before I got caught. I bit my lower lip and slowly turned around. "Uh, home... I have to go shower, change, deal with my overbearing brother... then head to work."

I'd never woken up to Mrs. Gallagher... wait, Amelia... A smile curved up on my lips. I'd never woken up to Amelia sleeping right next me before.

"How about breakfast?" she said.

I was about to respond when I noticed the inviting smile on her lips and realized I was fully naked. "I could use some breakfast," I said, failing to conceal my joy.

I had exposed a fraction of my heart to her and soared, so I refused to let myself submit to weakness. I had to admit though, knowing Amelia responded to confidence both empowered and motivated me.

She sat up on the bed and looked me up and down. "You think your boss could give you the day off?" she asked with a bit of a crooked smile.

I stood upright, ran both my hands through my hair, combing it back over my shoulders with my fingers and took in a deep breath, pushing my chest forward and intentionally, slightly, parted my legs. "You tell me," I said in a low seductive voice.

She threw her head back on the pillow and released a soft laugh as she pulled the bedsheets and tightly clenched them between her legs as though smothering her yearning. "Get over here," she said.

I laughed and got back on the bed, a bit too eagerly. I'd never seen this side of her before. She'd always been so unapproachable.

Now, she had this upward curve in her eyes which widened when she smiled. I'd always found her so breathtakingly beautiful; I'd never imagined there being an extension to that beauty. But there it was; the greatest discovery of my life and in it, a flower that bloomed from the seed.

As my heartbeat started to grow in speed and intensity, I watched her, realizing for the very first time, she was exposing a vulnerable side of herself to me.

When our lips recaptured, the kiss was so deeply intense and her lips so delicately soft, I could feel the hairs of my skin rising.

Her hands, even though free to roam about my body, stayed still along my waist, almost as if she was afraid to explore me further. Something about that simple touch made me feel like I could never live without it.

I broke the kiss and slightly pulled away just enough to meet her gaze and that was when it occurred to me. I was falling in love with her. This stunning enigma had captured my heart.

The realization hit me harder than I expected and a wave of panic traveled through me. "Wait," I said.

I had no idea why I exercised my willpower at that exact, intimate moment. I was naked and on top of her while she was covered by a white satin sheet from her chest down, but still managed to be the loveliest sight I'd ever come across.

"What's wrong?" she asked.

I closed my eyes shut as thoughts spiraled across my head. Had I really put enough thought into this whole thing? I wanted her, desperately. She made me strong, better, brave and powerful. I liked being that person.

My feelings for her were way beyond anything I'd ever experienced before. I'd felt it grow from mere attraction to admiration but now, it was something stronger, something deeper.

"I have these two meetings I can't get out of," the coward in me said. "I'm sorry, but I have to go." I got off of her and almost fell face first on the carpeted floor, as I got off the bed and reached for a robe to cover myself up.

It was a grave moment of fear.

"Olivia," Amelia said as she sat up.

I needed to get out of there. I needed to put my thoughts in order. It was so irresponsible of me to fall for her when I knew she'd never reciprocate my feelings.

"Livvy…" Her soft calm voice stopped me.

I faced her as my heartbeat violently pounded in my chest. She'd never called me Livvy before.

"What's going on?" she asked.

A wave of overwhelming emotion took complete control of me and I realized I wasn't just falling in love with her; I'd already passed that point.

"There's nothing I'd love more than to spend more time with you, but I still have responsibilities," I said as my heart continued to pound loudly in my chest.

She smiled lightly and nodded.

"Are we still on for tonight?" I asked.

I knew she was eventually going to break my heart. Not because she'd want to, or because she was my boss or a married woman with kids, but because I knew she'd never see me the way that I saw her.

She slowly got out of bed, fully exposing herself as the bedsheet slid down her body and my jaw dropped. She closed the distance between us, just barely touching me and said in that sultry voice that haunted my dreams. "That's entirely up to you."

My eyes hungrily feasted on her as she moved past me, gently and lightly running her hand over my belly then she stopped and faced me. Her hand rose up my belly, to the valley between my breasts, over my throat to my neck and rested on my chin.

"You dropped something," she said, gently moving my jaw to close my mouth, then smiled, reaching for the robe I was still clutching in my hands. She covered herself up and went to the bathroom.

A bittersweet pain moved through me and went to settle on the spot between my legs. I groaned in sexual yearning because it was self-inflicted and fell backwards on the bed, tightly clenching my legs together to relieve the ache.

That incredibly sexy image of her was going to haunt me for the rest of my natural life. I bit my lower lip to alleviate my longing and took a deep calming breath as I got to my feet, grabbed a sheet to cover myself and went to search for my clothes.

Mrs. Gallagher had taken me on the balcony, creating one of my most alluring sexual encounters yet. So I found my dress and undergarments exactly where I'd left them the previous night.

As I put them on, I fondly remembered her reaction when I'd stripped out of the dress. I hadn't planned it. I hadn't even known I'd end up at her penthouse. I'd been thinking about her. I thought about her all the time. It was the constant wondering and the waiting that made me grow anxious and drove me to her.

Luckily, I found the same guy at the front desk during my first night there and getting the key to the penthouse became an easier task.

I was always afraid Mrs. Gallagher would rebuff me, but even though she never opened up to me, I was still slowly getting to know her and knew there was a part of her that cared about me.

I finished dressing up and turned around to head to the bedroom to bid her goodbye and found her leaning against the threshold of the corridor, silently watching me.

I smiled at her, wondering if she was thinking about our night together on the balcony and she smiled back. She'd kissed me with a ruthless passion, the kind that I was always the one exercising when fighting so hard to maintain control. I'd loved it.

I walked up to her, feeling that familiar sexual ache rising to the surface again.

"Are you going to deal with your brother?" she asked.

"Yes, when I get off work." I knew she was concerned about me, and to be honest, I was afraid he'd disrupt the life I'd made for myself, so I needed to deal with him as soon as possible.

"Good," she said.

I moved closer and circled my arms around her waist as her scent filled me. She always smelled so damn good. Did she produce that delicious scent? Or had she worn it so long it was now ingrained in her?

"I must go now, before my body decides to stay," I said.

She leaned close and kissed me very lightly, just lightly enough for me to deepen the kiss, which I did because my body and my desire for her always drew out this horny savage in me.

I gently pinned her against the wall and explored her lips. When my hands found an opening into her robe, she stopped the kiss. "If you go any further, you'll never get to work," she said against my lips.

My senses came back and my brain restarted. That sexual ache in me had intensified. But she was right. If I opened that robe and started to explore her, I was never going to leave for work. I pecked her lips and forced myself to step back.

"I'll see you tonight," I said as I left the penthouse.

It took every ounce of strength in me to physically leave her side.

I got a cab home and was surprised to find my apartment in the same neat way I'd left it. Greg was a messy character who'd always had someone cleaning up after him.

I assumed he was still sleeping in the guest bedroom and went to get ready. Forty minutes later when I was ready and about to leave the apartment, I found him in the living room with a bowl of cereal.

"Well, well, well, look at you," he said, pointing at me with a spoon. "You never came back home last night."

It was still a little early and James was going to pick me up in another ten minutes so I went to the kitchen to make myself some coffee. "Of what concern is it of yours?" I asked.

He rolled his eyes and rested his head back on the couch. "Just curious about this life you lead," he said.

I watched him, recalling my conversation with Mrs. Gallagher. "When I get back, I'm taking you to a motel."

"Still against me staying here, I see."

The fresh smell of the brewing coffee lifted my spirits.

"Liv, I'm not going to do anything untoward against you," he said. "I meant what I said. I just came to check up on you."

"And now that you have, isn't it time you left?"

"We've barely had a conversation."

"What would you call this?"

He groaned, got to his feet and approached me. "Why are you acting like this towards me? I'm your brother, for God's sake."

He had an innocent look on his face that my mother or his girlfriend would've fallen for, but not me. I knew him better. "I know you, Greg. People like you don't change."

I poured the coffee into a cup and took my first savored sip. When I met his gaze, I could see the concealed disdain. That was the Greg I knew.

"Why don't you tell me the real reason why you don't want me here? You've got this mysterious little life that doesn't come easy, how did that really happen?"

I took my purse, retrieved some dollar bills and placed them right next to him. "I don't want to find you here when I get back."

He smiled smugly as he stretched out his hand over the countertop and instead of reaching for the money, he took my coffee. "I'm not leaving town, Liv. Not until I figure out what you're trying to hide from me." He took a sip and started walking back to the couch. "Oh, you still want this?" he asked, pointing to the coffee with that smug look on his face.

I wanted to hurl something at him for his irritating presence and even more annoying behavior. "It was nice seeing you, Greg. Thanks for reminding me why I can't stand being around you."

I took my purse and headed for the door. "If I don't find you gone by the time I get back, I'll have you removed." I lived in a safe and secure building where unwanted visitors could be easily ridden of.

My encounter with Greg left an unpleasant taste in my mouth and I was a bit pissed he'd actually managed to provoke me with something as trivial as taking my coffee.

I found James waiting for me when I got downstairs and the rest of my day seemed to slowly drag by. My meetings felt like they lasted forever, but I wasn't in the right state of mind so that might've been the reason why.

I was distracted by my discovery earlier that morning. I told myself that I was merely infatuated, but every time thoughts of my time with Mrs. Gallagher flashed in my mind, a warm tingling feeling would overcome me.

I wondered how she'd react if she ever found out. I was almost certain she'd abruptly end things between us because this wasn't what either one of us had bargained for.

My conversation with her the previous night replayed itself in my mind. I'd told her I couldn't stop thinking about her and her response had confirmed she'd noticed I had feelings for her.

I'd condemned myself when I'd told her that nothing was going to stop me from developing feelings for her because I hadn't known at the time, that I already had.

I'll never be able to give you more than this. These were the words that tortured me during the day. Why couldn't she give me more? Was it because what we had was nothing but a meaningless affair to her? Apart from our professional relationship, was her interest in me purely sexual?

The questions drove me so crazy, they delved into untouched waters; her marriage to Mr. Gallagher.

She hadn't stated reasons why there would never be more between us, so I wondered if it may have had something to do with her feelings for him. Did she still love him? Did they still share a bed?

As the questions spiraled in my head, I came to realize how sadly little I knew about Mrs. Gallagher and how now, I wanted to focus myself on that particular part of her.

Here and now...The echo of my own voice replayed the words which had revealed I may have had a little influence on Mrs. Gallagher than I imagined. *We get to have equal say.* I had no idea where I got the guts to put myself on an equal footing with her. *Here and now, Mrs. Gallagher, you're mine and I'm yours.* But I meant what I said.

I had been terrified, but once again, I'd somehow managed to take some of that power back. If I continued on this path, I knew there wasn't anything I couldn't do.

Chapter Forty-One

"Your mom and I have been growing apart for years," Patrick said.

He'd called me earlier on during the day to talk. I'd had to put off my meetings to go meet him because he took first priority, and this was the conclusion we'd come to after our conversation.

"Wait, what're you talking about?" Anna asked.

"They want to separate, stupid," Jonah said bitterly.

"Wait, what? No," Anna said.

Patrick and I had met to discuss the real nature of our relationship. As he spoke, trying to explain it to Anna, our dialogue replayed itself in my head.

"I know what you came from, Amelia. Over the years, I've come to understand you more and more. This is not coming from bitterness, its coming from an honest place," he said.

"Patrick——."

"No, let me finish."

Maybe it was better to let him get whatever he needed out of his chest.

"I wanted you to love me, Amelia. I wanted it so desperately it felt like I couldn't live without it. Adrianna was our little miracle. We were a family again, do you remember?"

His words took me back in time and I smiled as I nodded. "She was a clumsy little thing, wasn't she?" I said.

He nodded with a smile on his face. "Yes, she was."

We both went silent, almost as though our memories had synchronized and we were on the same plane again. Then he yanked me back to reality with the ugliest memories in my mind.

"Your mother was trying to turn you into a weapon, Amelia. A weapon she could use against any corporate giant, as long as it worked in her favor. She wanted to turn you into a machine. How you were capable of being with me, baring our children, loving and nurturing them into what they are today is beyond me."

I tightened my jaw.

This was information I was already aware of. I'd never thought anyone would ever come to possess it, let alone speak of it, but after all that time I'd spent with Patrick, it didn't surprise me he was aware of it.

"That guarded humanity I saw in you when I realized the kind of life you'd had, it's what has kept me by your side. Though we haven't touched or kissed in years, just having you in my life has been enough for me."

"Patrick, stop." I couldn't stand to hear anymore.

"I love you, Amelia. It may not show, but I do and I need you to know that."

I gritted my teeth. "What do you want from this?" I said in a bit of irritation.

"I want to set you free," he said.

Set me free? Did he think he was my savior? "Are you kidding me?" I asked. "What does that even mean?"

He laughed softly as he closed his hands over mine, gently and warmly squeezing them, an act that felt strange to me. "It may be a little too late, but I don't want you to feel obligated to me anymore."

"What are you saying?" I asked, pulling my hands away.

"I think we should get a divorce," he said.

I was stunned for a minute.

"We've grown so far apart, Amelia. I don't know who you are anymore. You don't know who I am. Jonah and Adrianna are the reason we've stayed together this long. But they're both grown up now. They'll understand."

I had no words.

"The first time I saw you, I knew I'd spend every single day of my life loving you. I know you've given me everything you could've given anyone else. But I think its time we sought after something that would make us both individually happy... apart."

I agreed. I wanted Patrick to be happy. He'd been so good and patient with me.

"I think that would be best," I said.

"Adrianna might take this a little harder than Jonah but in time, I think she'll understand. They don't know you the way I do. They don't know what you've been through."

"They should never find out, Patrick. I want to protect them from that knowledge and ironic as this may seem, I want them to retain the relationship they have with Kathy because they've somehow managed to make a somewhat decent being out of her."

For some reason, we both laughed at some mutual silent agreement.

"Anna, would you rather we stay together and continued to be miserable or parted ways and tried to seek happiness from someplace else?" Patrick asked, drawing me back to the present.

"I want you both to be happy," she said.

We turned our attention to Jonah, but he only shrugged his shoulders in nonchalance.

When Patrick and I were alone later on, it felt strangely comfortable.

"I know we've both gone through some things we'd rather not speak of, but doesn't it feel like the first breath of fresh air, in a long time?" Patrick asked.

It was too good to be true and I had no idea what to do with it, but yes it did. "It does," I said. "Is it supposed to feel this way?"

Even though we'd spent so many years practically apart, the finality in this separation felt wholesomely liberating. Our lives wouldn't have to change, but knowing we had the freedom to do anything we both wanted without worrying about hurting or humiliating each other felt incredible.

"I think so," he said.

We were talking in his study. He'd poured us both some whisky and this was the most peaceful we'd been around each other in a very long time.

"So what happens now?" I still wasn't fully aware of the formal norms to follow when it came to some things.

"To be honest, I don't know," he said.

"I don't want this to affect the family in any negative way. We've managed to stay out of the spotlight for a long time and I'd really like it if it continued that way." I didn't want Adrianna and Jonah to get hurt.

"As long as we stay united, everything is going to be okay," he

said.

I took a deep breath and relaxed.

Hours later when it was about to hit midnight, I was at the penthouse thinking about my afternoon. I was concerned about Jonah and Adrianna.

Even though Anna took the separation the hardest, I couldn't help thinking about Jonah. He'd always been like me. Always seeking success and trying so hard not to feel things that profoundly affected him.

I'd made sure he grew up in as normal an environment as he could, but there was a part of myself in him that I saw every time I looked into his eyes. A part that I looked at with sadness because I didn't know how help.

The elevator doors opened.

I knew it was Olivia since we'd made plans to meet up, but I wasn't sure I was in the best mood to spend the night with her. Earlier on that morning, she'd left me in a bit of confusion but I hadn't had time to think about it because of my day with Patrick.

I saw her walk inside and stop when her gaze met mine. That look in her eyes resembled the one I'd noticed in the morning. I thought it was curiosity and fear, but at that moment, it was something else, something more.

I was standing outside the balcony in the warm midnight air. I'd been lost in thought while blankly staring at the bright countless stars in the sky but now, I was looking at Olivia, lost in not only how beautiful I found her to be, but also, how seeing her managed to somehow shift my axis.

She never took her eyes off me as she placed her bag on the couch and approached me. I watched her as she stepped out to join me on the balcony, came to stand so close, we were just a couple of inches apart.

"Hi," she said.

I smiled.

She smiled back and closed the gap between us with a kiss I didn't know I'd been anticipating. I responded, caressing her soft lips with my own as her arms gently moved around my waist, and our mutual passion took over.

When we pulled apart, I was breathless. I hadn't enjoyed something as simple as a kiss with anyone in such a long period of time until Olivia had come along for, whenever we kissed, some sort of life seemed to bloom from it.

"I've been looking forward to this all day," she said.

I guess I had been too, I just hadn't been as acutely aware of it.

"Are you okay?" she asked.

I quickly nodded. I hadn't expected my day to be as eventful as it had turned out to be. "I'm fine," I pecked her lips, which was strange how easily comfortable it was for me to perform such an act.

Olivia slightly pulled away and stared out into the sky and took a breath of the warm night air. She turned her attention back to me when her eyes opened and said softly, "I can't remember a night I've spent by your side that hasn't been this beautiful."

Sometimes the intensity in her eyes coupled up by the truth she spoke frightened me. "Why don't I get us something to drink?" I said, pulling away from her before she had a chance to respond.

I resented how she had the power to make me feel like I was twenty-one again. She made me nervous, got me excited, made me question myself but above all, when she looked at me sometimes, it felt like everything I desired was in her eyes.

I got us a nice expensive bottle of red wine and two glasses and rejoined her at the balcony. She silently watched me as I uncorked the bottle and poured the wine into the glasses.

"I'm sorry about the way I ran out this morning," she said.

I knew she'd wanted to stay but she'd had a job to do and going to work when I'd offered her a chance not to, had only gone to prove how serious she was with her responsibilities. "You don't have to be sorry for that," I said.

She took a sip of the wine and a smile crept up my lips from the look of appreciation that came across her face.

"This is nearly orgasmic," she said.

I held up my glass and said, "It's a 1999 Romanée-Conti."

"I'd never had anything close to vintage wine before, this must be expensive," she said.

I shook my head and shortly after realized that what was expensive to her wasn't expensive to me. I'd never lived without money. Whatever struggle she'd ever had to live through was something I'd probably never come to understand.

She had a thoughtful look across her face before she spoke.

"When my brother showed up, he mentioned something that sounded odd," she said.

I nodded, thinking she was going to ask me for help but from the expression on her face, I could tell she was more interested in something else.

"He said my school loans had all been paid in full. I went by to confirm today and he was right."

I waited for her question.

"Did you pay it off?" she asked.

"I'd never been able to lie to her. "Yes," I said.

"Why? I'm making money now. I could have paid it off myself."

She seemed very bothered by the knowledge. "I wanted you to have a fresh start."

"You've done so much for me already. Please don't take this the wrong way, but I'm not a wounded creature that you always have to rescue. I know you mean well and I so deeply appreciate it, but you have to stop. Let me handle things on my own, how will you ever fully trust me if you're always taking care of things for me?"

She made a valid argument, but I'd paid off her loans when I'd gotten her the professors. It had been supposed to be a new start for her. She worked so hard, I didn't want her to have anything holding her back. "You're right. I'm sorry."

She studied me for a long while before she spoke, then looked into the horizon. I could tell she had something on her mind, but I didn't want to risk asking incase she said something I wasn't ready to deal with.

"You know at first, when you started doing all these amazing things for me, I used to be so happy and I felt so lucky. When I saw Rex again and realized what you'd done for him, my heart almost burst in joy." She turned to face me, her eyes more serene than I'd ever seen them.

"I know you have a plan and to be honest, I used to doubt you and your motive, but not anymore. I just want to know; do you care about me?"

I thought about what the answer would mean, how it'd affect our current relationship, maybe even change its course, but that soft sincere look in her eyes practically forced the answer right out of my lips.

"Yes," I said, but I needed her to understand this didn't change the nature of our relationship. "But this doesn't mean anything changes between us."

"I understand," she said with a smile on her lips.

If she understood, then why did she seem so pleased? "Do you really?"

She gently reached for my hand and moved closer to me so that we were almost touching. "Yes, and for now it's all I need to know." She closed the space between us and planted a light kiss over my neck, sending tantalizing shivers of arousal through me.

It seemed no matter what I said she always had an upper hand. Her confidence was awe-inspiring and again, it felt focused on the wrong thing but at that moment, it didn't feel right for me to correct her.

"You know someday, someone is going to tell our story," she said softly as she slowly pulled away.

"Yeah?" I said, indulging her.

"The author, whom I presume will be a woman, will probably have one of those weird English surnames, like …Belchambers."

I laughed and asked, "And how do you presume she'll conclude this story?"

Her face grew a bit serious as she shook her head. "To be honest, I don't think she'll know until the very last page."

I placed my hand over the nape of her neck and slowly pulled her closer, leaning my forehead against hers.

I really couldn't start thinking about how our lives would end up. My marriage had just ended and while that should've felt like an open way to do whatever I wanted, I couldn't lose focus on the plans I had for Olivia. Unfortunately, that put what we were doing and everything else aside.

Chapter Forty-Two

I was dying to tell her how I truly felt, and if the circumstances had been different, I would've happily done so. I couldn't help wonder if this roadblock between us would ever come down.

I wanted her more than I'd ever wanted anything else in life, but I was a realist and after thinking it all through, I knew this was all we'd probably ever have. So instead of pining and thinking about things that would most likely just end up hurting me, I focused on the present and the present couldn't have been more beautiful.

I wanted to get to know Amelia, and I wanted her to know me.

We sat down on the lounge seats as I sipped on the expensive wine she'd poured us and wondered if I should ask direct questions.

"I've always wondered how you came to run all these businesses." I'd tried to learn more about her from the internet but the scattered information was completely unreliable.

"How many businesses do you think I run?" she asked.

"To my knowledge, I'd have to say Winston Enterprises, Price Healthcare and I know you have shares in your husband's business." I tried to sound as casual as possible because I wanted her to voluntarily offer the information I needed to fill in the blanks.

"Winston Enterprises is an old family business which has passed on from one generation to the next," she said.

"I kinda figured that. You must've started working for the business pretty early." I was watching her in the moonlight glow, trying to capture her facial expressions because I wanted to absorb every second of that conversation. For some reason, it felt like this was the most open she'd ever be with me.

"I did, but it was expected of me. If I'd had brothers or sisters, it probably would have been different. But after my dad died, all the pressure fell on me."

She had a flash of sadness but it disappeared almost as fast as it had appeared.

"I'm sorry."

She shook her head, brushing it off. "It was a long time ago."

"Irrespective, you must've grown up very fast because of what was expected of you," I said, trying not to give her a chance to think about stopping the conversation because of how guarded she was. I was even surprised I'd come this far.

She went silent for a while and I thought I'd lost the connection, but she said softly and distantly, "I had to."

"I know back then things were very different, but something tells me you must've kicked ass," I said.

She turned to face me with a small smile on her face.

"You did, didn't you?" I asked.

She nodded.

I admired the fact that she wasn't a showy or bragging type of person. Somehow, over the years, she'd managed to retain that humility in its sincerest form.

I didn't know much about her involvement with healthcare, there had never really been any publicly documented information about it but in a past, vague conversation, she'd mentioned something that I remembered.

I had asked her if she'd gone into healthcare because she felt she hadn't done enough charity, and she'd said someone she'd known had gone into it. When I'd asked further, she'd said she couldn't talk about it.

I wondered if she was ready now. "How did you end up owning Price Healthcare?"

I was looking at the most beautiful and natural form of reality I'd ever been graced with; the countless stars, bright misty moon on the dark blue-grey stained canvas of a sky, which held everything in place to create this magical view.

I knew, because just the previous night, she'd made love to me in its glorious presence and it had been absolute heaven. So yes, I understood why she loved the penthouse. It wasn't just because of its location, extravagance or magnificence; it was also because of the amazing view during the right seasons.

"I didn't," she said.

I turned to face her with questions, hoping she'd offer me a detailed explanation.

"Someone I knew did. I just helped her acquire it," she said.

For a moment, I was lost. Every explanation that could exist lived and passed through my mind but none of it made sense.

"Who was the original owner of Price Healthcare?" I asked.

She took a deep breath, got to her feet and walked over to the railing of the balcony.

Whoever this person was, she must've played a very big role in Amelia's life which partly explained why in a past attempt to know her she'd refused to answer me.

"Was it someone you cared about?" I asked, getting to my feet and making my way over to her.

"Yes," she said.

I replayed every detail of my conversation with her that night in my mind.

"Were you together?" From the expression across her face, I could tell it was someone who had been very special to her and for some silly reason I was jealous of her.

"Yes." I gritted my teeth, but before I could respond, she continued, "I was about to turn twenty-one when we met. She was unlike anyone I'd ever known at the time." Amelia seemed to zone out as she spoke. "But she died and I didn't even know she'd been sick. Her name was Isabel Price." She released an angry laugh.

I wanted to speak, but the anger in her laugh quickly translated to pain in my mind and somewhere in my heart. I didn't know what to say and at the same time, selfish reasons kept me from interfering with her momentum because I wanted to learn more.

She took a long while to talk after that, but I waited, patiently, because this is who she was, the person I was so desperate to get to know.

"You remind me of her," she said softly.

Suddenly every sentence and conversation that had ever been spoken between us ran through my mind making me realize I reminded her of someone she'd greatly cared about.

"Did you love her?" At that moment, it didn't feel like it was about me, it felt like it was about something bigger, greater than me or what I reminded her of.

She turned to face me and took a breath as she said, "I didn't know what love meant, but looking back after everything I've been through, I'd have to say yes. I think I did."

My heart ached for this Isabel. If she'd lived long enough to know Amelia had loved her, maybe things would've been different. I wasn't quite sure how, but something told me, not everything would've worked out the way it had.

"I'm sorry she's gone. I'm sorry you lost her. I'm sorry she lost you," I said softly as I moved closer to her, hoping she'd let me try to offer her some form of comfort.

"I'm sorry too," she said, but she never sought any comfort from me. She just turned away and frozenly continued staring at the sky, lost in the past, but the sky to me, had turned into a meaningless blur.

"She left you Price Healthcare," I said.

It took a moment for her to answer because for a short while, it was like she was trying to set herself free from the past. "Yes," she said.

"She sounds like she was an exceptional person." It only took a moment or two to realize the only other Price-related business I was aware of was Price Industries and the company was worth billions.

Amelia took a deep slow breath, then said, "She was working on developing a cure for cancer. She wanted to save lives. She wanted to live, but her cancer was extremely aggressive. By the time we met, by the time she owned Price Healthcare, she knew she wasn't going to make it but she kept strong and fought on." There was such a deep sadness in her as she spoke.

I couldn't believe she was telling me something about herself I never would've imagined existed.

"I tried so much to hate her for not telling me, but when I went to visit her and saw her, I understood for the first time, how it felt like to be normal, to be human, to feel and to be helpless and I despised it."

I saw myself living the story through her words, and my heart broke for her.

"We've worked for years on a cure but still haven't developed the perfect remedy. At times I feel like I failed her," she said.

I wanted to reach out to her, but something told me she wouldn't eagerly welcome me, so I stood by her side, quietly wishing I could take her in my arms.

"Amelia," I said softly, "I'm sure you've done your best."

Seeing this fragile part of her was ironically refreshing. She'd always been this strong, focused and controlled boss lady to me. Only shortly after we'd started sleeping together had I noticed there was more to her than what she projected to the world.

Knowing that she was sharing something so intensely personal with me only made my feelings for her stronger. That vulnerability she exposed to me was a part of herself I doubted she'd ever let the world see.

"Did you ever fall in love again?" I asked.

She slowly shook her head.

"What about Mr. Gallagher?" I said cautiously, knowing I was treading on a sensitive path.

"I loved him the best way I knew how," she said.

It sounded like she'd loved Isabel more than she ever loved her husband. My hands shook nervously because of the question I wanted to ask next and I was glad for the dim illumination because she couldn't see it.

"Are you two...?" I tried to think of a better way to phrase it. "Do you get intimate with him?" My heart raced and I wasn't sure if it was because I had actually managed to voice the question or whether I was afraid to learn her answer.

She looked at me for a long time before she answered. "No," she said.

I exhaled in joy and relief. I'd never known such knowledge would bring me so much peace or happiness. My heart seemed to expand at the thought of knowing I wasn't sharing her with anyone else.

"Have you been intimate with other people?" I asked.

She placed her hand over mine. "I think that's enough with the questions for today," she said.

I was a little disappointed, but she'd already told me more than I'd hoped to get from her and that was good enough for now. It was nice spending time with her, just getting to know her.

I couldn't help wonder if she'd ever shared that part of herself with anyone else, but thinking it all through, it became apparent what type of people she was accustomed to.

Isabel Price had come from a wealthy and powerful family and had single-handedly acquired a billion-dollar company. Patrick Gallagher had also come from a rich family and his success grew by the day.

These were the only two people I was aware of who Amelia had been with. One she'd loved, the other she'd married. I had no doubt they'd both immensely loved her.

Amelia and I had a connection but I would never be able to measure up to the standards of these two. Whatever she felt for me, she'd made clear would never see the light of day outside that penthouse.

The thought was depressing because I wanted to be with her and even that I wasn't supposed to tell her. I was just an employee and someone she had sexual rendezvous with. She'd never look at me the same way she'd looked at Isabel.

A memory crossed my mind and I remembered the party in Paris where I'd met Zola. Her friend, Jonathan, had posed a question, which at the time had sounded absurd. He'd asked if I was Amelia's new pet.

I'd not understood his question, but now, thinking about it made me wonder. Did Amelia do this sort of thing often? Did she pick out who she wanted to engage in an illicit affair with then walk away? Was that what she was doing with me? Was she using me for sex?

Have you been intimate with other people? The last question I'd asked her rang in my mind and her answer resounded with an ominous chant which left a chilling effect in me.

"Where are you?" She asked, placing her hand over mine and I looked up and took a deep breath. I laughed nervously and shook my head.

"I'm right here." Maybe I was over-thinking it. I was the one who'd gone after her. She could have her pick of both men and women, why would she choose me? Someone who had absolutely nothing to offer her?

God, even my attempts to comfort myself were in vain. They left me feeling worse about the whole situation.

"Hey," she touched my face and my focus fell on her gorgeous face.

Would she ever pick someone like me in any one of her lifetimes?

"What's wrong?" her voice was so soft and calm, it soothed me.

"Nothing, just some stupid thoughts floating through my mind," I said.

"You want to share?"

Her warm palm was on my cheek and my body was drawing incredible heat from it. "We've shared enough tonight," I said, leaning close to kiss her.

She met me halfway and all my disturbing thoughts instantly vanished. With everything else forgotten, her arms came around my body and she whisked me into the wonderful world we created together.

Chapter Forty-Three

I left the penthouse on Sunday afternoon feeling like my time with Mrs. Gallagher had ended far too soon but despite that, I left with a big smile on my face.

Being with her had been different this time. She'd taken the lead and unlocked a part of herself I hadn't expected to see. Despite my disturbing thoughts, it felt like she and I had grown closer.

Since it was still early, I wanted to get home, change and go see Rex. We didn't spend as much time together as we desired and I terribly missed him. I didn't know if I was ready to share what had happened between me and Amelia, but I figured I'd know when I saw him.

I got home, took a quick shower and went to Rex's art studio. I assumed he'd be there because he was always working, and I wasn't wrong. He had a huge canvas hanging vertically on one side of his wall and his hands were covered in paint. From the look of things, he'd been working on it for a while.

The sight made me think of Jaime. She'd probably look at the painting and see something profound because she was an artist. All I saw was a mixture of paint smeared across the canvas bringing together colors to create something that appeared to be really complex.

I watched him from the door for a while as he worked. All of his attention was fully focused on his work. He was using his hands to paint, and was standing on a medium height ladder to reach the top. He was wearing a pair of overalls, which might as well have been part of the painting because it was covered in paint.

"Hey, how long have you been standing there?"

His voice startled me because I was stuck in a trance, watching the way his hands moved against the canvas, almost as though he was in a duel with his creativity.

"Uhm, I don't know, a few of seconds, maybe. How do you do that?" I said as I got inside.

"Do what?" he asked, watching me from the position I'd found him in.

"It's like something was controlling you, like you were under a spell." I approached him, getting closer to the painting he was working on. I regretted having walked in on him because I interrupted his flow.

He smiled, getting down from the ladder. He reached for a towel and started wiping the paint from his hands. "I don't know, something just moves in me."

I turned to face him and smiled as that tender feeling of having missed him and being around him again embraced me.

"A hug?" he said, opening up his arms.

I took in the poor state of his appearance and laughed as I shook my head, "Maybe after you take a shower."

He came closer to me and pecked my cheek. "You look good, Liv."

"I wish I could say the same about you," I said, pointing at him from top to bottom.

"Come on, chicks dig this messed up, artistic look. They find it deep," he said.

I couldn't help laughing. "It's deep when you're working. Not so much when you stop for a chat, which by the way I should be apologizing for. I'm sorry for interrupting your flow. If you want I could come by later."

"Are you kidding me, sit down."

I went and took a seat.

"You want something to drink. I've got water and a couple of beers."

"No, I'm good."

"How're you holding up between work and studies?" he asked.

"Would you believe me if I told you that I actually like it?"

He came and sat beside me. "Knowing you the way I do? I would believe it."

"It's challenging and exhausting, but when I get home really late in the evening, I love knowing I'm doing something meaningful with my life. I finally have direction and zero baggage."

"I can imagine. The last few years you've struggled so much. It's refreshing to know there's nothing trying to get in the way of that."

I was about to agree when the thought of my brother's unexpected and unwelcome appearance crossed my mind.

"What?" Rex said.

I groaned and leaned back against the couch. He knew all about my brother so I knew what his reaction would be even before I told him. "Remember how last time we talked, I said I'd send money home to start helping out?"

He nodded.

"My brother found out and showed up at my apartment a couple of days ago."

"You gotta be kidding me!"

"He claimed he only came to check up on me but I know him better, so I told him he couldn't stay with me and gave him some money to go live in a motel or something."

"When is he leaving?"

"He said he wanted to stay in New York for a while, try out his luck."

"I hope he doesn't cause you any trouble."

"Me too," I said, recalling Amelia's words. I'd hate to see you show weakness when it comes to your brother, someone you know will hurt you at any opportunity he gets. "I don't want Amelia to think I'm weak after everything that's happened."

"Amelia?"

I turned to face Rex, realizing I'd slipped because he was still unaware of the progress I'd made with Mrs. Gallagher. "Uhm, there's something you need to know."

I took a deep breath and watched his anxious expression, wondering how he'd take the news.

"Ame—. Mrs. Gallagher and I, are sort of involved," I said, and bit into my lower lip.

"What!" The shock was evident on his face and his voice.

"That whole speech you made after you got back from your cruise gave me the courage to go after her."

"Wow, how long has it been going on?"

"Since the corporate gala party."

He had a thoughtful look on his face. "Didn't we spend the

following afternoon together?"

I slowly nodded.

"Why didn't you tell me then?"

"It all happened so fast. I wanted to absorb it, to really believe it. I mean, before then we'd only flirt, touch, and sometimes kiss. I showed up at her penthouse unannounced and I swear I thought she'd turn me away. I'd wanted her for so long there was an excruciating ache inside of me."

"I can't believe you're telling me this just now."

"I've wanted to tell you but I've been so preoccupied since then." He exhaled and went silent for a moment.

"I'm sorry, Rex. I didn't intentionally keep it from you."

"So what exactly do you mean when you say you're sort of involved?"

"We're sleeping together," I said, wishing there was more to it.

He watched me for a couple of seconds then smiled widely at me. "How's it like? I mean, how do you feel? You must be ecstatic!"

"It's mind-blowing and I wish I could say I couldn't be happier but it's a complicated situation. But I can't complain. She has started to open up to me and I'm getting to know her. She's letting me into her world."

"Oh, my God. Liv, you're in love with her."

His statement caught me off guard because I didn't expect him to confront me with feelings that were only known to me. "I am," I said.

"Does she feel the same way?" he asked.

The question made me think about everything Amelia had ever said to me regarding our situation and it felt like a nail had been forcefully jammed into my heart. The impact was so powerful, I involuntarily tore up.

"Oh, Livvy." Rex reached for my hand and gently massaged it.

"The situation is complicated," I said as I wiped away the tears. "She's married, so her family comes first."

"She cares about you though, right?"

I nodded. "That's what she said, but I can't help wanting more." I knew what I'd been getting myself into when it had all started, so I didn't know why I was getting all emotional. "I feel so stupid." I reached for a tissue in my purse to dab the tears and got to my feet in an attempt to compose myself.

"You shouldn't, Liv. Who knows, things could change." He said as he stood up and approached me.

"Change would require her to reciprocate my feelings for her. It would require her to leave her husband, tell her kids, her friends and probably even the public; a public that greatly loves and respects her for her high family values. Does that sound like something that could happen in this lifetime?" I asked, trying to swallow the painful ball that had settled in my throat.

"You never know."

"I think what makes it worse is the thought that I may not be the first person she's done this with, which means I'm disposable to her."

Rex closed his hand over mine and slowly turned me to face him. I tried to keep it together but the pitiful look in his eyes broke me and tears streamed down my cheeks.

He took me in his arms and I momentarily forgot his clothes were full of paint. Since I was already in his arms, I relaxed and held him back, letting him console me the best way he knew how.

"You met in a world where you two would never naturally have met. You got to be in a position many people have envied, and you've gotten to know her in a way that most people can only dream of. You two were destined to meet and in this lifetime Livvy, if you ask me, anything is possible."

I tightened my hold on him at his comforting words and let the calm settle back in. When we pulled apart, he took the tissue in my hand and dabbed it over my tears.

I was a little surprised to see my outfit was still in good condition. I touched his overalls and realized the paint had dried up. When he noticed, he smiled at me and gently ran the back of his hand over my cheek.

"She'll fall in love with you. She'd be crazy not to," he said.

I took a deep relaxing breath and exhaled. Rex took my hand and led me back to the couch. "Tell me more about your time together," he said.

"Well, the sex is amazing!" I said and we both broke into laughter as we settled back down on the seat.

I didn't go much into detail about our sexual encounters. I only told him mostly about the experiences I'd left out in the period of time Amelia and I had started getting close.

When we were done and he was back on track on everything that had happened in my life, I felt guilty for having kept him in the dark for so long because he was such a wonderful and supportive friend.

"Someday some lucky girl is going to snatch you up. I hope it'll never change our relationship," I said.

"Never," he said.

He'd never been in a serious relationship and whenever he tried dating, for some reason it never worked out. I hoped there was a special girl out there for him who'd be able to appreciate him for the amazing person that he was.

I went back to my apartment later on in the evening, leaving Rex to continue with his painting. Spending time with him, opening up to him and sharing my feelings made me feel a whole lot better.

He hadn't been up to much since the last time we'd met so he didn't have much to fill me in on.

After I ordered some take out for dinner, I hit the books. Healthcare, I'd come to learn, wasn't that much different from Business Administration. It was the languages I was having a little trouble with but I knew with extra effort and a little bit of time, I'd come to excel.

Halfway through, I heard a knock on the door and went to open, expecting my food delivery but was met by my brother. He stared back at me with that smug look on his face and I tightened my jaw, wondering what he was there for.

"Aren't you going to invite me in?" he asked.

"What do you want?" I asked.

He pushed the door open and walked in right past me. His arrogance irritated me.

"You need a little attitude adjustment towards me or I may not be so nice to you," he said.

"When I asked you to leave, I was hoping I wouldn't have to see you again quite so soon."

"That's a mean thing to say," he said as he walked over to the coffee table where my laptop and some of my books were laid out. He picked up one of the books, scanned through it and deliberately closed the page I'd been studying.

I gritted my teeth, trying not to appear upset because I knew he derived joy from the cruelty. "Why are you here?" I asked.

"To let you know that I discovered your dirty little secret," he said.

I tried not to react but my heart palpitated. "I really don't have time for this."

"You don't have time for your family but you have time to go screw your rich old boyfriend?" he said accusingly.

"What are you talking about?"

"Come on, Livvy. I followed you to work yesterday. I followed you to that huge mansion. I know who lives there. That penthouse you spent the night at, it belongs to the guy who owns the house, doesn't it? What's his name? Gallagher? Patrick Gallagher?"

My heart almost stopped. He thought I was having an affair with Mr. Gallagher? I didn't know what worried me more, that he'd gotten so close to discovering the truth, or that he could use the inaccurate knowledge to manipulate me.

"Greg, you don't know what you're saying."

"It all makes sense now; this apartment, the fancy clothes, jewelry, and the job. Do you even work or does he just pay you to screw him?"

I was so insulted by his remark, I walked right up to him and smacked him hard across the face. "Do not disrespect me," I said.

He ran his hand over his cheek and gave me a menacing look. "I hit a nerve there, huh?" he said. "I told you I'd figure out this mysterious little life you lead."

"Whatever you think you know, it's wrong."

"It can't be, I can tell by the look in your eyes."

"What do you expect to gain from this? What is your goal? Are you trying to find something that you can use to hurt me? Is that why you're still here? Is that why you're taunting me right now?"

"This mightier than thou attitude you've got going is not a good look on you," he said, cupping my chin in his hand.

I knocked it away and created distance between us. "You're my older brother. You're supposed to set an example and be my role model but all you've ever done was take, take, take without regard for anything or anyone else."

"Is that what you think?" he asked.

"It's what I know."

"Yeah, well while you've been in New York for the past four years, dad has had two heart attacks and a mild stroke. What have you done to help him? What have you done to be there for the family?"

I was stunned into silence.

"You've been shacking up with your boss, living this fancy little life, forgetting you left your family behind. And what, you thought some money would help bridge the distance? You thought it'd help make it feel like you care?"

I sat down on the couch, deaf to everything he was saying because I was still stuck at the first statement he had delivered about my father. "Why didn't you tell me this when you first got here? You said he had a cold, that there was nothing to worry about."

"Mom didn't have the heart to tell you. She didn't want you to worry."

"She didn't want me to worry? Its two heart attacks and a stroke! You had every right to tell me." I got back to my feet, oblivious to the fact that I had raised my voice.

"What difference would it have made?" he asked in nonchalance.

I wanted to smack him again. "I would've come home."

"And done what?"

"Something," I said hopelessly.

I was almost certain he'd kept that piece of information to himself in order to use it at the appropriate time when it'd cause the most damage.

"Get out," I said.

"What?"

"Get the fuck out of my house!" I screamed.

He walked past me and left the apartment. A minute later when I was pacing back and forth fuming in rage, I heard another knock on the door. Thinking it was Greg again, I yanked the door open and was met by a surprised expression of the delivery guy.

I paid him, tossed the food on the table and after calming myself, I called home. When I heard my mother's voice, the anger flew out of me and tears of sadness engulfed me.

"I'm so sorry I haven't been a good daughter," I said.

"Oh, honey, what's going on?" she asked.

"Greg just told me about dad's heart attacks and stroke. Why didn't you tell me? And don't say it's because you didn't want me to worry."

"They were minor heart attacks and a mild stroke. He's doing much better now."

"It doesn't matter, Mom. He's my dad. I love him. I care about every single thing that happens to both of you."

"Honey, I'm sorry. I know how hard you work. I just didn't want to add any more stress onto that."

Tears fell freely from my eyes now that there was no one around to see me express myself. "Is he there? Can I talk to him?"

"Sure," she said.

A moment later, his voice came on the phone. "Hi honey," he said.

"Hi Dad."

"How are you?" He asked.

"I'm fine, Dad. How about you?"

"I'm alright. I couldn't help overhear some of the conversation with your mother. I don't want you to worry yourself over this whole thing now, you hear? I'm strong, and I'm not going anywhere."

I tried hard not to sob as I held onto my mouth to silence myself. "I love you, Dad," I said weakly.

"Your mother and I love you too, very much."

"I'll try and see if I can get some time off from work and come see you."

"That would be nice, we'd really like that."

I took a deep shaky breath. "Can you put Mom back on?"

"Sure sweetheart."

"Livvy?" Mom said.

"Mom, promise me you'll tell me first thing if anything else happens. Please promise me," I pleaded.

"I will, sweetheart. I'm so sorry."

"I'm sorry too," I said.

"Are you and Greg getting along?"

I couldn't tell her the truth. "We're trying."

"Good, that's good to hear."

"I have to go now. I'll call soon, okay?"

"Okay."

"I love you, Mom."

"I love you too, sweetheart."

I curled up into a ball on the couch long after we'd hang up thinking about them both. I was terrified to think it might have taken a tragedy for mom to tell me about dad. I felt guilty because I didn't call home as often as I should have and the fact that it had taken Greg to make me realize it made me feel sick.

Chapter Forty-Four

During the following couple of days, I tried to keep myself focused but I couldn't stop thinking about my dad. I was extremely concerned for his health and knew I wouldn't be able to relax until I saw him.

I was hoping I could talk to Mrs. Gallagher and ask her to give me the weekend off so that I could fly home and go spend some time with my parents, but I was too busy and the timing was always lousy because whenever we saw each other one of us was always rushing off.

She called me to her office on Wednesday afternoon when I got back from a meeting. I was emotionally drained and a bit tired because of the worry and stress.

I tried not to think about what Greg had said about me sleeping with Patrick Gallagher, but I couldn't help worrying about how he'd use it against me. I wanted to tell Mrs. Gallagher but something told me not to, because of the impact it would have on our relationship.

"You wanted to see me," I said when I walked into her office.

"Yes, please take a seat."

I approached her desk and took a seat across from her.

"You want to tell me what's been going on? You seem distracted lately," she said.

I couldn't believe she'd noticed. I guess I hadn't done a very good job of hiding it. "It's just family related problems," I said.

"Is it Greg?" she asked.

I quickly shook my head. "It's my parents." I took a breath "I recently found out that my dad has been sick and no one told me. He's suffered two minor heart attacks and a mild stroke."

"What? How come no one told you?"

I groaned at my parents' poor reasons. "They said they didn't want me to worry but now I can't seem to do anything but worry."

"How did you find out?"

My conversation with my brother passed through my mind. "My brother and I were arguing and he told me out of spite."

"Shouldn't you have gone back home by now to check up on your dad? I'm sure that would worry you less," she said.

"I've been meaning to ask you if I could, but we've both been so busy."

"Olivia, you should always put your family above everything else. You can take my private jet and leave first thing tomorrow morning. How long do you need to stay?"

I replayed her words in my head just to make sure I'd not misheard her.

"Livvy?"

The touch of concern in her voice was sweet. "Uhm, I can report back to work Monday morning," I said.

"Okay, you can postpone your meetings and take a short break from your other duties. As for your studies, I'd recommend video chats since it'll be inappropriate to take your professors back home with you. But if you want to spend the entire time with your family and put off your studies for a few days, it's all up to you."

If she was trying to make me love her even more, she'd flawlessly succeeded. "You have no idea how much this means to me, thank you so much."

She smiled and said, "You have nothing to thank me for. Now, tomorrow morning, James will take you directly to the airstrip. I'll give you the pilot's information so that you can communicate about the travel arrangements. If your brother wants to come along, you can ask him to join you."

She was being so kind and generous. Did she really expect me not to fall for her? Even if I hadn't emotionally been there yet, this was a battle I would've lost. I was no match for her. She knew how to go after my heart.

I could have said the words right there and then, but I enjoyed being with her too much to spoil it. I think that was also why I didn't want to tell her about what Greg had discovered. I didn't want to risk losing her.

"Better?" she asked with that effortless upward curve of her lips.

"Much, much better," I said.

"Good," she said.

I wanted to go around that large desk and kiss her, but there was a reason for boundaries. So I got to my feet and walked out of her office with my spirits high. I couldn't wait to call home and tell them I was going.

I considered telling Greg to go back with me because once I left him in St. Paul, he wouldn't cause me any more trouble in New York, but traveling there in my boss' private jet was only going to fuel his suspicions so I decided against it.

"I know it's late, I just needed to talk to someone," I said to Rex over the phone later on that night after I got home from my studies.

"Hey, you can call me anytime, you know that," he said.

"I had a big fight with my brother last night," I said, and shortly after, filled him in on what had happened.

"He thinks you're having an affair with Mr. Gallagher?" he asked in disbelief.

I'd put Rex on my cell phone's loudspeaker and I was lying back on the couch blankly scrolling through a textbook. "I'm worried he might do something stupid."

"Have you told Mrs. Gallagher?"

"I can't."

"So how're you going to handle this?"

I groaned and closed the textbook, placing it over my chest. "I don't know."

"You know him best, what do you think he wants? How do you think he'll use the information against you?"

The most likely thing was extortion, but if I gave him money, he was going to confirm his suspicions and I was constantly going to keep on paying him off. I couldn't do that. "I can't even think about that right now, Rex. My dad is my number one priority. Mrs. Gallagher told me I could use her private jet to go home for a few days and see him."

"Hey, I have an idea."

"What?" I said, closing my eyes as I massaged my temple with my fingertips.

"How about I come with you?"

I sat up at his suggestion. "What about your painting and school?"

"They'll still be here when I get back."

I smiled. "Are you serious? You'd come to St. Paul with me?"

"Yeah, you're going through a hard time and you can use a friend."

"Oh, Rex, that will be great."

"Good, I'm going to start packing right now," he said, reminding me that I needed to do the same.

"Shit, me too," I said. "Okay, listen, we're leaving tomorrow sometime around ten. The flight is about two hours, and we're getting back on Sunday evening."

"Okay, no problem."

We hang up, hoping to resume the conversation the following day. I had already called the pilot and made all the necessary arrangements. I hadn't called my parents because I wanted to surprise them and much as I resented my brother, I was looking forward to seeing how big my nephew, Riley, had gotten.

Greg's girlfriend, Sandra, and I had a bit of a tense relationship but we always tried to get along. She was devoted to Greg for reasons I couldn't understand but I hadn't seen or spoken to her in a while, so I didn't know if her relationship with my brother had changed.

James picked up Rex from his place before he came to get me the following day. My body was already agitated because my daily routine had been tampered with, but I was excited to know I was going home to see my parents.

"Oh, my goodness!" Rex said when we entered the airplane.

I went and settled down on my seat as he moved around, looking at the beautiful and extravagant piece of aircraft. If I hadn't already traveled in Mrs. Gallagher's private jet, I would've been as impressed as he was.

"When I'm rich and famous, I'm getting one of these," he said as he moved from one seat to another. "This is her private jet?"

I nodded, leaning back on my seat as I watched him in amusement. "One of many, there's a bedroom back there," I said, pointing to the back.

"Nooo!" he said in disbelief as he got to his feet and leapt to the back.

I laughed to myself, waiting for takeoff.

"It even has a shower! Did you know that?" he asked in

excitement.

"I knew," I said, eager to get home and see my parents.

"This is awesome," Rex said when he came to settle down right across from me.

"I know. Mrs. Gallagher is very generous."

"No wonder you're in love with her," he said.

"Hey!" I sat up and turned to him. "Don't just throw that around," I said.

"Was I supposed to whisper it? There's no one here," he said in a low voice as he scanned the area.

"It's just that..." I leaned back on the seat and stretched out my feet. "I haven't fully confronted it yet, that's all."

When we took off, he came and sat right next to me. "What do you think she'd do or say if you told her?" he asked.

"Told her that I've fallen in love with her?"

He nodded.

"Seeing as she's already expressed that nothing could ever come of this, my most likely guess would be that she'd end it."

"I know there's a lot going on and a lot to consider, but I think she cares about you a little more than you want to make yourself believe." He gestured at the aircraft.

I was glad he was going home with me. He'd finally get to meet my parents and know where I lived.

I was thinking about my house and wondering if anything had changed back home when the flight attendant came to serve us breakfast. I didn't have an appetite since I wasn't used to eating anything in the morning, so Rex ate while I indulged in a nice hot cup of coffee.

"How long has it been since you were last there?" Rex asked.

"Almost two years," I said in a bit of shame.

"Wow, that's a long time."

"I know. It's no wonder they haven't been telling me what's been going on."

"I doubt that's their reasoning."

"It's not, but deep down I can't help feel like it is. When Greg and I were fighting the other day, he said something that I can't stop thinking about. He said that I forgot I left my family behind."

"But you didn't, Liv."

"Every time I think about it, I keep telling myself the same thing. But he said something that made sense. No amount of money will help bridge the distance I've created between me and my parents."

"It's not like you chose to live that way. Liv, everything has just started coming together for you. The moment you were in a position to help, you did."

"If something serious were to happen to either one of your parents, how long do you suppose it'd take for the news to reach you?"

He looked thoughtful for a moment, and then he placed his hand over mine on the armrest. "They love you and you may not like to hear this, but I think their reasons were valid."

I pulled my hand away. "How can you say that?" I thought he understood me.

"Liv, put yourself in their position. They saved up for your education and halfway through, the expenses became so increasingly much, they were unable to continue doing so which forced you to go out, find work, and pay for yourself. As a parent, wouldn't you want to focus on what helps rather than what doesn't?"

I wanted to be upset but he made a lot of sense.

"I've been so busy putting my life together, it didn't occur to me that I had other people counting on me," I said.

"Hey, they're not your responsibility. They're your parents. Their job is to take care of you, to protect you and that's exactly what they've done."

I closed my eyes and took a deep calming breath. Rex was being a friend. He was delivering the hard truth in the best way he knew how. I couldn't help wonder how my parents would treat him.

"I didn't have any close friends growing up so my parents have never met anyone of importance to me before. I'm telling you this because I don't know what's going to happen when we get there."

Rex laughed softly. "Don't worry. Parents love me."

He was a great guy and I had no doubt my parents would love him. The problem was, they were most likely going to think he was my boyfriend. "Rex, you don't understand."

"What?"

"They might assume we're together, like a couple."

He laughed nervously, "So, I'll be your beard."

"My beard?"

"You know, your pretend boyfriend to divert suspicion."

"Are you being serious right now?"

"What? I'm not good enough to play your boyfriend?"

I chuckled. "Actually, that's a great idea." Just incase Greg ever mentioned my alleged affair with Mr. Gallagher, my parents would already be aware of Rex, the guy I was supposedly dating.

Ugh, I wished I could come out to them and tell them the truth. I hated having to lie but I was afraid of how they'd take it if they ever knew.

What if they rejected me and turned their back on me? They were the only family I had. I couldn't lose them. Not over something as trivial as my sexuality.

There was no need to tell them. We lived two states apart. I could go on pretending. It wasn't hurting anyone.

When we arrived, it was a little past noon. We got a cab and in half an hour, we were stopping right outside my house. Nothing seemed to have changed. My parents had bought the house in the late nineties and my dad had beautifully renovated it with some help from Greg.

The landscaping on the yard had improved, which I assumed was my mom's doing since she loved gardening and the house had a bit of a rustic look that gave it an overall lovely appearance.

It was a contemporary four-bedroom maisonette, with three bathrooms, a dining room, a living room with a fireplace and a kitchen that featured a nice breakfast area. The windows offered the lovely view of the area and one of the lakes in the neighborhood.

Rex and I walked up the entrance and opened the door. The high level of security in the area made homeowners a little reckless because they never felt the need to lock their doors.

When we entered into the foyer, which offered access to the living room and dining room, the familiar scent of the house embraced me and I took a deep breath, smiling at the welcoming feeling of being home.

"Nice place," Rex said.

"Oh, my God! Livvy, is that you?"

I heard my mom's voice before I could respond to Rex.

"What're you doing here?" She asked when I turned to face her. Her unchanging graceful face was a sight for sore eyes.

I walked over to her and she took me in her arms. A warm sensation went through me and I tightened my hold on her. God, I'd missed her.

"I wanted to see you guys. I've missed you so much."

We pulled apart and she looked at me as she slowly ran her hands over my face. "We've missed you too. You look wonderful." She pulled me back in her embrace and I held back tears. "It's so good to see you. I can't believe you're really here. Why didn't you tell me you were coming?"

"It was a last-minute trip and I wanted to surprise you guys."

"You seem to have succeeded," she said.

"Oh, I'd like you to meet Rex. Rex, this is my mother," I said.

"It's lovely to meet you, Mrs. Williams."

They shook hands.

"It's nice to meet you too," Mom said.

"Oh, where's dad?" I asked in excitement.

"In his study. Go see him, he'll be very happy to see you," she said as she let go of my hand.

"You have a beautiful home, Mrs. Williams." I heard Rex say as I went in search of my father.

I didn't want to startle him so I gently knocked on the door and walked in a second later. When his gaze met mine, I saw shock register on his face and a moment later, he got to his feet and approached me.

"Dear Lord! I'm I dreaming?" he asked.

I met him halfway and stopped when we were standing just inches apart. "You're not dreaming, dad. I'm really here," I said.

He exhaled and I jumped in his arms. For some reason I felt like a little girl again and tears streamed down my face at the reminder of his delicate condition.

"What are you doing here?" he asked over my shoulder.

"I was worried. I had to come see you," I said.

We slowly pulled apart. "What about your work?"

"It's fine. I took some time off."

He pecked my cheek and closed his hand over mine as we headed back to the living room where my mother and Rex were.

"Judy, look who's here," he said with a smile on his face.

"I know, Robert. Isn't it a wonderful surprise?"

"Dad, this is Rex. We go to school together," I said.

"You have an exceptional daughter, Sir," Rex said as shook my dad's hand.

"I'll go make some tea," Mom said.

We sat down and much as I didn't want to bring it up so soon, I had to ask. "Dad, how are you doing?"

"I'm fine, honey. You shouldn't worry yourself."

I couldn't help it. I was going to take him to the hospital later on to make sure everything was fine. I hoped he wouldn't refuse to go with me because he could be stubborn at times. "Two heart attacks and a stroke are the exact kinds of things I should worry about."

"The doctor said I'm fine," he said.

"For my peace of mind, can I please take you for a checkup?" I said.

My mom came back to the room. She had a bit of a worried expression, but when she looked at me, it disappeared. It felt like they were hiding something from me.

"I was just at the hospital the other day," he said.

"Please, Dad. Do this for me," I said pleadingly.

He tightened his jaw and reluctantly nodded. "Tomorrow, not today," he said.

"Honey, where's Greg? Shouldn't he have come back with you?" mom asked.

"He said he wanted to try out his luck in New York," I said.

"Try out his luck doing what?" Dad asked.

Exploiting my situation, I wanted to say. "I don't know."

"Is he okay?" mom asked.

I shared a look with Rex and nodded. "He's fine."

We spent the next few hours talking and catching up. I told them how I was doing in school but failed to mention I had private professors. I told them I had a great job working for Mrs. Gallagher but didn't go into detail about it.

They got to know a little bit about Rex and I could tell from the way they looked at him and treated him, they thought there was more between us than friendship.

Later on, I went to help my mom prepare a late lunch while Rex bonded with my dad.

"Where's Sandra and Riley?" I asked.

"Sandra works at a grocery store in town and Riley is in school."

"Sandra got a job?"

"Yes, when Riley started kindergarten," she said.

That was good. It meant they were less reliant on my parents.

"What does Greg do when he's here?"

"Some odd jobs here and there," she said.

I didn't know what I'd expected to hear. Later on after lunch, I showed Rex to the guest bedroom and shortly after, I went up to my room to freshen up.

Everything was just as I had left it. My bed, the desk I'd used for my homework, the closet with old clothes that no longer fit and the bathroom. It wasn't much and the room wasn't that big but when I'd lived there, that small room had been my universe.

I'd never known my life would come to change quite so drastically. If I had never started working for Mrs. Gallagher, my world would have still been that small.

I ran a quick bath and after changing into warm comfortable clothes, I called my professors to inform them how we'd conduct our next three sessions.

When I was done, I found Rex downstairs looking through the framed family pictures which were hanging on one side of the living room wall.

"Look at how adorable you were as a kid," he said, pointing to a picture of me when I'd been ten.

I went over to him and scanned the wall. My parents had added new pictures of Riley and Sandra. Riley must have been four or five. He'd been very young the last time I'd seen him. I couldn't wait to see him when he got back from kindergarten.

"Let's go for a walk," I suggested.

I wanted to show him the neighboring lake which was a walking distance away.

The neighboring houses were some distance apart so it was hard to know the people living on the same street but after years of living in the same house, my parents had gotten to know most of them.

"I love your house, but this place looks like such a lonely place to grow up," Rex said when we left the house. I'd told my parents earlier that we'd be going out for a walk so they wouldn't worry.

"It kinda was. Most people made friends in school, church and any other place that had a large gathering."

"How come you didn't get close to anyone?"

"I was always afraid my family would find out the truth about me and making friends meant I'd have to lie and pretend to be something I wasn't. I was scared someone would discover my sexual orientation and tell my parents, who were respected, church-going members of the community."

"That's no way to live, Livvy."

"That's why I wanted to start afresh in New York."

"Guess that makes sense."

He placed his arm over my shoulder and I automatically leaned into him, placing my arm around his waist. I'd never been so comfortable with anyone else apart from him.

"So, where are we going?" he asked.

"To one of my favorite places, Lake Phalen."

"Cool."

We walked in silence for a while and my thoughts somehow found their way to Mrs. Gallagher. I wondered what she was doing, if she was with her family or by herself at the penthouse. I wondered if she'd thought of me at all that day, if she missed me.

"You're thinking about her, aren't you?" Rex said.

"How did you know?" I asked as I looked up to see his face.

"The melancholic look on your face. When you talk about her, it's usually with love, joy and sadness."

"Earlier on I was thinking about how small my world used to be when I lived here. I never imagined one day my life would turn out this way. Being here, where it all started is a bit overwhelming."

"I know what you mean. I feel the same when I go back home. New York feels like a whole different planet."

"I hope you have better luck at this whole love thing. One of us should be happy."

"Livvy," he stopped and turned me to face him. "I'll only seek out my own happiness when I know without a doubt you've found your own," he said as he gently ran the back of his hand over my cheek.

"You can't put your happiness on hold for me. It's a dumb thing to do."

He smiled and pecked my forehead. When he lingered, I closed my eyes and a selfish part of me wished he'd been a woman. I had no doubt I would've fallen in love with him.

"Why couldn't you have been a woman?"

He laughed at the question.

"Why couldn't you have been straight?" he asked.

I laughed at his question and we continued walking along.

We got to the lake a few minutes later. Since it was in the fall, the weather was lovely, the leaves had changed color and started falling making the overall atmosphere look like something out of a romantic flick.

"Wow, I see why you love it. I can see myself standing here with a canvas painting this entire scenery. The birds, the sky, the trees and homes in the distance, the lake with its changing colors when the sun hits it just right."

"I used to love coming here because I always found serenity. There was no chaos in my world, but there was always a storm in my heart and mind."

"What's there now?"

I reached for a rock on the ground. "A different kind of storm." I bounced the rock four times on the lake, like I had so many times before in the past.

"How did you do that?" Rex asked, trying to bounce a rock on the lake, only for it to disappear.

"It's all in the wrist. You have to flick it." I reached for another rock and showed him how. He got two bounces when he tried and continued practicing as I went to sit down some distance away from the damp ground.

He kept trying until he got three bounces, then he came and sat beside me.

"For someone who creates such complex beauty by the stroke of your hand, you sure suck at bouncing rocks on water."

"Before I leave, I will have learned to bounce four."

"Try six and I'll take you out to dinner on our last night here."

"You've got yourself a deal."

I wasn't sure how long we stayed by the waterside but when we left, it was a little late. We went back home to find Riley and Sandra had returned. Riley was a handsome young boy, but since he didn't seem to remember me, he was a bit apprehensive towards me. I hoped to win over before we left.

Sandra's reception towards me was warmer than I expected, which was a little surprising. She wasn't shocked to discover Greg was still in New York and I didn't bother to explain why since I assumed they kept in touch.

I went to help mom prepare dinner while Sandra went to clean up Riley. When she was done, she came to join us while Rex and Riley bonded. My father was at his usual chair watching something on television.

The whole setup made me a bit nostalgic because I knew I'd greatly miss it when I went back to New York. We had a bit of conversation while we had dinner and Rex was kind enough to help with the dishes.

Around eight, I went up to my room for my video chat sessions with my professors and by one, when we were done, I was drowsing off in my bed.

Chapter Forty-Five

The following day after breakfast, I took my dad for his medical checkup and though the doctor said his health had improved, I couldn't help being worried because he expressed a lot of concern.

We spent most of the morning together and in the afternoon, I took Rex around town in my dad's truck to show him the area. I showed him where I'd attended elementary and high school, some of the other lakes around the area, a few waterfalls, and hang out joints where people went for leisure.

When we went back home, I joined my mom outside where she was gardening. I tried to get her to tell me what was troubling dad but she kept a steady smile on her face and assured me there was nothing to worry about.

Later on when Sandra came home from work, I went to play with Riley who was a bit more receptive towards me. It was hard to believe that something so beautiful had come from my brother.

I experienced a certain kind of peace I hadn't felt in a long time during dinner, and realized it was the warmth that came from being surrounded by family.

That night around eight, I was on my computer studying, telling myself I'd try as much as possible to make trips back home when my world stopped being so crazy.

On Saturday, Rex, Sandra, Riley and I went out to the Mall of America for some fun. Sandra and I only went for a few rollercoaster rides, but Rex and Riley continued on.

When we were seated some distance away having coffee, Sandra finally asked what I knew my parents were still wondering. "Is he your boyfriend?"

I hesitated in my response because I didn't want to lie. "He's my best friend."

"He's a good guy and he seems to care a great deal about you," she said.

We'd never really been much of friends, but since she was making the effort, I tried to meet her halfway. "How are you and Greg doing?"

I asked.

She pursed her lips, took a breath and exhaled. "It hasn't been easy. Your brother can be very difficult to deal with."

I was surprised to hear her say so because she'd always been loyal to him. "I'm sorry, Sandra."

"Don't be. I knew the type of person he was when we got together. I don't know, I guess I thought I could change him. When I failed and discovered I was pregnant with Riley, I thought he'd change." She released a painful laugh.

"Maybe one day he will," even as I said it, I knew it was wishful thinking. Greg would always be a selfish screw-up. I didn't even understand why Sandra continued to stay with him.

"That look in your eyes, I see it in so many people who know us," she said.

"Why not leave him?"

"Because of Riley, and your parents."

I looked at her in confusion.

"I never used to be like this. I was hotheaded, reckless and selfish. I didn't care about anything or anyone. When you've gone through countless foster homes, knowing that no one wants you, the constant rejection gets to your head. Greg and I, we were never meant to be anything serious. We were just having fun. But we never got to the finish line where we were meant to part ways."

I was surprised she was opening up to me. I had never known this about her.

"I knew your parents thought I was trouble, but they never treated me differently. When I discovered I was going to have Riley, I realized I had to clean up my act. I wanted to be a proper parent for him and I thought Greg would want the same thing too. I didn't realize until later on that he was already the best version of himself. By then, I'd bonded with your parents and Riley had been born. I had nothing to go back to."

I couldn't believe how much I'd misjudged her over the years. I'd never thought much of her, but she seemed to genuinely care about my family.

"I have the family I never had while growing up. I got a chance to change my outcome. If you were me, would you leave?" she asked.

I shook my head.

After a short while of silence, she asked, "How is he doing in New York?"

"He's okay," I said.

"What's he doing?"

I bit the side of my lower lip and shrugged my shoulders. "I don't know. He just said he was going to try out his luck."

"Do you think he's capable of change?"

I wanted to say yes to cheer her up. "To be honest, I don't know."

She leaned back against her chair and turned her attention back to Rex and Riley.

"I'm sorry I failed to make the effort to be more understanding towards you," I said.

"It's fine."

I watched Rex and Riley as they screamed while the rollercoaster did a three-sixty degree turn and my heart almost stopped in fear.

I thought about everything Sandra had said and it suddenly occurred to me that she might have had an idea of what was happening with my dad. "Do you know why dad has been getting sick?" I asked.

She looked at me and asked, "You don't know?"

I shook my head, hoping she'd tell me.

"He took a loan and he hasn't been able to meet the payments so the bank is putting a lot of pressure on him, threatening foreclosure on the house."

"Oh, my God. What was the loan for?"

"After he used up the savings on your studies, he took a loan to keep helping you out. With both his salary and Judy's, he thought he'd be able to cover the payment but it wasn't enough. Extra shifts haven't done much to help either."

"Why didn't they tell me? I could've helped out." I felt horrible, but I was pissed at the important information they chose to keep from me.

"I guess they felt like they had failed you."

"That will never be possible."

"I thought Greg would've told you. He was so angry when he

found out about it. When he came to New York after you sent that cheque, I assumed that would be the purpose of his visit."

Why hadn't he told me? Or was this the reason he'd been snooping into my life, trying to find an angle to exploit in order to get some money?

"I'm not going to let anyone take the house," I said.

I didn't ask my parents about it when we got back home. I just looked at them with more love than I could possibly put into words and vowed I'd make everything right.

On my last day there, I went out shopping with Sandra and Riley. I got the kid a lot of toys and managed to penetrate Sandra's pride, getting her some new clothes and shoes.

Afterwards, we did some shopping for household items, and since it was Sunday and my parents were out, I went to my dad's study and got a few of the foreclosure letters from the bank.

In the afternoon, Rex and I went back to the lake. I told him everything I'd learned and as usual, he was a wonderful supportive friend. After staying there for a while, he reminded me of the deal we'd made.

He threw two rocks, only managing to bounce it four to five times on the water but on his third try, he succeeded and bounced it six times as per our deal.

"You've been practicing, haven't you?" I asked.

"I had to. I wanted to beat your record."

"My record?" I asked.

"Yeah, have you ever bounced more than six?"

I laughed and took a couple of rocks. I'd been bouncing rocks all my childhood. "Stay alert, count this," I said, positioning my body at an angle and relaxing my wrist. When I threw the first rock, it bounced off seven times. When I threw the second one, it bounced off nine times. From my memory, the best I'd ever done was twelve and I had never beat that record.

"How the hell did you do that and what was that position? You didn't show me how to do that," Rex complained.

"Does a magician reveal his tricks?"

He groaned as we started heading back to the house. My parents were probably already back home and I wanted to spend a little more time with them before I took Rex out for dinner because afterwards, we were going to head straight to the airstrip.

"Don't worry, you still get your dinner," I said.

When we got back home, I sat both my parents down and explained to them how important they were to me. I tried to put them in my position and asked them how they would feel if something were to happen to me and no one told them about it.

They were not too pleased by the idea so they promised to be more transparent with information. I talked to Sandra as well and told her I'd keep in touch in case my parents failed to divulge any important stuff.

Afterwards, I played with Riley and his exciting new toys and when it was time, I tearfully said goodbye to them. Leaving was harder than I thought it would be and when Rex and I were having dinner, he seemed to sense my sadness.

"You have a wonderful family, Liv," he said.

I almost broke into tears because it was just occurring to me how much I'd taken them for granted.

"They all love you so much," he said, reaching for my hand over the table.

We stayed at the restaurant for a couple of hours and when we were done with dinner, we took a cab to the airstrip where we found the pilot waiting for us.

We slept through the short flight to New York and when we woke up, I asked Rex to spend the night at my apartment. He wanted to take the guest bedroom but since neither one of us was able to sleep when we got to the apartment, he came to my bedroom and we fell asleep watching a movie.

Instead of going straight to the office on Monday, I attended some of the meetings I'd been forced to put off because of my travel. Sometime around two in the afternoon, I headed to the mansion hoping to run into Mrs. Gallagher. I was disappointed to find her absent, so I resumed with my duties.

Around six when I was heading home, I asked James. "How's everything been around here?" I'd only been gone a few days but it felt like it had been longer.

James met my gaze over the rearview mirror and said, "Everything's been fine." He focused back on the road.

I nervously fiddled with the items on my lap. "How's Mrs. Gallagher? I didn't see her today." I wanted to know if she'd traveled or if she was around.

"She's okay, but well, you know how busy her life is."

I wanted to inquire more but there was no point because James probably didn't have the answers I was seeking. When he dropped me off, I felt like my life had gone back to its normal routine.

The following day, I called the bank my dad owed money in order to figure out how to settle the loan and learned that payments for the loan had not been made for the last nine months.

In order to fix the problem, I paid a one-off lumpsum that would keep my dad's bank foreclosure threats at bay, and had them deduct three quarters of my salary for the next six months until the loan was fully settled. I didn't have many expenses so I knew I'd survive on what remained.

I was leaving the office that evening when I ran into Mrs. Gallagher down the hallway. My heart immediately picked up pace at the sight of her and it felt like forever since I'd last seen her, and I didn't realize how much I'd missed her until that very moment.

She silently observed me and a small automatic smile rose on my lips. She looked as beautiful as usual in a black pantsuit that hugged her firm sexy body. Seeing her reminded me of our sexual encounters and something animalistic in me fought to reach out and take her in my arms.

"Hello, Olivia," she said. "Would you mind stepping into my office?"

I nervously followed after her, wondering how she still had that effect on me. After closing the door, I approached her desk and stopped some distance away as I exhaled in an attempt to calm myself.

"How was your trip?" she asked as she turned to face me,

effortlessly leaning against her desk.

"It was good," I said.

"How's your dad?"

"I took him for a checkup and the doctor said he's doing well. I think everything is going to be fine." Without the pressure from the bank, he could relax and focus on other things that were less stressful.

"That's good to hear. How're you doing?"

"Much better," I said, slowly placing my purse on the seat right next to her. I wished we were at the penthouse so that I could tell—. No, show her just how much I'd missed her. "Uh, Rex accompanied me to St. Paul," I said, trying to focus my mind on the conversation.

"Oh, he did?" she said.

I thought I saw something flicker in her eyes but I wasn't sure. "My nephew, Riley is in kindergarten. He was a baby last time I saw him and now he's all grown up."

She nodded with a faint smile and asked, "Did Greg come too?"

I shook my head. "No, I didn't want him to think..." It immediately occurred to me what I'd just been about to say and shook my head again. "No, he didn't."

She continued looking at me. I was dying to go to her, to tell her how much I'd missed her, to just touch her. "Mrs. Gallagher," I said nervously.

"I'm glad your trip back home was fruitful," she said.

It felt as if she'd known what I'd been about to say. I reminded myself I needed to be bold and brave and said, "I need to see you." I wanted to be with her, but those were the words that came out.

We'd crossed the stage where fear crippled me. I didn't understand why a few days apart felt like I was back where it had all started. "I've missed you," I said. "If I wasn't so overwhelmed from seeing you again," I took a step towards her. "I'd be kissing you right now."

She silently watched me then said softly, "I'm not stopping you."

Her words were as unexpected as the surge of energy that burst through me upon hearing them. In my fight to contain that energy, I took a slow step forward and closed the distance between us. My lips captured hers in a kiss and my arms naturally moved around her waist.

The soft feel of the light movement of hers lips against mine felt like heaven had opened up and was smiling upon me. After everything that had happened since Greg's last visit, being at the reciprocating end of that amazing kiss was exactly what I needed.

When we pulled apart, I could literally feel my heart expanding in my chest. God, I loved her.

She touched my face, gently trailing her palm over my cheek as she gazed deep into my eyes and for a moment, I felt like there was a chance she could reciprocate my feelings for her.

I didn't get to find out because we were interrupted. We immediately parted and created physical distance between us as a strange man I'd never seen before walked into the office.

I noticed Amelia's tension and discomfort at his presence and wondered who he was to her. After a moment of awkward silence, I reached for my purse and excused myself.

I didn't fail to notice how he looked at me as I walked past him. He had a bit of a smirk on his face, which I found weird because since I'd started working for Mrs. Gallagher, I'd never met anyone who didn't hold her in high regard.

On my way home, I couldn't help wondering if the strange man had witnessed anything that had happened between me and Amelia. Who was he? What was he doing at the Gallagher mansion? Why did Amelia seem to have such animosity towards him? The questions continued in my head.

When I got home, I groaned in frustration at finding Greg waiting for me outside my apartment. "What're you doing here? Haven't I expressed in every way and form possible, that I don't want you here?" I asked as I opened my door. I couldn't deal with him right now.

"I'm going back home," he said.

I stopped and turned to look at him to see if he was serious. "What?"

"I'm going back to St. Paul."

I was so pleased to hear that I almost wanted to hug him, but the repulsion I felt towards him was greater than my relief. "Good, I'm glad to hear that."

"Yeah, I need two hundred and fifty grand."

I thought I heard him wrong until I met his serious expression and ran the words across my head again. When I realized he was being serious, I couldn't stop myself from laughing. It was like a reflex I couldn't control. "You actually think that I have a quarter million dollars stacked up somewhere for you to just... demand for it?"

"Whether you have it or not, I don't really care. All you need to do is ask your rich sugar daddy to give it to you," he said.

"Do you listen to yourself when you talk?" I asked him. "Greg, I'm your sister. We want the same thing. We should be working together, not against each other."

"All I know is that mom and dad put everything they had on you; their entire lives' work and savings. They put everything on the line for you. It's going to five years since you came to New York, Olivia. You're doing far much better than I expected. All your school loans are paid for. You're living in a fancy apartment, which by the look of it, appears to be ten times more than our house and what have you given back?"

I could tell by his tone he was upset and from everything I'd learned when I'd been home, he probably had every right to be. "Greg, I had no idea what was going on. If I'd known, I would've tried to help out sooner. That is my goal now."

He looked at me in bewilderment and after a couple of seconds, shook his head saying. "No, you have a great thing going here. Two hundred and fifty grand is little to ask for. Look at your life," he gestured to the apartment.

If he only knew how hard my life had been. How long I'd been forced to defer on my classes because I couldn't afford to pay the fees. If he only knew that the only reason why I had reached that point in my life was because of Mrs. Gallagher. I didn't even deserve to be there. She had propelled me to levels I hadn't even prepared myself for.

"You have forty-eight hours," he said.

I walked up close to him and looked into his eyes. "I went home, Greg. I saw mom, dad, Riley and Sandra. I know the bank is threatening foreclosure on the house. I realize you're desperate, but do you really think blackmailing me is the right way to go? Do you think that I wouldn't have tried to help if I'd known these things were taking place back home?" I spoke with the same emotion I'd felt when I'd realized how much my parents had given up to make sure I had a proper education.

"I don't know," he shook his head, taking a step away from me. "All I know is that I need to clean up your mess."

"My mess?"

"You think it was easy for them to let you leave? Let you come here, spend all they had, so that you could what? Go to NYU?"

I didn't realize until that moment, how hard it must have been for my parents to let me go.

"Now we're all paying for that. You have two days, Liv. Forty-eight hours." He headed for the door and swung it open.

"Or else what?" I asked before he could leave.

"I'll tell the Gallaghers the truth and who knows, maybe the world too." He slammed the door.

I collapsed back on the couch and as much as I wanted to be upset with him, I understood the root of his anger. My parents had sacrificed everything to give me the education I needed in order for me to be successful. Their efforts had only worked halfway and practically left them with nothing. If Greg wanted money, it wasn't for himself. It was for the family.

I understood him but where the hell was I supposed to get a quarter million dollars in forty eight hours?

Chapter Forty-Six

"What do I need to do to permanently get rid of you?" I asked in agitation.

"Come on, Amelia. We're family."

I felt violated by the very sound of his voice saying my name. It was Wednesday afternoon and I didn't know if it was the heat or his unbearable presence. "Eric, you need to go back home."

I'd always been extremely uncomfortable around him. For some reason I'd always thought the thousands of miles between us had created two different realms for us, which meant we could live in the same world without ever having to see or speak to each other.

He'd aged as gracefully as my mother and would've probably been good looking for a man in his fifties, had it not been for his skinny physical posture and his pronounced facial features.

He'd shown up the day Olivia and I had reunited after her trip back from St. Paul. The moment I'd seen his face, I'd recalled our last encounter, ten years ago, which was something I tried hard to block from my memory.

I'd been sleeping in my bedroom at the mansion. I hadn't been aware he was around. He'd gone over my head and asked Patrick if he could spend a couple of nights at the mansion because he was in town for business.

I hadn't been aware of his trip or his stay until the creepy encounter. I'd had that eerie feeling that someone was watching me and on opening my eyes, I'd found him lying in my bed, watching me sleep.

"What the hell are you doing?" I asked in panic as I scrambled out of bed and reached for a robe to cover myself.

"Haven't you missed me?" he asked, unfazed by my shock.

He was fully clothed, which was a relief but the suggestive look in his eyes made me uncomfortable and I tightened my robe.

"What are you doing in my bedroom in the middle of the night while I sleep?"

"I didn't see you when I arrived."

"So you thought you could waltz in here and get on my bed?"

"I didn't want to wake you. You looked so beautiful and peaceful while you slept. You haven't aged a day, Amelia."

"Get out of my bedroom," I said.

He got to his feet and I was glad for the large bed separating us because I didn't fully trust his intentions.

"I just wanted to check up on you," he said.

"You could have done that in the morning. You didn't need to attempt to give me a heart attack."

"I'm sorry."

"Please, just leave."

He watched me silently for a moment then walked out. I rushed over to the door and locked it. I'd never felt the need to lock it before because the mansion was my home and I was safe, but knowing he'd been in bed with me made me feel completely violated.

The following morning after breakfast, I talked to Patrick, telling him what had happened the previous night and he asked Eric to leave. Eric tried to reach out to me after that, but I never wanted to see or hear from him again.

"Why do you hate me so much? I've never done anything to hurt you," he said now as he stood across my desk.

"We've never gotten along, Eric. Have you suddenly forgotten that?"

"We were young back then. The competition and everything else brought out the worst in me. I'm not that guy anymore. It's what I was trying to tell you last time we saw each other. We're grownups now. There's never been any need for animosity between us."

"If that's the case, couldn't you have chosen a more conventional way of seeing me that night instead of climbing into bed while I slept?"

"I crossed the line and I'm sorry about that."

I couldn't tell if he was being genuine but his apology didn't change the way I felt about him. "Okay, so what're you doing in New York?" I asked.

"I needed a bit of a change of atmosphere. Connie and I divorced a while back."

"I'm sorry to hear that."

"Yeah, well, there's nothing we can do about it." He approached my desk and looked at me as he stopped short and asked, "May I?"

I nodded and he took a seat. I'd never seen him this way. The divorce must've taken a greater toll on him than he let on. Still, I didn't believe for one second his show of humility was genuine.

"What's been going on with you? Kathy used to keep in touch. She'd mention you, say how you were doing and talk about your kids. She really loves them and you," he said.

I had no idea what to say to him. "Look, Eric, I'm sorry about everything but..."

"I get it. You don't have to say anything. I just hope this can be the beginning of something."

"What do you mean?"

"We can try and be friends."

I wasn't sure I was interested in anything that had to do with him. Whether he'd changed or not, I appreciated his attempt but I could never trust him. "How long will you be in New York?"

"I'm not sure, but while I'm here, I'd really like it if we could talk sometime."

I wasn't sure how I felt about that.

"Baby steps, I get it."

I was glad he could read me and I didn't have to actually have to say the words.

"I'll be staying at Kathy's."

I nodded.

He got to his feet and headed for the door. When he opened it, he turned to face me, smiled and said, "It's really nice to see you, Amelia."

When I didn't respond, he looked down and stepped out, shortly after, he closed the door. I exhaled and leaned back against my chair. I didn't understand his change of attitude towards me. He'd always been so unusual.

Seeing him again made me wonder if he'd seen anything when he'd walked in on me and Olivia. He hadn't acted like it, and I'd been too disturbed by his presence to concern myself with what he had or hadn't seen.

Nonetheless, it had been a close call and it had reminded me why I didn't like to risk anything intimate happening between me and Olivia in case of such an instance.

I'd missed Olivia. I'd tried to downplay it when we'd seen each other down the hallway and, in my office, but looking into her soulful eyes and seeing what she felt for me on display lowered my guard.

For some reason it had become increasingly easier to be around her since that night at the penthouse when I'd opened up to her about Isabel. I assumed it was because she was the first person I'd ever felt comfortable enough to share something so extremely personal with about myself.

It was odd to think at that point in my life, she knew me better than anyone else had ever gotten the chance to. I didn't know what was happening to me, why I kept drawing her in when I meant to push her away.

I didn't want to have to end up hurting her. But at the same time, I wanted to be selfish because I'd never had what we shared with anyone else. Someone I could actually talk to, someone who looked at me the way she did; like I was her moon and her stars. I wanted that, and I didn't want to have to give it up.

I kept telling myself it was my time to experience something profound, my time to feel good, my time to be happy and Olivia came with that package, but there was so much standing in the way.

I had lived my life. She was just starting hers. I would never be able to give her what she needed in the long run, especially considering the fact that my family would always come first.

And that was the other thing, I had a family. Olivia would eventually desire to have one too. So she needed to be with someone her own age. Someone who could give her everything I couldn't.

If only I'd had a normal upbringing. My life would've turned out so different. I probably would've fallen in and out of love several times. I'd have experienced the kind of joy people derived from small things. I'd have laughed, danced and made love more.

I would have been brave and daring as Olivia was. She made me feel like I'd missed out on so much because everything she brought to my life was emotionally heightened. I wished for one day, I could be an ordinary human being.

My thoughts were interrupted by the light knock on the door. A moment later, Olivia stepped inside. She looked at me for a few seconds, then approached my desk with some files in her hands.

"I'm sorry to bother you. I need you to sign some documents from some of the meetings I've taken for you." She seemed a little nervous as her gaze darted from my face to the documents in her hands.

She looked lovely in a beautiful white official dress that snugly fit her figure, strikingly accentuating her slender curves. The dress reached just right above her knees, exposing her legs, which looked long and endless in the six-inch heels she was wearing.

Her long hair was falling over her shoulders to her back in curls and though she was wearing little make-up, I found her very attractive. This made me go back to my earlier thoughts about wanting to be ordinary for a day.

I wanted to try out something new, take a risk and experience that spike of adrenaline. I got to my feet and went around my desk to where she was standing. I liked the way she was looking at me in fascination, desire and curiosity.

I stretched out my hand and took the documents from her hands, slowly placing them on my desk. I hadn't seen her all day and it had been over a week since we'd been sexually intimate. I missed her touch, her passion and her overpowering desire when we got too close.

Before I could proceed, I moved past her and headed to the door. When I turned the lock, I faced her and smiled in amusement because she was still standing in the same position I'd left her in.

I walked up to her, placed my hand over her waist and slowly turned her to face me. Her eyes had that restrained fire in them. "I was thinking about how interesting it'd be if I could be an ordinary human being for just a day," I said, trailing my hand up from her waist to her ribs.

She released a ragged breath and smiled. "That would be interesting," she said.

"If you were in my position, what would you suggest I do?" I gently leaned her back against my desk as I moved my hands down to her legs.

"Well, what you're doing for starters," she said, placing her arms around my waist. "It'd be interesting to see you go out on an ordinary date with me."

"A date?" I asked, laughing softly as I leaned close and placed a light kiss on her neck.

"Yes, a date. I'd love for you to experience a little part of my world."

"What would that require, exactly?" I asked.

"For you to give up a few luxuries; no driver, no fancy restaurant and no comfort zone, which means a nightcap at my apartment afterwards."

"A nightcap at your apartment? What if your friend or your brother shows up?"

She looked worried and thoughtful for a second then she said, "Rex is busy working on a painting and I have a feeling I won't see my brother for the next thirty-six hours."

"That's precise." She looked certain and I didn't want to put much thought into it because if I was going to do this, I'd have to adjust my attitude a little and maybe try and worry less.

"Will you go out on a date with me tonight?" she asked.

I laughed and asked, "What about your studies?"

"I can take a break."

I remembered my earlier thoughts about wanting to experience joy from small things and wondered if it was really possible.

Olivia made the choice for me when she closed the distance separating us and kissed me, reminding me why my thoughts had taken that route in the first place.

Her kiss was soft but demanding and it sent shivers of arousal through my body. I could tell she missed our erotic encounters as much as I did, but we were in my home and the only reason I'd locked the door was because I'd wanted us to have a little privacy.

I parted her lips and deepened the kiss, seeking to calm the storm brewing in me as one of my hands moved securely around her waist and the other sought for buried treasures along the curve of her knee.

When she released a soft sigh and circled her arms around my neck, my desire for her intensified and I knew I had to stop before we went too far but being there with her felt so sinfully good, I couldn't bring myself to physically pull away.

My hand started a slow journey up her leg, under her dress and she moaned against my lips. I was dying to make love to her, to explore every inch of her body like I had so many times before, but I was glad when she broke the kiss.

"I don't want to stop this, but we said it could never happen here," she said as she gently panted.

I was pleased by her candor.

"Let's save it for the date," she said.

I laughed as I slowly pulled my hand from under her dress and let go of her, physically creating distance between us.

"I'll pick you up from the penthouse at eight," she said as she straightened herself out and quickly composed herself.

"Olivia?" I said when she was preparing to leave my office.

I took a pen, signed the documents she'd brought in with her and handed them back to her. It was amusing to see the effect I seemed to have on her. It made something strange move within me.

Long after she'd left my office, I was seated back on my chair wondering how the date would turn out as a voice quietly reminded me that this was going to be my first real date. The unexpected excitement that followed made me feel silly.

Chapter Forty-Seven

I nervously waited for Amelia outside the penthouse. I couldn't believe I was taking her out on a date. I was so excited. I'd even somehow managed to put my troubles out of my mind.

Initially I'd planned to take her to the Angelika film centre to watch an indie movie then I'd hoped we could go to the Village Vanguard for some jazz music, but I'd decided to go for something easier and more casual.

I wanted to show her the part of New York that I loved. I knew she'd seen a lot and nothing I was going to show her was new, but it was the spending of quality time together that I was excited about.

So after much thought, I decided I was going to take her to Washington Square Park for an outdoor movie screening. If she loved classic movies as much as I did, then I was certain she'd enjoy the movie which was showing.

There were food trucks there so I was looking forward to seeing her eat something I was more accustomed to, like a grilled cheese sandwich or a burger, hotdog or even a corndog. I doubted they sold salads.

After the date, I was hoping we could grab some drinks then take a walk under the stars while we talked and headed back to my apartment.

When she stepped outside the building, my heart started pounding and I grew nervous. I took in her stunning frame, quenching my eyes with the sight of her and I wondered how I'd ever gotten so lucky.

She was casually dressed in a pair of blue skinny jeans, which were tucked under stylish ankle length boots, a loose-fitting top that gave her an air of laid-back elegance and a silk scarf around her neck. Her hair was freely falling over her shoulders and she was carrying a clutch purse in one hand.

"Too casual?" she asked, pulling me out of my trance.

"No." I made my way over to her and pecked her cheek in greeting. "Perfect," I said and led her to the cab.

When we were inside, I gave the driver the address and a moment later, we were on the road.

"I hope you like what I have planned," I said as I turned to face her.

"I'm sure I will." Her confidence in me was elating.

"I like this carefree side of you."

My heart was racing because I was sitting so close to her.

She'd surprised me that afternoon when she'd locked the door to her office and taken me in her arms. Whenever I was around her, I felt like I was floating on a magical cloud because everything between us was so surreal.

Never in my wildest dreams had I ever thought Amelia and I would come to get so close. I couldn't help wondering if her past lovers had ever felt that way about her. I knew the importance wasn't in how they'd felt, but how she'd felt about them in return. But being knowledgeable about her dating record, well, particularly the families and the wealth they'd come from, I couldn't help wonder if I was setting myself up to fail.

I didn't know why these thoughts chose that moment to run through my mind when before I'd done nothing but excitedly looked forward to the date.

"What're you thinking about?" Amelia said.

I turned to find her looking at me. I didn't want to tell her what was going through my mind so I struggled to come up with something to say, then took a deep breath and told her the truth. "I'm sorry, I'm just a little nervous."

"Don't be, you've been on dates before, isn't this the easy part?" she asked.

I smiled at her. "It's supposed to be, but you're not exactly an ordinary date."

"Pretend I am. Tell me what you'd be doing right about now," she suggested.

"I'd be trying to get to know you, where you're from, what you do, just basically get a layout of the sort of person you are."

"I see."

"I'd be interested in knowing about your past relationships, how they were like and why they ended." The problem was, I couldn't ask her these questions because even though I had some of the answers, I doubted she'd be willing to reveal the rest because she was always so guarded.

"Let's start with you," she said.

"Me?"

She nodded.

I wondered if she'd open up to me if I opened up to her and decided to give it a try. "Okay, what exactly would you like to know?"

"Tell me about the last person you were with," she said.

I couldn't remember being with anyone else other than Jaime. We hadn't been a couple and we hadn't slept together but in the period of time we'd known each other, I'd liked her, maybe even cared for her.

I bit my lower lip now and wondered whether I should tell Amelia about her. I didn't know how she'd take knowing I'd gotten close to someone she'd hired me to work with.

"The last person I was with was Jaime Bryce. Nothing significant happened between us but over the short period of time we got to spend together, I came to like her."

Amelia shifted in her seat. I thought I saw something move across her face but I wasn't sure. "What ended it?" she asked.

"I don't know. One day she just told me she couldn't see me anymore."

"Did you two ever get intimate?"

I shook my head. "We kissed a few times, but that was as far as it went."

"Would you have wanted to be with her?"

It felt like it had been such a long time ago. "At the time, yes. She was sensational."

She looked like she wanted to say something, but she didn't. Instead she faced forward and looked out the window, asking, "Where are we going?"

"Uhm, Washington Square Park. I found out there was an outdoor movie screening so I thought it'd be fun to watch a classic film together," I said, observing her expression.

"Sounds like fun," she said, though her voice was lacking its earlier joy.

"Did I say something wrong?" I asked.

"No," she shook her head. "No, it's not you."

"What is it?"

When she didn't speak, I reached for her hand and gently squeezed it.

"I may have had something to do with Ms. Bryce ending things with you," she said.

"What?" I asked in confusion as I pulled my hand away.

"I sensed there may have been more between you."

I watched her in surprise.

"I'd seen your potential and I didn't want you to get distracted so I asked her to focus on what was important to her."

I didn't know how the news made me feel. I'd gotten over it but I hadn't imagined Mrs. Gallagher had played a role in it.

"I'm sorry, Olivia. I didn't know at the time that what you felt for her was quite so strong."

I didn't know what to say.

"If you want to cancel tonight, I'll understand."

Was she kidding? I was in love with her. Jaime was in the past, Amelia was my present. So far, Amelia hadn't done anything to hurt me. If she thought what she'd done was for the greater good, I couldn't be mad at her for that.

I closed my hand over hers and smiled, "We're here."

I paid the cab driver when he stopped and we stepped out. It was a beautiful night and I didn't want anything to spoil it.

"You're not upset?" she asked.

"No, Amelia. I'm not upset. All that's in the past and right now I'm really enjoying my present."

She rewarded me with a smile.

"Would you like something to eat?" I asked as we followed the trail leading to the screening area. There were food trucks and vendors all over so we had our pick of choice in food and beverage.

Since the movie was starting in twenty minutes, there was a live band playing music and entertaining the crowd that had already gathered. I'd bought my movie tickets online so after snacking we were just going to pick a spot, sit and enjoy the film.

"Chicken quesadilla," she said.

I was pleased with her choice. I went and put forward her order while I got myself some chicken enchiladas. Ten minutes later, we were seated on a blanket I'd been carrying in my bag at a nice, comfortable and private spot enjoying the delicious food and some non-alcoholic beverages.

"I don't think I've ever done anything like this before," Amelia said as she looked up to watch the stars while she slowly ate.

"You must have done some crazy exciting things in your time."

"No, not really." She shook her head. "Almost everything I've ever done was already decided for me before I was old enough to walk."

"I guess it comes with running an empire," I said.

She nodded.

It was a dark but warm night and the stars were casting down a glow, dimly illuminating us. It was perfect because no one could recognize Amelia or interfere with our date, which gave us the freedom to be ourselves.

The live band was playing slow soft music which was rather soothing and seemed to create an atmosphere charged with romance. Most people there were couples who were cuddling in comfortable positions that suited them.

"What's the name of the movie showing?" Amelia asked.

"Black Orpheus, it's a 1959 film based on a play which was an adaptation of the Greek legend of Orpheus and Eurydice."

"Sounds good," she said.

A few minutes later, the live band winded up and shortly after, the movie started. I couldn't help recalling the time when Amelia had taken me to the Opera and my reaction afterward. This was nothing like that, but if she was anything like me, I knew she'd enjoy the film.

When the movie ended, I was pleased to see Amelia's expression. I could tell she'd enjoyed it even before she mentioned it.

"That was wonderful," she said.

"Yeah, it was." I was ecstatic because it meant we had a little more in common.

The warm night air had changed to thick and musky as though foretelling of coming rain.

"It feels good being out here," she said.

I wanted to grab her and kiss her but I wasn't one for public displays of affection and I had a feeling that neither was she. "It feels good being with you," I said.

She looked at me for a couple of seconds then turned her attention back on the street as we crossed the road.

"Do you want to go grab some drinks?" I asked, hoping one of these days she'd positively respond to me.

"Yeah."

I took her to a little comedy club to watch standup comedians because I wanted to see her laugh and when we got there, we found an empty table at a corner directly facing the stage.

The show had already started and by the time we were seated, a waiter had come to serve us. We ordered a bottle of red wine and he brought it back as soon as possible. After pouring it into our wine glasses, he left us alone and we turned our attention to the stage.

I didn't know how long we stayed there, but from seeing Amelia laugh, I could have easily traded everything to stay there with her in that moment for all of eternity. The comedians were really good. I'd always laughed whenever I frequented the place with Rex, but it was the glorious sound of Amelia's laughter that distracted me for most of the show.

Somewhere along it all, it occurred to me that was the first time I'd ever seen her laugh without restraint. It was magical and she was absolutely beautiful.

"You know that was the first time I've ever heard you laugh like that?" I said when we were leaving.

"It's the first time I've laughed that hard in a long time," she admitted.

It was almost midnight but my apartment was only a ten-minute walk. Since I was concerned about her, I asked, "It's a little late, you want us to grab a cab?"

"It's a lovely night, let's walk."

New York was the city that never slept so even at such a late hour, there were still people on the streets. Not as many as there would have been during the day, but some. The city was moderately safe since such an hour was still early by some people's standards, so it was safe for us to walk.

As we headed back to my apartment on the brightly lit streets of New York, we walked in comfortable silence for a while and then she asked. "Did you manage to deal with your brother?"

I exhaled at the question because Greg was the last thing I wanted to think about. How was I supposed to tell her that my own brother was blackmailing me? "I'm still working on it," I said.

I'd decided I wasn't going to give him any money because it would prove his suspicions true. I knew he'd be upset but I hoped we could talk it out and I could try and explain that I'd found out about the problems taking place back home and I was helping out the best way I could.

"Is he still bothering you?"

I wanted to say yes, I wanted to ask her for help but I couldn't drag her into my mess. "You know what? Let's not focus on the negative points in our lives tonight. I've had so much fun spending time with you, I don't want to ruin it," I said.

She looked at me as though she could see the contents in my brain and right at that moment, it started pouring. I grabbed her hand and pulled her away from the street so that I could shield her from the rain. When we found some shelter, we broke into laughter.

We were both a little damp, but neither one of us cared about that. I looked down the street to notice everyone else had disappeared, probably in search of shelter from the rain.

The tall buildings were going to shield us the rest of the distance to my apartment. I was going to tell Amelia so that we could proceed, but stopped when I noticed her looking into the distance.

"Amelia?" I said as I moved closer to her.

"I've never danced in the rain," she said in a low soft voice. Before I could respond, she surprised me when she stepped into the rain and spread her arms wide apart then looked up to the sky as the light showers started soaking her wet.

I watched in amazement as she started to move in synchronized motion to an imaginary tune. I'd never seen this side of her before, she looked like an angel.

I followed her lead and stepped into the rain, dancing right along with her. When she saw that I had joined her, she stopped for a second to watch me, laughed softly and reached out for me.

She placed one arm around my waist and held my hand with the other and together, we danced in the rain. It was like an out of body experience. I felt like I was standing some distance away watching the amazing moment, as we had fun.

When the dance slowed, her deep blue eyes gazed into mine and she captured my lips in a kiss. I wrapped my arms around her neck and she circled hers around my waist so that our bodies were touching from head to toe and we deepened the kiss.

It was like time stopped and even though it was raining, it felt like that moment only existed for the two of us. I could feel how she felt about me while she kissed me. I could feel the heat coming off her body. I could sense her fear and her excitement.

I could feel it all, and in that moment, I wasn't afraid to tell her how I felt. I didn't care about the repercussions. I didn't care about anything, but her.

"I'm in love with you, Amelia," I said softly when we pulled back from the kiss, my forehead leaning against hers.

She pulled away and even though she had all the power in the world to break my heart, I wasn't afraid. I looked deep into her eyes and said, "I love you."

I told myself I was prepared for what was to come, but I was a little caught off guard when she kissed me again, passionately, ruthlessly. She abruptly broke the kiss and closed her hand over mine.

We headed to my building and in a few minutes, we were in the elevator heading to my floor. The moment I unlocked the door and we got into my apartment, she fiercely took me back in her arms and immediately started to undress me.

I was in a dress that was tightly clinging onto my body because of the rain so it was a bit of a struggle for her to take it off. I had a similar problem with her clothes but we somehow managed and left a trail of damp clothes on the floor as we headed to my bedroom.

Her naked body was hot and slick against mine, which was a great turn on. When we got on the bed, her devouring kisses drew unimaginable sensations from my body. She started running her hands over me while she covered my body with hot kisses and I shuddered in pleasure.

It was like she wasn't even trying to restrain herself as her mouth covered my breast while her hands explored my being, leaving an arousing sensation that traveled downwards to meet at the apex of my pleasure.

My breathing was quick and shallow when her hands moved lower to go hover around my sex. She was barely touching me but everything going through me was so powerful I thought I'd climax if she did.

She lowered herself as she kissed my stomach and lower abdomen and then she parted my legs and positioned herself. When her tongue lightly moved over my folds, spasms started to take hold of me.

She waited a couple of seconds for me to relax, then applied a little more pressure and closed her mouth over me, using her tongue to drive countless waves of ricocheting sensations all through my body.

I thought I'd lose my mind or burst into a tiny million pieces as I trembled under her and I moaned her name while she continued to tease and flick my clitoris with her tongue until I couldn't take it anymore.

Uncontrollable spasms took hold of my body as a powerful orgasm seized me and I completely blacked out for several seconds as the sensations continued to reverberate through me.

God, was this how it was like being in love? Did everyone experience such a rush, or such powerful waves of pleasure? I wondered as Amelia lifted herself up and came to rest beside me.

"I don't want you to love me, Livvy," she said a while later.

I watched her sweet soft expression and asked. "Do you think it's something I can control?"

She ran her hand over my cheek and pecked my forehead. "It's something you must."

"I can't, Amelia. My heart has a mind of its own."

"We can never be more. Even this, what we're doing right now, it's too much, too risky."

"I wish you'd stop being so afraid."

She sat up. "I'm afraid for you, because I don't want to hurt you and I haven't done my best at controlling myself or this situation. I told you, my family comes first."

I sat up after her. "I get that, but when are you going to start putting yourself first. Your kids are grown up. They'd want you to be happy. They'd understand."

"No, they wouldn't. To do something so different would be confusing for them. To be this person, I'd have to give up everything."

"I'm willing to give up everything for you. I'm willing to risk my parents finding out that I'm in love with you." I placed my hand over her back and she got out of bed and pulled a bed sheet to conceal her nudity.

"Stop saying that."

"That I'm in love with you?" I asked as I got out of bed and reached for a robe. "I need you to understand that these are not just words to me. I've never felt this way about anyone else."

"Livvy, can't you see?" she asked as she headed to my walk-in closet. "You and I can never be together that way."

"I saw you tonight, Amelia. I saw how happy you were," I said as I followed after her.

"I was reckless. I shouldn't have done this. I shouldn't be here." She reached for some clothes and started getting dressed.

I felt like she was yanking my heart out of my chest with her bare hands. "I didn't plan to feel this way. It just happened. When I walked into your office that first day, seeing you for the very first time changed my life."

"I know right now the lines are seriously blurred, but at the end of the day no matter what I do, I'm still Amelia Gallagher. That's never going to change."

I didn't need the reality check; I knew who and what she was. I knew what she stood for. At that point, I didn't really expect anything from her. I just wanted her to accept my feelings for her and then we could move on from there. "I'm sorry, I shouldn't have said anything."

I'd probably spoilt everything and judging from the way she was reacting, this was most likely going to be the end of our affair. "Greg's going to be disappointed his blackmail's not going to amount to anything." If there was no affair for him to hold over my head, his blackmail was invalid.

"What did you say?" Amelia asked.

"I said I'm sorry, I shouldn't have said anything."

She'd found a pair of jeans, a top and a jacket that perfectly fit her. She pulled her hair over the jacket and approached me. "No, what did you say after that?"

I must have zoned out a bit because it occurred to me I'd mentioned Greg and blackmail in the same sentence. "I said that…" I hesitated. I'd never meant to let her know.

"Greg's blackmailing you?" she asked.

I turned to face away.

"What's he got on you?"

I bit my lower lip.

"Damn it, Olivia. Tell me," she said in a low firm voice.

I didn't know how she'd take it, but at this point, I had no choice but to tell her. "He thinks I'm having an affair with your husband."

"What? Why would he think that?"

"A while back he followed me to the mansion and later on to your penthouse. He thinks I'm sleeping with Mr. Gallagher. He doesn't know… he doesn't know it's you."

"Why didn't you tell me this sooner? For God sakes Olivia, we were out in public together. He could've been following you. He could've seen us."

I could tell she was upset, but I wanted to reassure her and tell her there was nothing to worry about. I knew my brother. Since he believed I was having an affair with Mr. Gallagher, he was too lazy to follow it up with real actual proof. He was probably somewhere getting drunk waiting for his payday.

"He didn't," I said as I headed back to the bedroom.

"How can you be so sure?" she asked as she followed after me.

"Because he thinks he's getting paid and he's coming back tomorrow night. Wherever he is, trust me, it's nowhere near us. You have nothing to worry about." I sat down on the bed where only a few moments ago I'd felt like I was in heaven.

"What does he want?" she asked.

"It doesn't matter," I said as I met her concerned gaze. I wondered if it was over the blackmail or the possibility of someone finding out about us. She watched me for a while then headed back to my closet. A moment later, she came out wearing a pair of closed comfortable shoes.

She walked over to me and placed a kiss on my head, lingering a bit. "Goodnight, Olivia." She walked out of my bedroom and moments later, I heard my living room door close.

I lay down on the bed and replayed our entire night in my head. When my thoughts obsessively circled around the last half hour, my heart started breaking at the possibility of it being our last time together and my eyes started tearing up.

Chapter Forty-Eight

The hardest part of going to work the following day was pretending that the previous night hadn't taken place, but I was determined to show courage instead of fear. I did my job and performed my duties like it was just any other day. I was keeping it all together and trying hard not to think about the most recent events that had occurred.

There was a part of me that wished I wouldn't see Mrs. Gallagher that day because I wasn't ready to face her just yet, but luck wasn't on my side. I ran into her around midday while I was heading out for a meeting. I wasn't sure if she was coming in, or going out, but part of me was wishing she was coming in. Once again, luck wasn't on my side.

"Hello Olivia," she said.

I straightened up, picturing our situation as a Band-Aid that quickly needed to be pulled off. "Mrs. Gallagher," I said.

James pulled up a plush Mercedes Benz S-class limo right in front of us and I stared at the luxury car in awe. James usually drove me around in a BMW which was very classy, but this monster of a car was a sight for sore eyes.

I looked at Mrs. Gallagher and wondered if we were supposed to travel together just as James came and opened the door for her. I stood in hesitation, unsure of what I was supposed to do.

"Get in, James will drop you off on the way," she said.

Quickly thinking on my feet, I shook my head and said, "Its okay, I'll get an Uber. I don't want to inconvenience you."

"You won't," she said.

Since I didn't have much of a choice, I got in the car and sat beside her. She had other drivers. I didn't see why she couldn't have someone else drive her wherever she was going. We didn't have to share the same car.

"How's your day?" she asked when we were on the road.

The question prompted my mind to revisit the previous night. How did she think my day was? I'd offered her my heart and she'd crushed it and on top of that, she was seated beside me, wearing that amazing fragrance that I loved and looking as wonderful as ever. "It's okay," I said.

She pressed a button on her side of the door and a tinted window came up to create privacy between us and James. "Olivia, I'm sorry last night didn't go as planned," she said.

I held my head up high and said, "Its fine, things happen." I was hurt, my heart was breaking but I was working and I needed to hold myself together. I promised myself I wouldn't break in front of her.

"Are you okay?"

What do you think? A voice said in my head as I looked at her and smiled. I didn't want her to see how much the situation was affecting me. "I'm fine, Mrs. Gallagher."

I stared outside the window, wishing, hoping she wouldn't say another word. "I'd like to offer my assistance regarding the situation with your brother," she said.

My hands quivered and I tightened my grip on the contents on my lap to keep her from noticing. "Because you care or because you might be implicated?" I asked.

She was silent for a moment, then she asked, "Does it matter?"

It mattered because I wanted to know she was offering her help because she cared about me. "I guess not," I said.

"What does he want from you?"

I took a breath and shook my head. "I appreciate you wanting to help, Mrs. Gallagher but with all due respect he's my brother. He's family." I looked at her, silently reminding her of her high family values. "I'll handle him."

"Can you at least tell me what he's demanding from you?" Her soft gaze was pulling at my heartstrings. This was the moment where I'd normally reach out and touch her, or kiss her, but I didn't know if I was allowed to do that anymore.

"Are we over?" I asked, resentful of how easy it seemed for her to throw everything we'd shared away. I wanted to know what she was thinking so that I could start my grieving process because waiting for something that would never come was probably going to destroy me.

"Olivia," she said.

"You know where I stand. I just want to know if we're on the same page."

"I'm sorry, but right now it's just too much."

I didn't think her answer would hurt me quite as much as it did. Her words tore my heart apart. "I understand," I said, even though I really didn't. But, I tried hard to control my breathing so that I wouldn't seem fazed by her words.

The moment the car came to a stop, I got out before James came to open the door for me and I quickly walked out. I rushed to the venue where my meeting was taking place and headed straight for the bathroom.

I dumped the contents in my hands on the sink, rushed to the bathroom and hurled. I didn't know why, maybe it was my body's way of absorbing shock, but after a few minutes, I was fine, a little queasy, but fine.

I got out of the bathroom and went to the sink to compose myself. I rinsed my mouth with some water, retouched my make-up and straightened up. I temporarily put Mrs. Gallagher out of mind, looked through the meeting notes and confidently stepped out and headed for my meeting.

I was glad I didn't see Mrs. Gallagher again for the rest of the day. The moment it clocked five, I was out of the office. Keeping busy helped because I didn't think about my breaking heart, but that only postponed the pain.

I figured dealing with it would be much more beneficial to me because it would promote healing, but the moment I was home, alone with my thoughts, I realized heartbreaks were not like ordinary problems.

I wanted to be angry with Mrs. Gallagher, but I couldn't be. She'd told me all along not to develop feelings for her and she'd constantly told me her family came first but I hadn't listened. I'd done this to myself. I was to blame.

But how did she expect me not to feel anything for her when she was such a magnificent woman? She'd taken me out of a tiny studio apartment, gotten me exceptional professors, paid off my student loans and now, she had me working at the heart of Price Healthcare, doing everything she'd normally do herself.

Apart from the work-related perks, she'd opened up to me, allowing me to see the real her. She'd told me about her past, about the one great love of her life and she'd touched me in a manner that no one else ever had.

Even as these thoughts crossed my mind, I felt my heart palpitating as my love for her continued to grow. The very idea of thinking I may never touch or kiss her again drove me mad and made me tear up again.

Images of our time together passed seamlessly through my mind. I could hear the sound of her laughter, the look of pure bliss in her eyes, the smooth velvet feel of her skin, the sweet soft taste of her lips and that powerful fragrance she always wore. God, this was torture.

I recalled all our conversations, every single moment she'd smiled or laughed, every time she'd looked at me with her soft blue eyes or brushed her hand against mine and each time she'd slept holding me in her arms.

I groaned in desperation, cursing my selective photographic memory because these thoughts would haunt me for the rest of my life.

How was I supposed to fall out of love with her when the mere thought of her only succeeded in making me love her more? How was I supposed to do so when we worked so close together?

Was she thinking about me? Did she care that I was hurting? Was there any chance she could be just a little bothered? Would she move on to someone else as though none of this had ever happened?

That last thought made me feel like I'd punched myself in the heart with Wolverine-like claws. I flinched in physical pain as I rolled on my bed, staring at the ceiling. I wondered if every night would be like this. Would I lie in my bed, the last place we'd made love, and torture myself with thoughts of her?

Would I helplessly torment myself with questions about where she was, what she was doing, who she was with, and if I ever crossed her mind? Or would this pain eventually come to pass?

Maybe it was so intense right now because it had just happened. Maybe in time, I'd manage to get her out of my mind, maybe even out of my heart. Right now, I just needed to keep myself busy and keep my mind occupied.

I got out of bed and went to take a shower. I needed to go meet my lecturer for my class.

When I was about to leave the apartment, my phone started ringing. I was going to let it go to voicemail but decided to pick it up.

"Hello," I said.

"Is this Olivia Williams?" a female voice asked.

"Yes, this is Olivia Williams."

"Do you know a Gregory Williams?"

I was still expecting him to show up later on that evening demanding his quarter million dollars. "He's my brother," I said.

"He was in a car accident earlier on today and he's admitted at St. John's Memorial Hospital."

My heart stopped. "What?"

"Ma'am, you need to get down here as soon as possible."

Greg was in a car accident?

"Ma'am?"

"Yeah, I'm on my way."

I was still holding the phone to my ear in shock, long after the woman had hung up. I should have asked if the accident had been serious. Oh, God, Greg. I quickly got to my feet and ran out of my apartment.

I hailed a cab when I got downstairs and on my way there, I called Rex and told him to meet me at the hospital. After everything that had happened, I needed someone for support.

I got to the hospital and immediately headed to the information desk. After confirming that Greg was admitted there, I was told to wait for his doctor to come tell me his condition.

"Livvy?" Rex arrived shortly after. I hadn't told him much over the phone, so when he took me in his arms then pulled back and started scanning me for signs of distress, I quickly filled him in.

"I got a call from the hospital informing me that Greg had been in a car accident. I'm waiting for his doctor to come tell me if he's going to be okay," I said.

"Olivia Williams?" I turned to face Greg's doctor, an intelligent looking middle-aged man.

"That's me," I said.

"I'm Dr. Alex Burgess. Your brother suffered multiple fractures. He's in the intensive care unit and he's still unconscious. We've done all we can for now. We'll know more when he regains consciousness," he said.

"Can I see him?"

"Yes, but for just a short while."

I took Rex's hand and was about to follow the doctor when he said, "I'm sorry, but only one person for now."

"Its okay, Liv. You go. I'll be right here waiting for you," Rex said.

I didn't know what to expect but when we walked into the small hospital room, I gasped in shock. He had bandages all over. His arms and legs were suspended in the air and he had a neck brace, with small cuts and scrapes all over his face.

"I'll leave you alone with him for a few minutes," Dr. Burgess said.

I moved closer to his hospital bed and closed my eyes, trying to imagine the pain he must have been in. It was so hard to see him lying there like that. What was I supposed to tell my parents, Sandra and Riley? How was I supposed to break the news to them?

I touched his short hair as I looked at his face. "What did you do, Greg?" I said softly, recalling how earlier I'd been dreading his visit. "You must get better, you hear me? You must do it for Riley and Sandra. They need you." I couldn't help wondering if his accident would've occurred had I let him stay with me as he'd wanted.

"Ms. Williams?" I turned at a nurse's voice. "You'll have to come see him later," she said.

"I'm here, Greg. I'm not going anywhere," I said, then leaned down and pecked his forehead.

A moment later, I walked out of his hospital room. I thought I was okay until I got to Rex and completely broke down. What the hell was happening? Everything had been going so well then just like that, it was all going to hell.

"He's in really bad shape, Rex. I have to call home. I have to tell them."

"Calm down first and then make the call," he said as he held me in his arms.

Later, when I was doing a little better, I made the dreaded call. My mom picked up the phone and grew instantly concerned when she heard my voice.

"I have some bad news, Mom," I said before I lost my nerve.

"What is it, Livvy?" she asked.

Rex squeezed my hand and I took a deep breath. "Greg is in the hospital. He was in an accident and he's hurt pretty bad."

"Oh God."

"The doctor says he suffered multiple fractures."

"Have you seen him?" she asked.

"The doctor let me see him a while ago for a few minutes."

"Stay with him, let him know we love him and please keep me updated," she said.

I could tell she was trying hard to sound strong. "I will, Mom."

When we hang up, I tried to imagine how she'd break the news to the family and my heart broke for them. I didn't know how long we stayed in the hospital after that, but later on, somewhere around ten, I remembered I'd forgotten to cancel my classes and called my professors. They seemed understanding after I told them what had happened.

When I joined Rex back in the waiting room, I went and sat beside him and leaned against his shoulder. I kept wondering how the accident had occurred. Had he run into a truck? Were there other casualties? What had really happened? The questions went on and on, making me resent the helplessness of the situation.

"Olivia?" I looked up at the familiar voice and stood up when I saw Mrs. Gallagher.

What was she doing there? How had she known? I turned to Rex and realized he must have been the one who'd called her. I hadn't gotten around to telling him that she'd ended things between us but I was certain if he'd known, he wouldn't have called her.

"I heard about what happened," she said.

Rex got to his feet and walked away, giving us some room to talk in private after gently and reassuringly squeezing my arm.

"How is Greg doing?" she asked.

"I wish I could say he's doing okay, but to be honest, I don't know.

He's still unconscious."

"Rex said he was involved in an accident."

"Yes, but I haven't been given much detail to go on."

She moved closer to me and placed her hand over my shoulder. "Don't worry. Everything is going to be okay." For some reason when she said that, I felt like there was some hope.

I took a step closer and wrapped my arms around her. Her arms settled warmly around me and for one consolatory second, I felt safe. After a moment, I pulled away, reminding myself that I wasn't supposed to do that. "Thanks for being here," I said.

"I don't want you to concern yourself with work tomorrow. Stay here with your brother. I'll take care of everything."

"Thank you."

"What's the name of his doctor?"

"Alex Burgess." I didn't know why she wanted to know Greg's doctor, but I wasn't going to deprive Greg of the much-needed assistance.

"Alright, I'll go talk to him, see if there's anything I can do."

When she left, Rex came back and placed his arm around my shoulders. We sat back down and I closed my eyes and prayed for my brother. I couldn't get the image of how he'd looked out of my mind.

"Mrs. Gallagher ended things between us," I told Rex, in an attempt to take my mind off of Greg.

"What? Why?" he asked.

I rubbed my temple with my forefingers in an attempt to soothe an oncoming migraine. "I told her I was in love with her." At the words, the pain which had been temporarily pushed aside returned.

"Oh, Livvy."

I got to my feet and hopelessly tossed my arms aside. "All this is my fault."

"No, none of this is your fault."

"Do you know there were moments in there when I truly believed we could be together? Can you believe how naïve my thinking was? I knew. I knew it would end this way. I knew she'd never choose me, but I made myself believe there was a chance," I said as I paced back and forth.

Rex stood up. "Liv, that is the natural order of falling in love."

"She felt right for me. She still does. But she's a married woman with a family." I laughed painfully. "What was I expecting, right? And then Greg shows up, assumes I'm having an affair with Mr. Gallagher and tries to exploit the situation, and now he's lying in a hospital bed and the doctors can't tell whether or not he's going to make it. I put this whole thing into motion." I was venting because I was angry and hurt.

He came and stood right in front of me, forcing my gaze to meet his. "Livvy that's far too great a burden to bear. As far as you and Mrs. Gallagher are concerned, your future with her is yet to be determined."

"Yet to be determined?" I moved away from him as a fire started to burn in me.

"She came here immediately she found out your brother was in the hospital. That woman in there, that's not your boss. She's someone you share something much more significant with. Putting her family first is her responsibility but that doesn't mean she doesn't care about you. As for Greg, you can't take the blame for his accident. Whether or not he'd been exploiting you, we never could have predicted this."

I exhaled in exasperation and leaned my back against the wall. I was angry with myself. This may not entirely have been my fault, but I had still played a great role in it.

"Livvy?" Amelia's voice pulled me from my misery. She walked up to me and said, "I've spoken to the doctor. Your brother is going to get the best possible care. He's been moved to a private wing where he'll be well monitored."

"I don't know what to say, Amelia."

"I wish I could do more."

"You've done enough. I'm sure my family would appreciate it."

"Did you tell them?" she asked.

"I called my mom earlier. She's terrified. I wish there was something I could do to ease this whole thing for her."

She reached for my hand and gently squeezed it in form of comfort. "I'll do all I can to help."

I met her soft calm gaze and thought about what Rex had just said.

Maybe she truly did care about me. "Thank you for everything."

"I have to go, but I'll check in as often as I can." She took a step closer to me, pecked my forehead then walked away, stopping to momentarily talk to Rex before she left.

"She told me to take care of you," he said.

Tears fell down my cheeks at the words and he took me back in his arms. We ended up spending the night at the hospital's waiting room and when morning came, we went to have breakfast at the Hospital's cafeteria. Since Greg's doctor wouldn't let us see him until the official visiting hours, I tried to talk Rex into going home because he still had his own responsibilities.

"Rex, why don't you go and carry on with your day? You can come by later."

"And leave you here all by yourself? No," he said.

Since I didn't really want him to leave, I didn't fight him on the matter. Sometime around mid-morning, I went to ask the doctor if there was any change, but he had nothing to report.

I was resting my head back against my chair when I heard my mom's voice. I thought I had imagined it until I searched the room and found my parents, Sandra and Riley at the entrance of the waiting room.

"Oh, my God." I ran over to them and hugged them all.

Rex seemed as surprised as I was when he saw them.

"Honey, tell us what happened," Dad said.

I told them everything I knew and shortly after, I went to call Greg's doctor to come explain the situation to them. Rex took Riley to the vending machine as I stood by my parents and Sandra.

Dr. Burgess must have seen their distress because he broke hospital protocol and allowed us all to go see Greg. He'd been moved to a bigger, better room, thanks to Amelia and even though his condition hadn't changed, I was hopeful.

"How did you guys get here?" I asked Sandra when we were alone.

"Someone sent by your boss came to get us on a private jet. We thought you arranged it."

Oh, Amelia. God, what was she doing? Didn't she know it was things like these that made it so easy for me to be in love with her?

Rex and Riley came to join us a moment later. I picked up the little boy and sat him on my lap. He still remembered me because we'd recently seen each other so he was sweet and friendly towards me. I hoped for his sake, as well as that of Sandra and my parents, Greg would recover.

Greg opened his eyes later on in the evening and after his doctor had checked him, he allowed us to go see him. He seemed happy to see the whole family there and I hoped that would give him the strength he needed to fight for his life.

Opening his eyes felt like a sign that he'd get better. My parents were destroyed to see him in such a broken condition and Sandra was holding back tears because Riley needed to see her strong.

He was too weak to speak, so he didn't say anything but my parents were fast to reassure him and offer him words of comfort. We gave him a few moments alone with Sandra but after that, no one left his side.

It felt like time stood still for most of it while we were there because there was little progress to report. I tried talking my family into going back to my place for a little bit of rest, but they didn't want to leave incase something happened, which was understandable because I didn't want to leave either.

Despite everything that had happened between me and Greg, he was still my brother and I was equally as concerned as my parents.

Sometime around midnight, Riley was sleeping in Sandra's arms, my parents were sleeping right next to each other and Rex was sleeping by himself. Sleeping in the waiting room seats was uncomfortable, but they didn't seem to mind.

I was standing by the window looking into the dark starless night. My mind, for once, was blank. All I'd done the whole day was think, so I was tired and I couldn't sleep.

It had been over twenty-four hours since I'd gotten to that hospital. The helpless situation my family was in made me feel useless. I left the waiting room and snuck out to go see Greg. I wasn't allowed to see him at such a late hour, but I didn't care.

I grabbed a seat and sat beside him as my mind traveled back in time. I thought of a time when things between us had been good and started reminding him of childhood stories of when we'd both been young and innocent.

He'd been protective of me while we'd been children. He'd been proud to have a younger sister he could play with and take care of. I didn't know when things had changed between us, but as children growing up, we'd been close.

"Do you remember the time when that kid, Joe, at school used to pull my pigtails? I came home crying and when you found out you went and told him if he ever touched me again, you'd break his teeth." I leaned my head over his bed and closed my eyes. I'd cried so much in the last forty-eight hours I didn't know if I had it in me anymore.

"Liv," his voice was weak, strained, but I heard him. I got to my feet and looked into his eyes. "I'm sorry," he whispered. "I'm sorry for everything."

Just when I thought I couldn't cry anymore, tears blurred my vision. "When you get better, I'd like for us to start over," I said.

He blinked a couple of times then closed his eyes again. With my hope renewed, I leaned over his bed again and fell asleep by his side.

I was woken up by the sound of beeping machines and before I knew what was going on, the room filled with nurses and doctors. One of them escorted me out and I watched in horror as they took him to an operating room.

"Ma'am, you need to go back to the waiting area," a nurse said.

"Is he going to be okay?" I asked in fear.

"Go be with your family. His doctor is working on him."

I stood there for some time, waiting, wondering, hoping and praying, then turned and headed back to the waiting area. Everyone had woken up and rushed to me the moment I entered the room.

"Livvy, where were you? What's going on?" Rex asked.

I looked at my parents and told them what I'd just seen. I didn't want to worry them, but they deserved to know what was happening to their son. I walked up to Sandra and Riley and wrapped my arms around them.

After waiting for what felt like eternity, the doctor came out, accompanied by the nurse who'd spoken to me earlier. I could tell the worst had happened by the look on their faces, but I waited, still hopeful.

"Greg had massive internal bleeding. We did everything we could, but he didn't make it. I'm sorry," he said.

The room fell silent and then my parents and Sandra broke into tears. Rex wrapped his arms around me and it wasn't long before I started crying too. My dad tried to console us all, but there was nothing he could say at that moment which could ease our pain.

Chapter Forty-Nine

I was tired of crying and hurting. I was tired of the pain and misery. I needed a break from it even if it was just for a few hours. Greg's body had been released to my family and was being taken back to St. Paul, where the funeral was going to take place.

My family had stayed in my apartment for a couple of days now and were preparing to head back home. They were taking care of the funeral arrangements and Mrs. Gallagher was kind enough to fly us all to St. Paul in her private jet.

The sadness surrounding us all was almost palpable. I wanted to get away from it but unfortunately, I was at the centre of all its madness. To give myself some space, I went to my office, at the Gallagher mansion where I knew I'd be alone.

It was a Tuesday afternoon. I should've been working but Mrs. Gallagher had been kind enough to give me as much time as I needed. The problem was, during all that time, I couldn't think about anything other than what had just happened.

My family was devastated and I resented knowing there was nothing I could do to ease the grieving period for them. I didn't know how long I sat there, lost in thought, but I was glad when Francis, the Gallagher butler, knocked on the door and a second later, stepped inside.

"Hello Ms. Williams," he said.

"Hi Francis."

"There is a young man asking for you downstairs."

It had to be Rex. He was the only person who knew me well enough to know where I'd go at a time such as this. "I'll be right down," I said.

He nodded and walked back out.

I tried to psych myself up, using that little voice in my head to scream continuously. *I'm okay. I'm strong. I'll get through this. My family will find a way to get through this. Just get past these next few days.*

When I thought I was strong enough, I got to my feet and headed for the door. I'd only just opened it when Mrs. Gallagher opened hers.

She seemed surprised to see me.

I blankly looked at her, unsure of what to say.

"Olivia, what are you doing here?" she asked.

"I'm sorry, I know this is your home, but I just needed a bit of a break from everything."

"Oh, sure, that's fine."

We stood awkwardly staring at each other for a few seconds and then she said, "Can I talk to you for a minute?"

I nodded and stepped back into my office, where she followed me. "Mrs. Gallagher, before you start, I just want to thank you for everything you've done for my family. This whole thing would have been extra harder without your involvement or your assistance," I said.

"Olivia, you don't have to thank me for that."

"I do." I took a deep breath. "You're my boss. Usual bosses don't extend these kinds of courtesies to their employees," I added.

"Livvy," she said as she stepped closer to me, stopping just the right amount of distance away. "You know you're more than that."

I knew I was. But whatever I was to her, it wasn't significant enough for her to accept what I felt, and from the turmoil I was going through at that moment, I didn't want to delude myself. "If you meant it when you said that you want me to stop loving you, I want you to stop with all these gestures. I appreciate them. God knows I do, but the only thing they do is make me love you more. So please, just stop."

She looked at me for a while then slowly nodded.

"I have to go, Rex is waiting for me."

"Please wait," she said when I walked past her.

I stopped and closed my eyes, wishing, praying she wouldn't say something that would pull me back to her.

"I'm sorry for everything that's happened."

I tightened my jaw, trying to hold myself together.

"I'm here for you if you need me," she said.

I could literally feel my heart constricting in my chest. What did that even mean, she was there for me when I needed her? "I won't settle for just a piece of your heart, Amelia. I need you, each and every single part of you. But we want different things and I get that. It breaks my heart, but God knows I get it."

I walked out of the office and after closing the door, I took a deep breath and held my tears back in. I was not going to cry. Not anymore. Not for her. When I was calm enough, I headed downstairs.

I found Rex talking to Adrianna and paused for a second to watch them. If it had been any other time, I would have thought they looked good together, but at that moment, there was just too much going on for me to pay attention.

"Hi Adrianna," I said as I approached them.

"Hi Olivia," she said.

Rex walked over to me and said, "It's time. Everything is ready. We have to go."

I nodded and headed out the door.

"It was nice meeting you, Adrianna," Rex said as he followed after me.

When we got out, he led me to where he'd parked my crappy little car, which he'd been using since I'd started working for Amelia. We drove straight to the airstrip, where I found my family waiting and an hour later, we were heading back to St. Paul.

The funeral took place two days later and all my family's friends were in attendance. The gloomy atmosphere suited the sad occasion and later, when everyone had left, we all silently sat down as a family for dinner.

The following day, we all seemed to mourn separately. It was as though we were all individually paying our respects to Greg in our own special way. Since Rex and I had to get back to New York, during our last night there when we were having dinner, I announced it to my family. They seemed more than understanding, which made it easy for us to leave.

I didn't want to bother Amelia, and after our last conversation, I thought it would be easier to take a commercial plane back home.

The following morning, I was back to work. Since I was desperate to keep myself occupied in order to avoid depressing thoughts, I called my professors and informed them I was ready to resume with my studies.

After that, I went to see Mrs. Gallagher in order to report back to work. She'd taken up some of my responsibilities and I wanted to let her know I was back in full swing.

I found her talking to that odd man who'd almost walked in on us. I still had no idea who he was and though I was a bit curious, I mostly just wanted to resume with my duties and try and move on with my life.

"I'm sorry. I don't mean to interrupt," I said as my gaze immediately settled on Mrs. Gallagher who seemed a bit tense as she sat behind her desk.

My gaze moved to the odd man, who was watching me now. He was tall and scrawny and though he didn't appear intimidating, there was something about him that felt a bit off.

"Eric, would you give us a minute," Mrs. Gallagher said.

I did not fail to notice that she addressed him by his first name.

"Sure," he had a small smile as he walked past me, which left me a little confused.

"I just wanted to report back to work," I said.

She got to her feet and came around her desk. "How are you doing?" she asked.

"I'm fine, just eager to resume with my responsibilities."

"Olivia."

I didn't imagine hearing her say my name after those difficult few days would affect me so much. "Please," I said softly.

"I've lost someone close to me. I know how hard it is," she said.

"Then you know that I need to focus my mind on something otherwise I'll go insane."

"I know," she said in a low voice that almost sounded like a whisper. "But Olivia, don't you want to talk about it?"

I knew she was trying to be helpful and I wished I could respond to her the way she wanted me to, but after all this time of being bold, brave and strong, I was just coming to realize that it wasn't a façade anymore.

I wasn't being this person for her. I was being this person for me. I was myself. I was brave, strong and confident. It had nothing to do with her anymore. This was the person I'd become and I was not going to submit to weakness any longer.

"That's the thing about friends, Mrs. Gallagher. I don't have to talk about it, they just …understand. That's why Rex is my best friend."

She observed me for a few moments then nodded. "I'll forward everything to you in a moment," she said.

"Thank you." I walked out before she could respond because I wanted to believe that I was stronger than this.

"Ms. Williams."

I came to a startling halt right outside Mrs. Gallagher's door when the odd man said my name.

"I'm sorry, I didn't mean to startle you," he said.

I quickly composed myself. "Sir?" I said.

"I'm Eric Gardner. Amelia's cousin," he said.

I raised my eyebrow, wondering if they were distant cousins because there was no trace of family resemblance. "Oh, I'm sorry. I didn't know. It's nice to meet you," I said.

"It's nice to meet you too."

We shook hands and when I went to pull away, it almost felt like he lingered a bit.

"You're her—. Her personal assistant, is that right?" he asked.

"Yes, sir."

He nodded as if satisfied by my answer and I headed back to my office.

I got right back to work and Mrs. Gallagher forwarded me notes and everything else I needed to know about what had happened in my absence. It was a busy day, and I was glad for it because I hardly had time to focus on the negative.

When I was preparing to leave for my evening classes, I was interrupted by a knock on my door. I opened to find two gentlemen clad in police uniform standing on the opposite side.

"Pardon me, Ma'am. I'm looking for Olivia Williams," one of them said.

"I'm Olivia Williams," I said, wondering what this was about.

"I'm Officer Garret, this is Officer Spade. We'd like to talk to you about Gregory Williams' accident. Would you mind if we come in for a moment?"

"My brother's accident?"

"Yes, Ma'am." The other policeman, Officer Spade, said.

"Uh, what's—. What's going on?" I asked as I let them in.

"Ms. Williams, I'm sorry to tell you this but it seems there was some sort of foul play involved in your brother's accident," Officer Garret said.

His words were so unexpected, I didn't respond for a while.

"Ma'am, do you understand?" Officer Spade asked.

"I'm sorry, what exactly do you mean?" I asked.

"Someone tampered with the brakes of your brother's car," Officer Garret said.

I took in his words and once I understood what they meant I asked, "Are you saying—. Are you saying that Greg was murdered?"

"Yes, Ma'am," he said.

I felt like my feet lost their balance as I staggered back in denial.

"We're looking further into the investigation and we'd like to know if there was anyone you might have been aware of, who had any motive to kill him," Officer Spade said.

My heartbeat had increased pace. I could hear the officers but it was like I couldn't comprehend their words. Who would want to kill Greg? He'd been in New York for such a short period of time.

"Ma'am?"

"He came to visit me from St. Paul, Minnesota, a few weeks ago. We hadn't seen each other in years since I moved here for school. I don't know who would have wanted to hurt him." Even if he'd crossed me, I wouldn't have attempted to physically harm him.

"And you don't know if he had any enemies? Someone who might have seen him as a threat?"

I shook my head. "No sir," I said.

"Okay, Ma'am. Thanks for your time. Here's my number incase you remember anything," Officer Spade said as he handed me his card.

After they were gone, the last question replayed itself in my head.

And you don't know if he had any enemies? Someone who might have seen him as a threat?

He'd been a threat to me but I hadn't had anything to do with his accident. Oh, God. Had Greg owed money to some dangerous criminals? Was that why he'd been blackmailing me for a quarter million dollars? No, no that couldn't be it. He'd been petty, but he never would have gotten himself involved in criminal activities.

Did it have anything to do with me? But how could it? The only person who'd known about Greg and his blackmail had been Rex and Amelia. Wait a minute, Amelia. Was she? No! I rejected the thought the moment it attempted to enter my mind.

Greg had probably gotten himself involved with some bad people and he'd ended up in trouble. There was no way his murder had anything to do with me. He must have gotten himself involved in shady dealings during his time in New York.

After thinking about it for a long time, I decided it'd just be easier to let the officers do their investigations. Until then, I would not rattle my family with the news. They had just laid a loved one to rest, to think someone had actually played a role in it would tarnish their image of Greg and destroy them.

"May I talk to you for a minute?" I said the following day. I'd just dropped off some files in Mrs. Gallagher's office and was on my way out when I decided to tell her about what I'd learned.

"Sure," she said.

I walked back over to her desk and tried to think of a way to put it. When she got to her feet, I took a breath and said, "Last night some police officers came to see me."

"Oh? About what?"

She looked concerned, but I tried not to let myself get distracted. "They came to see me about Greg. They said his brakes were tampered with, that his accident wasn't an accident. It was premeditated murder."

She was speechless for a while but I didn't blame her. I'd reacted in a similar fashion at the news.

"Do they know who's responsible?" she asked.

I watched her for a minute then slowly shook my head.

"I'm sorry."

"Me too," I said as I turned to leave.

"Olivia,"

I took another breath and faced her.

"Do you think I had something to do with it?"

I shook my head. "No, I don't think you'd cause me or my family any harm."

She pressed her lips together and slowly nodded. After a moment, she came around her desk and approached me. I stood still, calculating the distance from where I was standing, to the door.

"It must've been devastating for you to learn about Greg so soon after everything else you've been through," she said.

I wondered if everything else incorporated her breaking my heart. "He had his faults, but he didn't deserve to go that way."

"Do you know anyone who would've wanted to hurt him?"

I exhaled in an attempt to release some of the overwhelming emotions I was keeping at bay. "No, we weren't close. I had no idea where he went after he came to see me. I didn't care to find out. I just wanted him gone." I tightened my jaw, closed my eyes and told myself to breathe. "But not like this." I could sense her presence even before she touched my face.

"Olivia, I hope you don't blame yourself for any of this," she said.

"It doesn't matter."

"Of course, it does."

I opened my eyes and was a little surprised to see just how close she was standing next to me. "It's not your fault," she said.

"If I'd never sent that stupid cheque home—"

"You never would have known your father had been sick, you never would have made the time to go see your family. Livvy, his coming here prompted you to pay closer attention to what was happening back home. If you think you put this whole thing into motion, you couldn't be more wrong."

I took a deep breath as I let her words sway me and she gently took me in her arms. I relaxed in her embrace and clasped my arms around her. She felt like heaven and for the first time in the last few days, I felt safe, warm and less burdened.

When we pulled apart, she lightly ran her fingers over my cheek and my heart started its ridiculous dance of palpitation. God, would that ever stop? She moved tresses of my hair from my face and I released a shaky breath. I wanted her with every fragment of my being.

I leaned in, unsure of whether or not she'd pull me in or push me away, but she surprised me when she met me halfway and pressed her lips against mine. The kiss was intimately slow, but the heat growing in me was driving me to want to demand more.

The reminder that I couldn't, that this was all we'd probably ever have had me exercising my self-restraint. I broke the kiss and physically pulled away from her, creating a proper amount of distance between us as my mind started working again.

"I'd like you to transfer me to an office at Price Healthcare," I said, unsure of where the words came from.

"What?" she asked.

I tried to put my thoughts together and said, "I can't continue to work this closely to you. Every time I see you, I fall deeper in love with you. Every time I'm close to you, all I can think about is how much I'd love to take you in my arms and make love to you. I can't stop loving you. It's not a reversible thing that I can will myself to do. But I can force myself to bury it somewhere deep within myself and in order for me to do that, I need to distance myself from you." I swallowed a painful ball of air. What was I doing? Could I really go without seeing her for long periods of time?

"Olivia,"

"Please Amelia. It's the only way."

I could feel my heart breaking all over again, but I told myself this was the right thing to do. Amelia could never want me the way I wanted her. She had priorities which were more important than our affair.

"This is what you want?" she asked.

"No, but it's what I need."

She looked at me for a while then said, "I'll make the necessary arrangements."

A surge of emotions rushed through me. Did she have any idea how hard this was for me? Did she have it in her to want to fight for me?

I wanted her to tell me she'd work something out; that she wanted to be with me, that all she needed was time, but her answer was plain and simple.

"Thank you," I said and walked out of her office.

I told myself I wouldn't cry as I went back to my office. I sat down on my chair and stared at the laptop screen, then slowly, tears blurred my vision. I promised myself this was the last time I'd ever cry for her.

Chapter Fifty

It didn't take long for me to transfer Olivia to Price Healthcare. Within a couple of days, everything had been taken care of. She had a nice large office with a private conference area where she could hold her meetings without having to go out and I made sure James was still available for her transportation.

It had been a week now since she'd left the office across from mine and now that she had taken over my responsibilities at Price Healthcare, I was looking for someone to fill her newly vacated position.

I needed someone to do what Olivia had been doing during her earlier time working for me, which included traveling, planning events and handling my schedule. I'd interviewed several people, but none of them met my standards.

I didn't know why sometimes when my office door opened, I expected it to be Olivia. It was silly, but sometimes, my heart jumped then calmed in disappointment when it turned out to be someone else.

I knew I had treated her unfairly. She had been through so much and I was partly responsible for inflicting that pain when I'd rejected her. I had warned her there could never be more between us, but now I was disappointed in myself for not having done a better job of protecting her.

It hadn't come by surprise when during our date she'd announced she was in love with me. I'd seen it in her eyes way before then. I'd denied it during that time but looking back, I now realized that a part of me had thrived in it, which was why I'd never stopped the affair or myself.

Olivia had been my guilty pleasure, and now that she was gone, it felt like she had been something a lot more. I'd never denied that I'd cared for her, but I'd never wanted to question the extent of that care.

After our last encounter at her apartment, I admit her brother threatening to expose whatever at the time he'd thought he'd known, had caused a tremor of panic, but it had made it easier for me to end things with Olivia.

We'd gone too far. Our affair, or whatever it had been, had never been supposed to see the light of day. But something, forces stronger than me had been in control and no matter what I'd told myself, that spark between us had turned to fireworks.

I felt horrible for hurting her because shortly after, her brother's accident had taken place and then she'd lost him. I had wanted to be there for her, to somehow help ease her pain, but I'd only done what I'd been capable of, bringing her family to the hospital and making sure her brother was comfortable.

It had all seemed to happen so fast. Poor Olivia, seeing her at the hospital so sad and helpless had been so familiar and heartbreaking. I'd seen my younger self in her when I'd lost Isabel. I'd wanted to reach out, but having ended things between us had cut off that privilege.

Every time I'd seen her after that, a sadness I couldn't understand had taken root in me. I'd wanted to hold her, take away her pain and the excessive thought of her and what she'd been going through had made me angry at the world, angry at myself.

Our last encounter in my office had made me want so badly to shield her from her pain. I'd understood her need to want to push me away, but weirdly enough, I hadn't liked it. I'd wanted her to speak to me in order to know what was going through her mind and when she'd opened up, she'd been so vulnerable. I'd just wanted to comfort her. I hadn't planned on kissing her.

Her words after the kiss had startled me but I'd realized one thing, Olivia was far much stronger than I'd ever given her credit for, and that was how I was going to see and remember her, as a strong, brave soul.

The knock at my door pulled me from my reverie, and a moment later, Francis walked in. "Good afternoon, Madam," he said.

"Good afternoon, Francis."

"This just came for you by courier," he said as he handed me an envelope.

"Did it say who it was from?"

"No, Ma'am."

"Okay. Thank you."

He bobbed his head and walked back out.

I placed the envelope on the desk and my thoughts unsuccessfully trailed back to Olivia. I remembered our lovely date. I hadn't known what to expect but she'd managed to pleasantly surprise me.

The date had been perfect because everything she'd planned and everything we'd done had seamlessly unfolded, easily creating one of the most memorable and magical nights of my life.

My favorite part of the evening was when it had started raining. I'd never been spontaneous in my life. Dancing in the rain with Olivia and kissing as though nothing else would ever make me feel that soaring sense of freedom again, had been one of the most amazing experiences for me. After all, in the world I lived in, it was the little things that counted.

Something odd which had happened to me however, was the unexpected carnal need I'd developed for Olivia, shortly after she'd confessed her feelings for me. There had been this fiery look in her eyes, accompanied by a softness that I'd just wanted to keep to myself.

Everything had been perfect, up until that moment when my fears could no longer stay silent and I'd had to go and ruin it.

When Olivia had mentioned that Greg had been blackmailing her, I'd wanted to know what he wanted but his information had been based on pure speculation. Nonetheless, if someone had been keen enough, it wouldn't have taken long to discover the affair was with me, and not Patrick.

When Olivia had told me his accident had been caused by someone, I'd wondered if he'd made some enemies during his short stay in New York. But it didn't make any sense.

From the file I'd gotten from my private investigator when Olivia had started working for me, it didn't seem to suit his character to go do something so dangerous that it'd get him killed. I was curious to know what the police would uncover in their investigations.

Deciding to focus my mind back to work, I took the envelope and slowly opened it. When I turned it over and removed the contents, my eyes widened in shock as A4 sized photographs containing images of me and Olivia kissing in the rain fell on my desk.

I scanned through them one by one, wondering who, when and how. Had Greg taken these and had them mailed to me before he'd died? He was the only one who'd come close to discovering the truth and judging from this evidence, he seemed to have hit the jackpot.

Could he have followed us, taken the photos and had them mailed to me just hours before someone had killed him? It didn't seem to fit the timeline. By the time he must have taken the photos, printed them out and sent them to me, it would have been too late. He would have already been at the hospital, and it wasn't possible they would have taken this long to reach me. So it couldn't have been him.

It could however, very possibly be, the person who had killed him. If this person was capable of murder, there was very little such a person was incapable of. I searched the envelope for some sort of message, but there was nothing else inside other than the photographs.

What did this person want from me? Why had it taken him so long to send me these photos? Was he a threat to my family? To Olivia? Oh God, I immediately took my phone and dialed her number at the thought.

She answered on the first ring. "Mrs. Gallagher," she said.

The sound of her voice was soft and calm. "Hello Olivia," I said, picturing her seated behind her large desk.

"Hello."

I trailed my mind back to the matter at hand and said, "Are you okay?"

"I'm fine."

"I need to ask you something."

"Okay."

"Did Greg say anything to you before he died?"

She was silent for a while then asked, "You're calling me to ask about Greg?"

"I'm sorry, Olivia, but I need to know."

"He said," she seemed to choke on the words, "He said he was sorry for everything."

"He didn't say anything else?"

"No, why are you asking about this?"

I looked at the pictures in my hand. I didn't want to get her involved if she was not in any danger. Whoever had sent those pictures seemed only interested in me. "I just wanted to confirm something, I'm sorry to have distracted you from your work. Have a good afternoon," I said and hang up.

I was still trying to figure the whole thing out half an hour later, when Eric walked in through the door. His visits were becoming more frequent and his presence still bothered me.

"Eric, I can't talk to you right now," I said as I put the photographs back in their envelope.

"Something wrong?" he asked.

I tightened my jaw, resenting how he seemed to think his visits made it easier for me to be around him when in fact, he continued to irk me.

"What happened to your personal assistant?"

I looked up at him, wondering why he'd be interested in Olivia and then I looked at the envelope.

"I see you received my little present."

"You sent these?" I asked, holding up the envelope.

He smiled as he approached my desk. "Well, I needed some leverage for myself."

"Leverage for what?" I asked as I got to my feet.

"Kathy's grown weak and desperate. She doesn't seem to yield any power over you anymore. Her pathetic attempts to reach out to you created an opportunity for me and I took it." He seemed highly pleased with himself.

"Eric, what are you talking about? What does this have to do with my mother?"

"She wanted to see you happy, there was a threat, so she told me to get rid of it."

His words started taking meaning but I refused to believe him or any of what he was saying. "Did you have anything to do with Greg's accident?" I asked in denial but the look on his face said it all. "You killed Olivia's brother?"

"I didn't care for him until I realized why Kathy wanted him out of the picture. He was a threat to your happiness. Old Kathy has grown soft with age. Suddenly she seems to care about what makes you happy.

"So she told me to get rid of him, but before I did, I wanted to know why she wanted him gone so I followed you. Imagine my surprise, when I saw you and your young and pretty personal assistant lip-locking in the middle of the night, out in the streets as if you had no care in the world." He sat down on one of the seats facing my desk and leaned back into the leather.

"Let me get his straight, Kathy told you to kill Greg?" I asked because I wanted to be sure. Had my mother lost her mind?

"Yes," he said.

A leopard couldn't change his spots, I had known Eric was still the same filthy bastard I'd grown up resenting. "And she told you to do this because she knew about me and Olivia?" Was there anything that woman didn't know? How was she still one step ahead of me?

"Look, it doesn't matter. I just want what's mine."

"And what is that?"

He got to his feet and leaned over my desk as I pulled back in disgust. I was glad the desk was standing between us.

"I'm just asking for what I'm entitled to. A seat on the board, a better position in the company here in New York and last but not least, I know this little part is going to make Kathy very happy," he said, grinning from ear to ear. "I want you to merge Price Healthcare and Winston Enterprises."

I wasn't surprised by his conniving ways.

"Kathy has always treated me like a lapdog because of you. She's never thought I was capable of anything because you always overshadowed me, but now, she's going to see what I can do."

"And you think blackmailing me into giving you what you want is going to achieve that? You think you'll finally have her love and approval?"

He pulled back and started pacing. "Do you have any idea what she took me from?" He stopped and looked at me. "Of course not, you've never cared to find out. Well, I'm going to tell you. Kathy took me from her cousin, a drug addicted sonofabitch with a mean streak. My mother had died during childbirth so there was no one else to take care of me. My old man, he wasn't afraid to express his frustrations with life on me using his belt or pretty much anything else he got his hands on. Kathy gave me a chance at life and I swore I'd make her proud but I couldn't do that with you constantly taking over my spotlight."

"It was never yours to begin with, Eric."

"You've had things handed to you all your life. You don't know how it's like to work your ass off for something."

"Are you kidding me?"

"Price Healthcare for instance, it was a half a billion-dollar company that was just handed to you."

I took a deep breath, unsure I had the patience to continue talking to him anymore because he seemed to believe what he was saying, and it felt like I was wasting my breath, so I let him ramble on.

"You had everything, Amelia. Kathy may never have known how to express herself but she's always been proud of you. She's always loved you. But you don't care, you never have. She loves your family and all you've ever done was push her away, create distance between them. You've been punishing her for years for something she couldn't help."

He clearly had no idea what he was talking about. He didn't know Kathy the way I did. "You're her family, how much effort has she put into getting close to your kids?" I asked.

"That doesn't matter. My kids are grateful for what they have and they know she cares."

"Because she sees them, talks to them as often as she can, because she's interested in their lives, what they're doing, what they're studying, who they're dating?" I asked.

"Maybe not that, but she cares. I know she does."

"The only person Kathy cares about is herself. You'd be wise to open your eyes and see this for yourself."

He gritted his teeth and approached me. He took the envelope and angrily slammed the photographs on my desk. "When Kathy sees that I can get her what she's wanted all along, she'll start to care."

He was psychotic.

"A seat on the board, a position in Winston Enterprises here in New York and a merger with Price Healthcare."

"And you think I'm just going to hand these things over to you because you have pictures of me in a compromising situation with a Price Healthcare employee?"

"Yes, if you don't want them plastered all over the media. I'm talking the internet, magazines, newspapers and every other form of media station out there. The world will be talking about this. Patrick and your kids are going to be at the center of it and your beautiful, young Olivia will be on a very unpleasant receiving end of this whole scandal. Oh, and you should know, I have a video of your little dance in the rain."

He smirked as though realizing he had me exactly where he wanted me.

"You just admitted to killing Greg, Eric."

"I also said your mother sent me to do it. You can't implicate me without implicating her."

"What makes you think I won't go to the police with any of this?"

"Kathy is your mother. You'd never do that to her, or your kids. Your high family values betray you," he said as he walked out of my office.

I sat back on my chair, running his words through my head. I didn't care much about what Patrick would think, after all, the divorce proceedings were well on their way. What worried me was how Jonah and Adrianna would take the news if they found out, and how this whole thing would affect Olivia and her family.

It wasn't really a big deal that I was with a woman in those photographs; it was the particular woman I had been photographed with. She was a young beautiful employee who, the media would say I'd exploited and taken advantage of, or they could twist the story to say she'd taken advantage of me to get money or a position in my company.

God, what had I done? No, wait, this was my mother's doing. The shock started to register now that I was alone. Kathy was responsible for Greg's death. How could she have known? At the thought, I called James to pull up the car so that I could go talk to her.

Chapter Fifty-One

I was a little nervous to face my mother. Our last exchange had not been very pleasant and now, after what I'd come to learn, I was dreading being in her presence again.

I had always known she was capable of anything but I'd never thought she could commit murder and worse, manipulate someone as emotionally starved for her affection as Eric into doing it for her. What purpose did Greg's death serve her?

On my way to her house, I wondered what reasons she'd offer for having committed such a heinous crime. Eric had probably revealed a tad too much. He'd probably never meant to tell me the truth about the crime, but his greed had blinded him because he'd seen an opportunity he could exploit.

But what if this had been Kathy's plan all along? She'd always had her eye on Price Healthcare. What if she was the one behind what Eric was doing? No, it didn't make any sense. She no longer had any say over what happened at Winston Enterprises. Even if she wanted the merger, it would serve her no purpose now. The only people who would benefit from it would be my kids.

When I pressed the doorbell, one of my mother's employees answered it and let me in. I went to wait in the large living room and poured myself a glass of scotch for my nerves while I waited.

I had no idea what she did with her time. I didn't even know if she had any friends. She'd always been a stranger to me so I knew absolutely nothing about her life. But it would seem she kept a close eye on mine.

How had she known about me and Olivia? How had she known Greg had been blackmailing Olivia? What more did she know? Was she willing to hurt Olivia? The last thought gave me chills as she walked into the room.

"Amelia?" She sounded surprised.

I turned to face her to notice she looked different from the last time I'd seen her. She'd always had this ageless grace and poise, but now, I could see the lines forming below her eyes and a bit of a tired look across her face. She looked almost, fragile.

"It's so good to see you," she said as she approached me.

I took an involuntary step back when she reached out to touch me, refusing to let her physical appearance fool me. "Hello Kathy," I said.

"Are you still upset with me?" she asked.

Well, there seemed to be absolutely nothing wrong with her memory and I could bet she was still as acute as ever. I took a gulp of the shot of scotch I'd poured myself and placed the glass down, as the burning sensation made its way down my throat.

"Eric has been coming by to see me," I said, ignoring her question.

"Oh, he mentioned something about wanting to repair your relationship."

"There was never a relationship to start with."

"Well, that's too bad. I guess his visits have been fruitless then," she said as she came around me.

"How long have you been spying on me?" I asked, turning to face her because I wanted to see the look on her face when I discovered the truth.

"Spying on you?"

"Eric told me everything. He sent me this." I handed her the envelope. She hesitantly looked at me, took it and opened it. I watched her blank expression as she looked through the photographs. "Did you tell him to take these pictures?"

"No, of course not."

"He claims to have a video too, which he's going to expose if I don't agree to his terms."

"Which are?"

"He wants to be made a member of the board; he wants a position here in New York, and a merger with Price Healthcare."

She seemed a little surprised by the demands.

"He's not going to expose anything," she said, almost as though she was a hundred percent certain.

"He admitted to having killed Olivia's brother under your orders."

"Do you believe him?"

"I don't know. I need to hear the truth from you."

She placed the photos back in the envelope and placed it down on a table. She went and poured herself a glass of scotch and when she offered to refill mine, I turned it down. "I don't have anything to do with that," she said, pointing to the envelope before she took a gulp of the scotch and emptied the glass.

"Did you know about me and Olivia?" I asked, starting from the very beginning.

"Not at first," she said.

"What do you mean?"

"During our last conversation, there was something different about you. You'd always been cold to me, but never hostile. I wanted to know what was going on and I knew you'd never voluntarily tell me, so I took initiative."

"You started spying on me."

"I may have put you under light surveillance."

"May have?"

"You have to understand, I didn't realize how unhappy you were or how much losing Isabel still affected you."

My hands shook in contained anger because she had no right to speak Isabel's name.

"I've always wanted to be part of your life, Amelia. When I brought you back to New York, I thought we could find some way to start over. But you were so distant, so rebellious. I never knew how to reach out."

My memory trailed back to the past. There was nothing she was telling me I wasn't already aware of, but she was twisting the truth to fit herself. "You pushed me away when I tried to bridge the gap between us. Dad died and the first thing you did was send me to Germany."

"I wanted you to learn to be independent, to be strong on your own so that you'd never have to rely on anyone for anything."

"I guess your plan worked out a bit too well then, huh?" I said, refusing to let her try to appeal to me for understanding. "When I came back from Germany, I was all those things. You made the mistake of thinking I was someone you could control."

She turned to face away.

"Dressing me up, inviting me to those ridiculous parties to parade me around in attempts to find me a suitor? That's why you didn't let me properly mourn Isabel. You saw vulnerability, weakness and manipulated the situation and filled her place with Patrick."

"I thought he could make you happy."

"Stop it!" I said, gritting my teeth. She had an excuse for everything. "You destroyed my life. I do not know how you always somehow manage to crawl your way back in every time I kick you out."

"Amelia, can't you see? Can't you see that I'm trying to make it up to you?" She moved closer to me and I took a step back.

"How? How could you possibly make it all up to me?" I asked.

"By giving you a second chance at what you had with Isabel."

I looked at her in utter shock.

"I admit, I wasn't very supportive and to be honest, I could never really understand, but out of your marriage with Patrick, you had a full life and got two beautiful kids. I wasn't as good a mother to you as you are to them. When I found out about you and young Ms. Olivia—,"

She must have been trying really hard because I could still sense a tone of disapproval in her voice.

"I saw a change in you. I saw something I hadn't seen in your eyes in a long time. I didn't know what plans you had with Olivia, but I never intended to interfere. I figured, if she made you happy, even if it was just a little, you deserved it and I didn't want to take that away from you. I didn't want anyone to take that away from you."

"What did you do?" I asked.

"What any mother would do to protect their child. I made sure no one would get in the way of your happiness."

"So you had Eric get rid of Greg because you saw him as a threat to my happiness?"

She watched me in silence then a moment later, she turned around and went to pour herself another glass of scotch.

"I protected you," she said, her back to me.

"You had someone killed, and it wasn't just anyone."

She faced me at that moment then slowly walked up to me. She stretched out her hand and touched my face. This time, I didn't know why, but I let her gently trail the back of her fingers over my cheek. "I didn't realize until it was too late just how much I had failed you." She slightly smiled as she withdrew and took a step back.

"Mom, you didn't have to kill him. He had nothing substantial on me."

She looked at me and I saw her features soften. "You called me mom." I'd never seen her get emotional, and I didn't notice I'd addressed her differently until she pointed it out.

"Because of what you did, Eric saw a window of opportunity and he's now blackmailing me." I brushed her off.

She pursed her lips together and sadly looked away. "I didn't kill him."

"Eric did, following your orders."

"No one can prove that."

Maybe no one could, and Eric's word against hers meant nothing, but she'd failed in whatever she'd been trying to do. "I knew from the very beginning that whatever Olivia and I shared never had a chance. I was prepared for it to end. You see, I have lived my life, it may not necessarily be the way I would have wanted, but I've lived. I don't get to go back and correct my mistakes or reshape my life. I don't get to put everything I've known aside to start anew.

"But Olivia, her life is just beginning. Her dreams are just starting to come true. It was wrong for you to take someone she loved away from her. You caused her and her family unimaginable pain, and whatever your reasons are, deep down you know taking Greg's life was the wrong way to go. What you did, it was all for nothing."

"She loves you," she said.

"That doesn't matter anymore because you took it away from me when you had her brother killed. There is no way she could ever forgive me for this." Now there was a sentence I never thought I'd use.

"She doesn't have to know. You could still…"

"Nothing!" I didn't mean to raise my voice, but I was upset and she kept on going, almost as if she didn't know when to stop. "There's nothing anymore. The police will find out. It may not come from me, but the truth will come to light."

"Why not go tell them yourself?"

I looked at her, wondering the same question as I took a deep breath and started to leave.

"Amelia."

I stopped. "Because of you," I said as I took a breath and headed out.

"So you do care about me." I heard her say.

"You don't make it easy," I said to myself as I left her house.

I couldn't believe she'd had someone killed because she'd thought she was trying to make me happy. Why couldn't she have been a normal parent? And what was I supposed to do with this information?

I couldn't go to the police with it. Kathy may have been a lot of horrible things, but she was still my mother and though it was hard to believe, I thought she was being honest when she said she was trying to help make things up for me.

Every single part of our conversation was disturbing and it was hard to believe that after years of being so manipulative and distant, she'd ended up being so oddly supportive. Granted her support had been offered in the wrong way, but she'd tried.

I wanted to stay mad at her and hate her for it, but I'd seen something in her I'd never seen before; care and well, her royally screwed up interpretation of love which shockingly was for me. But what kind of poisonous care was that, it drove her to kill someone? And how could she possibly believe she'd done it to safeguard my happiness?

And after all she'd done over the years, how was I still willing to protect her? I could have James drive me straight to the police station and report her and Eric. So what was stopping me? What was wrong with me? How had I gotten so weak?

She was my mother, so there was a part of me that would always have a soft spot for her no matter what she'd done, but still. She'd gone a bit too far this time. It didn't matter what her reasons were.

How much was Olivia going to resent me once she found out? When I'd asked her if she thought I had anything to do with her brother's death, she'd said no. What would she say now when she found out that in fact I did? I wasn't directly involved, but I was still tied to it. God, I couldn't think about that right now.

I needed to figure out a way to be one step ahead of Eric. I couldn't report him to the police without implicating my mother, so that was out of the question and while I could give him a powerful position in our New York branch of Winston Enterprises, I couldn't meet his other two demands.

Winston Enterprises was a family owned business. It was meant to go down to Jonah and Adrianna and their children thereafter. Not to Eric and unfortunately, not to any of his children, which made his second demand impossible. When it came to his third demand, merging Price Healthcare to Winston Enterprises was never going to happen and there was no room for negotiation.

I groaned as I looked out the window. I couldn't believe I was actually thinking about this. How much damage could a video really do? Why not just let him leak it? Because of Olivia, a little voice said in my head.

After obsessively thinking about the matter, I called Jonah and Adrianna and informed them we were going to have dinner together. Jonah had an apartment in the city where he spent most of his time because it was convenient for work, and when Adrianna wasn't busy traveling and picking up every new skill she came across, she spent most of her time with friends or in the five-star presidential suite hotel the Gallagher family owned in the city.

We all had our own individual lives and no one seemed bothered by it. After talking to Kathy, I decided I didn't want to be the kind of mother she had been. I wanted my kids to know me, the real me, because they deserved to know the truth. However they were going to take it, in the end, I knew they'd come to appreciate the fact that they'd heard it from me first.

When they showed up and we were all seated during the second course of the meal, Anna asked, "Where's dad? I thought he'd be joining us too."

I should have invited him, but I only had the energy to deal with Jonah and Anna. After we'd decided to divorce, it didn't feel like I owed him much of anything.

"I thought it could be just us, tonight," I said.

"Mom, that's pretty much how it's been in the past," Jonah said.

I laughed nervously and tried to think about how I'd start. "There is something I need to tell you both and I didn't think it involved your father."

They were both indulging in the meal, but stopped when I spoke.

"What is it, Mom?" Jonah asked in concern.

"You know that your grandmother and I have never had an easy relationship," I started and they both nodded. "We were never really close because we thought the business demanded a lot from us individually... But I'd like to think we're different. I've tried my best to have a transparent relationship with both of you so that you feel you can always trust me and know that no matter what, I'm always here for you."

"We know that," Anna said.

I took a breath, wondering where I should start. "I lost someone when I was young; someone I deeply cared about." I looked at them both, not in an attempt to gauge their reaction, but in order to meet them straight in the eye when I told them the truth. "I married your father afterwards, who was kind, loving and patient and we had you both, which was the greatest gift life could have ever given us."

They had stopped eating and were both watching me now, listening intently. "My life was set, that was it for me, or at least that was what I thought. So I wholly dedicated myself to you and to my work. I didn't think there would ever be more to my life other than that," I said, wondering if they understood.

"What about dad? Didn't he make you happy?" Anna asked.

"For a time yes, and I did everything I could to make him equally happy, but there was always something missing."

"Did it have to do with the person you lost?" Jonah asked.

I didn't know whether to say yes or no.

"Mom, you and dad are getting a divorce. We're old enough to understand what that means," Anna said. "You've grown apart, things are different now. We know that."

God, I wished it was that easy. "The person I lost... her name was Isabel."

I could see the confusion in their faces.

"What are you saying?" Jonah asked.

"Mom?" Anna asked after her brother.

"She was the only other person I'd ever been with before your father," I said.

"Why are you telling us this now?" Jonah asked.

"Because there has been someone else." They both silently watched me, not waiting for further explanation, but seeking deeper understanding from what I'd just said.

"So someone discovered this and wants to expose it and that's why you're telling us," Jonah said, with a little more hostility than I expected. He'd always been smart so I wasn't surprised his first guess was so accurate.

"The reason why I'm telling you is because I love and respect you both and I want you to hear it from me first," I said.

"What? That you're a lesbian?" he said in rage as he got to his feet.

I didn't know how to respond to him. It was an ironic situation because the way he looked at me and spoke to me was the same way I'd spoken to my mother on several occasions.

"Jonah, let me explain" I said.

"This is the real reason why you're getting a divorce, isn't it?"

I got to my feet at that point but I wasn't sure if it was to defend myself or to submit to his accusations. He was my flesh and blood, what could I possibly do or say?

"You're a disgrace," he said.

His words delivered a hurtful blow. How could he say that to me? Why wasn't he more willing to understand the situation?

"I'm not going to be part of this," he said as he left the room.

I wanted to stop him, but I didn't know what I'd say. I turned to face Anna, who was still seated. "I'm sorry," I said.

She got up, walked over to me and surprised me when she wrapped her arms around me. After a few moments, she pulled away and met my gaze. "Was Jonah right? Did someone discover this and is threatening to expose it?" she asked.

I didn't want her to worry or concern herself with problems I could easily handle. My only intention of coming clean with them was to make sure the truth came from me. "Don't worry about that. I'd never let anyone hurt this family."

She smiled faintly. "I know," she said. "When you're ready to tell me more about this other person, I'll be right here."

I watched her leave the room, confused by the turn of events. I'd had no expectations from telling them the truth, but I'd thought Anna would have the same reaction as Jonah. If she was willing to be patient and understanding with me, I had some hope Jonah would come around as well. He just needed a little bit of time.

When I was up in my room preparing for bed, I wondered how I'd face Olivia. She deserved to know the truth, but I didn't know how I'd tell her. How did you tell someone you cared about that your own mother ordered their loved one's death? How did one even start such a conversation?

Olivia was going to resent me, there was no doubt about it but she needed to know the truth. She was an innocent party to all of this and my world had sucked her in and destroyed her family.

I still couldn't believe my mother had played such a big role in this. I'd blamed her for so many things in my life. I couldn't believe it took something so dangerous and reckless for her to show me that she cared.

The thoughts went on and on in my head, forcing me to stay up all night. In the morning, I prepared myself and headed to Price Healthcare. I told myself I was prepared for however Olivia was going to handle the news.

When I stepped into Price Healthcare, Isabel's face came to mind. I wondered if she'd be proud to see how much her empire had grown. When I got to Olivia's office floor, I was met by two receptionists who immediately recognized me.

One of them led me to Olivia's office and quickly announced my visit before she walked out and left us alone. I hadn't told her I was coming, so the surprise registered on her face was expected.

Her office was spacious and elegantly furnished and she looked great behind that large desk. She seemed to fit in perfectly with her surroundings.

"Hello Olivia," I said.

"Ame—. Mrs. Gallagher." She got up, stepped away from her desk and approached me. When she stopped in front of me, she leaned close and a warm sensation traveled through me when she lightly pecked my cheek.

"I wasn't expecting you," she said.

"I know. I'm sorry for showing up unannounced."

"No, it's fine. Would you like to take a seat?"

I shook my head, telling myself that what I needed to tell her wouldn't take long. If only I knew how to start.

"Would you like some refreshment?" she asked.

"No, Olivia. But thank you. I need to talk to you about something."

"Okay."

I walked away from her and took a deep breath as everything I needed to say scrambled through my brain. "I told Jonah and Anna about Isabel."

"You did?" The surprise in her voice was evident. "How did that go?"

"It could have been worse. Jonah didn't take it too well, but Anna was understanding. I told them there had been someone else after Isabel and their father and Jonah assumed that was why we're getting a divorce."

"You're getting a divorce?"

I turned to face her, recalling I'd never told her about it.

"What do you mean you told them there had been someone else?" she asked.

I walked over to the large window behind her desk exposing the magnificent view of the city and said, "I didn't tell them it was you, Olivia but they're aware of your existence."

"That's a start," Olivia said as she came to stand beside me.

"It's not," I said.

"You're getting a divorce, you told them about me, why isn't that a start?" she asked, turning me to face her.

"Because there are a lot of other things at play, Olivia. Things we can't control." I wanted to touch her soft lovely features, but pushed away the urge when I reminded myself about all the other things she needed to know.

"I don't understand."

She was looking at me with such earnestness, I didn't know if I had it in me to destroy what she felt for me. "I'm responsible for what happened to your brother."

She looked momentarily confused. "What are you talking about?"

"My cousin, Eric, he was the one who tampered with the brakes of the car."

She shook her head as though she couldn't fathom the information. "Why?"

I wondered if I'd be putting her in danger if I told her everything. "Look, I know this is a lot to take in but right now, that is all I can tell you. Eric followed us that night we went out on a date and took pictures of us. He wants something from me."

"Why would he kill Greg if it was you he was after?"

"It's complicated, Olivia. I can't tell you everything right now because I can't give you information that might put you in danger. All you need to know is that he's going to pay for this."

I was disgusted with myself for protecting Kathy, but I didn't know what she was capable of and if she was willing to hurt Olivia. Another part of me I wanted to deny was, Olivia not knowing about my mother's involvement kept her from hating me.

She looked frightened, which made me wonder if I should have told her anything at all. The news were unsettling but I didn't want her to live in fear. "Livvy, I'm not going to let anyone hurt you. If it'll make you feel safer, I'll hire you a bodyguard."

"I just don't—, I don't understand. How could he have known about us? About Greg?" she said.

"I'll explain it all in detail when this is all over."

"Have you told the police? Have you told them he killed Greg?"

I took a breath. "No," I said.

"Why not?"

I could tell she was agitated and I knew she wanted justice, but there was a better way of dealing with the situation. "Do you trust me?" I asked as I moved closer to her.

I could see the terror and confusion in her eyes as she nodded. "Yes."

"Eric will pay for this. I'll make sure he does."

"What are you going to do?"

"That's not important. I just want you to know that everything is going to be okay. I'm not going to let anything happen to you." I reached out and touched her cheek and she moved closer and slowly wrapped her arms around me.

I closed my arms around her in an attempt to reassure her, inwardly resenting Kathy for interfering because I knew Olivia would never look at me the same way again.

Chapter Fifty-Two

"I miss you," I said, momentarily forgetting everything we'd just talked about because it felt so good to be in her arms again.

The distance wasn't working the way I had hoped. It hadn't been long but I was already going crazy from missing her and thinking about her.

"Olivia, coming to work at Price Healthcare was the right thing for you to do," she said as she pulled back.

It felt like she was squeezing the life out of my heart because she was underestimating the intensity of my love for her.

"In time, you'll barely think of me."

How could she think that? "You're wrong. What I feel for you…" I choked on the words, wondering if there was any better way to put it. "Amelia, it's very plain and simple. My heart belongs to you."

She moved closer and gently trailed her fingers over my face then leaned her forehead against mine. "You have to stop saying things like that."

"Why? Why do I have to stop?"

"Because I don't know how long I can keep on pretending that it doesn't feel good to hear it." She pulled her head back, meeting my gaze.

"I want to be with you," I said.

"Livvy, you're young, too young for me. You'll need things I can't give you. So please stop making this harder than it has to be and just move on."

"Will you? Will you move on from me?"

She closed her eyes and took a deep breath. When she met my gaze again, she opened her mouth to speak, then stopped. After a moment of what appeared to be like an internal battle, she resignedly said, "I don't know if I'll ever be able to."

A wave of emotion and confusion rushed through me.

"Livvy, you're special to me in ways that even I fail to understand. But a lot has happened and some of it may end up making you look at me differently. Right now, I just need you to know that I care a great deal about you."

I didn't know what she meant. Why did she think I'd ever look at her differently? She'd been nothing short of amazing since the very moment I'd started getting to know her. "If you care about me as much as you say you do, why can't you work past whatever it is that's in the way and let me make you happy? Don't you want that? Don't you want me?"

She shook her head as though she was fighting herself. "I do, Livvy but—."

"No, no buts. I'm dying to be with you. I miss your kisses, your touch, your laugh, your smile. I miss the feel of your body lying next to mine. I miss the way you make me feel and I swear, I thought the distance would make this whole thing easier but it hasn't. I love you and I don't think that's going to change, so I'm going to wait for you."

She kissed me at the passionate declaration and I immediately responded. If my world had come crashing down at that moment, I would have died happy.

"You're making this too hard," she said against my lips.

"I'm not giving up on you without a fight."

She brushed her lips against mine and I responded, trying hard to contain my desire for her. When she pulled away, she broke all physical contact and emptiness occupied the space she'd temporarily filled with joy.

"Bye, Liv."

I watched her in dismay as she exited my office and went and sat down, leaning back against the sleek comfortable leather seat I was still trying to get used to, as I deeply inhaled.

I didn't know what to do, I was deeply in love with her and seeing her, talking to her and being so close to her made me feel so nostalgic for the time when things had been good between us.

It was a little comforting to know that she felt something powerful for me, but not entirely because she was determined to push me away. I wished she could have been just a little bit miserable as I was from being away from her, that way she could understand how difficult it was to not see her quite as often as I had before.

I groaned in frustration, thinking back to our conversation. I was very confused by the information she'd offered but I wasn't blind to the fact that she'd left out some of the details.

I couldn't understand Eric's motive if his vendetta was against Amelia. Why kill someone who was not even directly linked to her? What had he had to gain by killing Greg?

If he wanted to hurt Amelia, wouldn't he have gone after someone who was close to her? I doubted he'd harm her kids because they were his relatives so the only other person he could have gone after would have been …me? The thought gave me chills.

How much did he know about the nature of my relationship with Amelia? Was he willing to come after me? Maybe that bodyguard Amelia had mentioned wasn't such a bad idea.

If there was a chance he might have been aware of my love affair with Amelia, could he also have known about Greg's blackmail? No, no, it didn't quite fit.

What had Amelia left out of her explanation? She'd said she didn't want to offer information that could potentially put me in danger. What could it have been that she feared me knowing would risk my life?

The more I thought about it, the more unsettled I grew. Part of me wished she could have told me, the other part wanted to trust that she knew what she was doing.

"You're so naïve."

"I can't believe you'd say that," I said.

Colin was seated opposite me as we had dinner on a Friday evening. We'd met through Amelia when she'd chosen him to train me on being her personal assistant, and then again at the corporate gala dinner.

"No, I mean seriously," he said, trying to chew after a bite of his burger. "You're brilliant and clearly Mrs. Gallagher can see that. How could you not expect some sort of turbulence in your transition?" he asked.

"Well," I said in defense but couldn't come up with one proper response. God, I *was* naïve.

The turbulence I was experiencing was coming from my new colleagues and apart from my secretary and the receptionist; everyone else I met in attempts to acquaint myself with had a hostile attitude towards me.

I thought I was giving off the wrong vibe, which was met with hostility when all I was trying to do was fit in with the rest of my colleagues. I'd made dinner plans with Colin so that he could better explain it to me, since he worked at Price Healthcare.

"Some of these people have worked for Price Healthcare for decades. They've never heard of you, but suddenly, you're occupying a large corner office. It's only logical for them to feel threatened," he said.

I'd stopped picking at my French fries and was now watching him.

"You're not just her personal assistant anymore. You're her right-hand man and you need to understand that the corporate world is full of sharks. These people will eat you alive."

"So what exactly I'm I supposed to do?"

"Enjoy your coveted position," he said with a smile.

I smiled back and resumed eating.

I hadn't had a single moment to myself since I'd moved to Price Healthcare. I had constant back to back meetings with acquaintances, investors and basically every other important person in the Healthcare industry but I wasn't complaining since I needed to occupy every free second of my day with something to avoid the constant, overwhelming thought of Amelia.

My studies were also progressing very fast because I was extremely determined to finish up with school and since my classes were dependent on my schedule, I created more time, studying up until late and whichever free minute I got.

My professors were always available for me, which was a great advantage but what pleased me the most was the fact that I was passing and at this rate, I knew it'd take me half the time to graduate

I never heard from Amelia again, but she hired me a bodyguard as she'd assured me she would. It was uncomfortable knowing someone was following me wherever I went, but it was for my safety so I couldn't complain.

His name was Jerry and he kept a proper amount of distance. Since most of what I did took place in my office, I didn't move around a lot so sometimes I barely noticed him.

Three weeks after my talk with Amelia, I attended Rex's graduation. I was a little envious of him because I wished I could be in his place, but with the speed at which my studies were progressing, I knew it was just a matter of time.

"I should've been more appreciative of the time we spent together," Rex said. Instead of going out partying and celebrating like everyone else, he decided to go back to the office with me.

"I'm sorry, I know I've been scarce," I said.

"It's fine. I understand. Who's that guy who keeps following you around?" he asked.

"Oh, that's Jerry, my bodyguard."

"Why do you need a bodyguard?"

I didn't want to alarm him. "Comes with the territory," I said playfully as I motioned at the office.

"Holy hell, look at this place!" he said as he moved around.

I wasn't used to the space, the elegance and well, the luxury, but my work kept me so busy, I barely paid attention to the surroundings.

"When you told me about your change of address, I never pictured anything quite like this," he said as he headed to the large window that exposed the amazing view of the Big Apple.

"Neither did I. I thought I'd be stuffed up in some dark, humid, dusty corner office."

"Really?" He turned to face me.

"Okay, maybe not that dark," I said.

He broke into soft laughter and approached me. "How are you holding up?"

"It's a little overwhelming but I'm hanging in there."

"You miss her?"

Rex knew me far too well, but his love and concern for me was always comforting, which made it easy for me to confide in him. "Every second of everyday."

"Creating distance between you was a huge step and you're very brave and strong for doing it."

"But it's not working, Rex. She's moving on with her life and I am still stuck where we left off. She calls and I get tremors of excitement. My heart beats so fast at the sound of her voice I fear I might get a heart attack."

"Has she come to see you?"

"Once, about three weeks ago. She told me that she told her kids about us. I thought it was a turning point, but she thinks there's too much standing in the way."

"Livvy, maybe you should seriously start to consider moving on. I know it's hard because it's still fresh. I know it's painful because you're in love with her, but maybe you should start thinking about living your life without her. I really hate seeing you hurt over her."

The idea of never being with her again was frightening, but she'd made her stand very clear. She cared about me, she always would, but the circumstances were too complicated.

Rex gently wrapped his arms around me at the sadness that overcame me. I didn't know why it hit me so hard when the words came from him.

"I know something that might cheer you up," he said softly.

"What?" I asked.

"Frank booked a spot for me at a silent auction art event. It'll take place this coming weekend. I'd love it if you'd be there."

I let go of him. "My office could use a Brexton Phillips painting."

He smiled. "You're going to buy my art?"

"Yeah, now that I'm able to, I'd like to start showing you my support. I hold a lot of meetings here with some very important people and displaying your work on my wall could get you interested buyers."

"That would be amazing."

"I love the last painting I found you working on. Will it be at the auction?"

"Yes."

"Awesome, I'm going to get that one."

"It won't come cheap, Liv."

"I'll outbid every interested buyer."

He laughed as he pulled me close and pecked my forehead.

"Ms. Williams, your five o'clock is here." My secretary announced over the intercom.

"That's my cue to leave," Rex said. "I'll come pick you up on Saturday at six."

I nodded.

"Bye Ms. Williams," he said, mimicking my secretary.

I laughed at his silliness and told my secretary I was ready to take the meeting.

Time moved at such fast speed, I didn't notice it was Saturday until Rex called me to remind me he was picking me up. I had to wrap up work and rush home to change and by the time he was arriving, I was just finishing up.

I was in a short beautiful black dress that slightly exposed my cleavage. I wore the rose pendant necklace Amelia had given me and with my hair freely cascading down my shoulders, my look was simple but elegant.

Rex was in a semiformal outfit that gave him a serious but handsome look.

"I can't believe we're still moving around in this crappy little car," I said when he opened the door to my car. It served as a reminder of how far I'd come, but at that stage in our lives, we needed a better mode of transport.

"What are you talking about? I love this car," he said as he got in.

"We should sell it and get something better. You're becoming a big shot artist. You can't move your work around in this contraption."

He smiled as he pulled out of parking. When we got on the road, I looked through the rearview mirror and saw Jerry's car following behind us.

"I like the big shot artist part," Rex said.

I smiled back at him and relaxed in my seat, wondering who would be at the event. I'd attended so many art events so far, I was almost certain we'd run into people we'd met in the past.

"Do you remember how our lives were before all this started?"
I nodded.

"We've come so far, Liv. I have you to thank for all of this."

"Me? I haven't done anything. You're the one who is constantly working to create the next masterpiece."

"It all started with you. Do you know what I'd be doing right now?"

"What?"

"I'd be looking for a job while I struggle to figure out how to get my work out there. I feel horrible for getting so mad at you when Mrs. Gallagher reached out to help me."

"This is just the beginning. Your career will soar to heights you never imagined."

He reached out and squeezed my hand. "Your confidence in me is inspiring."

We got to the venue a while later.

It wasn't as big an event as some of the ones we'd attended in the past. Instead, it was small but intimate. The artists whose works were being auctioned were very popularly known in the art world.

It was always amazing being surrounded by people who had so much creativity and at this point, it was probably just a matter of time until I became an art enthusiast myself.

"I'm going to look for Frank, are you going to be okay on your own for a while?" Rex asked.

"Yeah, I'm fine."

He nodded and walked away.

The art was well displayed with names of artists and the silent auction papers were clearly set out on a table. For a small and intimate event, there was quite a number of people present. I wondered if all the artists were also in attendance.

I got myself a glass of champagne and was about to start browsing when I saw Adrianna. Our gazes met at the same time. What was she doing there? I thought Amelia was the art lover in the family. Wait, was Amelia also present?

"Olivia, hello," she said.

"Hi Adrianna, what are you doing here?"

"I organized the event," she said.

I looked at her in surprise. "You did?"

"Why are you so surprised?"

I didn't know why I'd always thought of her as a bit of a wild child. I knew Jonah was the serious responsible one in the family, but I'd never imagined Adrianna taking on a serious role.

"I can't find him," Rex said, interrupting us, which I was grateful for.

"Rex, you remember Adrianna? You two met at the Gallagher Residence," I said.

I thought I saw him tense up a bit as I turned to face Adrianna to notice a hint of a smile on the corners of her lips.

"Nice to see you again, Anna."

Anna? Was I missing something?

"You too, Rex."

I smiled to myself as their awkward silence stretched out and I cleared my throat. "I'm going to refill my drink," I said, walking away before they noticed my glass was still full. Did they like each other? I wondered as I studied them from a distance. They looked good together.

"Livvy?"

Surprised by the familiar voice, I turned around and froze when my gaze fell on Jaime. She was as stunning as usual, in a beautiful flowered dress that hugged her body and exposed her curves.

"Hi Jaime," I said, remembering Amelia's confession. Jaime had cut contact with me because she'd had to, not because she'd wanted to.

"How are you?" she asked.

Last time we'd met, it had been at an event much like this. It had felt a bit odd carrying out a conversation with her but now that I knew why she'd ended things between us so abruptly, I felt like I was the one who owed her an apology.

"I'm okay," I said, trying to silence the chaos inside of me.

"It's good to see you," she said.

I wondered what to say, but I must have taken too long to respond because she nodded and walked away from me. I turned around, deeply inhaled and took a long sip of my champagne as I searched the room for Rex.

He was still talking to Adrianna and I didn't want to interrupt so I headed for the art pieces on display, searching for the piece I'd told him I'd buy as I tried to figure out how I'd talk to Jaime.

When I found it, I realized people had started bidding and added my own bid. Rex joined me a while later.

"Frank's not here," he said.

"Oh?" I said, "Did you get a chance to thoroughly look around?" I teased.

"Okay, just say it."

"You like Adrianna!"

He shushed me and looked around to see if anyone had heard. "It's not like that."

"Why don't you tell me exactly how it's like then?"

"Okay, look. I never thought I'd see her again after we met that first time at her house. Seeing her here tonight caught me off guard."

"Why don't you ask her out?"

"She's Amelia Gallagher's daughter. Girls like her don't go out with guys like me."

"What is that supposed to mean? You're an amazing guy and any woman would be lucky to be with you. Plus, didn't you notice the way she was looking at you? She likes you."

He looked at me thoughtfully for a moment then laughed.

I was pleased to see him like that. "Did you get her number?"

He nodded.

"Good, ask her out when this is over."

I saw him searching the room and my gaze followed his, unexpectedly falling on Jaime's across the room.

"Jaime's here," he said.

"I know. We talked a while back and I didn't know what to say. After finding out Mrs. Gallagher was the reason behind her pulling away from me, I feel like I owe her an apology."

He turned to face me. "I don't think you owe her an apology since you did nothing wrong, but I do think you should talk to her. Its time you started moving on."

"Are you saying that I should start things up with her again?" I didn't think that was a very good idea. Anything I did would most likely end up hurting her because I didn't know if I could be with someone else when I was still so deeply in love with Amelia.

"I think you should stop holding on to the past and go over there and talk to her."

"And say what exactly?"

"It'll come to you," he said and gave me a little shove, forcing me to keep walking.

I made my way over to her art display and started slowly perusing, while she carried out conversation with one of the guests in attendance. She was extremely gifted so I wasn't surprised to see all the bids on her work.

"Did you take a real interest in art or are you here to support Rex?" She came to stand right beside me as I studied one of her magnificent landscape paintings. "I think a little bit of both," I said.

I turned to face her and found her watching me with a familiar look on her face.

"Why didn't you tell me?" I asked.

"Tell you what?"

"That Mrs. Gallagher asked you to stay away from me?"

She raised her eyebrow in surprise. "How did you find out?" she asked.

"Does it matter?"

She shook her head. "I guess not. I'm sorry. I tried, the last time we saw each other but I didn't think you'd care to learn the truth."

I wondered what would have happened between us had I never fallen in love with Amelia. Would we still have been together? Would I have been there supporting her, as I was Rex?

"I've missed you," she said.

I met her soft gaze and bit my lower lip.

"I've missed you too." I missed how easy it had been to be around her, to talk to her, to have her look at me with pure interest and curiosity. Things between us would have progressed so calmly as compared to the turbulence I had faced at the hands of Amelia.

"Are you seeing someone?" she asked.

I thought about Amelia. "I was, but it's over now." I was always going to love her, but she'd made it clear we could never be together. I'd said I'd wait for her, fight for her, but I wasn't so sure she'd ever want me the same way I wanted her.

"You want to talk about it over coffee sometime?"

"No," I said as I shook my head. "I don't want to talk about it." A look of understanding came across her face. "But coffee sounds good." We smiled at each other.

We were interrupted by someone who wanted to talk to her, so I left to give her space, made a bid I knew no one would beat on the landscape painting and walked back to Rex's art with a smile on my face.

I went and outbid the last person who'd bid on my Brexton Phillips painting just as Rex came to talk to me.

"By the look on your face, I'd say it went well," he said.

I nodded. "She asked me out."

"That's awesome! The first step to moving on. I'm so happy for you."

He seemed more excited than I was.

Pleased as I was though, I couldn't help thinking whatever I was starting was doomed to fail but every time I looked at Jaime to find her looking back at me, a spark of hope flickered.

I stayed close to my painting until the auction ended and I was the top bidder on both Rex's and Jaime's paintings. When it was over, I went over to Jaime to say goodnight and as soon as she wrapped up talking to yet another guest, she came over to talk to me.

"You're very popular tonight," I said.

"I'm sorry. I haven't attended a silent auction in years. Most of these people are just old friends," she said.

"Hi Jaime," Rex said when he joined us.

"Hi Rex," she said.

Before anyone of us could talk, Adrianna came to talk to Rex. I was happy he'd taken the initiative to put himself out there. It was about time he got himself a girlfriend.

"Since you spent so much on my painting, how about we decide early that coffee will be on me," Jaime said.

I laughed at the joke, and when I was about to respond, Adrianna said, "Excuse me, Olivia. I'm sorry to interrupt." I looked at her, then turned my gaze to Rex but I couldn't read him because he looked as confused as I was.

"Where'd you get that pendant?" she asked.

I ran my fingers over the rose pendant and raised an eyebrow when I realized how she recognized it. I was tongue-tied because I didn't know how to answer. How could I tell her Amelia had given it to me?

When Adrianna noticed my hesitation, her eyes widened in what appeared to be surprise and understanding. "You're the one she was talking about," she said.

My shock slowed my thinking as I remembered Amelia telling me her kids knew of my existence but didn't know my identity. I wanted to deny whatever she thought she knew but I couldn't think fast enough.

"You and my mother?" she said, then shook her head in disbelief as she walked away. Rex went after her and I was left standing awkwardly, knowing Jaime had a few questions for me.

"You and Mrs. Gallagher?" Jaime asked.

I looked at her in guilty silence and she scoffed as she shook her head.

"That certainly explains a lot."

"It's over, she ended it so it doesn't matter," I said.

"Are you still in love with her?"

I couldn't answer.

"See Liv, it does. It matters." She walked away and I could feel my heart starting to break.

I couldn't believe the first single step I'd taken towards moving forward had landed me flat on my face. How was Amelia still influencing my personal life when she was the one who'd left me?

I ran out of the building and hailed a cab, ignoring Rex when I heard him call after me. I wanted to cry, to scream, to curse, but instead, I headed to Mrs. Gallagher's penthouse. I was so upset I had no idea what I was going there to do.

Thoughts and emotions tore through me during my ride to the penthouse and by the time I was paying the driver, I was too rattled to move. It took me a few minutes to catch my breath and when I did, I was unsure of whether I should have been there at all.

I got into the elevator and when the doors opened, I walked in and found Mrs. Gallagher standing out the balcony. I'd almost forgotten how much it affected me to see her in one of those silky robes and nightgowns she wore to bed.

She seemed surprised to see me, which was fitting because I shouldn't have been there.

"Liv, is everything okay?" she asked in concern as she approached me. I was a little taken aback until she touched my face and lightly ran her fingers over my cheeks, wiping away tears I was unaware I'd shed.

I pulled back and recalled what had happened as I tried to push down a painful ball of air from my throat.

"What happened?" she asked.

I closed my eyes shut in an attempt to fight the tears and took a deep breath. When I tried to speak, I choked on my words and took another breath, turning away from her because I couldn't look at her while I spoke.

"Did you know Adrianna organized a silent art auction?" I asked.

"She told me about it. What does that have to do with what's going on?" I'd never heard impatience in her voice until that moment.

"Rex was one of the artists whose work was being auctioned, so I accompanied him. I saw Jaime," I faced her at this juncture to gauge her reaction but my eyes were blurry from the tears I was fighting back so I couldn't hold her gaze, much less read her.

"Rex encouraged me to make the first step at moving on from you, so I went and talked to her. We hit it off and it was going well up until Adrianna saw this pendant you gave me and put two and two together." I saw the look of surprise that came across her face. "She knows about us and she said it in front of Jaime."

A mix of emotions went through me and I fought to keep them at bay. I wasn't sure whether I was more concerned about Adrianna finding out about us, or the frightening idea of being in emotional captivity for all of eternity.

"I want to stop hurting over you, Amelia. But how do I do that when the first thing I do in an attempt to stop it lands me flat on my face?" I took a deep breath. "I hate this and it doesn't even seem to affect you. You're going on with your life as if I never even existed."

"Don't you say that Olivia. You know it's not true."

"That's the thing, I don't know. I've never been in love but you've done this sort of thing before. I was someone else's replacement and after this, there will be someone else to take my place."

She walked up to me and made me face her. "You're no one's replacement and this isn't easy for me either." She tossed her arms aside and hopelessly stepped back.

"I've never been with anyone quite like you, Livvy. Before you came into my life I led this void, plain, colorless life. I felt like I was in constant suspended animation. Just doing what I was meant to do, never feeling or seeking anything outside what I knew.

"Then you stepped into my world and knocked everything off balance. You kissed me and I felt like my heart had been electrocuted. It started beating again. Every single day after that, I fought myself because I was so confused. I'd never experienced anything quite so different."

She'd never expressed herself to me before, not like this.

"Imagine seeing color for the very first time, learning to enjoy it, to let it be apart of you and let it fully consume you only to realize you'll have to let it go and resume with life in that void, plain, colorless world like none of it ever existed. With that knowledge, wouldn't you want to create some sort of resistance?"

After taking a long deep breath, she said in a low sad voice, "As far as I'm concerned Livvy, there was no one else before you and there will be no one else after you."

Her words hit me so hard, tears started falling down my cheeks. I didn't know who I felt sorrier for, me or her.

We both turned towards the penthouse when we heard clapping and my gaze widened when I saw Eric. Amelia walked back inside and I followed after her, quickly wiping away my tears.

"So the ice queen does have a heart after all," he said in a mocking tone.

What was he doing there? Hadn't Amelia said she'd take care of him? Had he somehow managed to evade her since the last time they'd seen or spoken to one another?

Amelia walked over to the phone and Eric pulled out a gun, pointing it to her. "No, no, no, get away from the phone," he warned, motioning her with the gun.

She came and stood in front of me, almost as if shielding me from him. I closed my hand over her arm and she held me back, showing me to stand behind her and stay still.

"Eric, what do you think you're doing?" she asked.

"You turned Kathy against me when all I tried to do was help, and then you put a manhunt for me. What did you think was going to happen?" he asked, waving the gun as he spoke.

"Whatever happened between you and Kathy was between the two of you, I had nothing to do with it. Now why don't you let Olivia get out of here and then you and I can talk about this," she said.

I wasn't going anywhere without knowing if she was going to be okay. This man had killed Greg. I doubted he'd hesitate pulling the trigger when it came to Amelia. He looked so resentful towards her.

"No one's going anywhere," he said. "I've done everything Kathy ever asked of me and you've done nothing but resent her and disrespect her. Merging Price Healthcare and Winston Enterprises was the only thing she ever wanted and I told you to do it or I'd expose your nasty little affair to the public. But you didn't listen. Instead, you went and told her garbage about me and she kicked me out like a dog."

"The only thing I did was confront her."

"Confront her about what? Ordering me to get that guy out of the way? She did that for you. You should be grateful to her for what she's willing to do to ensure your happiness."

I pulled back in shock and asked. "What's he talking about?"

"Oh, you haven't told your young lady friend what your mother made me do for you?" he asked.

"Eric, there's another way of doing this," Amelia said.

"Shut up!" he yelled and the room fell silent.

"Olivia, can I call you Olivia?" he asked as he walked towards us and Amelia continued to shield me from him. "I'm going to tell you something you don't know about your precious Amelia."

He continued nearing us and grabbed my arm, forcefully pulling me away from Amelia as he pointed the gun to my head, motioning her to stay back. I was terrified because a madman was holding us at gunpoint.

When he created enough distance between us, I tried not to show fear and held Amelia's assuring gaze.

"This heartless cold bitch has been the bane of my existence since the day I met her." He sounded so bitter and angry. I kept my eye on his hand as he continued frantically waving the gun at Amelia while he spoke.

"The problem was, she couldn't get hurt because she had no weaknesses and I couldn't hurt her without hurting Kathy. But you worked your way around that one for me, didn't you?" he asked Amelia, slowly moving his hand to point the gun right at me.

"Eric, please. It's not too late. You can have it all. You can have your merger, and you can join the board. Anything you want," Amelia said, expressing fear for the first time.

"She's the precious little gem I can use to cause you misery, harm and pain like you've done me and Kathy over the years," he said.

I stared at the gun as my heart pounded loudly in my chest, afraid for my life because he seemed so sure about what he was about to do.

"She's your weakness."

"Eric, please point the gun at me. Olivia has nothing to do with this. You're right about everything. I'm to blame. I should've been better for mom and for you. I'm sorry for all that I've done," she said.

Eric watched her for a minute then broke into laughter. "Oh, you have no idea how good this feels. You must really care about her," he said, moving closer to me.

As terrified as I was, I wanted the gun to stay aimed at me instead of Amelia because I now understood why she'd pushed me away so many times in the past.

I had become a weakness to her and now Eric was using that against her. If we ever came out of this alive, Amelia was going to push me away for good. Today it was Eric, tomorrow it'd be someone else. I was a threat to her.

"Shoot me." I didn't want to see Amelia lower her guard to protect me when I was partly responsible for everything that was happening. All she'd ever done was care for me and it took such a dangerous occurrence for me to see it, to believe it.

"What?" Eric said.

"Liv, what are you doing?" Amelia asked in a panic.

"Oh, she's good. I see why you like her," he said.

"I said shoot me." I moved closer to him.

"Olivia, stop it!" Amelia said.

He aimed the gun at my chest and I was certain he was going to pull the trigger because an evil cynical look came across his face and he tightened the hold on the gun.

"I love you, Amelia," I said and closed my eyes right at the same time a shot was fired.

Chapter Fifty-Three

I heard two gunshots and saw both Olivia and Eric fall down on the floor. Jerry, Olivia's bodyguard was standing some distance away with smoke coming out of his gun, which explained where the second shot had come from.

I rushed over to Olivia in horror as Jerry carefully approached Eric's limp body and kicked the gun from his hand while he called for an ambulance.

"Livvy?"

Her hand was on her stomach, covering the place where Eric had shot her. My heart clenched in my chest when I saw her covered in blood. How could she stand in front of a madman and tell him to shoot her? What had she been thinking?

"I'm sorry," she said.

"Shh, it's okay. Don't talk. An ambulance is on its way. You're going to be fine." Grave fear embraced me at the thought of history repeating itself. "I can't lose you too," I said, placing my robe over the wound as I applied pressure to stop the bleeding.

It destroyed me to see her tearing up as she tried to speak. "I couldn't—I couldn't let him hurt you," she said.

I leaned close and pecked her forehead as I fought back tears. "You shouldn't have done that, Livvy," My voice shook and I took a deep breath. I was in another helpless situation at the verge of losing someone else I deeply cared about.

"Its okay, no one—," She struggled to speak. "No one will ever use me to hurt you again."

Was that why she'd told Eric to shoot her? Because she'd thought she was keeping people like him from using her as a weapon against me?

"I finally understand you now," she said, wincing in pain. "I—I understand everything."

"Where is that ambulance?" I yelled at Jerry as tears started streaming down my face.

A few minutes later, paramedics walked in and rushed over to

Olivia. She was unconscious and covered in blood. I watched in horror as they worked on her, unsure of what I was supposed to do.

When they finally took her out in a gurney, I went to my bedroom, quickly changed and followed after them. Jerry called the police and stayed behind as James drove me to the hospital.

When we got there, Olivia was immediately taken to an operating room and I had no choice but to helplessly wait as I thought of a million ways I could have handled the situation.

I should've protected her better. I should've put two bodyguards on her. I should've reported Eric to the police the moment he'd confessed to killing Greg. I should've done more.

No one will ever use me to hurt you again. Her words rang through my mind. God, had she thought she was going to die? That couldn't happen. She couldn't die. I wasn't going to let it happen.

"I need to know what's happening to the young woman who was brought in with a gunshot wound," I said to the nurse at the reception desk.

"Are you two related?"

'No, but she was with me when it happened. She was taken to an operating room. I need to know how she's doing," I said in desperation.

"Ma'am, I'm sorry but we cannot divulge the information to you unless you're family."

I gritted my teeth in anger and read the nurse's nametag. "Christy Stellar, I am Amelia Gallagher. I'm a member of the board in this hospital. If you don't give me the information I need, I will have you fired on the spot and make sure you never work in a hospital again. Do you understand me?"

She quickly nodded. "I'll—I'll go check for you." She rushed off.

I took a deep breath and a moment later, she came back. "Mrs. Gallagher, the doctors are still working on her," she said. "Are you hurt? Can I check you for injuries?"

I looked at my hands to notice they still had Olivia's blood as the image of her lying bleeding in my arms replayed itself in my head.

I walked away and went to wash up in the bathroom. As the water ran over my hands, washing away the blood, the last couple of hours went through my head. God, what had I done? This was all my fault.

None of this would've ever happened if I'd been more careful. Now Olivia was lying in a hospital bed and I didn't even know if she was going to make it. What if she succumbed to her injuries? What if she bled out on the operating table?

Tears blurred my vision as the time I'd shared with her flashed through my mind. She'd been so patient, kind and loving with me. What had I done to deserve her? Even at the end when she'd known Eric would pull the trigger, she'd still boldly declared her love for me.

My knees unbuckled and I sat and curled up in a corner. I couldn't lose her. I'd lost Isabel before I'd ever even known I'd been losing her. I'd spent my life with sorrow buried deep inside of me. If I lost Olivia, I was going to die. I couldn't live in a world where she didn't exist.

"Mom?"

I looked up at Adrianna's voice. What was she doing there?

"My God, Mom, are you okay?" She rushed over to me and wrapped her arms around me and I broke down.

"What— what are you doing here?" I managed.

"I went to the penthouse to talk to you and I found policemen there. One of the men told me what had happened and where you were. I came here immediately. Are you okay?"

She pulled back to look at me and I closed my eyes, trying to block the tears and I shook my head.

"They told me Eric shot Olivia."

He'd fired his gun a second before Jerry had shot him.

"I need to know how she is," I said as I got up and wiped away my tears.

I went back to the waiting area and found Rex there. I'd been so wrapped up in my own grief I'd forgotten to tell the people Olivia loved what had happened.

"What's going on, Mrs. Gallagher? These people won't tell me," he said as he rushed over to me when he saw me. "Is it true? Did someone really shoot Livvy? Please tell me it's a lie."

I composed myself and placed my arm over his shoulder. "Rex, it's true."

"No," he said as he shook his head and moved away from me. "How could you let that happen? You were supposed to protect her." His grief quickly turned to anger.

"She couldn't have prevented this, Rex," Anna said.

"You were supposed to protect her," he said as he pulled away from Anna when she went to offer him comfort.

He had no idea how horrible I felt about everything. "It's true. I was."

I turned and walked away, heading back to the reception area to find out if there was any word about Olivia.

"I'm sorry, there's no news yet. I'll bring her doctor to you as soon as we know something," Nurse Christy said.

I went and sat down by myself and started praying. Olivia had to get better. She had to walk out of that operating room alive. She had to look at me again, smile at me again. She had to kiss me again, touch me again, hold me again and tell me she loved me again. She just had to and this time, I was going to happily embrace it all and tell her that I too lov—.

"Mrs. Gallagher?"

I looked up at Rex.

"I'm sorry. Liv means everything to me. I just can't imagine life without her."

I nodded and he sat down beside me.

"She's going to be okay, right?" he asked.

"She has to be," I said wondering how he'd found out about Olivia and it occurred to me he'd met Anna at the silent auction. It seemed she had taken a liking to him as she stood some distance away watching us.

"Mrs. Gallagher," I stood up when Christy approached me with a doctor beside her. "This is Doctor Freeman."

"Mrs. Gallagher, I'm the doctor to the young woman who was brought in earlier with a gunshot wound to the stomach," he said. "Can I talk to you in private please?" He looked at Rex and I shook my head.

"Whatever it is, you can tell me in front of him." He was the closest thing to family Olivia had in the city and he needed to know what was going on.

The doctor nodded. "The bullet went straight through. It didn't hit any vital organs, but she lost a lot of blood. We've done all we can for now and she's under close observation."

"I want the best possible care for her and I want to be informed of the slightest change," I said.

He nodded.

"Can we see her?" Rex asked.

"For just a few minutes," he said.

Christy, the nurse, took us to Olivia's room. I stayed at the door as Rex walked in and a flashback of me going to see Isabel passed through my mind. Things had been so different back then. I hadn't even known how deeply I'd cared for Isabel until it had been too late.

What if I went to see Olivia and she never woke up again? What if I never got to see the light in those beautiful green eyes again? I leaned against the wall and placed my hand over my heart.

"It's okay."

I heard Rex say as he closed his hand over mine and led me inside. It was strangely comforting to know I wasn't alone.

"She's a fighter. She's going to be okay. She wouldn't leave us when she knows how much we still need her," he said.

Her eyes were closed and she looked like she was sleeping peacefully, apart from the machines attached to her body and the beeping sound coming from one of them.

I looked at Rex who was holding her hand as he closely watched her. His confidence in her recovery inspired hope in me.

"We'll all be here when you wake up, Liv." He pecked her forehead. "I'll leave you alone with her," he said and walked out.

After a moment, I took a breath and approached her bed. I sat beside her and closed her hand in mine. "I'm so sorry, Liv. This was never supposed to happen to you. You have so much to live for." I lightly ran my fingers over her cheek.

"You have to wake up." I bit my lower lip as my heartbeat increased pace. "You have to wake up because I can't live without you." I had never thought I'd ever say those words to anyone and I'd never known just how much I'd mean it.

"I can't lose you, Liv." I leaned forward and placed a light kiss on her lips. "Please open your eyes so that we can start our lives together." Tears started falling from my eyes again.

"If this is the afterlife I don't want to wake up."

I pulled back and found her opening her eyes. She had a faint smile on her lips.

A wave of overwhelming relief washed over me. "Oh, my God. You're awake."

"Are you okay? Did he hurt you?" she asked.

She was lying in a hospital bed with a gunshot wound on the stomach and she was asking if *I* was okay? My heart fluttered as I leaned forward and kissed her. "You took a bullet for me," I said. "No one has ever made such a sacrifice for me. No one has ever loved me like you do."

She didn't say anything. She just smiled at me and closed her eyes again. I went and called her doctor, who, after examining her, said she was stable and all we had to do now was wait.

I was massively relieved she hadn't taken a turn for the worse and even if it was just a couple of minutes, I was glad she'd opened her eyes.

Rex was happy to hear the news as well and after consulting him on whether we should inform Olivia's parents about what had happened, we decided after everything they'd been through with Greg, we'd inform them when Olivia was better.

When I went back to the waiting area, I found Kathy seated with Anna. I couldn't believe her nerve. She was responsible for every bad thing that had happened to me and Olivia. How could she even show her face?

"What are you doing here?" I asked.

"I found out about what happened and thought I could come show my support," she said.

"Anna, please give us a moment."

She got up and went to Rex.

"Because of you, two people are dead and one of them is lying in a hospital bed. You did this. Everything you touch, you destroy."

"Amelia, I tried to help get Eric."

"You pushed him over the edge. You're the reason he's dead."

"No," she said.

"Before he shot Olivia, he was talking about how much he wanted the merger because he wanted to make you proud. He loved you, Kathy. He loved you more than anyone else ever will but all you did was take advantage and exploit him."

"No." She took a step back.

"He shot Olivia because he knew this was the only way he could hurt me without hurting you." I took a step closer to her. "Look at what your love does, Mother. Look at all the pain and chaos you've caused."

She weakly sat down as tears started falling from her eyes and I walked away from her without any thought of comforting her.

I approached Anna and she came and wrapped her arms around me. I closed my arms around her and held her back. I couldn't believe I had survived such an emotional rollercoaster.

Chapter Fifty-Four

I reclined my bed to a comfortable sitting position and restlessly scanned through the channels on the television in my private hospital room, thinking about how the last two weeks had set me back in my work and studies.

Sure, I was recovering from a gunshot wound, but I kept telling my doctor I was okay enough to leave the hospital and go home but neither he nor Amelia were having it.

She was kind enough to make sure all my needs were met, but what I really needed was to get out of that bed I'd been confined to the last two weeks, and go back to my life.

Amelia and I hadn't talked much since the incident, mostly because I'd been unconscious, and I barely remembered anything due to the heavy sedation but the drugs were wearing off now and I was itching to get back to the world.

I hadn't had the courage to take a look at the wound because of the terror and shortness of breath I experienced from both memories and nightmares.

Every time I recalled Amelia's face when Eric fired the shot, my heart broke for her. I'd been informed of his passing and though I was vague on details, I was waiting for the right time to ask Amelia what exactly had happened.

Their conversation had revealed details I'd been unaware of and sometimes I wondered if I'd imagined it. So much had taken place that night, it felt like it had happened to someone else.

"Olivia?" I turned towards the door at the feminine voice and my heart picked up pace. "Hi," Adrianna said as she walked in.

"Hi," I said.

"How are you doing?"

I turned off the television and shrugged my shoulders, wondering why she'd come to see me. During our last encounter she'd discovered about my affair with her mother. Was she there to confront me? "I've been better," I said.

"It's good to see you awake."

Had she visited me while I'd been unconscious? "Yeah, two days now."

She smiled, slowly and carefully approaching my bed.

"Look, I'm sorry about the way you found out about me and Ame—your mother."

"It's okay. We talked. She explained everything to me."

I raised my eyebrow. "She did?"

"Yes."

I couldn't help being curious about what she'd said.

"I probably shouldn't be here. You're not supposed to be under any strain."

I didn't mind the strain. What had Amelia told her and was she okay with it?

She sat down on the chair next to my bed and looked at me. "What did you do to her?" she asked.

"What?"

"It's just that I've—." She looked away. "I've never seen her like that before. I can't stop thinking about it. They way I found her. She's always been this strong unbreakable person to me. To see her the way she was that night... it haunts me."

"How—," I nervously played with the tag on my wrist. "How was she?"

"Distraught, broken, terrified," she said.

Amelia's image came to mind as that fateful night replayed itself in my mind. If Eric had shot her I would've died. I didn't regret getting him to shoot me instead. "It was a traumatic experience."

"You really love her."

I met her gaze and slowly nodded.

"Well, however you two decide to proceed, I want you to know that anyone who's willing to take a bullet for my mother deserves her. You have my full support."

I was so taken aback by her words, I found myself speechless.

The door opened a moment later and Rex stepped inside. He hesitated at the door when he saw Adrianna, then approached me.

"Hi Anna," he said.

"Hi Rex," she said.

He came around my bed and lightly pecked my cheek as he closed his hand over mine.

"I'm going to leave you two alone. I wish you a quick recovery Olivia," Adrianna said as she left the room.

"How are you doing?" Rex asked when we were alone.

"Much, much better, do you think you can sign the release forms for me?"

He raised his eyebrow. "My God, Liv. You've barely been conscious for forty eight hours."

I groaned and moved over to create room for him to sit. He carefully got on the bed and placed his arm around my shoulders as I leaned back against him.

"What's happening between you and your Anna?" I asked, wondering how much I'd missed out on.

"Nothing so far."

"Why not? I thought you two hit it off."

"Everything has been at a standstill."

"How come?"

"You got shot, Liv. I almost lost you."

"But you didn't. I'm still here. So stop making excuses. She likes you."

"Okay, I'll call her."

"No, go catch up with her right now and ask her out for a cup of coffee."

"But I just got here."

"Does it look like I'm going anywhere?"

He blankly stared at me.

"Go," I said.

He got off the bed and reluctantly walked out of my hospital room. I laughed at him and a piercing pain shot through my stomach, spreading all over my body. A nurse had given me pain medication a bit earlier, I wondered if it was wearing off. I didn't want to ask for more incase they decided to sedate me again. I hated knowing time was passing me by and I resented falling asleep.

Later when I was tired of stressing about the work I'd have to go back to and the delay in my studies, I attempted to get out of bed.

Amelia had hired me a nursing assistant to perform minimal physical therapy to reduce limb weakness during the time I'd been unconscious so physically, I was strong enough to move on my own.

Carefully, without straining myself, I got my feet off the bed and held my breath, trying to ignore the pinch of pain from my stomach created by the movement. I supported myself on the bed as I got down and placed my hand over the wound.

It hurt more than I wanted to admit to myself as I slowly made my way over to the wheelchair just a little distance away. I was pleased with myself for the progress, but the joy was short-lived when Amelia walked in and saw me.

"Oh, my God! What are you doing?"

I opened my mouth to speak but failed to form words.

"Get back in bed." She came over to me and offered assistance as she slowly led me back to the bed. She helped me sit back down and pressed the distress button. A moment later, a nurse walked in and I groaned in frustration.

"What were you trying to do?" she asked.

"Escape," I said dryly.

She smiled at me as the nurse inspected the wound. "I need to change the dressing on the wound because you're bleeding. You're still recovering, Olivia, you need to take it easy," she said as she leaned me back against the bed.

I stared up at the ceiling as she worked on the wound, wondering if it would leave an unsightly scar. Amelia was silently standing beside me as she observed the nurse. When she found me looking at her, she reached for my hand and gently squeezed it.

The nurse offered me pain medication before she left us alone and I turned my attention to Amelia.

"I know being confined to this bed is frustrating for you, but it's for your own good. You woke up yesterday, you can't start moving around quite yet otherwise you'll disturb the wound and it'll take longer to heal," she said softly.

"I'm just a little restless. I hate being idle."

"I know, Liv. Just please, give it a little bit of time."

"Can I at least resume with my studies? My body may not be up for it right now but my mind is still active and alert."

"I'll talk to your doctor and see what he says."

"Don't let them sedate me again. I have memory lapses and I keep having recurring nightmares about that night. After the shooting, I don't remember much of anything else until yesterday when I woke up. It's all hazy in my head."

When she didn't respond, but instead continued looking at me, I wondered if there was something I was missing. "What is it?"

She hesitated and shook her head, "Uh, it's nothing."

I could tell there was something she was keeping from me and since I was lucid enough to know I'd remember this part, I reached for her hand and met her soft gaze. "I know it was stupid to ask him to shoot me instead, but I would've died if he'd shot you, Amelia."

"It was stupid," she said. "You could have died, Livvy."

"All I could think about at that moment was protecting you."

"It almost cost your life."

"I'd do it again."

She raised her eyebrow and pulled away from me. After a moment she said, "If you hadn't made it… there wouldn't have been a life to go back to." She turned her back to me. "When I thought I was going to lose you, I realized just how much you meant to me."

When she turned to face me and I saw tears in her eyes, my entire body shook in emotion. "Amelia," I tried to get out of bed to go to her.

"God, what are you doing?" She rushed over to my side. When I leaned back on the bed, she sat down beside me and met my gaze. I gently reached out and wiped the tears from her eyes.

"I'm sorry," I said.

She smiled, then leaned close and brushed her lips against mine. When I responded, she lightly touched my cheek and slightly pulled back.

I was almost afraid to ask. "What does this mean?"

She pulled back to look at me then released a soft laugh. "It means that from now on," She trailed her thumb over the outline of my jaw. "You're mine and I'm yours."

My heart fluctuated in disbelief.

"It means that I've stopped fighting what's between us." She took a breath and met my gaze. "It means that I love you."

I watched her in surprise. I couldn't believe she was finally saying everything I'd ever dreamed of hearing from her.

"I've never said that to anyone or meant it more than I do now."

I couldn't help tearing up at her words. I had wanted her for so long. I'd waited, cried and hurt and she was finally there, telling me she wanted me back. Telling me she loved me. "I can't believe this is happening."

She kissed me and a wave of warmth swarmed through me. I had to be dreaming. This couldn't be real. Amelia loved me.

"Say it again," I said.

She smiled and whispered softly against my lips. "I love you." Had I died and gone to heaven because if so, then God truly did work wonders.

The moment was interrupted by Rex, who looked instantly embarrassed when he realized what he'd just walked in on. "I'm sorry, I didn't mean to…" he started.

"It's okay," Amelia said as she got to her feet. "I'll go talk to your doctor, see if we can do something to make you more comfortable," she said.

I barely heard what she said because I was still stuck in the moment. She surprised me when she planted a light kiss on my lips in front of Rex, then she left the room.

"She loves me," I screamed.

Rex started laughing. "What?"

"She said she loves me." Had I been able to, I would've gotten to my feet and danced around the room. "This has got to be the best day of my life."

Rex came over to me and hugged me. "That's amazing. You truly deserve to be happy."

I took a deep breath, trying to calm myself because I was completely overwhelmed. My heart raced at the thought of finally getting to spend my life with Amelia.

"Thanks, Rex." My lips were stuck in a permanent smile. "Okay, tell me, how did it go with Adrianna?"

He retook his earlier position on my bed. "It was a little awkward at first, we're not used to being around one another but after talking, we realized we had a lot in common, which made it easy. We're going out for dinner tomorrow night."

"That's great, Rex. I really hope it works out for both of you."

He laughed and said, "A crazy thought just passed through my mind."

"What?"

He looked at me and laughed some more, which made me even more curious. "If you and Mrs. Gallagher got married, and Adrianna and I got married, you'd sort of be like my mother-in-law."

I playfully punched his shoulder and laughed along with him.

"On a serious note though, I believe it when she says she loves you. The night this all happened, anyone could tell how worried she was about you."

There was a part of me that had thought I wouldn't live to see another day but the idea of my parents losing another child, Rex grieving and everything that had been unfinished between me and Amelia, all of it just kept me strong.

"What happened that night Liv?" he asked.

"Eric, Amelia's cousin, was responsible for Greg's accident."

He looked at me in surprise and I told him everything Amelia had shared with me. "After Adrianna discovered the truth about me and Amelia, and Jaime found out, I got really upset and went to see Amelia. Eric showed up while we were talking and aimed a gun at her. She'd put a manhunt on him and hired me a bodyguard because she was unsure of how far he was willing to go. While they were talking..." The details started running through my mind.

"Eric admitted it was Kathy, Amelia's mother, who'd ordered him to kill Greg." I trembled at the memory. "He wanted to hurt Amelia but he could never do so without hurting Kathy because he loved her. My presence in Amelia's life created an opportunity for him, I was her weakness. He was going to use me as a weapon against her. At that moment, I realized why Amelia had always kept me at a distance. I didn't want anyone else to ever use me to hurt her again so I told him," I exhaled. "I told him to shoot me."

"Oh my God."

"I was just thinking about protecting her. When he shot me…" I remembered all the blood, Amelia holding me in her arms with fear and terror in her eyes and then silence and darkness.

Rex pulled me in his arms.

"Amelia's mother had my brother killed," I said in a bit of a panic.

"Did Amelia know?" he asked.

Her conversation with Eric that night made it pretty clear. "Yes."

My thoughts kept twirling around Amelia, Eric and her mother, long after Rex had left. I understood Eric's vendetta against Amelia, but I didn't know how Kathy fit into all of it.

Why would she have Greg killed? Was that part of the information Amelia had withheld from me thinking she was protecting me? I was up most of the night trying to think of every possible angle I could make sense out of the situation but nothing plausible came to mind.

The following day when I woke up, it was around noon. I found Amelia seated silently on the chair next to my bed. I was happy to wake up to her beautiful face.

"Hey, how long have you been sitting there?" I asked.

Her blue eyes had never been brighter as she looked up and met me with a smile, making my heart palpitate. How could she still do that?

"It's not important," she said as she reached out and took my hand in hers.

My gaze stayed locked in hers for a while as the memory of her declaring her love for me replayed itself. She got up and sat next to me on the bed.

"How are you feeling?" she asked.

"Happy," I said.

She laughed softly. "I mean how are you feeling, physically?"

"I'm okay."

"Good, I spoke to your doctor. Since I know how much you hate it here, I managed to convince him to let me take you home. I've hired two nurses to care for you, and your doctor will pay you regular visits to make sure you're improving."

She never ceased to amaze me. "That's great, Amelia. Thank you."

"You're very welcome."

"When will I get to see you?" I asked, knowing once I was back in my apartment with a bit of normalcy, things would easily go back to the way it was before and with everything that had happened, I wasn't sure what Amelia had planned for us.

"I'm assuming probably every day since we're going to be sharing the same bed, that's when neither one of us is traveling or working," she said.

The gunshot hadn't killed me but I was pretty sure if I grew any happier, that would most likely be the end of me. "We're going to live together?" I asked, trying hard to contain my joy.

"My realtor is looking for a place for us."

"What about the penthouse?"

"I'm going to sell it."

"Why?"

She grew a little more serious. "You got shot there. Eric died there. You sure you'd want to live in a place that has such bad memories?"

"Amelia, that penthouse also has great memories. I love the balcony because that was where you opened up to me and shared something about yourself. I love the hallway because that was where I saw you for the first time and knew I never wanted to make love to anyone else. I love the bedroom because that was where I looked at you one morning and knew I'd fallen in love with you. No other place will ever hold such wonderful memories of us together," I said.

She smiled at me and planted a kiss on the back of my hand. "Then I'll have your things moved there. That is if you'd like to live with me."

"There's nothing I'd love more."

She leaned close and kissed me. "Liv, there are still things I may not be able to give you," she said when we pulled apart.

"Amelia, you're everything I'm ever going to need."

"I love you, Liv."

"I love you too."

Epilogue

After I acknowledged and embraced how I felt about Olivia, it felt like my whole life changed. I didn't realize how sad my life had been until I discovered how wonderful it was like being with someone who made me feel so much.

Sometimes it was too overwhelming because it was like floodgates had opened upon my heart and soul and everything I'd avoided feeling in the past was flowing through every single pore of my being.

When I was with Olivia, sometimes I looked at her and couldn't believe that one person could have so much love.

We had lived together for almost a month now, and every single day I woke up next to her, I felt like I'd been bestowed a priceless gift. She evoked feelings in me I had never known I had.

"I can't believe I'm almost graduating," she said. "I never thought this day would come."

She was seated on one of the stools along the kitchen island going through her laptop and I was on my desk going through some work-related documents.

During the time we'd been living together, she'd done nothing but study from morning, noon and night and I was proud of her because she was so determined to finish up with her studies.

"I can't wait to go back to work," she said, meeting my gaze from the distance. "You will let me go back to work, won't you?"

She got upset sometimes because I didn't think she was recovered enough to go back, but I understood her frustration. "As soon as Dr. Freeman says you're fit enough to handle the pressure."

"I've been fit enough for weeks. The wound is almost fully healed and I don't need the pain medication anymore. I can move around by myself and apart from a little discomfort, I'm fine."

I stopped what I was doing to look at her. "Liv, it's admirable how focused you've been with your studies. You've done what in six months most people take a year or longer to do. Take a short break, breathe and prepare yourself because what's coming will be an avalanche of work that will require more from you than you can handle right now."

She sadly turned her back to me. I wanted to make her happy but her health meant more to me. "Liv," I got to my feet and approached her.

When she looked at me, the events that had taken place at the penthouse that night quickly flashed through my mind. I still thought about it every time I passed that spot in the living room. I'd had the carpet replaced but that didn't erase what had happened.

"Let's give it one more week. I can't risk anything bad happening to you." I moved closer to her and gently touched her cheek.

"I'm sorry. It's just that I don't want to be forgotten. I'd just started meeting everyone at the office and I keep thinking the little turbulence I was experiencing would be over by now." She closed her hand over mine.

"Olivia, everyone will know who you are when you go back to Price Healthcare."

"What do you mean?" she asked.

I'd been waiting for the perfect opportunity to reveal the plans I had for her, but this seemed as good a time as any. "When you go back to work, you're not just going to be another executive. You're going to be the president of the company."

She looked at me in disbelief. "What?"

"When Isabel left me Price Healthcare, she trusted me to continue with the work she'd started and now I'm passing the torch onto you. You'll have all the people and resources you need at your disposal to help run the business."

"Amelia, I don't know what to say."

"That's why I need you to be in your best health when you go back to work because everything is going to change. You're going to be running a billion dollar company." I'd made the decision to let her take over from me when I'd seen what she could do during the time she'd worked for me. I'd been waiting for her to finish up with school so that she could take over the business and now that she was graduating, the timing couldn't be more perfect.

"Oh my God."

"Do you understand now? Do you see why I need you to be fully recovered?"

She nodded, smiling happily at me which warmed my heart.

"I'm going to announce it to the board, the employees and the world one week from now."

"Wait, won't your family be upset with this decision?"

"I'm sure they will be, but Price Healthcare is not their company. It's mine and soon, it's going to be yours."

"What if they think you're doing this because we're together?"

I leaned my forehead against hers. "People will always have something to say, especially when they discover that I'm in love with a woman but what they think and what they say is never going to change my mind."

"I still can't get used to that," she said.

"To what? You, saying those amazing words."

I leaned close and captured her lips in a kiss. She responded, unrestrainedly expressing her love and passion and I wrapped my arms around her, moving intimately close.

We hadn't been sexually intimate since before she'd gotten shot so we were both completely starved and being close and unable to do it was torture. I wanted her with a hunger I'd never experienced for anyone before but I always stopped myself when our kisses became far too fervent because I didn't want her to strain herself.

I also felt her holding back when we got too close to getting intimate and something told me she was uncomfortable because of the scar the gunshot had left behind.

When I moved my hands over the curve of her waist, she broke the kiss and pulled back while she struggled to maintain her breathing. I wanted her to know she was beautiful and she had nothing to be shy about.

"Livvy, I want to make love to you." I touched her chin and made her meet my gaze. "The only reason I haven't is because I haven't wanted to strain you. The moment your doctor tells me you're okay, I'm going to tear off your clothes and make you mine once again. Do you hear me?"

She smiled at me and nodded.

"You're beautiful and you have absolutely nothing to be ashamed of. This scar," I placed my hand over it and she covered it with her hand. I slowly moved my hand under her top, touching it for the first time. "It's just that, a scar, which makes absolutely no difference over how much I'll still want you even after I see it, do you understand?"

She kissed me, expressing everything she'd been holding back and quickly turned me on. She wrapped her arms around my neck and I held her closer as her lips passionately explored mine.

"Olivia, if you don't stop I'm going to lose all control," I said in between her arousing kisses.

"Do it."

I trembled under her touch when her hands started exploring my body. "What?"

"Lose control."

I slightly pulled back to meet her aroused gaze.

"I've missed making love to you so much and you're right, the scar was making me feel insecure but now that I know your reasons for holding back, I don't have to restrain my desire for you anymore. So lose control, Amelia and make love to me."

I was afraid that if I started, I'd never be able to stop.

"Make me yours."

I closed the distance and recaptured her lips in another kiss. I had to remind myself to take it easy on her because I didn't want to hurt her. "Let's go to the bedroom."

The day I went back to Price Healthcare, Amelia made her announcement of electing me as her successor and it was all over the media. I took over her office and all her responsibilities and as she'd said, it came as an avalanche of work.

Having her as my mentor made things easier but during those first few weeks, it was so overwhelming I almost told her she'd made a mistake and I wasn't ready, but it was like she sensed it because she was quick to reassure me and offer assistance wherever I needed it.

It took me a bit of time to settle into my new role as the president of such a huge company, but everyone became so accommodating, which I figured was because I was their boss now.

I knew it'd take some getting used to and transitioning from an executive to such a huge role did take a bit of a toll on me, but Amelia was extremely understanding.

The thought of knowing I was going home to the woman I loved was always titillating and getting to see her lovely face after a long day of work was one of the favorite part of my days.

She'd taught me to expect the unexpected and while I was ready and prepared for anything that came my way, I didn't expect a visit from Jonah. He showed up in my office one evening while I was just about to head home.

Our first and only interaction had been at his house while I'd still been Amelia's personal assistant. So much time had passed and so much had changed. Adrianna was aware of the nature of my relationship with Amelia, but I wasn't sure if Jonah knew.

Adrianna expressed surprise when Amelia offered me the powerful position at Price Healthcare, but she tried to be supportive and I understood because it couldn't have been easy for her to see her mother with another woman.

I didn't know what the rest of Amelia's family thought about our relationship or my new position but she never wavered in her belief in me. It was because of her confidence in my skills that I worked so hard.

"Hi Jonah," I said cautiously.

He looked a bit more intimidating than the last time I'd seen him, probably because I knew he wasn't there to exchange pleasantries.

"Olivia," he said, slowly and comfortably approaching my desk.

"How can I help you?" I asked.

He was dressed in a suit and his hands were tucked in his pants pockets as he looked around my office.

"I've been trying to figure out how my mother could promote you from such a lowly position to a significant one in her jewel of a company." He paused to look at me. "At some point," he started pacing from side to side. "I thought she'd lost her mind and once she knew what a mistake she was making, she'd rescind the offer and keep the business in the family as she's done with Winston

Enterprises, which I'm sure you're aware of."

I stood upright and waited for him to get to the point.

"Adrianna gave me a bit of news I wasn't expecting, but it all made sense to me. Now frankly, I don't care about what my mother does with her personal life, but I do care greatly about how my family's wealth is distributed."

He looked at me as though he expected me to respond but I had absolutely nothing to say to him. I hadn't gotten the position through favor. I had worked and still continued to work for it. If that made him feel insecure about the distribution of his family's wealth, that was on him. I wasn't going to apologize or back down.

"Don't get too comfortable behind that seat. But try and enjoy this moment, because it's not going to last." He finished and after silently observing me, he walked out.

I took a breath and sat back on my seat. I couldn't say I hadn't expected some backlash, but it was only going to make me want to succeed even more. I had to show Amelia she hadn't made a mistake offering me such a great opportunity.

I wasn't going to tell her about Jonah's visit unless it was absolutely necessary. If his drive and passion equaled that of Amelia's, I knew it was going to be tough fighting him every second of the way, but as long as I had Amelia's support, I believed everything was going to be fine.

When I got home, I found Amelia at her desk talking on the phone. She was always busy with Winston Enterprises business so I tried as much as I could not to get in the way.

After putting my things down, I approached her and lightly pecked her lips. My heart still raced whenever I saw her and remembered she was finally mine. When she put down the phone, she approached me while I was pouring myself a glass of wine.

I finally had everything I'd ever wanted and I was extremely happy but there was more to Amelia than I knew. We'd never talked about her mother's involvement in Greg's murder and after Jonah's visit that evening, I felt a little more driven to want to discuss it. I wanted to know her family better so that I knew what I was going to have to deal with.

"How was your day?" she asked as she took the glass of wine from me.

I took another glass and filled it up. "It was good, though coming home to you is always my favorite part."

Her divorce had been finalized, which pleased me greatly because it wasn't one of those long, dragged out messy separations but mostly, it made me glad because she seemed so at ease with it.

"Do you think we can talk for a minute," I said.

She looked at me as though she sensed it was something serious and led me to the living room couch. When we were comfortably seated, I took a breath and said, "When you and I finally got together, I promised myself I'd find a way to tell my family about us. I've been holding off on telling them because I'm frightened of how they'll react."

"Liv, you don't have to tell them, especially if you think they'll take it badly.'

"How did your mom take it when she found out about you and Isabel?"

"She married me off to Patrick the first opportunity she got after Isabel was out of the picture."

I stared at her and she started laughing.

"Things were far too different back then. I was different. My mother is a very complicated woman. She's nothing like your parents."

I nodded, thinking that when the time was right, I'd be brave enough to tell them. Amelia didn't seem to mind.

"Liv, I know we haven't had a chance to talk about what happened with my mother and her involvement in Greg's death," she said.

I nodded.

"To be completely honest, I've been afraid of losing you once you had all the details and I don't want that to happen."

"That's never going to happen."

She seemed a little uncomfortable as she said, "My relationship with my mother has always been very complicated," she resumed to tell me about her history with her mother, Eric's involvement and how everything had played out to the very end where he'd shot me.

"She's not a threat to us anymore. After everything that happened, it seems like she had a bit of a mental breakdown. I have people taking care of her at her estate. I know she doesn't deserve it but——."

"She's your mother," I said in understanding.

"She's my mother," Amelia said calmly, almost sadly.

"I know you didn't play any role in Greg's death, Amelia. I know that if it was up to you, he'd be alive. One of the reasons why I fell in love with you was because you always did everything you could to make me happy. I want you to know that I'll do the same for as long as we're together. I will do everything in my power to make you as happy as you make me."

She smiled and leaned forward to kiss me. She was a bit more expressive now, which was wonderful because we'd grown so comfortable around one another.

"I love you," she said against my lips and goosebumps traveled all through my body. I doubted I'd ever get used to hearing her say that.

"I love you too."

End

ABOUT THE AUTHOR

Kerry Belchambers is a poet, playwright, writer and author of the Goldie Award nominated novel *Cresswell Falls*. She's also published well received romantic fiction books such as *After Sunset* and *Finding You*.

In the last decade, Kerry has spent time reading and writing romance novels with beautifully woven storylines and unforgettable characters.

She has completed a comprehensive course in writing and has traveled through Africa and America. Currently, she lives with her partner and canine son, Lexa.

Made in the USA
Middletown, DE
13 April 2023